I0831543

The Helmet of Navarre

The Helmet of Navarre

Bertha Runkle

ÆGYPAN PRESS

This text from the edition published in 1901 by The Century Company of New York.

The Helmet of Navarre
A publication of
ÆGYPAN PRESS

www.aegypan.com

To My Mother

Press where ye see my white plume shine amidst the ranks of war,
And be your oriflamme today the Helmet of Navarre.

Lord Macaulay's "Ivry."

I

A flash of lightning.

At the stair-foot the landlord stopped me. "Here, lad, take a candle. The stairs are dark, and, since I like your looks, I would not have you break your neck."

"And give the house a bad name," I said.

"No fear of that; my house has a good name. There is no fairer inn in all Paris. And your chamber is a good chamber, though you will have larger, doubtless, when you are Minister of Finance."

This raised a laugh among the tavern idlers, for I had been bragging a bit of my prospects. I retorted:

"When I am, Maître Jacques, look out for a rise in your taxes."

The laugh was turned on mine host, and I retired with the honors of that encounter. And though the stairs were the steepest I ever climbed, I had the breath and the spirit to whistle all the way up. What mattered it that already I ached in every bone, that the stair was long and my bed but a heap of straw in the garret of a mean inn in a poor quarter? I was in Paris, the city of my dreams!

I am a Broux of St. Quentin. The great world has never heard of the Broux? No matter; they have existed these hundreds of years, Masters of the Forest, and faithful servants of the dukes of St. Quentin. The great world has heard of the St. Quentins? I warrant you! As loudly as it has of Sully and Villeroi, Trémouille and Biron. That is enough for the Broux.

I was brought up to worship the saints and M. le Duc, and I loved and revered them alike, by faith, for M. le Duc, at court, seemed as far away from us as the saints in heaven. But the year after King Henry III was murdered, Monsieur came to live on his estate, to make high and low love him for himself.

In that bloody time, when the King of Navarre and the two Leagues were tearing our poor France asunder, M. le Duc found himself between the devil and the deep sea. He was no friend to the League; for years he had stood between the king, his master, and the machinations of the Guises. On the other hand, he was no friend to the Huguenots. "To seat a heretic on the throne of France were to deny God," he said. Therefore he came home to St. Quentin, where he abode in quiet for some three years, to the great wonderment of all the world.

Had he been a cautious man, a man who looked a long way ahead, his compeers would have understood readily enough that he was waiting to see how the cat would jump, taking no part in the quarrel lest he should mix with the losing side. But this theory jibed so ill with Monsieur's character that not even his worst detractor could accept it. For he was known to all as a hotspur – a man who acted quickly and seldom counted the cost. Therefore his present conduct was a riddle, nor could any of the emissaries from King or League, who came from time to time to enlist his aid and went away without it, read the answer. The puzzle was too deep for them. Yet it was only this: to Monsieur, honor was more than a pretty word. If he could not find his cause honest, he would not draw his sword, though all the curs in the land called him coward.

Thus he stayed alone in the château for a long, irksome three years. Monsieur was not of a reflective mind, content to stand aside and watch while other men fought out great issues. It was a weary procession of days to him. His only son, a lad a few years older than I, shared none of his father's scruples and refused point-blank to follow him into exile. He remained in Paris, where they knew how to be gay in spite of sieges. Therefore I, the Forester's son, whom Monsieur took for a page, had a chance to come closer to my lord and be more to him than a mere servant, and I loved him as the dogs did. Aye, and admired him for a fortitude almost more than human, in that he could hold himself passive here in farthest Picardie, whilst in Normandie and Île de France battles raged and towns fell and captains won glory.

At length, in the opening of the year 1593, M. le Duc began to have a frequent visitor, a gentleman in no wise remarkable save for that he was accorded long interviews with Monsieur. After these visits my lord was always in great spirits, putting on frisky airs, like a stallion when he is led out of the stable. I looked for something to happen, and it was no surprise to me when M. le Duc announced one day, quite without warning, that he was done with St. Quentin and would be off in the morning for Mantes. I was in the seventh heaven of joy when he added that he should take me with him. I knew the King of Navarre was at Mantes – at last we were going to make history! There was no bound to my golden dreams, no limit to my future.

But my house of cards suffered a rude tumble, and by no hand but my father's. He came to Monsieur, and, presuming on an old servitor's privilege, begged him to leave me at home.

"I have lost two sons in Monsieur's service," he said: "Jean, hunting in this forest, and Blaise, in the fray at Blois. I have never grudged them to Monsieur. But Félix is all I have left."

Thus it came about that I was left behind, hidden in the hay-loft, when my duke rode away. I could not watch his going.

Though the days passed drearily, yet they passed. Time does pass, at length, even when one is young. It was July. The King of Navarre had moved up to St. Denis, in his siege of Paris, but most folk thought he would never win the city, the hotbed of the League. Of M. le Duc we heard no word till, one night, a chance traveler, putting up at the inn in the village, told a startling tale. The Duke of St. Quentin, though known to have been at Mantes and strongly suspected of espousing Navarre's cause, had ridden calmly into Paris and opened his hôtel! It was madness – madness sheer and stark. Thus far his religion had saved him, yet any day he might fall under the swords of the Leaguers.

My father came, after hearing this tale, to where I was lying on the grass, the warm summer night, thinking hard thoughts of him for keeping me at home and spoiling my chances in life. He gave me straightway the whole of the story. Long before it was over I had sprung to my feet.

"Do you still wish to join M. le Duc?" he said.

"Father!" was all I could gasp.

"Then you shall go," he answered. That was not bad for an old man who had lost two sons for Monsieur!

I set out in the morning, light of baggage, purse, and heart. I can tell naught of the journey, for I heeded only that at the end of it lay Paris. I reached the city one day at sundown, and entered without a passport at the St. Denis gate, the warders being hardly so strict as Mayenne supposed. I was dusty, foot-sore, and hungry, in no guise to present myself before Monsieur; wherefore I went no farther that night than the inn of the Amour de Dieu, in the Rue des Coupejarrets.

Far below my garret window lay the street – a trench between the high houses. Scarce eight feet off loomed the dark wall of the house opposite. To me, fresh from the wide woods of St. Quentin, it seemed the desire of Paris folk to outhuddle in closeness the rabbits in a warren. So ingenious were they at contriving to waste no inch of open space that the houses, standing at the base but a scant street's width apart, ever jutted out farther at each story till they looked to be fairly toppling together. I could see into the windows up and down the way; see the people move about within; hear opposite neighbors call to each other. But across from my aerie were no lights and no people, for that house was shuttered tight from attic to cellar, its dark front as expressionless as a blind face. I marveled how it came to stand empty in that teeming quarter.

Too tired, however, to wonder long, I blew out the candle, and was asleep before I could shut my eyes.

Crash! Crash! Crash!

I sprang out of bed in a panic, thinking Henry of Navarre was bombarding Paris. Then, being fully roused, I perceived that the noise was thunder.

From the window I peered into floods of rain. The peals died away. Suddenly came a terrific lightning-flash, and I cried out in astonishment. For the shutter opposite was open, and I had a vivid vision of three men in the window.

Then all was dark again, and the thunder shook the roof.

I stood straining my eyes into the night, waiting for the next flash. When it came it showed me the window barred as before. Flash followed flash; I winked the rain from my eyes and peered in vain. The shutter remained closed as if it had never been opened. Sleep rolled over me in a great wave as I groped my way back to bed.

II

At the Amour de Dieu.

When I woke in the morning, the sun was 6shining broadly into the room, glinting in the little pools of water on the floor. I stared at them, sleepy-eyed, till recollection came to me of the thunderstorm and the open shutter and the three men. I jumped up and ran to the window.

The shutters opposite were closed; the house just as I had seen it first, save for the long streaks of wet down the wall. The street below was one vast puddle. At all events, the storm was no dream, as I half believed the vision to be.

I dressed speedily and went downstairs. The inn-room was deserted save for Maître Jacques, who, with heat, demanded of me whether I took myself for a prince, that I lay in bed till all decent folk had been hours about their business, and then expected breakfast. However, he brought me a meal, and I made no complaint that it was a poor one.

"You have strange neighbors in the house opposite," said I.

He started, and the thin wine he was setting before me splashed over on the table.

"What neighbors?"

"Why, they who close their shutters when other folks would keep them open, and open them when others keep them shut," I said airily. "Last night I saw three men in the window opposite mine."

He laughed.

"Aha, my lad, your head is not used to our Paris wines. That is how you came to see visions."

"Nonsense," I cried, nettled. "Your wine is too well watered for that, let me tell you, Maître Jacques."

"Then you dreamed it," he said huffily. "The proof is that no one has lived in that house these twenty years."

Now, I had plenty to trouble about without troubling my head over night-hawks, but I was vexed with him for putting me off. So, with a fine conceit of my own shrewdness, I said:

"If it was only a dream, how came you to spill the wine?"

He gave me a keen glance, and then, with a look round to see that no one was by, leaned across the table, up to me.

"You are sharp as a gimlet," said he. "I see I may as well tell you first as last. Marry, an you will have it, the place is haunted."

"Holy Virgin!" I cried, crossing myself.

"Aye. Twenty years ago, in the great massacre – you know naught of that: you were not born, I take it, and, besides, are a country boy. But I was here, and I know. A man dared not stir out of doors that dark day. The gutters ran blood."

"And that house – what happened in that house?"

"Why, it was the house of a Huguenot gentleman, M. de Béthune," he answered, bringing out the name hesitatingly in a low voice. "They were all put to the sword – the whole household. It was Guise's work. The Duc de Guise sat on his white horse, in this very street here, while it was going on. Parbleu! that was a day."

"Mon dieu! yes."

"Well, that is an old story now," he resumed in a different tone. "One-and-twenty years ago, that was. Such things don't happen now. But the people, they have not forgotten; they will not go near that house. No one will live there."

"And have others seen as well as I?"

"So they say. But I'll not let it be talked of on my premises. Folk might get to think them too near the haunted house. 'Tis another matter with you, though, since you have had the vision."

"There were three men," I said, "young men, in somber dress –"

"M. de Béthune and his cousins. What further? Did you hear shrieks?"

"There was naught further," I said, shuddering. "I saw them for the space of a lightning-flash, plain as I see you. The next minute the shutters were closed again."

"'Tis a marvel," he answered gravely. "But I know what has disturbed them in their graves, the heretics! It is that they have lost their leader."

I stared at him blankly, and he added:

"Their Henry of Navarre."

"But he is not lost. There has been no battle."

"Lost to them," said Maître Jacques, "when he turns Catholic."

"Oh!" I cried.

"Oh!" he mocked. "You come from the country; you don't know these things."

"But the King of Navarre is too stiff-necked a heretic!"

"Bah! Time bends the stiffest neck. Tell me this: for what do the learned doctors sit in council at Mantes?"

"Oh," said I, bewildered, "you tell me news, Maître Jacques."

"If Henry of Navarre be not a Catholic before the month is out, spit me on my own jack," he answered, eying me rather keenly as he added:

"It should be welcome news to you."

Welcome was it; it made plain the reason Monsieur's change of base. Yet it was my duty to be discreet.

"I am glad to hear of any heretic coming to the faith," I said.

"Pshaw!" he cried. "To the devil with pretences! 'Tis an open secret that your patron has gone over to Navarre."

"I know naught of it."

"Well, pardieu! my Lord Mayenne does, then. If when he came to Paris M. de St. Quentin counted that the League would not know his parleyings, he was a fool."

"His parleyings?" I echoed feebly.

"Aye, the boy in the street knows he has been with Navarre. For, mark you, all France has been wondering these many months where St. Quentin was coming out. His movements do not go unnoted like a yokel's. But, i' faith, he is not dull; he understands that well enough. Nay, 'tis my belief he came into the city in pure effrontery to show them how much he dared. He is a bold blade, your duke. And, mon dieu! it had its effect. For the Leaguers have been so agape with astonishment ever since that they have not raised a finger against him."

"Yet you do not think him safe?"

"Safe, say you? Safe! Pardieu! if you walked into a cage of lions, and they did not in the first instant eat you, would you therefore feel safe? He was stark mad to come to Paris. There is no man the League hates more, now they know they have lost him, and no man they can afford so ill to spare to King Henry. A great Catholic noble, he would be meat and drink to the Béarnais. He was mad to come here."

"And yet nothing has happened to him."

"Verily, fortune favors the brave. No, nothing has happened – yet. But I tell you true, Félix, I had rather be the poor innkeeper of the Amour de Dieu than stand in M. de St. Quentin's shoes."

"I was talking with the men here last night," I said. "There was not one but had a good word for Monsieur."

"Aye, so they have. They like his pluck. And if the League kills him it is quite on the cards that the people will rise up and make the town lively. But that will not profit M. de St. Quentin if he is dead."

I would not be dampened, though, by an old croaker.

"Nay, maître, if the people are with him, the League will not dare –"

"There you fool yourself, my springald. If there is one thing which the nobles of the League neither know nor care about it is what the people think. They sit wrangling over their French League and their Spanish League, their kings and their princesses, and what this lord does and that lord threatens, and they give no heed at all to us – us, the people. But they will find out their mistake. Some day they will be taught that the nobles are not all of France. There will come a reckoning when more blood will flow in Paris than ever flowed on St. Bartholomew's day. They think we are chained down, do they? Pardieu! there will come a day!"

I scarcely knew the man; his face was flushed, his eyes sparkling as if they saw more than the common room and mean street. But as I stared the glow faded, and he said in a lower tone:

"At least, it will happen unless Henry of Navarre comes to save us from it. He is a good fellow, this Navarre."

"They say he can never enter Paris."

"They say lies. Let him but leave his heresies behind him and he can enter Paris tomorrow."

"Mayenne does not think so."

"No; but Mayenne knows little of what goes on. He does not keep an inn in the Rue Coupejarrets."

He stated the fact so gravely that I had to laugh.

"Laugh if you like; but I tell you, Félix Broux, my lord's council-chamber is not the only place where they make kings. We do it, too, we of the Rue Coupejarrets."

"Well," said I, "I leave you, then, to make kings. I must be off to my duke. What's the scot, maître?"

He dropped the politician, and was all innkeeper in a second.

"A crown!" I cried in indignation. "Do you think I am made of crowns? Remember, I am not yet Minister of Finance."

"No, but soon will be," he grinned. "Besides, what I ask is little enough, God knows. Do you think food is cheap in a siege?"

"Then I pray Navarre may come soon and end it."

"Amen to that," said old Jacques, quite gravely. "If he comes a Catholic it cannot be too soon."

I counted out my pennies with a last grumble.

"They ought to call this the Rue Coupebourses."

He laughed; he could afford to, with my silver jingling in his pouch. He embraced me tenderly at parting, and hoped to see me again at his inn. I smiled to myself; I had not come to Paris – I – to stay in the Rue Coupejarrets!

III

M. le Duc is well guarded.

I stepped out briskly from the inn, pausing now and again to inquire my way to the Hôtel St. Quentin, which stood, I knew, in the Quartier

Marais, where all the grand folk lived. Once I had found the broad, straight Rue St. Denis, all I need do was to follow it over the hill down to the river-bank; my eyes were free, therefore, to stare at all the strange sights of the great city – markets and shops and churches and prisons. But most of all did I gape at the crowds in the streets. I had scarce realized there were so many people in the world as passed me that summer morning in the Town of Paris. Bewilderingly busy and gay the place appeared to my country eyes, though in truth at that time Paris was at its very worst, the spirit being well-nigh crushed out of it by the sieges and the iron rule of the Sixteen.

I knew little enough of politics, and yet I was not so dull as not to see that great events must happen soon. A crisis had come. I looked at the people I passed who were going about their business so tranquilly. Every one of them must be either Mayenne's man, or Navarre's. Before a week was out these peaceable citizens might be using pikes for tools and exchanging bullets for good mornings. Whatever happened, here was I in Paris in the thick of it! My feet fairly danced under me; I could not reach the hôtel soon enough. Half was I glad of Monsieur's danger, for it gave me chance to show what stuff I was made of. Live for him, die for him – whatever fate could offer I was ready for.

The hôtel, when at length I arrived before it, was no disappointment. Here one did not wait till midday to see the sun; the street was of decent width, and the houses held themselves back with reserve, like the proud gentlemen who inhabited them. Nor did one here regret his possession of a nose, as he was forced to do in the Rue Coupejarrets.

Of all the mansions in the place, the Hôtel St. Quentin was, in my opinion, the most imposing; carved and ornamented and stately, with gardens at the side. But there was about it none of that stir and liveliness one expects to see about the houses of the great. No visitors passed in or out, and the big iron gates were shut, as if none were looked for. Of a truth, the persons who visited Monsieur these days preferred to slip in by the postern after nightfall, as if there had never been a time when they were proud to be seen in his hall.

Beyond the grilles a sentry, in the green and scarlet of Monsieur's men-at-arms, stood on guard, and I called out to him boldly.

He turned at once; then looked as if the sight of me scarce repaid him.

"I wish to enter, if you please," I said. "I am come to see M. le Duc."

"You?" he ejaculated, his eye wandering over my attire, which, none of the newest, showed signs of my journey.

"Yes, I," I answered in some resentment. "I am one of his men."

He looked me up and down with a grin.

"Oh, one of his men! Well, my man, you must know M. le Duc is not receiving today."

"I am Félix Broux," I told him.

"You may be Félix anybody for all it avails; you cannot see Monsieur."

"Then I will see Vigo." Vigo was Monsieur's Master of Horse, the staunchest man in France. This sentry was nobody, just a common fellow picked up since Monsieur left St. Quentin, but Vigo had been at his side these twenty years.

"Vigo, say you! Vigo does not see street boys."

"I am no street boy," I cried angrily. "I know Vigo well. You shall smart for flouting me, when I have Monsieur's ear."

"Aye, when you have! Be off with you, rascal. I have no time to bother with you."

"Imbecile!" I sputtered. But he had turned his back on me and resumed his pacing up and down the court.

"Oh, very well for you, monsieur," I cried out loudly, hoping he could hear me. "But you will laugh t'other side of your mouth by and by. I'll pay you off."

It was maddening to be halted like this at the door of my goal; it made a fool of me. But while I debated whether to set up an outcry that would bring forward some officer with more sense than the surly sentry, or whether to seek some other entrance, I became aware of a sudden bustle in the courtyard, a narrow slice of which I could see through the gateway. A page dashed across; then a pair of flunkeys passed. There was some noise of voices and, finally, of hoofs and wheels. Half a dozen men-at-arms ran to the gates and swung them open, taking their stand on each side. Clearly, M. le Duc was about to drive out.

A little knot of people had quickly collected – sprung from between the stones of the pavement, it would seem – to see Monsieur emerge.

"He is a bold man," I heard one say, and a woman answer, "Aye, and a handsome," ere the heavy coach rolled out of the arch.

I pushed myself in close to the guardsmen, my heart thumping in my throat now that the moment had come when I should see my Monsieur. At the sight of his face I sprang bodily up on the coach-step, crying, all my soul in my voice, "Oh, Monsieur! M. le Duc!"

Monsieur looked at me coldly, blankly, without a hint of recognition. The next instant the young gentleman beside him sprang up-and struck me a blow that hurled me off the step. I fell where the ponderous wheels would have ended me had not a guardsman, quick and kind, pulled me out of the way. Someone shouted, "Assassin!"

"I am no assassin," I cried; "I only sought to speak with Monsieur."

"He deserves a hiding, the young cur," growled my foe, the sentry. "He's been pestering me this half-hour to let him in. He was one of Monsieur's men, he said. Monsieur would see him. Well, we have seen how Monsieur treats him!"

"Faith, no," said another. "We have only seen how our young gentleman treats him. Of course he is too proud and dainty to let a common man so much as look at him."

They all laughed; the young gentleman seemed no favorite.

"Parbleu! that was why I drew him from the wheels, because *he* knocked him there," said my preserver. "I don't believe there's harm in the boy. What meant you, lad?"

"I meant no harm," I said, and turned sullenly off up the street. This, then, was what I had come to Paris for – to be denied entrance to the house, thrown under the coach-wheels, and threatened with a drubbing from the lackeys!

For three years my only thought had been to serve Monsieur. From waking in the morning to sleep at night, my whole life was Monsieur's. Never was duty more cheerfully paid. Never did acolyte more throw his soul into his service than I into mine. Never did lover hate to be parted from his mistress more than I from Monsieur. The journey to Paris had been a journey to Paradise. And now, this!

Monsieur had looked me in the face and not smiled; had heard me beseech him and not answered – not lifted a finger to save me from being mangled under his very eyes. St. Quentin and Paris were two very different places, it appeared. At St. Quentin Monsieur had been pleased to take me into the château and treat me to more intimacy than he accorded to the highborn lads, his other pages. So much the easier, then, to cast me off when he had tired of me. My heart seethed with rage and bitterness against Monsieur, against the sentry, and, more than all, against the young Comte de Mar, who had flung me under the wheels.

I had never before seen the Comte de Mar, that spoiled only son of M. le Duc's, who was too fine for the country, too gay to share his father's exile. Maybe I was jealous of the love his father bore him, which he so little repaid. I had never thought to like him, St. Quentin though he were; and now that I saw him I hated him. His handsome face looked ugly enough to me as he struck me that blow.

I went along the Paris streets blindly, the din of my own thoughts louder than all the noises of the city. But I could not remain in this trance forever, and at length I woke to two unpleasant facts: first, I had no idea where I was, and, second, I should be no better off if I knew.

Never, while there remained in me the spirit of a man, would I go back to Monsieur; never would I serve the Comte de Mar. And it was equally obvious that never, so long as my father retained the spirit that was his, could I return to St. Quentin with the account of my morning's achievements. It was just here that, looking at the business with my father's eyes, I began to have a suspicion that I had behaved like an insolent young fool. But I was still too angry to acknowledge it.

Remained, then, but one course – to stay in Paris, and keep from starvation as best I might.

My thrifty father had not seen fit to furnish me any money to throw away in the follies of the town. He had calculated closely what I should need to take me to Monsieur, with a little margin for accidents; so that, after paying Maître Jacques, I had hardly two pieces to jingle together.

For three years I had browsed my fill in the duke's library; I could write a decent letter both in my own tongue and in Italian, thanks to Father Francesco, Monsieur's Florentine confessor, and handle a sword none so badly, thanks to Monsieur; and I felt that it should not be hard to pick up a livelihood. But how to start about it I had no notion, and finally I made up my mind to go and consult him whom I now called my one friend in Paris, Jacques the innkeeper.

'Twas easier said than done. I had strayed out of the friendly Rue St. Denis into a network of dark and narrow ways that might have been laid out by a wily old stag with the dogs hot on him, so did they twist and turn and double on themselves. I could make my way only at a snail's pace, asking new guidance at every corner. Noon was long past when at length I came on laggard feet around the corner by the Amour de Dieu.

Yet was it not fatigue that weighted my feet, but pride. Though I had resolved to seek out Maître Jacques, still 'twas a hateful thing to enter as suppliant where I had been the patron. I had paid for my breakfast like a lord, but I should have to beg for my dinner. I had bragged of Monsieur's fondness, and I should have to tell how I had been flung under the coach-wheels. My pace slackened to a stop. I could not bring myself to enter the door. I tried to think how to better my story, so to tell it that it should redound to my credit. But my invention stuck in my pate.

As I stood striving to summon up a jaunty demeanor, I found myself gazing straight at the shuttered house, and of a sudden my thoughts shifted back to my vision.

Those murdered Huguenots, dead and gone ere I was born, had appeared to me as plain as the men I passed in the street. Though I had beheld them but the space of a lightning-flash, I could call up their faces like those of my comrades. One, the nearest me, was small, pale, with pinched, sharp face, somewhat ratlike. The second man was conspicuously big and burly, black-haired and-bearded. The third and youngest – all three were young – stood with his hand on Blackbeard's shoulder. He, too, was tall, but slenderly built, with clear-cut visage and fair hair gleaming in the glare. One moment I saw them, every feature plain; the next they had vanished like a dream.

It was an unholy thing, no doubt, yet it held me with a shuddery fascination. Was it indeed a portent, this rising of heretics from their unblessed graves? And why had it been shown to me, true son of the Church? Had anyone else ever seen what I had seen? Maître Jacques had hinted at further terrors, and said no one dared enter the place. Well, grant me but the opportunity, and I would dare.

Thus was hatched in my brain the notion of forcing an entrance into that banned house. I was an idle boy, foot-loose and free to do whatever mad mischief presented itself. Here was the house just across the street.

Neglected as it was, it remained the most pretentious edifice in the row, being large and flaunting a half-defaced coat of arms over the door. Such a house might well boast two entrances. I hoped it did, for there was no use in trying to batter down this door with the eye of the Rue Coupejarrets upon me. I turned along the side street, and after exploring several muck-heaped alleys found one that led me into a small square court bounded on three sides by a tall house with shuttered windows.

Fortune was favoring me. But how to gain entrance? The two doors were both firmly fastened. The windows on the ground floor were small, high, and iron-shuttered. Above, one or two shutters swung half open, but I could not climb the smooth wall. Yet I did not despair; I was not without experience of shutters. I selected one closed not quite tight, leaving a crack for my knife-blade. I found the hook inside, got my dagger under it, and at length drove it up. The shutter creaked shrilly open.

A few good blows knocked in the casement. I followed.

I found myself in a small room bare of everything but dust. From this, once a porter's room, I fancied, I passed out into a hallway dimly lighted from the open window behind me. The hall was large, paved with black and white marbles; at the end a stately stairway mounted into mysterious gloom.

My heart jumped into my mouth and I cringed back in terror, a choked cry rasping my throat. For, as I crossed the hall, peering into the dimness, I descried, stationed on the lowest stair with upraised bludgeon, a man.

For a second I stood in helpless startlement, voiceless, motionless, waiting for him to brain me. Then my half-uttered scream changed to a quavering laugh, as my eyes, becoming used to the gloom, discovered my bogy to be but a figure carved in wood, holding aloft a long since quenched flambeau.

I blushed with shame, yet I cannot say that now I felt no fear. I thought of the panic-stricken women, the doomed men, who had fled at the sword's point up these very stairs. The silence seemed to shriek at me, and I half thought I saw fear-maddened eyes peering out from the shadowed corners. Yet for all that – nay, because of that – I would not give up the adventure. I went back into the little room and carefully closed the shutter, lest some other meddler should spy my misdeed. Then I set my feet on the stair.

If the half-light before had been full of eerie terror, it was naught to the blackness now. My hand on the rail was damp. Yet I mounted steadily.

Up one flight I climbed, groped in the hot dark for the foot of the next flight, and went on. Suddenly, above, I heard a noise. I came to an instant halt. All was as still as the tomb. I listened; not a breath broke the silence. It never occurred to me to imagine a rat in this house of the dead, and the noise shook me. With a sick feeling about my heart I went on again.

On the next floor it was lighter. Faint outlines of doors and passages were visible. I could not stand the gloom a moment longer; I strode into the nearest doorway and across the room to where a gleam of brightness outlined the window. My shaking fingers found the hook of the shutter and flung it wide, letting in a burst of honest sunshine. I leaned out into the free air, and saw below me the Rue Coupejarrets and the sign of the Amour de Dieu.

The next instant a cloth fell over my face and was twisted tight; strong arms pulled me back, and a deep voice commanded:

"Close the shutter."

Someone pushed past me and shut it with a clang.

"Devil take you! You'll rouse the quarter," cried my captor, fiercely, yet not loud. "Go join monsieur." With that he picked me up in his arms and walked across the room.

The capture had been so quick I had no time for outcry. I fought my best with him, half strangled as I was by the cloth. I might as well have struggled against the grip of the Maiden. The man carried me the length of the house, it seemed; flung me down upon the floor, and banged a door on me.

IV

The three men in the window

I tore the cloth from my head and sprang up. I was in pitch-darkness. I dashed against the door to no avail. Feeling the walls, I discovered myself to be in a small, empty closet. With all my force I flung myself once more upon the door. It stood firm.

"Dame! but I have got into a pickle," I thought.

They were no ghosts, at all events. Scared as I was, I rejoiced at that. I could cope with men, but who can cope with the devil? These might be villains – doubtless were, skulking in this deserted house, – yet with readiness and pluck I could escape them.

It was as hot as a furnace in my prison, and as still as the grave. The men, who seemed by their footsteps to be several, had gone cautiously down the stairs after caging me. Evidently I had given them a fine fright, clattering through the house as I had, and even now they were looking for my accomplices.

It seemed hours before the faintest sound broke the stillness. If ever you want to squeeze away a man's cheerfulness like water from a rag, shut him up alone in the dark and silence. He will thank you to take him out into the daylight and hang him. In token whereof, my heart welcomed like brothers the men returning.

They came into the room, and I thought they were three in number. I heard the door shut, and then steps approached my closet.

"Have a care now, monsieur; he may be armed," spoke the rough voice of a man without breeding.

"Doubtless he carries a culverin up his sleeve," sneered the deep tones of my captor.

Someone else laughed, and rejoined, in a clear, quick voice:

"Natheless, he may have a knife. I will open the door, and do you look out for him, Gervais."

I had a knife and had it in my hand, ready to charge for freedom. But the door opened slowly, and Gervais looked out for me – to the effect that my knife went one way and I another before I could wink. I reeled against the wall and stayed there, cursing myself for a fool that I had not trusted to fair words instead of to my dagger.

"Well done, my brave Gervais!" cried he of the vivid voice – a tall fair-haired youth, whom I had seen before. So had I seen the stalwart blackbeard, Gervais. The third man was older, a common-looking fellow whose face was new to me. All three were in their shirts on account of the heat; all were plain, even shabby, in their dress. But the two young men wore swords at their sides.

The half-opened shutters, overhanging the court, let plenty of light into the room. It had two straw beds on the floor and a few old chairs and stools, and a table covered with dishes and broken food and wine-bottles. More bottles, riding-boots, whips and spurs, two or three hats and saddle-bags, and various odds and ends of dress littered the floor and the chairs. Everything was of mean quality except the bearing of the two young men. A gentleman is a gentleman even in the Rue Coupejarrets – all the more, maybe, in the Rue Coupejarrets. These two were gently born.

The low man, with scared face, held off from me. He whose name was Gervais confronted me with an angry scowl. Yeux-gris alone – for so I dubbed the third, from his grey eyes, well open under dark brows – Yeux-gris looked no whit alarmed or angered; the only emotion to be read in his face was a gay interest as the blackavised Gervais put me questions.

"How came you here? What are you about?"

"No harm, messieurs," I made haste to protest, ruing my stupidity with that dagger. "I climbed in at a window for sport. I thought the house was deserted."

He clutched my shoulder till I could have screamed for pain.

"The truth, now. If you value your life you will tell the truth."

"Monsieur, it is the truth. I came in idle mischief; that was the whole of it. I had no notion of breaking in upon you or anyone. They said the house was haunted."

"Who said that?"

"Maître Jacques, at the Amour de Dieu."

He stared at me in surprise.

"What had you been asking about this house?"

Yeux-gris, lounging against the table, struck in:

"I can tell you that myself. He told Jacques he saw us in the window last night. Did you not?"

"Aye, monsieur. The thunder woke me, and when I looked out I saw you plain as day. But Maître Jacques said it was a vision."

"I flattered myself I saw you first and got that shutter closed very neatly," said Yeux-gris. "Dame! I am not so clever as I thought. So old Jacques called us ghosts, did he?"

"Yes, monsieur. He told me this house belonged to M. de Béthune, who was a Huguenot and killed in the massacre."

Yeux-gris burst into joyous laughter.

"He said my house belonged to the Béthunes! Well played, Jacques! You owe that gallant lie to me, Gervais, and the pains I took to make him think us Navarre's men. He is heart and soul for Henri Quatre. Did he say, perchance, that in this very courtyard Coligny fell?"

"No," said I, seeing that I had been fooled and had had all my terrors for naught, and feeling much chagrined thereat. "How was I to know it was a lie? I know naught about Paris. I came up but yesterday from St. Quentin."

"St. Quentin!" came a cry from the henchman. With a fierce "Be quiet, fool!" Gervais turned to me and demanded my name.

"Félix Broux."

"Who sent you here?"

"Monsieur, no one."

"You lie."

Again he gripped me by the shoulder, gripped till the tears stood in my eyes.

"No one, monsieur; I swear it."

"You will not speak! I'll make you, by Heaven."

He seized my thumb and wrist to bend one back on the other, torture with strength such as his. Yeux-gris sprang off the table.

"Let alone, Gervais! The boy's honest."

"He is a spy."

"He is a fool of a country boy. A spy in hobnailed shoes, forsooth! No spy ever behaved as he has. I said when you first seized him he was no spy. I say it again, now I have heard his story. He saw us by chance, and Maître Jacques's bogy story spurred him on instead of keeping him off. You are a fool, my cousin."

"Pardieu! it is you who are the fool," growled Gervais. "You will bring us to the rope with your cursed easy ways. If he is a spy it means the whole crew are down upon us."

"What of that?"

"Pardieu! is it nothing?"

Yeux-gris returned with a touch of haughtiness:

"It is nothing. A gentleman may live in his own house."

Gervais looked as if he remembered something. He said much less boisterously:

"And do you want Monsieur here?"

Yeux-gris flushed red.

"No," he cried. "But you may be easy. He will not trouble himself to come."

Gervais regarded him silently an instant, as if he thought of several things he did not say. What he did say was: "You are a pair of fools, you and the boy. Whatever he came for, he has spied on us now. He shall not live to carry the tale of us."

"Then you have me to kill as well!"

Gervais turned on him snarling. Yeux-gris laid a hand on his sword-hilt.

"I will not have an innocent lad hurt. I was not bred a ruffian," he cried hotly. They glared at each other. Then Yeux-gris, with a sudden exclamation, "Ah, bah, Gervais!" broke into laughter.

Now, this merriment was a heart-warming thing to hear. For Gervais was taking the situation with a seriousness that was as terrifying as it was stupid. When I looked into his dogged eyes I could not but think the end of me might be near. But Yeux-gris's laugh said the very notion was ridiculous; I was innocent of all harmful intent, and they were gentlemen, not cutthroats.

"Messieurs," I said, "I swear by the blessed saints I am what I told you. I am no spy, and no one sent me here. Who you are, or what you do, I know no more than a babe unborn. I belong to no party and am no man's man. As for why you choose to live in this empty house, it is not my concern and I care no whit about it. Let me go, messieurs, and I will swear to keep silence about what I have seen."

"I am for letting him go," said Yeux-gris.

Gervais looked doubtful, the most encouraging attitude toward me he had yet assumed. He answered:

"If he had not said the name –"

"Stuff!" interrupted Yeux-gris. "It is a coincidence, no more. If he were what you think, it is the very last name he would have said."

This was Greek to me; I had mentioned no names but Maître Jacques's and my own. And he was their friend.

"Messieurs," I said, "if it is my name that does not please you, why, I can say for it that if it is not very high-sounding, at least it is an honest one and has ever been held so down where we live."

"And that is at St. Quentin," said Yeux-gris.

"Yes, monsieur. My father, Anton Broux, is Master of the Forest to the Duke of St. Quentin."

He started, and Gervais cried out:

"Voilà! who is the fool now?"

My nerves, which had grown tranquil since Yeux-gris came to my rescue, quivered anew. The common man started at the very word St. Quentin, and the masters started when I named the duke. Was it he whom they had spoken of as Monsieur? Who and what were they? There was more in this than I had thought at first. It was no longer a mere question of my liberty. I was all eyes and ears for whatever information I could gather.

Yeux-gris spoke to me, for the first time gravely:

"This is not a time when folks take pleasure-trips to Paris. What brought you?"

"I used to be Monsieur's page down at St. Quentin," I answered, deeming the straight truth best. "When we learned that he was in Paris, my father sent me up to him. I reached the city last night, and lay at the Amour de Dieu. This morning I went to the duke's hôtel, but the guard would not let me in. Then, when Monsieur drove out I tried to get speech with him, but he would have none of me."

The bitterness I felt over my rebuff must have been in my voice and face, for Gervais spoke abruptly:

"And do you hate him for that?"

"Nay," said I, churlishly enough. "It is his to do as he chooses. But I hate the Comte de Mar for striking me a foul blow."

"The Comte de Mar!" exclaimed Yeux-gris.

"His son."

"He has no son."

"But he has, monsieur. The Comte de –"

"He is dead," said Yeux-gris.

"Why, we knew naught –" I was beginning, when Gervais broke in:

"You say the fellow's honest, when he tells such tales as this! He saw the Comte de Mar – !"

"I thought it must be he," I protested. "A young man who sat by Monsieur's side, elegant and proud-looking, with an aquiline face –"

"That is Lucas, that is his secretary," declared Yeux-gris, as who should say, "That is his scullion."

Gervais looked at him oddly a moment, then shrugged his shoulders and demanded of me:

"What next?"

"I came away angry."

"And walked all the way here to risk your life in a haunted house? Pardieu! too plain a lie."

"Oh, I would have done the like; we none of us fear ghosts in the daytime," said Yeux-gris.

"You may believe him; I am no such fool. He has been caught in two lies; first the Béthunes, then the Comte de Mar. He is a clumsy spy; they might have found a better one. Not but what that touch about ill-treatment at Monsieur's hand was well thought of. That was Monsieur's suggestion, I warrant, for the boy has talked like a dolt else."

"I am no liar," I cried hotly. "Ask Jacques whether he did not tell me about the Béthunes. It is his lie, not mine. I did not know the Comte de Mar was dead, and this Lucas of yours is handsome enough for a count. I came here, as I told you, in curiosity concerning Maître Jacques's story. I had no idea of seeing you or any living man. It is the truth, monsieur."

"I believe you," Yeux-gris answered. "You have an honest face. You came into my house uninvited. Well, I forgive it, and invite you to stay. You shall be my valet."

"He shall be nobody's valet," Gervais cried.

The grey eyes flashed, but their owner rejoined lightly:

"You have a man; surely I should have one, too. And I understand the services of M. Félix are not engaged."

"Mille tonnerres! you would take this spy – this sneak –"

"As I would take M. de Paris, if I chose," responded Yeux-gris, with a cold hauteur that smacked more of a court than of this shabby room. He added lightly again:

"You think him a spy, I do not. But in any case, he must not blab of us. Therefore he stays here and brushes my clothes. Marry, they need it."

Easily, with grace, he had disposed of the matter. But I said:

"Monsieur, I shall do nothing of the kind."

"What!" he cried, as if the clothes-brush itself had risen in rebellion, "what! you will not."

"No," said I.

"And why not?" he demanded, plainly thinking me demented.

"Because I know you are against the Duke of St. Quentin."

Whatever they had thought me, neither expected that speech.

"I am no spy or sneak," said I. "It is true I came here by chance; it is true Monsieur turned me off this morning. But I was born on his land and I am no traitor. I will not be valet or henchman for either of you, if I die for it."

I was like to die for it. For Gervais whipped out his sword and sprang for me. I thought I saw Yeux-gris's out, too, when Gervais struck me over the head with his sword-hilt. The rest was darkness.

V

Rapiers and a vow.

I came to my senses slowly, to hear loud, angry voices. As I opened my eyes and stirred, the room reeled from me and all was blank again. Awhile after, I grew aware of a clashing of steel. I lay wondering thickly what it was and why it had to be going on while my head ached so, till at length it dawned on my dull brain that swords were crossing. I opened my eyes again, then.

They were fighting each other, Yeux-gris and Gervais. The latter was almost trampling on me, Yeux-gris had pressed him so close to the wall. Then he forced his way out, and they drove each other round in a circle till the room seemed to spin once more.

I crawled out of the way and watched them, bewildered, absorbed. I had more reason to thrill over the contest than the mere excellence of it, – which was great, – since I was the cause of the duel, and my very life, belike, hung on its issue.

They were both admirable swordsmen, yet it was clear from the first where the palm lay. Anything nimbler, lighter, easier than the swordplay of Yeux-gris I never hope to see in this imperfect world. The heavier adversary was hot, angry, breathing hard. A smile hovered over Yeux-gris's lips; already a red disk on Gervais's shirt showed where his cousin's sword had been and would soon go again, and deeper. I had forgotten my bruise in my interest and delight, when, of a sudden, one whom we all had ignored took a hand in the game. Gervais's lackey started forward and knocked up Yeux-gris's arm. His sword flew wide, and Gervais slashed his arm from wrist to elbow.

With a smothered cry, Yeux-gris caught at his wound. Gervais, ablaze with rage, sprang past him on his creature. The man gaped with amazement; then, for there was no time for parley, leaped for the door. It was locked. He turned, and with a look of deathly terror fell on his knees, crouched up against the doorpost. Gervais lunged. His blade passed clean through the man's shoulders and pinned him to the door. His head fell heavily forward.

"Have you killed him?" cried Yeux-gris.

"By my faith! I meant to," came the answer. Gervais was bending over the man. With an abrupt laugh he called out: "Killed him, pardieu! He has come off cheap."

He raised the fellow's limp head, and we saw that the sword had passed just over his shoulder, piercing the linen, not the flesh. He had swooned from sheer terror, being in truth not so much as scratched.

Gervais turned to his cousin.

"I never meant that foul trick. It was no thought of mine. I would have turned the blade if I could. I will kill Pontou now, if you say the word."

"Nay," answered the other, faintly; "help me."

The blood was pouring from his arm; he was half swooning. Gervais and I ran to him and, between us, bathed the cut, bandaged it with strips torn from a shirt, and made a sling of a scarf. The wound was long, but not deep, and when we had poured some wine down his throat he was himself again.

"You will not bear me malice for that poltroon's work, Étienne?" Gervais asked, more humbly than I ever thought to hear him speak. "That was a foul cut, but it was no fault of mine. I am no blackguard; I fight fair. I will kill the knave, if you like."

"You are ungrateful, Gervais; he saved you when you needed saving," Yeux-gris laughed. "Faith! let him live. I forgive him. You will pay me for my hurt by yielding me Félix."

Gervais looked at me. While we had worked side by side over Yeux-gris he seemed to have forgotten that he was my enemy. But now all the old suspicion and dislike came into his face again. However, he answered:

"Aye, you would have been the victor had it not been for Pontou. You shall do what you like with your boy. I promise you that."

"Now that is well said, Gervais," returned Yeux-gris, rising, and picking up his sword, which he sheathed. "That is very well said. For if you did not feel like promising it, why, I should have to begin over again with my left hand."

"Oh, I give you the boy," Gervais repeated rather sullenly, turning away to pour himself some wine.

I could not but wonder at Yeux-gris, at his gaiety and his steadfastness. He had hardly looked grave through the whole affair; he had fought with a smile on his lips and had taken a cruel wound with a laugh. Withal, he had been the constant champion of my innocence, even to drawing his sword on his cousin for me. Now, with his bloody arm in its sling, he was as debonair and careless as ever. I had been stupid enough to imagine the big Gervais the leader of the two, and I found myself mistaken. I dropped on my knee and kissed my savior's hand in all gratitude.

"Aha," said Yeux-gris, "what think you now of being my valet?"

Verily, I was hard pushed.

"Monsieur," I said, "I owe you much more than I can ever pay. If you were any man's enemy but my duke's, I would serve you on my knees. But I was born on the duke's land and I cannot be disloyal. You may kill me yourself, if you like."

"No," he answered gravely, "that is not my métier."

Gervais laughed.

"Make me that offer, and I accept."

Yeux-gris turned to him with that little hauteur he assumed occasionally.

"You are helpless, my cousin. You have passed your word."

"Aye. I leave him to you."

His sullen eyes told me it was no newborn tenderness for me that prompted his surrender. Nor had I, truth to tell, any great faith in the sacredness of his word. Yet I believed he would let me be. For it was borne in upon me that, despite his passion and temper, he had no wish to quarrel with Yeux-gris. Whether at bottom he loved him or in some way dreaded him, I could not tell; but of this my fear-sharpened wits were sure: he had no desire to press an open breach. He was honestly ashamed of his henchman's low deed; yet even before that his judgment had disliked the quarrel. Else why had he struck me with the hilt of the sword?

"I leave him to you," he repeated. "Do as you choose. If you deem his life a precious thing, cherish it. When did you learn a taste for insolence, Étienne? Time was when you were touchy on that score."

"Time never was when I did not love courage."

"Oh, it is courage!" With a sneer he turned away.

"Gervais," said Yeux-gris, "have the kindness to unlock the door."

Gervais wheeled around, his face an angry question.

Yeux-gris answered it with cold politeness:

"That Félix Broux may pass out."

"By Heaven, he shall not!"

"You gave your word you would leave him to me. Did you lie?"

"I do leave him to you!" Gervais thundered. "I would slit his impudent throat; but since you love him, you may have him to eat out of your plate and sleep in your bosom. I will put up with it. But go out of that door till the thing is done, sang dieu! he shall not!"

"If he goes straight to the duke, what then? He will say he found us living in my house. What harm? We are no felons. Let him say it."

"And put Lucas on his guard?" returned Gervais. He was angry, yet he spoke with evident attempt at restraint. "Put Lucas on the trail? He is wary as a cat. Let him get wind of us here, and he will never let us catch him."

"Well," said Yeux-gris, reluctantly, "it is true. And though I will not have the boy harmed, he shall stay here. I will not put a spoke in the wheel. We will take no risks till Lucas is shent. The boy shall be held prisoner. And afterward –"

"I will come myself and let him out," said Gervais, and laughed.

I glanced at my protector, not liking to think of that moment, whenever it might be, "afterward." He went up to Gervais.

"My cousin, are we friends or foes? For, faith! you treat me strangely like a foe."

"We are friends."

"I am your friend, since it is in your cause that I am here. I have stood at your shoulder like a brother – you cannot deny it."

"No," Gervais answered; "you stood my friend, – my one friend in that house, – as I was yours. I stood at your shoulder in the Montluc affair – you cannot deny that. I have been your ally, your servant, your messenger to mademoiselle, your envoy to Mayenne. I have done all in my power to win you your lady."

A shadow fell over Yeux-gris's open face.

"That task needs a greater power than yours, my Gervais."

He regarded Gervais with a rueful smile, his thoughts of a sudden as far away from me as if I had never set foot in the Rue Coupejarrets. He shook his head, sighing, and said, with a hand on Gervais's shoulder: "It's beyond you, cousin."

Gervais brought him back to the point.

"Well, I've done what I could for you. But you don't help me when you let loose a spy to warn Lucas."

"He shall not go. You know well, cousin, you will be no gladder than I when that knave is dead. But I will not have Félix Broux suffer because he dared speak for the Duke of St. Quentin."

"As you choose, then. I will not touch a hair of his head if you keep him from Lucas."

Once more he turned away across the room. My bewilderment was so great that the words came out of themselves:

"Messieurs, is it Lucas you mean to kill?"

Yeux-gris looked at me, not instantly replying. I cried again to him:

"Monsieur, is it Lucas or the duke?"

Then Yeux-gris, despite a gesture from Gervais, who would have told me nothing I might ask, exclaimed:

"Why, Lucas!"

He said it in such honest surprise and with such a steady glance that the heavy fear that had hung on me dropped from me like a dead-weight, and suddenly I turned quite dizzy and fell into the nearest chair.

A dash of water in the face made me look up, to see Yeux-gris standing wet-handed by me.

"Mon dieu!" he cried, "you were as white as the wall. Do you love so much this Lucas who struck you?"

"No," I said, rising; "I thought you meant to kill the duke."

"Did you take us for Leaguers?"

I nodded.

He spoke as if actually he felt it important to set himself right in my eyes.

"Well, we are none. We are no politicians, but private gentlemen with a grudge to pay. I care not what the parties do. Whether we have the Princess Isabelle or Henry the Huguenot, 'tis all one to me; I am not putting either on the throne. So if you have got it into your head that we are plotting for the League, why, get it out again."

"But you are enemies to the Duke of St. Quentin?"

He answered me slowly:

"We do not love him. But we do not plot his death. He goes his way unharmed by us. We are gentlemen, not bravos."

"And Lucas?"

"Lucas is my cousin's enemy, and, being a great man's man, skulks behind the bars of the Hôtel St. Quentin and will not face my cousin's sword. So to reach him takes a little plotting. Do you believe me?"

I looked into his grey eyes, that had flashed so hotly in my defense, and I could not but believe him.

"Yes, monsieur," I said.

He regarded me curiously.

"The duke's life seems much to you."

"Why, monsieur, I am a Broux."

"And could not be disloyal to save your life?"

"My life! Monsieur, the Broux would not seek to save their souls if M. le Duc preferred them damned."

I expected he would rebuke me for the outburst, but he did not; he merely said:

"And Lucas?"

"Oh, Lucas!" I said. "I know nothing of him. He is new with the duke since my time. I do not owe him anything, save a grudge for that blow this morning. Mon dieu, monsieur, I am thankful to you for befriending me. Dying for Monsieur is all in a day's work; we expect to do that. But, my faith, if I had died just now, it would have been for Lucas."

At this moment a long groan came from the end of the room. We turned; the lackey was waking from his swoon, under the ministration of Gervais. He opened his eyes; their glance was dull till they fell upon his master. And then at once they looked venomous.

Gervais kicked him into fuller consciousness.

"Get up, hound. It is time to meet Martin."

The wretch scrambled shakily to his feet, and stood clutching the door-jamb and eying Gervais, terror writ large on his chalky countenance. Yet there was more than terror in his face; there was the look you see in the eyes of a trapped animal that watches its chance to bite. Yeux-gris cried out:

"You dare not send that man, Gervais."

"Why not?"

"Because the moment he is clear of the house he will betray you. Look at his face."

"He shall swear on the cross!"

"Aye. But you cannot trust the oath of such as he."

"What would you? We must send."

"As you will. But you are mad if you send him."

Gervais pondered a moment, his slower wits taking in the situation. Then he seized the man by the collar, fairly flung him across the room into the closet, and bolted the door upon him.

"I will settle with him later. But you are right. We cannot send him."

Yeux-gris burst into laughter.

"My faith! we could not have more trouble if we were heads of the League than this little duel of yours is giving us. Why, what if we are seen? I will go."

Gervais started.

"No; that will not do."

"Eh, bien, then, what will you propose?"

But it was someone else who proposed. I said to Yeux-gris:

"Monsieur, if all your purpose is against Lucas and no other, I am your man. I will go."

"What, my stubborn-neck, you?"

"Why, monsieur, I owe you a great debt. While I thought you meant ill to M. le Duc, I could not serve you. But this Lucas is another pair of sleeves. I owe him no allegiance. Moreover, he nearly killed me this morning. Therefore I am quite at your disposal."

"Now, I wonder if you are lying," said Gervais.

"I do not think he is lying," Yeux-gris said. "I trow, Gervais, we have got our messenger."

"You tell me to beware of Pontou because he hates me, and then would have me trust this fellow?" Gervais demanded with some acumen.

I said: "Monsieur, you do not seem to understand how I come to make this offer."

"To get out of the house with a whole skin."

I had a joy in daring him, being sure of Yeux-gris.

"Monsieur," I said, "I should be glad to leave this house with my skin whole or broken, so long as I left on my own feet. But you have mentioned the very reason why I shall not betray you. I do not love you and I do not love Lucas. Therefore, if you and M. Lucas are to fight, I ask nothing better than to help the quarrel on."

He stared at me with an air more of bewilderment than aught else, but Yeux-gris's ready laughter rang out.

"Bravo, Félix! I am proud of you. That is an idea worthy of Cæsar! You would set your enemies to exterminate each other. And I asked you to be my valet!"

"Which do you wish to see slain?" demanded the black Gervais.

I answered quite truthfully:

"Monsieur, I shall be pleased either way."

I know not how he relished the answer, for Yeux-gris cried out at once:

"Bravo, Félix, you are a paragon! I have not wit enough to know whether you are as simple as sunshine or as deep as a well, but I love you."

"Monsieur," I answered, as I think, very neatly, "if I am a well, truth lies at the bottom."

"Well, Gervais?" demanded Yeux-gris.

Gervais bent his lowering brows on his cousin.

"Do you say, trust him?"

"Aye, I would trust him. For never yet did villain turn honest, nor honest man false, in one short hour. When he was asked to serve against the duke he showed his stuff. He was no traitor; he was no coward; he was no liar. I think he is not those now."

Gervais was still doubtful.

"It is a risk. If he betrays –"

"What is life without risks?" cried Yeux-gris. "I thought you too good a gambler, Gervais, to falter before a risk."

"Well," Gervais consented, "I leave it to you. Do as you like."

Yeux-gris said at once to me:

"This Lucas, as I told you, is too cowardly to meet my cousin in open fight. Since he got the challenge he has never stuck his nose out of doors without two or three of the duke's guard about him. Therefore we have the right to get at him as we can. We have paid a man in the house to tell of his movements. He is to fare out secretly at night on a mission for M. le Duc, with one comrade only. M. Gervais and I will interrupt that little journey."

"Very good, monsieur. And I?"

"You will meet our spy and learn the hour of the expedition. Last night, when he told us of the plan, it had not been decided."

"Then he will be the other man I saw in the window? I shall know him."

"You have sharp eyes and a sharp brain, youngster. But he will not know you. Therefore you can say you come from the shuttered house in the Rue Coupejarrets. You will meet him in the little alley to the north of the Hôtel St. Quentin. Do you know your way to the hôtel? Well, then, you are to go down the passageway between the house and M. de Portreuse's garden – you cannot mistake it, for on two sides of the house is the street, on the third the garden, and on the fourth the alleyway. Halfway down the alley is an arch with a small door. In that arch our man, Louis Martin, will meet you. Do you understand?"

I repeated the directions.

"You have learned your lesson. You will ask him the hour – only that."

"And you will take oath not to betray us," commanded Gervais.

I took out the cross that hung on my rosary. I was ready to swear. Gervais prompted:

"I swear to go and come straight, and speak no word to any but Martin."

With all solemnity I swore it on my cross.

"That oath will be kept," said Yeux-gris. He held out a sudden hand for the cross, which I gave him, wondering.

"I swear that we mean no harm whatsoever to the Duke of St. Quentin." He kissed the cross and flung the chain back over my neck.

At last I saw the door unlocked. Yeux-gris even returned to me my knife.

"Au revoir, messieurs."

Gervais, sullen to the last, vouchsafed no answer, but Yeux-gris called out cheerily, "Au revoir."

VI

A matter of life and death.

Nothing in life can be so sweet as freedom after captivity, safety after danger. When I gained the open street once more and breathed the open air, no one molesting or troubling me, I could have sung with joy. I fairly hugged myself for my cleverness in getting out of my plight. As for the combat I was furthering, my only doubt about that was lest the skulking Lucas should not prove good sword enough to give trouble to M. Gervais. It was very far from my wish that he should come out of the attempt unscathed.

But as I went along and had more time to ponder the matter, other doubts forced themselves into my reluctant mind. Put it as I pleased, the affair smacked too much of secrecy to be quite savory. It was curious, to say the least, that an honest encounter should require so much plotting. Also, Lucas, coward and rascal though he might be, was Monsieur's man, doing Monsieur's errand, and for me to mix myself up in a plot against him was scarcely in keeping with my vaunted loyalty to the house of St. Quentin. My friend Gervais's quarrel might be just; his manner of procedure, even, might be just, and yet I have no right to take part in it.

And yet Monsieur had signified plainly enough that he was no longer my patron. For my birth's sake I might never work against him, but I was free to do whatever else I chose. Monsieur himself had made it necessary for me to take another master, and assuredly I owed something to Yeux-gris. I had reason to feel confidence in his honor; surely I might reckon that he would not be in the affair unless it were honest. Lucas was like enough a scoundrel of whom Monsieur would be well rid. And lastly and finally and above all, I was sworn, so there was no use worrying about it. I had taken oath, and could not draw back.

I hurried along to the rendezvous, only pausing one moment at the street-corner to buy sausages hot from the brazier, which I crammed into my mouth as I ran. But after all was there no need of haste; the little arch, when I panted up to it, was all deserted.

No better place for a tryst could have been found in the heart of busy Paris. Only the one door opened into the alley; M. de Portreuse's high garden wall, forming the other side of the passage, was unbroken by a gate, and no curious eyes from the house could look into the deep arch and see the narrow nail-studded door at the back where I awaited the rat-faced Martin.

I stood there long, first on one foot and then on the other, fearful every moment lest someone of Monsieur's true men should come along to demand my business. No one appeared, either foe or friend, for so long that I began to think Yeux-gris had tricked me and sent me here on a fool's errand, when, all at once, a low voice said close to my ear:

"What seek you here?"

I jumped on finding at my side a little, pale, sharp-faced man – the man of the vision. He had slipped through the door so suddenly and quietly that I was once more tempted to take him for a ghost. He eyed me for a bare second; then his eyes dropped before mine.

"I am come to learn the hour," said I.

"Did you not hear the chimes ring five?"

"Oh, no need for disguise. I am come from the two in the Rue Coupejarrets. They bade me ask the hour."

He favored me with another of his shifty glances.

"What hour meant they?"

I said bluntly, in a louder tone:

"The hour when M. Lucas sets out on his secret mission."

"Hush!" he cried. "Hush! Don't say names aloud – his or the other's."

"Well," I said crossly, "you have kept me waiting already more time than I care to lose. How much longer before you will tell me what I came to know?"

He looked at me sharply for another brief instant before his eyes slunk away from mine.

"You should have a password."

"They gave me none. They told me to say I came from the shuttered house in the Rue Coupejarrets, and that would be enough."

"How came you into this business?"

"By a back window."

He gave me another suspicious glance, but making nothing by it, he rejoined:

"Eh bien, I trust you. I will tell you."

He clutched my arm and drew me to the back of the arch, where the afternoon shadows were already gathered.

"What have you for me?" he demanded.

"Nothing. What should I have?"

"No gold?"

"No."

"He promised me ten pistoles today. He did not give them to you?"

"I tell you, no."

"You are a thief! You have them!"

He stepped forward menacingly; so did I. He then fell back as abruptly.

"Nay, it was a jest; I know you are honest. But he promised me ten pistoles."

"He did not give them to me," I said. "Perhaps he was not so convinced of my honesty. He will doubtless pay you afterward."

"Afterward!" he retorted in a high key. "By our Lady, he shall pay me afterward! The gutters will run gold then, will they? Pardieu! I will see that a good stream flows my way. But one cannot play today with tomorrow's coin. He said I should have ten pistoles when I let him know the hour."

"I cannot mend that. It lies between you and him. I have not seen or heard of any money."

Martin edged up close to the door of retreat and waxed defiant.

"Then all I have to say is, he may go whistle for his news."

Now, had I but thought of it, here was an easy road out of a bad business. If Martin would not tell the hour of rendezvous, Lucas was saved, Monsieur's interests not endangered, yet at the same time I was not forsworn. But touch pitch and be defiled. You cannot go hand and glove with villains and remain an honest man. I returned directly:

"As you choose. But M. Gervais carries a long sword."

He started at that and made no instant reply, seeming to be balancing considerations. Then he gave his decision.

"I will tell you. But your M. Gervais is wrong if he thinks I can be slighted and robbed of my dues. I know enough to make trouble for him, and I know where to take my knowledge. He will not find it easy to shut my mouth afterward, except with good broad gold pieces."

"Enfin, are you telling me the hour?" I said impatiently. I was ill at ease; my only wish was to get the errand done and be gone.

He laid a hand on my shoulder and made me bend to him, and even then spoke so low I could scarce catch the words.

"They have fixed positively on tonight. They will leave by this door and take the route I described last night to M. Gervais. They will start as soon as the streets are quiet, sometime between ten and eleven. They must allow an hour to reach the gate, and the man goes off at twelve.

In all likelihood they will not set out before a quarter of eleven; M. le Duc does not care to be recognized."

So they planned to kill Lucas at Monsieur's side? Yeux-gris had not dared to tell me that. But he had looked me straight in the face and sworn on the cross no harm was meant to M. le Duc. Natheless, the thing looked ugly. My heart leaped up at the next words:

"Also Vigo will go."

"Vigo!"

"Not so loud! You will have the guard on us! Yes, he is to go. At first Monsieur did not tell even him, he desired to keep this visit to the king so secret. But this morning he took Vigo into his confidence, and nothing would serve the man but to go. He watches over Monsieur like a hen over a chick."

"Then it will be three to three," I said. I thought of Gervais, Yeux-gris, and Pontou, for of course I would take no part in it.

"Three to two; Lucas will not fight."

Lucas must be a poltroon, indeed!

"But Vigo and Monsieur –" I began.

"Aye, they are quick enough with their swords. Your side must be quicker, that's all. If you are sudden enough you can easily kill the duke before he can draw."

Talk of words like thunderbolts! All the thunder of heaven could not have whelmed me like those words. Yeux-gris and his oaths! It *was* the duke, after all!

I could not speak. I looked I know not how. But it was dusky in the arch.

"It sounds simple," he went on. "But, three of you as you are, you will have trouble with Vigo. That is all. I have told you all. I must get back before I am missed. Good luck to the enterprise."

Still I stood like a block of wood.

"Tell M. Gervais to remember me," he said, and opening the door, passed in. I heard him lock and bolt it after him, and his footsteps hurrying down the passageway.

Then I came to myself and sprang to the door and beat upon it furiously. But if he heard he was afraid to respond. After a futile moment that seemed an hour I rushed out of the arch and around to the great gate.

The grilles were closed as before, but the sentry's face, luckily, was strange to me.

"Open! open!" I shouted, breathless. "I must see M. le Duc!"

"Who are you?" he demanded, staring.

"My name is Broux. I have news for M. le Duc. Let me in. It is a matter of life and death."

"Why, I suppose, then, I must let you in," that good fellow answered, drawing back the bolts. "But you must wait here till –"

The gate was open. I took base advantage of him by sliding under his arm and shooting across the court up the steps to the house. The door stood open, and a couple of lackeys lounged on a bench in the hall.

"M. le Duc!" I cried. "I must see him."

They jumped up, the picture of bewilderment.

"Who are you? How came you here?" cried the quicker-tongued of the two.

"The sentry opened for me. Where am I to find M. le Duc? I must see him! I have news!"

"M. le Duc sees no one today," the second lackey announced pompously.

"But I must see him, I tell you," I repeated. I had completely lost what little head I ever had; it seemed to me that if I could not see M. le Duc on the instant I should find him weltering in his gore. "I must see him," I cried, parrotlike. "It is a matter of life and death."

"From whom do you come?"

"That's my affair. Enough that I come with news of the highest moment. You will be sorry if I you do not get me quickly to M. le Duc."

They looked at each other, somewhat impressed.

"I will go for M. Constant," said the one who had spoken first.

Constant was Master of the Household; M. le Duc had inherited him with the estate and kept him in his place for old time's sake. He was old, fussy, and self-important, and withal no friend to me.

"I had rather you fetched Vigo," I said.

"Oh, Vigo will not come. He is with Monsieur. If I bring M. Constant, it is the best I can do for you."

I had recovered myself sufficiently by this time to remember the nature of lackeys, and gave the messenger the last silver piece I had in the world. He regarded it contemptuously, but pocketed it and departed in leisurely fashion up the stairs.

The other was not too grand to cross-examine me.

"What sort of news have you? Do you come from the king?" he asked in a lowered voice.

"No."

"From M. de Valère?"

"No."

"Then who the devil are you?"

"Félix Broux of St. Quentin."

"Ah, St. Quentin," he said, as if he found that rather tame. "You bring news from there?"

"No, I do not. Think you I shall tell you? This news is for Monsieur."

"It won't reach Monsieur unless you learn politeness toward the gentlemen of his household," he retorted.

We were getting into a lively quarrel when Constant appeared on the stairway – Constant and the lackey who had fetched him, and two more lackeys, and a page, all of whom had somehow scented that something was in the wind. They came flocking about us as I said:

"Ah, M. Constant! You know me, Félix Broux of St. Quentin. I must see M. le Duc."

Constant's face of surprise at me changed to one of malice. Down at St. Quentin he had suffered much from us pages, as a slow, peevish old dotard must. I had played many a prank on him, but I had not thought he would revenge himself at such time as this. He looked at me with a spiteful grin, and said to the men:

"He lies. I do not know him. I never saw him."

"Never saw me, Félix Broux!" I cried, completely taken aback.

"No," maintained Constant. "You are an impostor."

"Impostor! Nonsense!" I cried out. "Constant, you know me as well as you know yourself. I say I must see the duke; his life is in danger!"

Constant was paying off old scores with interest.

"An impostor," he yelled shrilly, "or else a madman – or an assassin."

"That is the truth," said someone, laying a heavy hand on my shoulder.

I turned; two men of the guard had come up, my friend of just now and my foe of the morning. It was the latter who held me and said:

"This is the very rascal who sprang on Monsieur's coach-step in the morning. M. Lucas threw him off, else he might have stabbed Monsieur. We were fools enough to let him go free. But this time he shall not get off so easy."

"I am innocent of all thought of harm," I cried. "I am M. le Duc's loyal servant. I meant no harm this morning, and I mean none now. I am here to save Monsieur's life."

"He is here to kill Monsieur; he is an assassin!" screamed Constant. "Flog him, men; he will own the truth then!"

"I am no assassin!" I shouted, struggling in their grasp. "Let me go, villains, let me go! I tell you, Monsieur's life is at stake – Monsieur's very life, I tell you!"

They paid me no heed. Not one of them – save hat lying knave Constant – knew me as other than the shabby fellow who had acted suspiciously in the morning. They were dragging me to the door in spite of my shouts and struggles, when suddenly a ringing voice spoke from above:

"What is this rumpus? Who talks of Monsieur's life?"

The guards halted dead, and I cried out joyfully:

"Vigo!"

"Yes, I am Vigo," the big man answered, striding down the stairs. "Who are you?"

I wanted to shout, "Félix Broux, Monsieur's page," but a sort of nightmare dread came over me lest Vigo, too, should disclaim me, and my voice stuck in my throat.

"Whoever you are, you will be taught not to make a racket in M. le Duc's hall. By the saints! it's the boy Félix."

At the friendliness in his voice the guards dropped their hands from me.

"M. Vigo," I said, "I have news for Monsieur of the gravest moment. I am come on a matter of life and death. And I am stopped in the hall by lackeys."

He looked at me sternly.

"This is not one of your fooleries, Félix?"

"No, M. Vigo."

"Come with me."

VII

A divided duty.

That was Vigo's way. The toughest snarl untangled at his touch. He had more sense and fewer airs than any other, he saw at once that I was in earnest; and Constant's voluble protests were as so much wind. The title does not make the man. Though Constant was Master of the Household and Vigo only Equery, yet Vigo ruled every corner of the establishment and every man in it, save only Monsieur, who ruled him.

He said no word to me as we climbed the broad stair; neither reproved me for the fracas nor questioned me about my coming. He would not pry into Monsieur's business; and, save as I concerned Monsieur, he had no interest in me whatsoever. He led the way straight into an antechamber, where a page sprang up to bar our passage.

"No one may enter, M. Vigo, not even you. M. le Duc has ordered it. Why, Félix! You in Paris!"

"I enter," said Vigo; and, sweeping Marcel aside, he knocked loudly.

"I came last night," I found time to say under my breath to my old comrade before the door was opened.

The handsome secretary whom I had taken for the count stood in the doorway looking askance at us. He knew me at once and wondered.

"You cannot enter, Vigo. M. le Duc is occupied."

He made to shut the door, but Vigo's foot was over the sill.

"Natheless, I must enter," he answered unabashed and pushed his way into the room.

"Then you must answer for it," returned the secretary, with a scowl that sat ill on his delicate face.

"*You* shall answer for it if it turns out a mare's nest," said Vigo, in a low, meaning voice to me. But I hardly heard him. I passed him and Lucas, and flew down the long room to Monsieur.

M. le Duc was seated before a table heaped with papers. He had been watching the scene at the door in surprise and anger. He looked at me with a sharp frown, while the deer-hound at his feet rose on its haunches growling.

"Roland!" I said. The dog sprang up and came to me.

"Félix Broux!" Monsieur exclaimed, with his quick, warm smile – a smile no man in France could match for radiance.

I had no thought of kneeling, of making obeisance, of waiting permission to speak.

"Monsieur," I cried, half choked, "there is a plot – a vile plot to murder you!"

"Where? At St. Quentin?"

"No, Monsieur. Here in Paris. In the streets tonight, when you go to the king."

Monsieur sprang to his feet, his hand on his sword. Lucas turned white. Vigo swore. Monsieur cried:

"How, in God's name, know you that?"

"You have been betrayed, Monsieur. Your plan is known. You leave the house tonight, near a quarter of eleven, to go in secret to the king. You leave by the little door in the alley –"

"Diable!" breathed Vigo.

"They set on you on your way – three of them – to run you through before you can draw."

"But, ventre bleu! Monsieur is not alone."

"No; he walks between you and M. Lucas."

Not one of them spoke. They stared at me as if I were something uncanny. I, a raw country boy, disclosing a perfect knowledge of their most intimate plans!

"How know you this?" Monsieur demanded of me. But he was not looking at me. His keen glance went first to Lucas, then to Vigo, the two men who had shared his confidence. The secretary cried out:

"You cannot think, Monsieur, that I betrayed you?"

Vigo said nothing. His steady eyes never left Monsieur's face.

"No," answered Monsieur to Lucas, "I cannot think it." And to Vigo he said: "I shall accuse you when I accuse myself. But – none knew this thing save our three selves." And his gaze went back to Lucas.

"It is not likely to be he," I said, impelled to be just to him though I did not like him, "for they meant to kill him as well."

Lucas started, then instantly recovered himself.

"A comprehensive plot, Monsieur," he said, with a smile.

"Then who was it?" cried Monsieur to me. "You know. Speak."

"There is a spy in the house – an eavesdropper," I said, and then paused.

"Aye?" said Monsieur. "Who?"

Now the answer to this was easy, yet I flinched before it; for I knew well enough what Monsieur would do. He feared no man, and waited on no man's advice. And if he was a good lover, he was a good hater. He would not inform the governor, and await the tardy course of justice, that would probably accomplish – nothing. Nor would he consider the troubled times and the danger of his position, and ignore the affair, as many would have deemed best. He would not stop to think what the Sixteen might have to say to it. No; he would call out his guards and slay the plotters in the Rue Coupejarrets like the wolves they were. It was right he should, but – I owed my life to Yeux-gris.

"His name, man, his name!" Monsieur was crying.

"Monsieur," I returned, flushing hot, "Monsieur –"

"Do you know his name?"

"Yes, Monsieur, I know his name, but –"

Monsieur looked at me in surprise and frowning, impatience. Quickly Lucas struck in:

"Monsieur, I have grave doubts of the boy's honesty."

"Doubts!" cried Monsieur, with a sudden laugh. "It is not a case for doubts. The boy states facts."

He seated himself in his chair, his face growing stern again. The little action seemed to make him no longer merely my questioner, but my judge.

"Now, Félix Broux, let us get to the bottom of this."

"Monsieur," I began, struggling to put the case clearly, "I learned of the plot by accident. I did not guess for a long time it was you who were the victim. When I found out that, I came straight here to you. Monsieur, there are four men in the plot, and one of them has stood my friend."

"And my assassin!"

"He is a black-hearted villain!" I acknowledged. "For he swore no harm was meant to you. He swore it was only a private grudge against M. Lucas. But when one of them let out the truth I came straight to you."

"That is likely true," said Vigo, "for he was ready to kill the men who barred his way."

"You were in a plot to kill my secretary!"

"Ah, Monsieur!" I cried.

"You – Félix Broux!"

I curled with shame.

"M. Lucas had struck me," I muttered; "I thought the fight was fair enough. And they threatened my life."

Monsieur's contemptuous eyes shriveled me as flame shrivels a leaf.

"You – a Broux of St. Quentin!"

Lucas, who had watched me close all the while, as they all three did, said now:

"I believe he is a cheat, Monsieur. There is no plot. He has learned of your plan through the eavesdropper he speaks of and thinks to make credit out of a trumped-up tale of murder."

"No," answered Monsieur. "You may think that, Lucas, for he is a stranger to you. But I know him. He was a fool sometimes, but he was never dishonest. You used to be fond of me, Félix. What has happened to make you consort with my enemies?"

"Ah, Monsieur, I love you. I have always loved you," I cried. "I am not lying now, nor cheating you. There is a plot. I learned it and came straight to you, though I was under oath not to betray them."

"Then, in Heaven's name, Félix," burst out Vigo, "which side are you on?"

Monsieur began to laugh.

"That is what I should like to know. For, by St. Quentin, I can make nothing of it."

"Monsieur," insisted Lucas, "whatever he was once, I believe him a trickster now."

Monsieur bent his keen eyes on me.

"No; he is plainly in earnest. Therefore with patience I look to get some sense out of this snarl of a story. Something is there we have not yet fathomed."

"Will Monsieur let me speak?"

"I have done naught but urge you to do so for some time past," he answered dryly.

"Monsieur, you know my father would not let me leave St. Quentin with you, three months back. But at length he said I should come, and I reached Paris last night and, since it was late, lodged at an inn. This morning I came to your gate, but the guard would not let me enter. I was so mad to see you, Monsieur, that when you drove out I sprang up on your coach-step –"

"Ah," said Monsieur, a new light breaking in upon him, "that was you, Félix? I did not know you; I was thinking of other matters. And Lucas took you for a miscreant. Now I *am* sorry."

If I had been a noble he could not have spoken franker apology. But at once he was stern again. "And because my secretary took you in all good faith for a possible assassin and struck you to save me, you turn traitor and take part in a plot to set on him and kill him! I had believed that of some hired lackey, not of a Broux."

"Monsieur, I was wrong – a thousand times wrong. I knew that as soon as I had sworn. And when I found it was you they meant, I came to you, oath or no oath."

"There spoke the Broux!" cried Monsieur with his brilliant smile. "Now you are Félix. Who are my would-be murderers?"

We had come round in a circle to the place where we had stuck before, and here we stuck again.

"Monsieur, I would tell you all before you could count ten – tell you their names, their whereabouts, everything – were it not for one man who stood my friend."

The duke's eyes flashed.

"You call him that – my assassin!"

"He is an assassin," I was forced to answer; "even Monsieur's assassin – and a perjurer. But – but, Monsieur, he saved my life from the other, at the risk of his own. How can I pay him back by betraying him?"

"According to your own account, he betrayed you."

"Aye, he lied to me," I said brokenly. "Yet Monsieur, if it were your own case and one had saved your life, were he the scum of the gutter, would you send him to his death?"

"To whom do you owe your first duty?"

"Monsieur, to you."

"Then speak."

But I could not do it. Though I knew Yeux-gris for a villain, yet he had saved my life.

"Monsieur, I cannot."

The duke cried out:

"This to me!"

There was a silence. I stood with hanging head, the picture of a shame-faced knave. Shame so filled me that I could not look up to meet Monsieur's sentence. But when I had remembered the good hater in Monsieur, I should have remembered, too, the good lover. Monsieur had been fond of me at St. Quentin. As I waited for the lightning to strike, he said with utmost gentleness:

"Félix, let me understand you. In what manner did this man save your life?"

Now that was like my lord. Though a hot man, he loved fairness and ever strove to do the just thing, and his patience was the finer that it was not his nature. His leniency fired me with a sudden hope.

"Monsieur, there are four of them in the plot. But one cannot be as vile as the others, since he saved my life. Monsieur, if I tell you, will you let that one go?"

"I shall do as I see fit," he answered, all the duke. "Félix, will you speak?"

"If Monsieur will promise to let him go –"

"Insolence, sirrah! I do not bargain with my servants."

His words were like whips. I flinched before his proud anger, and for the second time stood with hanging head awaiting his sentence. And again he did what I could not guess. He cried out:

"Félix, you are blind, besotted, mad. You know not what you do. I am in constant danger. The city is filled with my enemies. The Leagues hate me and are ever plotting mischief against me. Every day their mistrust and hatred grow. I did a bold thing in coming to Paris, but I had a great end to serve – to pave a way into the capital for the Catholic king and bring the land to peace. For that, I live in hourly jeopardy, and risk my life tonight on foot in the streets. If I am killed, more than my life is lost. The Church may lose the king, and this dear France of ours be harried to a desert in the civil wars!"

I had braced myself to bear Monsieur's anger, but this unlooked-for appeal pierced me through and through. All the love and loyalty in me – and I had much, though it may not have seemed so – rose in answer to Monsieur's call. I fell on my knees before him, choked with sobs.

Monsieur's hand lay on my head as he said quietly:

"Now, Félix, speak."

I answered huskily:

"Would Monsieur have me turn Judas?"

"Judas betrayed his *master.*"

It was my last stand. My last redoubt had fallen. I raised my head to tell him all.

Maybe it was the tears in my eyes, but as I lifted them to M. le Duc, I saw – not him, but Yeux-gris – Yeux-gris looking at me with warm good will, as he had looked when he was saving me from Gervais. I saw him, I say, plain before my eyes. The next instant there was nothing but Monsieur's face of rising impatience.

I rose to my feet, and said:

"Kill me, Monsieur; I cannot tell."

"Nom de dieu!" he shouted, springing up.

I shut my eyes and waited. Had he slain me then and there it were no more than my deserts.

"Monsieur," said Vigo, immovably, "shall I go for the boot?"

I opened my eyes then. Monsieur stood quite still, his brow knotted, his hands clenched as if to keep them off me.

"Monsieur," I said, "send for the boot, the thumbscrew, whatever you please. I deserve it, and I will bear it. Monsieur, it is not that I will not tell. It is something stronger than I. I *cannot.*"

He burst into an angry laugh.

"Say you are possessed of a devil, and I will believe it. My faith! though you are a low-born lad and I Duke of St. Quentin, I seem to be getting the worst of it."

"There is the boot, Monsieur."

Monsieur laughed again, no less angrily.

"That does not help me, my good Vigo. I cannot torture a Broux."

"There Monsieur is wrong. The lad has been disloyal and insolent, if he is a Broux."

"Granted, Vigo," said M. le Duc. But he did not add, "Fetch the boot."

Vigo went on with steady persistence. "He has not been loyal to Monsieur and his interests in refusing to tell what he knows. And if he goes counter to Monsieur's interests he is a traitor, Broux or no Broux. He has no claim to be treated as other than an enemy. These are serious times. Monsieur does not well to play with his dangers. The boy must tell what he knows. Am I to go for the boot, Monsieur?"

M. le Duc was silent for a moment, while the hot flush that had sprung to his face died away. Then he answered Vigo:

"Nevertheless, it is owing to Félix that I shall not walk out to meet my death tonight."

The secretary had stood silent for a long time, fingering nervously the papers on the table. I had forgotten his presence, when now he stepped forward and said:

"If I might be permitted a suggestion, Monsieur –"

Monsieur silenced him with a sharp gesture.

"Félix Broux," he said to me, "you have been following a bad plan. No man can run with the hare and hunt with the hounds. You are either my loyal servant or my enemy, one thing or the other. Now I am loath to hurt you. You have seen how I am loath to hurt you. I give you one more chance to be honest. Go and think it over. If in half an hour you have decided that you are my true man, well and good. If not, by St. Quentin, we will see what a flogging can do!"

VIII

Charles-André-Étienne-Marie.

Unpleased, but unprotesting, Vigo led me out into the anteroom. Those men who judged by the outside of things and, knowing Vigo's iron ways, said that he ruled Monsieur, were wrong.

The big equery gave me over to the charge of Marcel and returned to the inner room. Hardly had the door closed behind him when the page burst out:

"What is it? What is the coil? What have you done, Félix?"

Now you can guess I was too sick-hearted for chatter. I had defied and disobeyed my liege lord; I could never hope for pardon or any man's respect. They threatened me with flogging; well, let them flog. They could not make my back any sorer than my conscience was. For I had not the satisfaction in my trouble of thinking that I had done right. Monsieur's danger should have been my first consideration. What was

Yeux-gris, perjured scoundrel, in comparison with M. le Duc? And yet I knew that at the end of the half-hour I should not tell; at the end of the flogging I should not tell. I had warned Monsieur; that I would have done had it been the breaking of a thousand oaths. But give up Yeux-gris? Not if they tore me limb from limb!

"What is it all about?" cried Marcel, again. "You look as glum as a Jesuit in Lent. What is the matter with you, Félix?"

"I have cooked my goose," I said gloomily.

"What have you done?"

"Nothing that I can speak about. But I am out of Monsieur's books."

"What was old Vigo after when he took you in to Monsieur? I never saw anything so bold. When Monsieur says he is not to be disturbed he means it."

I had nothing to tell him, and was silent.

"What is it? Can't you tell an old chum?"

"No; it is Monsieur's private business."

"Well, you are grumpy!" he cried out pettishly. "You must be out of grace." He seemed to decide that nothing was to be made out of me just now on this tack, and with unabated persistence tried another.

"Is it true, Félix, what one of the men said just now, that you tried to speak with Monsieur this morning when he drove out?"

"Yes. But Monsieur did not recognize me."

"Like enough," Marcel answered. "He has a way of late of falling into these absent fits. Monsieur is not the man he was."

"He does look older," I said, "and worn. I trow the risk he is running –"

"Pshaw!" cried Marcel, with scorn. "Is Monsieur a man to mind risks? No; it is M. le Comte."

I started like a guilty thing, remembering what Yeux-gris had told me and I, wrapped in my petty troubles, had forgotten. Monsieur had lost his only son. And I had chosen this time to defy him!

"How long ago was it?" I asked in a hushed voice.

"Since M. le Comte left us? It will be three weeks next Friday."

"How did he die?"

"Die?" echoed Marcel. "You crazy fellow, he is not dead!"

It was my turn to stare.

"Then where is he?"

"It would be money in my pouch if I knew. What made you think him dead, Félix?"

"A man told me so."

"Pardieu!" he cried in some excitement. "When? Who was it?"

"Today. I do not know the man's name."

"It seems you know very little. Pardieu! I do not believe M. le Comte is dead. What else did your man say?"

"Nothing. He only said the Comte de Mar was dead."

"Pshaw! I don't believe it. You believe everything you hear because you are just from the country. No; if M. le Comte were dead we should hear of it. Oh, certainly, we should hear."

"But where is he, then? You say he is lost."

"Aye. He has not been seen or heard of since the day they had the quarrel."

"Who quarreled?"

"Why, he and Monsieur," answered Marcel, in a lower voice, pointing to the door of the inner room. "M. le Comte has been his own master too long to take kindly to a hand over him; that is the whole of it. He has a quick temper. So has Monsieur."

But I thought of Monsieur's wonderful patience, and I cried:

"Shame!"

"What now?"

"To speak like that of Monsieur."

"Enfin, it is true. He is none the worse for that. But I suppose if Monsieur had a cloven hoof one must not mention it."

"One would get his head broken."

"Oh, you Broux!" he cried out. "I have not seen you for half a year. I had forgotten that with you the St. Quentins rank with the saints."

"You – you are a hired servant. You come to Monsieur as you might come to anybody. With the Broux it is different," I retorted angrily. Yet I could not but know in my heart that any hired servant might have served Monsieur better than I. My boasted loyalty – what was it but lip-service? I said more humbly: "Pshaw! it is no great matter. Tell me about the quarrel."

"And so I will, if you're civil. In the first place, there was the question of M. le Comte's marriage."

"What! is he married?"

"Oh, by no means. Monsieur wouldn't have it. You see, Félix," Marcel said in a tone deep with importance, "we're Navarre's men now."

"Of course," said I.

"I suppose you would say 'of course' just like that to Mayenne himself. You greenhorn! It is as much as our lives are worth to side openly with Navarre. The League may attack us any day."

"I know," I said uneasily. Every chance word Marcel spoke seemed to dye my guilt the deeper. "But what has this to do with M. le Comte's marriage?" I asked him.

"Why, he was more than half a Leaguer. Perhaps he is one now. Some say he and Monsieur were at daggers drawn about politics; but I warrant it was about Mlle. de Montluc. They call her the Rose of Lorraine. She's the Duke of Mayenne's own cousin and housemate. And we're king's men, so of course it was no match for Monsieur's son. They say Mayenne himself favored the marriage, but our duke wouldn't hear of it. However, the backbone of the trouble was M. de Grammont."

"And who may he be?"

"He's a cousin of the house. He and M. le Comte are as thick as thieves. Before we came to Paris they lodged together. So when M. le Comte came here he brought M. de Grammont. Dare I speak ill of Monsieur's cousin, Félix? For I would say, at the risk of a broken head, that he is a sour-faced churl. You cannot deny it. You never saw him."

"No, nor M. le Comte, either."

"Why, you have seen M. le Comte!"

"Never. The only time he came to St. Quentin I was laid up in bed with a strained leg. I missed the chase. Don't you remember?"

"Why, you are right; that was the time you fell out of the buttery window when you were stealing tarts, and Margot got after you with the broomstick. I remember very well."

He was for calling up all our old pranks at the château, but it was little joy to me to think on those fortunate days when I was Monsieur's favorite. I said:

"Nay, Marcel, you were telling me of M. le Comte and the quarrel."

"Oh, as for that, it is easy told. You see M. le Comte and this Grammont took no interest in Monsieur's affairs, and they had very little to say to him, and he to them. They had plenty of friends in Paris, Leaguers or not, and they used to go about amusing themselves. But at last M. de Grammont had such a run of bad luck at the tables that he not only emptied his own pockets but M. le Comte's as well. I will say for M. le Comte that he would share his last sou with anyone who asked."

"And so would any St. Quentin."

"Oh, you are always piping up for the St. Quentins."

"He should have no need in this house."

We jumped up to find Vigo standing behind us.

"What have you been saying of Monsieur?"

"Nothing, M. Vigo," stammered the page. "I only said M. le Comte —"

"You are not to discuss M. le Comte. Do you hear?"

"Yes, M. Vigo."

"Then obey. And you, Félix, I shall have a little interview with you shortly."

"As you will, M. Vigo," I said hopelessly.

He went off down the corridor, and Marcel turned angrily on me.

"Mon dieu, Félix, you have got me into a nice scrape with your eternal chanting of the praises of Monsieur. Like as not I shall get a beating for it. Vigo never forgets."

"I am sorry," I said. "We should not have been talking of it."

"No, we should not. Come over here where we can watch both doors, and I'll tell you the rest before the old lynx gets back."

We sat down close together, and he proceeded in a low tone to disobey Vigo.

"Enfin, as I said, the two young gentlemen were quite sans le sou, for things had come to a point where M. le Duc looked pretty black at any application for funds – he has other uses for his gold, you see. One day Monsieur was expecting someone to whom he was to pay a thousand pistoles, and to have the money handy he put it in a secret drawer in his cabinet in the room yonder. The man arrives and is taken to Monsieur's private room. Monsieur gives him his orders and goes to the cabinet for his pistoles. No pistoles there!"

Marcel paused dramatically. "And what then?" I asked.

"Well, it appears he had once shown M. le Comte the trick of the drawer, so he sent for him – not to accuse him, mind you. For M. le Comte is wild enough, yet Monsieur did not think he would steal pistoles, nor would he, I will stake my oath. No, Monsieur merely asked him if he had ever shown anyone the drawer, and M. le Comte answered, 'Only Grammont.'"

"And how have you learned all this?"

"Oh, one hears."

"One does, with one's ears to the keyhole."

"It behooves you, Félix, to be civil to your better!"

I made pretence of looking about me.

"Where is he?"

"He sits here. I am page to the Duke of St. Quentin. And you?"

"Touché!" I admitted bitterly enough. Little Marcel, my junior, my unquestioning follower in the old days, was now indeed my better, quite in a position to patronize.

"Continue, if you please, Marcel. Yet, in passing, I should like to ask you how much you heard our talk in there just now."

"Nothing," he answered candidly. "When they are so far down the room one cannot hear a word. In the affair of the pistoles they stood near the cabinet at this end. One could not help but hear. As for listening at keyholes, I scorn it."

"Yes, it is well to scorn it. People have an unpleasant trick of opening doors so suddenly."

He laughed cheerfully.

"Old Vigo caught us, certes. Let's see, where was I? Oh, yes, then Monsieur put on his proud look and said, if it was a case of no one but his son and his cousin, he preferred to drop the matter. But M. le Comte got out of him what the trouble was and went off for Grammont, red as fire. The two together came back to Monsieur and denied up and down that either of them knew aught of his pistoles, or had told of the secret to anyone. They say it was easy to see that Monsieur did not believe Grammont, but he did not give him the lie, and the matter came near dropping there, for M. le Duc would not accuse a kinsman. But then Lucas gave a new turn to the affair."

"How long has Lucas been here, Marcel? Who is he?"

"Oh, he's a rascal of a Huguenot. Monsieur picked him up at Mantes, just before we came to the city. And if he spies on Monsieur's enemies as well as he does on this household, he must be a useful man. He has that long nose of his in everything, let me tell you. Of course he was present when Monsieur missed the pistoles. So then, quite on his own account, without any orders, he took two of the men and searched M. de Grammont's room. And in a locked chest of his which they forced open they found five hundred of the pistoles in the very box Monsieur had kept them in."

"And then?"

Marcel made a fine gesture.

"And then, pardieu! the storm broke. M. de Grammont raved like a madman. He said Lucas was the thief and had put half the sum in his chest to divert suspicion. He said it was a plot to ruin him contrived between Monsieur and his henchman, Lucas. It is true enough, certes, that Monsieur never liked him. He threatened Monsieur's life and Lucas's. He challenged Monsieur, and Monsieur declined to cross swords with a thief. He challenged Lucas, and Lucas took the cue from Monsieur. I was not there – on either side of the door. What I tell you has leaked out bit by bit from Lucas, for Monsieur keeps his mouth shut. The upshot of the matter was that Grammont goes at Lucas with a knife, and Monsieur has the guards pitch my gentleman into the street. Then M. le Comte swore a big oath that he would go with Grammont. Monsieur told him if he went in such company it would be forever. M. le Comte swore he would never come back under his father's roof if M. le Duc crawled to him on his knees to beg him."

"Ah!" I cried; "and then?"

"Marry, that's all. M. le Comte went straight out of this gate, without horse or squire. And we have not heard a word of either of them since."

He paused, and when I made no comment, said, a trifle aggrieved:

"Eh bien, you take it calmly, but you would not had you been here. It was an altogether lively affair. It wouldn't surprise me a whit if some day Monsieur should be attacked as he drives out. He's not one to forget an injury, this M. Gervais de Grammont."

At the name, intelligence flashed over me, sudden and clear as last night's lightning-gleam. Yet this thing I seemed to see was so hideous, so horrible, that my mind recoiled from it.

"Marcel," I stammered, shuddering, "Marcel –"

"Mordieu! what ails you? Is someone walking on your grave?"

"Marcel, how is M. le Comte named?"

"The Comte de Mar? Oh, do you mean his names in baptism? Charles-André-Étienne-Marie. They call him Étienne. Why do you ask? What is it?"

It was a certainty, then. Yet I could not bring myself to believe this horrible thing.

"I have never seen him. How does he look?"

"Oh, not at all like Monsieur. He has fair hair and grey eyes – que diable!"

For I had flung open Monsieur's door and dashed in.

IX

The honor of St. Quentin.

Monsieur was seated at his table, talking in a low tone and hurriedly to Lucas. They started and stared as I broke in upon them, and then Monsieur cried out to me:

"Ah, Félix! You have come to your senses."

"I will tell Monsieur all, the whole story."

He tested my honesty with a glance, then looked beyond me at Marcel, standing agape in the doorway.

"Leave us, Marcel. Go downstairs. Leave that door open, and shut the door into the corridor."

Marcel obeyed. Monsieur turned to me with a smile.

"Now, Félix."

I had hardly been able to hold my words back while Marcel was disposed of.

"Monsieur, I knew not, myself, the names of those men. Now I have found out. They –"

My eyes met the secretary's fixed excitedly upon me and the words died on my tongue. Even in my rage I had the grace to know that this was no story to tell Monsieur before another.

"I will tell Monsieur alone."

"You may speak before M. Lucas," he rejoined impatiently.

"No," I persisted. "I must tell Monsieur alone."

He saw in my face that I had strong reasons for asking it, and said to the secretary:

"You may go, Lucas."

Lucas protested.

"M. le Duc will be wiser not to see him alone. He is not to be trusted. Perchance, Monsieur, this demand covers an attack on your life."

The warning nettled my lord. He answered curtly:

"You may go."

"Monsieur –"

"Go!"

Lucas passed out, giving me, as he went, a look of hatred that startled me. But I did not pay it much heed.

"Well!" exclaimed Monsieur.

But by this time I had bethought myself what a story it was I had to tell a father of his son. I could not blurt it out in two words. I stood silent, not knowing how to start.

"Félix! Beware how much longer you abuse my patience!"

"Monsieur," I began, "the spy in the house is named Martin."

"Ah!" cried Monsieur. "So it is Louis Martin. How he knew – But go on. The others –"

"I lay the night in the Rue Coupejarrets, not far from the St. Denis gate," I said, still beating about the bush, "at the sign of the Amour de Dieu. Opposite is a closed house, shuttered with iron from garret to cellar. You can enter from a court behind. It is here that they plot."

Monsieur's brows drew together, as if he were trying to recall something half remembered, half forgotten.

"But the men," he cried, "the men!"

"They are three. One a low fellow named Pontou."

"Pontou? The name is nothing to me. The others?" He was leaning forward eagerly. I knew of what he was thinking – the quickest way to reach the Rue Coupejarrets.

"There are two others, Monsieur," I said slowly. "Young men – noble."

I looked at him. But no light whatever had broken in upon him.

"Their names, lad!"

Then, seeing him unsuspecting, the fury in my heart surged up and covered every other feeling. I burst out:

"Gervais de Grammont and the Comte de Mar."

He looked me in the face, and he knew I was telling the truth. Unexpected as it was, hideous as it was, yet he knew I was telling the truth.

I had seen cowards turn pale, but never the color washed from a brave man's face. The sight made my fingers itch to strangle that grey-eyed cheat.

With a cry Monsieur sprang toward me.

"You lie, you cur!"

"No, Monsieur," I gasped; "it is the truth."

He let me go then, and laid his hand on the collar of the dog, who had sprung to his aid. But Monsieur had got a hurt from which the dumb beast's loyalty could not defend him. He stood with bowed head, a man stricken to the heart's core. Full of wrath as I was, the tears came to my eyes for Monsieur.

He recovered himself.

"It is some damnable mistake! You have been tricked!"

My rage blazed up again.

"No! They tricked me once. Not again! Not this time. I knew not who they were till now, when I talked with Marcel. The two things fitted."

"Then it is your guess! You dare to say –"

"No, I know!" I interrupted rudely, too excited to remember respect. "Shall I tell what these men were like? I had never seen M. le Comte nor M. de Grammont before. One was broad-shouldered and heavy, with a black beard and a black scowl, whom the other called Gervais. The younger was called Étienne, tall and slender, with grey eyes and fair hair. And like Monsieur!" I cried, suddenly aware of it. "Mordieu, how he is like, though he is light! In face, in voice, in manner! He speaks like Monsieur. He has Monsieur's laugh. I was blind not to see it. I believe that was why I loved him so much."

"It was he whom you would not betray?"

"Aye. That was before I knew."

Thinking of the trust I had given him, my wrath boiled up again. Monsieur took me by the shoulder and looked at me as if he would look through me to the naked soul.

"How do I know that you are not lying?"

"Monsieur does know it."

"Yes," he answered after a moment. "Alas! yes, I know it."

He stood looking at me, with the dreariest face I ever saw – the face of a man whose son has sought to murder him. Looking back on it now, I wonder that I ever went to Monsieur with that story. I wonder why I did not bury the shame and disgrace of it in my own heart, at whatever cost keep it from Monsieur. But the thought never entered my head then. I was so full of black rage against Yeux-gris – him most of all, because he had won me so – that I could feel nothing else. I knew that I pitied Monsieur, yet I hardly felt it.

"Tell me everything – how you met them – all. Else I shall not believe a word of your devilish rigmarole," Monsieur cried out.

I told him the whole shameful story, every word, from my lightning vision to my gossip with Marcel in the antechamber, he listening in hopeless silence. At length I finished. It seemed hours since he had spoken. At last he said, "Then it is true." The greyness of his face drew the cry from me:

"The villain! the black-hearted villain!"

"Take care, Félix, he is my son!"

I got hold of my cross and tore it off, breaking the chain.

"See, Monsieur. That is the cross on which he swore the plot was not against you. He swore it, and Gervais de Grammont laughed! I swore, too, never to betray them! Two perjuries!"

I flung the cross on the floor and stamped on it, splintering it.

"Profaner!" cried Monsieur.

"It is no sacrilege!" I retorted. "That is no holy thing since he has touched it. He has made it vile – scoundrel, assassin, parricide!"

Monsieur struck the words from my lips.

"It is true," I muttered.

"Were it ten times true, you have no right to say it."

"No, I have none," I answered, shamed. I might not speak ill of a St. Quentin, though he were the devil's own. But my rage came uppermost again.

"I can bring Monsieur to the house in twenty minutes. Vigo and a handful of men can take them prisoners before they suspect aught amiss. They are only three – he and Grammont and the lackey."

But Monsieur shook his head.

"I cannot do that."

"Why not, Monsieur?"

"Can I take my own son prisoner?"

"Monsieur need not go," said I, wondering. In his place I would have gone and killed Yeux-gris with my own hands. "Vigo and I and two more can do it. Vigo and I alone, if Monsieur would not shame him before the men." I guessed at what he was thinking.

"Not even you and Vigo," he answered. "Think you I would arrest my son like a common felon – shame him like that?"

"He has shamed himself!" I cried. I cared not whether I had a right to say it. "He has forgotten his honor."

"Aye. But I have remembered mine."

"Monsieur! Monsieur cannot mean to let him go scot-free?"

But his eyes told me that he did mean it.

"Then," I said in more and more amazement, "Monsieur forgives him?"

His face set sternly.

"No," he answered. "No, Félix. He has placed himself beyond my forgiveness."

"Then we will go there alone, we two, and kill him! Kill the three!"

He laughed. But not a man in France felt less mirthful.

"You would have me kill my son?"

"He would have killed you."

"That makes no difference."

I looked at him, groping after the thoughts that swayed him, and catching at them dimly. I knew them for the principles of a proud and honor-ruled man, but there was no room for them in my angry heart.

"Monsieur," I cried, "will you let three villains go unpunished for the sake of one?" It was what I had meant to do, awhile back, but the case was changed now.

"Of two: Gervais de Grammont is also of my blood."

"Monsieur would spare him as well – him, the ringleader!"

"He is my cousin."

"He forgets it."

"But I do not."

"Monsieur, will you have no vengeance?"

Monsieur looked at me.

"When you are a man, Félix Broux, you will know that there are other things in this world besides vengeance. You will know that some injuries cannot be avenged. You will know that a gentleman cannot use the same weapons that blackguards use to him."

"Ah, Monsieur!" I cried. "Monsieur is indeed a nobleman!" But I was furious with him for it.

He turned abruptly and paced down the room. The dog, which had been standing at his side, stayed still, looking from him to me with puzzled, troubled eyes. He knew quite well something was wrong, and vented his feelings in a long, dismal whine. Monsieur spoke to him; Roland bounded up to him and licked his hand. They walked up and down together, comforting each other.

"At least," I cried in desperation, "Monsieur has the spy."

He laughed. Only a man in utter despair could have laughed then as he did.

"Even the spy to wreak vengeance on consoles you somewhat, Félix? But does it seem to you fair that a tool should be punished when the leaders go free?"

"No," said I; "but it is the common way."

"That is a true word," he said, turning away again.

I waited till he faced me once more.

"Monsieur will not suffer the spy to go free?"

"No, Félix. He shall be punished lest he betray again."

He passed me in his dreary walk. Half a dozen times he passed by me, a broken-hearted man, striving to collect his courage to take up his life once more. But I thought he would never get over the blow. A husband may forget his wife's treachery, and a mother will forgive her child's, but a father can neither forget nor forgive the crime of the son who bears his name.

"Ah, Monsieur, you are noble, and I love you!" I cried from the depths of my heart, and knelt to kiss his hand.

Monsieur laid that kind hand on my shoulder.

"You shall serve me. Go now and send Vigo here. I must be looking to the country's business."

X

Lucas and "Le Gaucher."

I cursed myself for a fool that I had carried the tale to Monsieur. It should have been my business to keep a still tongue and go kill Yeux-gris myself. For this last it was not yet too late.

Marcel was hanging about in the corridor, and to him I gave the word for Vigo. I tore away from his eager questionings and hurried to the gate.

In the morning I had not been able to get in, and now I could no more get out. By Vigo's orders, no man might leave the house.

Vigo was after the spy, of course. Monsieur knew the traitor now; he would inform Vigo, and the gates would be open for honest men. But that might take time and I could not wait five minutes. I had the audacity to cry to the guards:

"M. le Duc will let me pass out. I refer you to M. le Duc."

The men were impressed. They had a respect for me, since I had been closeted with Monsieur. Yet they dared not disobey Vigo for their lives. In this dilemma the poor sentry, fearful of getting into trouble whatever he did, sent up an envoy to ask Monsieur. I was frightened then. I had uttered my speech in sheer bravado, and was very doubtful as to how he would answer my impudence. But he was utterly careless, I trow, what I did, for presently the word came down that I might pass out.

The sun was setting as I hastened along the streets. I must reach the Rue Coupejarrets before dark, else there was no hope for me. A man in his senses would have known there was no hope anyway. Who but a madman would think of venturing back, forsworn, to those three villains, for the killing of one? It would be a miracle if aught resulted but failure and death. Yet I felt no jot of fear as I plunged into the mesh of crooked streets in the Coupejarrets quarter – only ardor to reach my goal. When, on turning a corner, I came upon a group of idlers choking the narrow ruelle, I said to myself that a dozen Parisians in the way could no more stop me than they could stop a charge of horse. All heels and elbows, I pushed into them. But, to my abasement, promptly was I seized upon by a burly porter and bidden, with a cuff, to mind my manners. Then I discovered the occasion of the crowd to be a little procession of choristers out of a neighboring church – St. Jean of the Spire it was, though I knew then no name for it. The boys were singing, the watchers quiet, bareheaded. They sang as if there were nothing in the world but piety and love. The last level rays of the sun crowned them with radiant aureoles, painted their white robes with glory. I shut my eyes, dazzled; it was as if I beheld a heavenly host. When I opened them again the folk at my side were kneeling as the cross came by. I knelt, too, but the holy sign spoke to me only of the crucifix I had trampled on, of Yeux-gris and his lies. I prayed to the good God to let me kill Yeux-gris, prayed, kneeling there on the cobbles, with a fervor I had never reached before. When I rose I ran on at redoubled speed, never doubting that a just God would strengthen my hand, would make my cause his.

I entered the little court. The shutter was fastened, as before, but I had my dagger, and could again free the bolt. I could creep upstairs and mayhap stab Yeux-gris before they were aware of my coming. But that was not my purpose. I was no bravo to strike in the back, but the instrument of a righteous vengeance. He must know why he died.

One to three, I had no chance. But if I knocked openly it was likely that Yeux-gris, being my patron, would be the one to come down to me. Then there was the opportunity, man to man. If it were Grammont or the lackey, I would boldly declare that I would give my news to none but Yeux-gris. In pursuance of this plan I was pounding vigorously on the door when a voice behind me cried out blithely:

"So you are back at last, Félix Broux"

At the first word I wheeled around. In the court entrance stood Yeux-gris, smiling and debonair. He had laid aside his sword, and held on his left arm a basket containing a loaf of bread, a roast capon, and some bottles, for all the world like an honest prentice doing his master's errand.

"Yes, I am back!" I shouted. "Back to kill you, parricide!"

He had a knife in his belt; the fight was even. I was upon him, my dagger raised to strike. He made no motion to draw, and I remembered in a flash he could not: his right arm was powerless. He sprang back, flinging up his burdened left as a shield, and my blade buried itself in the side of the basket.

As I stabbed I heard feet thundering down the stairs within. I jerked my knife from the wicker and turned to face this new enemy. "Grammont," I thought, and that my end had come.

The door flew open and, shoulder to shoulder like brothers, out rushed Grammont and – Lucas!

My fear was drowned in amaze. I forgot to run and stood staring in sheer, blank bewilderment. Crying "Damned traitor!" Gervais, with drawn sword, charged at me.

I had only the little dagger. I owe my life to Yeux-gris's quick wits and no less quick fingers. Dropping the basket, he snatched a bottle from it and hurled it at Gervais.

"Ware, Grammont!" shouted Lucas, springing forward. But the missile flew too quickly. It struck Grammont square on the forehead, and he went down like a slaughtered ox.

We looked, not at him, but at Lucas – Lucas, the duke's deferential servant, the coward and skulker, Grammont's hatred, standing here by Grammont's side, glaring at us over his naked sword.

I saw in one glance that Yeux-gris was no less astounded than I, and from that instant, though the inwardness of the matter was still a riddle to me, my heart acquitted him of all dishonesty, of all complicity. His was not the face of a parricide.

"Lucas!" he cried, in a dearth of words. *"Lucas!"*

I was staring at Lucas in thick bewilderment. The man was transformed from the one I knew. At M. le Duc's he had been pale, nervous, and shaken – senselessly and contemptibly scared, as I thought, since he was warned of the danger and need not face it. But now he was another man. I can think only of those lanterns I have seen, set with colored glass. They look dull enough all day, but when the taper within is lighted shine like jewels. So Lucas now. His face, so keen and handsome of feature, was brilliant, his eyes sparkling, his figure instinct with defiance. A smile crossed his face.

"Aye," he answered evenly, "it is Lucas."

M. le Comte appeared to be in a state of stupor. He could not for a space find his tongue to demand:

"How, in the name of Heaven, come you here?"

"To fight Grammont," Lucas answered at once.

"A lie!" I shouted. "You're Grammont's friend. You came here to warn him off. It's your plot!"

"Félix! The plot?" Yeux-gris cried.

"The plot's to murder Monsieur. Martin let it out. I thought it was you and Grammont. But it's Lucas and Grammont!"

Lucas hesitated. Even now he debated whether he could not lie out of it. Then he burst into laughter.

"It seems the cat's out of the bag. Aye, M. le Comte de Mar, I came to warn Grammont off. The duke will be here straightway. How will you like to swing for parricide?"

Yeux-gris stared at him, neither in fear nor in fury, but in utter stupefaction.

"But Gervais? He plotted with you? But he hates you!"

We gaped at Lucas like yokels at a conjurer. He made us no answer but looked from one to the other of us with the alertness of an angry viper. We were two, but without swords. I knew he was thinking how easiest to end us both.

M. le Comte cried: "You! You come from Navarre's camp, from M. de Rosny!"

"Aye. I have outwitted more than one man."

"Mordieu! I was right to hate you!"

Lucas laughed. Yeux-gris blazed out:

"Traitor and thief! You stole the money. I said that from the first. You drove us from the house. How you and Grammont –"

"Came together? Very simple," Lucas answered with easy insolence. "Grammont did not love Monsieur, your honored father. It was child's play to make an assignation with him and to lament the part forced on me by Monsieur. Grammont was ready enough to scent a scheme of M. le Duc's to ruin him. He had said as much to Monsieur, as you may deign to remember."

"Aye," said M. le Comte, still like a puzzled child, "he was angry with my father. But afterward he changed his mind. He knew it was you, and only you."

Lucas broke again into derisive laughter.

"M. de Grammont is as dull a dolt as ever I met, yet clever enough to gull you. He thought you must suspect. I dreaded it – needlessly. You wise St. Quentins! You cannot see what goes on under your very nose."

M. le Comte sprang forward, scarlet. Lucas flourished the sword.

"The boy there caught at a glance what you had not found out in a fortnight. He gets to the duke and blocks my game – for today. But if they sent him ahead to hold us till their men came up, they were fools, too. I'll have the duke yet, and I'll have you now."

He rushed at the unarmed Yeux-gris. The latter darted at Grammont's fallen sword, seized it, was on guard, all in the second before Lucas reached him. He might have been in a fortnight's trance, but he was awake at last.

I trembled for him, then took heart again, as he parried thrust after thrust and pressed Lucas hard. I had never seen a man fight with his left arm before; I had not realized it could be done, being myself helpless with that hand. But as I watched this combat I speedily perceived how dangerous is a left-handed adversary. In later years I was to understand better, when M. le Comte had become known the length of the land by the title "Le Gaucher." But at this time he was in the habit, like the rest of the world, of fencing with his right hand; his dexterity with the other he rated only as a pretty accomplishment to surprise the crowd. He used his left hand scarcely as well as Lucas the right; yet, the thrust sinister being in itself a strength, they were not badly matched. I stood watching with all my eyes, when of a sudden I felt a grasp on my ankle and the next instant was thrown heavily to the pavement.

Grammont had come to life and taken prompt part in the fray.

I fell close to him, and instantly he let go my leg and wound his arms around me. I tried to rise and could not, and we rolled about together in the wine and blood and broken glass. All the while I heard the sword-blades clashing. Yeux-gris, God be thanked! seemed to be holding his own.

Fighting Gervais was like fighting two men. Slowly but steadily he pressed me down and held me. I struggled for dear life – and could not push him back an inch.

I still held my knife but my arms were pinned down. Gervais raised himself a little to get a better clutch, and his fingers closed on my throat. One grip, and life seemed flowing from me. My arm was free now if I could but lift it. If I could not, nevermore should I lift it on this sunny earth. I did lift it, and drove the dagger deep into him.

I could not take aim; I could not tell where the knife struck. A gasp showed he was hit; then he clinched my throat once more. Sight went from me, and hearing. "It is no use," I thought, and then thought went, too.

But once again the saints were kind to me. The blackness passed, and I wondered what had happened that I was spared. Then I saw Grammont clutching with both hands at the dagger-hilt. After all, the blow had gone home. I had struck him in the left side under the arm. Three good inches of steel were in him.

He had turned over on his side, half off me. I scrambled out from under him. To my surprise, Yeux-gris and Lucas were still engaged. I had thought it hours since Grammont pulled me down.

As I rose, Yeux-gris turned his head toward me. Only for a second, but in that second Lucas pinked his shoulder. I dashed between them; they lowered their points.

"First blood for me!" cried Lucas. "That serves for today, M. le Comte. I regret that I cannot wait to kill you, but that will come. It is necessary that I go before M. le Duc arrives. Clear the way."

M. le Comte stood his ground, barring the alley. They glared at each other motionless.

Grammont had raised himself to his knees and was trying painfully to get on his feet.

"A hand, Lucas," he gasped.

Lucas gave him a startled glance but neither went nor spoke to him.

"I am not much hurt," said Grammont, huskily. Holding by the wall, he clambered up on his feet. He swayed, reeled forward, and clutched Lucas's arm.

"Lucas, Lucas, help me! Draw out the knife. I cannot. I shall be myself when the knife is out. Lucas, for God's sake!"

"You will die when the knife is out," said Lucas, wrenching himself free. He turned again to M. le Comte, and his eyes gleamed as he saw the blood trickling down his sleeve and the sword tremble in his hand.

"Come on, then," he cried to Yeux-gris.

But I sprang forward and seized the sword from M. le Comte's hand.

"On guard!" I shouted, and we went to work.

I could handle a sword as well as the next one. M. le Duc had taught me in his idle days at St. Quentin. It served me well now, and him, too.

The light was fading in the narrow court. Our blades shone white in the twilight as the weapons clashed in and out. I saw, without looking, Grammont leaning against the wall, his gory face ashen, and Yeux-gris watching me with all his soul, now and then shouting a word of advice.

I had had good training, and I fought for all there was in me. Yet I was a boy not come to my full strength, and Lucas was more than my match. He drove me back farther and farther toward the house-wall. Of a sudden I slipped in a smear of blood ('tis no lying excuse, I did slip) and lost my guard. He ran his blade into my shoulder, as he had done with Yeux-gris.

He would likely have finished me had not a cry from Grammont shaken him.

"The duke!"

In truth, a deepening noise of hoofs and shouts came down the alley from the street.

Lucas looked at me, who had regained my guard and stood, little hurt, between him and M. le Comte. He could not push past me into the house and so through to the other street. He made for the alley, crying out:

"Au revoir, messieurs! We shall meet again."

Grammont seized him.

"Help me, Lucas, for the love of Christ! Don't leave me, Lucas!"

Lucas beat him off with the sword.

"Every man for himself!" he cried, and sprang down the alley.

"It is not the duke," I said to Yeux-gris. "It is most likely the watch." I paled at the thought, for the watch was the League's, and Lucas by all signs the League's tool. It might go hard with us if captured. "Go through the house, M. le Comte," I cried. "Quick, if you love your life! I'll keep them at the alley's mouth as long as I can."

Not waiting for his answer, I rushed down the passage. At the end of it I ran against Lucas, who, in his turn, had bowled into Vigo.

Vigo.

I knew of old that it was easier to catch a weasel asleep than Vigo absent where he was needed; yet I did not expect to meet him in the alley. Monsieur, then, had changed his mind.

"Well caught!" cried Vigo, winding his arms round Lucas, who was struggling furiously for liberty. "Here, Maurice, Jules, I have number one. Ah, you young sinner! with your crew again? I thought as much. Tie the knots hard, boys. Better be quiet, you snake; you can't get away."

Lucas seemed to make up his mind to this, for he quieted down directly.

"So the game is up," he said pleasantly. "I had hoped to be gone before you arrived, dear Vigo."

We had both been deprived promptly of our swords and Lucas's wrists were roped together, but my only bond was Vigo's hand on my arm.

"Where are the others?" he demanded. "No tricks, now."

"Here," I said, and led the way down the passage. Maurice and Jules, with their prisoner, pressed after us, and half a dozen of the duke's guard after them. The rest stayed without to mind the horses and keep off the gathering crowd.

One of the men had a torch which lighted the red pavement. Vigo saw this first.

"Morbleu! is it a shambles?"

"That is wine," I said.

"They spilled wine for effect, they spilled so little blood!" Thus Lucas, speaking with as cool devilry as if he still commanded the situation. Vigo could not know what he meant but he asked no questions; instead, bade Lucas hold his tongue.

"I am dumb," Lucas rejoined, with a mock meekness more insolent than insolence. But we paid it no heed for M. le Comte came forward out of the shadows. He held his head well up but his face was white above his crimsoned doublet.

"M. Étienne! Are you hurt?" shouted Vigo.

"No, but he is." M. le Comte stepped aside to show us Grammont leaning against the wall.

"Ah!" cried Vigo, triumphantly. He and two of the men rushed at Gervais.

"You would not take me so easily but for a cursed knife in my back," Grammont muttered thickly. "For the love of Heaven, Vigo, draw it out."

With amazement Vigo perceived the knife.

"Who did it?"

"I."

"You, Félix? In the back?" Vigo looked at me as if to demand again which side I was on.

"He lay on me, throttling me," I explained. "I stabbed any way I could."

"I trow you are a dead man," Vigo told Grammont. "Natheless, here comes the knife."

It came, with a great cry from the victim. He fell back against Vigo's man, clapping his hand to his side.

"I am done for," he gasped faintly.

"That is well," said Vigo, carefully wiping off the knife.

"Yon is the scoundrel," Grammont gasped, pointing to Lucas.

"He will die a worse death than you," said Vigo.

Grammont looked from the one to the other of us, the sullen rage in his face fading to a puzzled helplessness. He said fretfully:

"Which – which is Étienne?"

He could no longer see us plain. M. le Comte came forward silently. Grammont struggled for breath in a way pitiable to see. I put my arm about him and helped the guardsman to hold him straighter. He reached out his hand and caught at M. le Comte's sleeve.

"Étienne – Étienne – pardon. It was wrong toward you – but I never had the pistoles. He called me thief – the duke. I beseech – your – pardon."

M. le Comte was silent.

"It was all Lucas – Lucas did it," Grammont muttered with stiffening lips. "I am sorry for – it. I am dying – I cannot die – without a chance. Say you – for – give –"

Still M. le Comte held back, silent. Treachery was no less treachery though Grammont was dying. All the more that they were cousins, bedfellows, was the injury great to forgive. M. le Comte said nothing.

How Grammont found the strength only God knows, who haply in his goodness gave him a last chance of mercy. Suddenly he straightened his sinking body, started from our hold, and tottered toward his cousin, both hands outstretched in appeal.

M. le Comte's face was set like a flint. The dying man faltered forward. Then M. Étienne, never changing his countenance, slowly, half reluctantly, like a man in a dream, held out his hand.

But the old comrades, estranged by traitory, were never to clasp again. As he reached M. le Comte, Grammont fell at his feet.

"He was a strong man," said Vigo. He turned Grammont's face up and added the word, "Dead." Vigo adored the Duke of St. Quentin. Otherwise he had no emotions.

But I was not case-hardened. And I – I myself – had slain this man, who had died slowly and in great pain. Vigo's voice sounded to me far off as he said bluntly:

"M. le Comte, I make you my prisoner."

"No, by Heaven!" cried M. Étienne, in a vibrating voice that brought me back to reality; "no, Vigo! I am no murderer. Things may look black against me but I am innocent. You have one villain at your feet and one a prisoner, but I am not a third! I am a St. Quentin; I do not plot against my father. I was to aid Grammont to set on Lucas, who would not answer a challenge. I have been tricked. Gervais asked my forgiveness – you heard him. Their dupe, yes – accomplice I was not. Never have I lifted my hand against my father, nor would I, whatever came. That I swear. Never have I laid eyes on Lucas since I left Monsieur's presence, till now when he came out of that door side by side with Grammont. Whatever the plot, I knew naught of it. I am a St. Quentin – no parricide!"

The ringing voice ceased and M. le Comte stood silent, with haggard eyes on Vigo. Had he been prisoner at the bar of judgment he could not have waited in greater anxiety. For Vigo, the yeoman and servant, never minced words to any man nor swerved from the stark truth.

I burned to seize Vigo's arm, to spur him on to speech. Of course he believed M. Étienne; how dared he make his master wait for the assurance? On his knees he should be, imploring M. le Comte's pardon.

But no thought of humbling himself troubled Vigo. Nor did he pronounce judgment, but merely said:

"M. le Comte will go home with me now. Tomorrow he can tell his story to my master."

"I will tell it before this hour is out!"

"No. M. le Duc has left Paris. But it matters not, M. Étienne. Monsieur suspects nothing against you. Félix kept your name from him. And by the time I had screwed it out of Martin, Monsieur was gone."

"Gone out of Paris?" M. Étienne echoed blankly. To his eagerness it was as if M. le Duc were out of France.

"Aye. He meant to go tonight – Monsieur, Lucas, and I. But when Monsieur learned of this plot, he swore he'd go in open day. 'If the League must kill me,' says he, 'they can do it in daylight, with all Paris watching.' That's Monsieur!"

At this I understood how Vigo came to be in the Rue Coupejarrets. Monsieur, in his distress and anxiety to be gone from that unhappy house, had forgotten the spy. Left to his own devices, the equery, struck with suspicion at Lucas's absence, laid instant hands on Martin the clerk, with whom Lucas, disliked in the household, had had some intimacy. It had not occurred to Vigo that M. le Comte, if guilty, should be spared. At once he had sounded boots and saddles.

"I will return with you, Vigo," M. le Comte said. "Does the meanest lackey in my father's house call me parricide, I must meet the charge. My father and I have differed but if we are no longer friends we are still noblemen. I could never plot his murder, nor could he for one moment believe it of me."

I, guilty wretch, quailed. To take a flogging were easier than to confess to him the truth. But I conceived I must.

"Monsieur," I said, "I told M. le Duc you were guilty. I went back a second time and told him."

"And he?" cried M. Étienne.

"Yes, monsieur, he did believe it."

"Morbleu! that cannot be true," Vigo cried, "for when I saw him he gave no sign."

"It is true. But he would not have M. le Comte touched. He said he could not move in the matter; he could not punish his own kin."

M. le Comte's face blazed as he cried out:

"Vastly magnanimous! I thank him not. I'll none of his mercy. I expected his faith."

"You had no claim to it, M. le Comte."

"Vigo!" cried the young noble, "you are insolent, sirrah!"

"I cry monsieur's pardon."

He was quite respectful and quite unabashed. He had meant no insolence. But M. Étienne had dared criticize the duke and that Vigo did not allow.

M. Étienne glared at him in speechless wrath. It would have liked him well to bring this contumelious varlet to his knees. But how? It was a byword that Vigo minded no man's ire but the duke's. The King of France could not dash him.

Vigo went on:

"It seems I have exceeded my duty, monsieur, in coming here. Yet it turns out for the best, since Lucas is caught and M. de Grammont dead and you cleared of suspicion."

"What!" Yeux-gris cried. "What! you call me cleared!"

Vigo looked at him in surprise.

"You said you were innocent, M. le Comte."

M. le Comte stared, without a word to answer. The equery, all unaware of having said anything unexpected, turned to the guardsman Maurice:

"Well, is Lucas trussed? Have you searched him?"

Maurice displayed a poniard and a handful of small coins for sole booty, but Jules made haste to announce: "He has something else, though – a paper sewed up in his doublet. Shall I rip it out, M. Vigo?"

With Lucas's own knife the grinning Jules slashed his doublet from throat to thigh, to extract a folded paper the size of your palm. Vigo pondered the superscription slowly, not much at home with the work of a quill, save those that winged arrows. M. Étienne, coming forward, with a sharp exclamation snatched the packet.

"How came you by my letter?" he demanded of Lucas.

"M. le Comte was pleased to consign it for delivery to Martin."

"What purpose had you with it?"

"Rest assured, dear monsieur, I had a purpose."

The questions were stormily vehement, the answers so gentle as to be fairly caressing. It was waste of time and dignity to parley with the scoundrel till one could back one's queries with the boot. But M. Étienne's passion knew no waiting. Thrusting the letter into his breast ere I, who had edged up to him, could catch a glimpse of its address, he cried upon Lucas:

"Speak! You were ready enough to jeer at me for a dupe. Tell me what you would do with your dupe. You dared not open the plot to me – you did me the honor to know I would not kill my father. Then why use me blindfold? An awkward game, Lucas."

Lucas disagreed as politely as if exchanging pleasantries in a salon.

"A dexterous game, M. le Comte. Your best friends deemed you guilty. What would your enemies have said?"

"Ah-h," breathed M. Étienne.

"It dawns on you, monsieur? You are marvelous thick-witted, yet surely you must perceive. We had a dozen fellows ready to swear that your hand killed Monsieur."

"You would kill me for my father's murder?"

"Ma foi, no!" cried Lucas, airily. "Never in the world! We should have let you live, in the knowledge that whenever you displeased us we could send you to the gallows."

M. le Comte, silent, stared at him with wild eyes, like one who looks into the open roof of hell. Lucas fell to laughing.

"What! hang you and let our cousin Valère succeed? Mon dieu, no! M. de Valère is a man!"

With a blow the guardsman struck the words and the laughter from his lips. But I, who no more than Lucas knew how to hold my tongue, thought I saw a better way to punish this brazen knave. I cried out:

"You are the dupe, Lucas! Aye, and coward to boot, fleeing here from – nothing. I knew naught against you – you saw that. To slip out and warn Martin before Vigo got a chance at him – that was all you had to do. Yet you never thought of that but rushed away here, leaving Martin to betray you. Had you stuck to your post you had been now on the road to St. Denis, instead of the road to the Grève! Fool! fool! fool!"

He winced. He had not been ashamed to betray his benefactor, to bite the hand that fed him, to desert a wounded comrade; but he was ashamed to confront his own blunder. I had the satisfaction of pricking, not his conscience, for he had none, but his pride.

"I had to warn Grammont off," he retorted. "Could I believe St. Quentin such a lack-wit as to forgive these two because they were his kin? You did better than you knew when you shut the door on me. You tracked me, you marplot, you sneak! How came you into the coil?"

"By God's grace," M. le Comte answered. He laid a hand on my shoulder and leaned there heavily. Lucas grinned.

"Ah, waxing pious, is he? The prodigal prepares to return."

M. Étienne's hand clinched on my shoulder. Vigo commanded a gag for Lucas, saying, with the only touch of anger I ever knew him to show:

"He shall hang when the king comes in. And now to horse, lads, and out of the quarter; we have wasted too much time palavering. King Henry is not in Paris yet. We shall do well not to rouse Belin, though we can make him trouble if he troubles us. Come, monsieur. Men, guard your prisoner. I misjudge if he is not cropful of the devil still."

He did not look it. His figure was drooping; his face purple and contorted, for one of the troopers had crammed his scarf into the man's mouth, half strangling him. As he was led past us, with a sudden frantic effort, fit to dislocate his jaw, he disgorged the gag to cry out wildly:

"Oh, M. l'Écuyer, have mercy! Have pity upon me! For Christ's sake, pity!"

His bravado had broken down at last. He tried to fling himself at Vigo's feet. The guards relaxed their hold to see him grovel.

That was what he had hoped for. In a flash he was out of their grasp, flying down the alley.

"To Vigo! Vigo is attacked," we heard him shout.

It was so quick, we stood dumfounded. And then we dashed after, pell-mell, tumbling over one another in our stampede. In the alley we ran against three or four of the guard answering Lucas's cry. We lost precious seconds disentangling ourselves and shouting that it was a ruse and our prisoner escaped. When they comprehended, we all rushed together out of the passage, emerging among frightened horses and a great press of excited men.

XII

The Comte de Mar.

"Which way went he?"

"The man who just came out?"

"This way!"

"No, yonder!"

"Nay, I saw him not."

"A man with bound hands, you say?"

"Here!"

"Down that way!"

"A man in black, was he? Here he is!"

"Fool, no; he went that way!"

M. Étienne, Vigo, I, and the guardsmen rushed hither and thither into the ever-thickening crowd, shouting after Lucas and exchanging rapid questions with everyone we passed. But from the very first the search was hopeless. It was dark by this time and a mass of people blocked the street, surging this way and that, some eagerly joining in the chase, others, from ready sympathy with any rogue, doing their best to hinder and confuse us. There was no way to tell how he had gone. A needle in a haystack is easy found compared with him who loses himself in a Paris crowd by night.

M. Étienne plunged into the first opening he saw, elbowing his way manfully. I followed in his wake, his tall bright head making as good an oriflamme as the king's plume at Ivry, but when at length we came out far down the street we had seen no trace of Lucas.

"He is gone," said M. le Comte.

"Yes, monsieur. If it were day they might find him, but not now."

"No. Even Vigo will not find him. He is worsted for once. He has let slip the shrewdest knave in France. Well, he is gone," he repeated after a minute. "It cannot be mended by me. He is off, and so am I."

"Whither, monsieur?"

"That is my concern."

"But monsieur will see M. le Duc?"

He shook his head.

"But, monsieur –"

He broke in on me fiercely.

"Think you that I – I, smirched and sullied, reeking with plots of murder – am likely to betake myself to the noblest gentleman in France?"

"He will welcome M. le Comte."

"Nay; he believed me guilty."

"But, monsieur –"

"You may not say 'but' to me."

"Pardon, monsieur. Am I to tell Vigo monsieur is gone?"

"Yes, tell him." His lip quivered; he struggled hard for steadiness. "You will go to M. le Duc, Félix, and rise in his favor, for it was you saved his life. Then tell him this from me – that some day, when I have made me worthy to enter his presence, then will I go to him and beg his forgiveness on my knees. And now farewell."

He slipped away into the darkness.

I stood hesitating for a moment. Then I followed my lord.

He slackened his pace as he heard footsteps overtake him, and where a beam of light shone out from an open door he wheeled about, thinking me a footpad.

"You, Félix?"

"Yes, monsieur; I go with M. le Comte."

"I have not permitted you."

"Then must I go in despite. Monsieur is wounded; I cannot leave him to go unsquired."

"There are lackeys to hire. I bade you seek M. le Duc."

"Is not monsieur a thought unreasonable? I cannot be in two places at once. Monsieur can send a letter. The duke has Vigo and a household. I go with M. le Comte."

"Oh," he cried, "you are a faithful servant! We are ridden to death by our faithful servants, we St. Quentins. Myself, I prefer fleas!" He added, growing angrier, "Will you leave me?"

"No, monsieur," said I.

He glowered at me and I think he had some notion of chasing me away with his sword. But since his dignity could not so stoop, he growled:

"Come, then, if you choose to come unasked and most unwelcome!"

With this he walked on a yard ahead of me, never turning his head nor saying a word, I following meekly, wondering whither, and devoutly hoping it might be to supper. Presently I observed that we were in a better quarter of the town, and before long we came to a broad, well-lighted inn, whence proceeded a merry chatter and rattle of dice. M. Étienne with accustomed feet turned into the court at the side, and seizing upon a drawer who was crossing from door to door dispatched him for the landlord. Mine host came, fat and smiling, unworried by the hard times, greeted Yeux-gris with acclaim as "this dear M. le Comte," wondered at his long absence and bloody shirt, and granted with all alacrity his three demands of a supper, a surgeon, and a bed. I stood back, ill at ease, aching at the mention of supper, and wondering whether I were to be driven off like an obtrusive puppy. But when M. le Comte, without glancing at me, said to the drawer, "Take care of my serving-man," I knew my stomach was safe.

That was the most I thought of then, I do confess, for, except for my sausage, I had not tasted food since morning. The barber came and bandaged M. le Comte and put him straight to bed, and I was left free to fall on the ample victuals set before me, and was so comfortable and happy that the Rue Coupejarrets seemed like an evil dream. Since that day I have been an easy mark for beggars if they could but manage to look starved.

Presently came a servant to say that my bed was spread in M. le Comte's room, and upstairs ran I with an utterly happy heart, for I saw by this token that I was forgiven. Indeed, no sooner had I got fairly inside the door than my master raised himself on his sound elbow and called out:

"Ah, Félix, do you bear me malice for an ungrateful churl?"

"I bear malice?" I cried, flushing. "Monsieur is mocking me. I know monsieur cannot love me, since I attempted his life. Yet my wish is to be allowed to serve him so faithfully that he can forget it."

"Nay," he said; "I have forgotten it. And it was freely forgiven from the moment I saw Lucas at my cousin's side."

"For the second time," I said, "monsieur saved my life." And I dropped on my knees beside the bed to kiss his hand. But he snatched it away from me and flung his arm around my neck and kissed my cheek.

"Félix," he cried, "but for you my hands would be red with my father's blood. You rescued him from death and me from worse. If I have any shreds of honor left 'tis you have saved them to me."

"Monsieur," I stammered, "I did naught. I am your servant till I die."

"You deserve a better master. What am I? Lucas's puppet! Lucas's fool!"

"Monsieur, it was not Lucas alone. It was a plot. You know what he said –"

"Aye," he cried with bitter vehemence. "I shall remember for some time what he said. They would not kill me to make my cousin Valère duke! He was a man. But I – nom de dieu, I was not worth the killing."

"It is the League's scheming, monsieur."

"Oh, that does not need the saying. Secretaries don't plot against dukedoms on their own account. Some high man is behind Lucas – I dare swear his Grace of Mayenne himself. It is no secret now where Monsieur stands. Yet the king's party grows so strong and the mob so cheers Monsieur, the League dare not strike openly. So they put a spy in the house to choose time and way. And the spy would not stab, for he saw he could make me do his work for him. He saw I needed but a push to come to open breach with my father. He gave the push. Oh, he could make me pull his chestnuts from the fire well enough, burning my hands so that I could never strike a free blow again. I was to be their slave, their thrall forever!"

"Never that, monsieur; never that!"

"I am not so sure," he cried. "Had it not been for the advent of a stray boy from Picardie, I trow Lucas would have put his purpose through. I was blindfolded; I saw nothing. I knew my cousin Gervais to be morose and cruel; yet I had done him no harm; I had always stood his friend. I thought him shamefully used; I let myself be turned out of my father's house to champion him. I had no more notion he was plotting my ruin than a child playing with his dolls. I was their doll, mordieu! their toy, their crazy fool on a chain. But life is not over yet. Tomorrow I go to pledge my sword to Henry of Navarre."

"Monsieur, if he comes to the faith –"

"Mordieu! faith is not all. Were he a pagan of the wilderness he were better than these Leaguers. He fights honestly and bravely and generously. He could have had the city before now, save that he will not starve us. He looks the other way, and the provision-trains come in. But the Leaguers, with all their regiments, dare not openly strike down one man, – one man who has come all alone into their country, – they put a spy into his house to eat his bread and betray him; they stir up his own kin to slay him, that it may not be called the League's work. And they are most Catholic and noble gentlemen! Nay, I am done with these pious plotters who would redden my hands with my father's blood and make me outcast and despised of all men. I have spent my playtime with the League; I will go work with Henry of Navarre!"

I caught his fire.

"By St. Quentin," I cried, "we will beat these Leaguers yet!"

He laughed, yet his eyes burned with determination.

"By St. Quentin, shall we! You and I, Félix, you and I alone will overturn the whole League! We will show them what we are made of. They think lightly of me. Why not? I never took part with my father. I lazed about in these gay Paris houses, bent on my pleasure, too shallow a fop even to take sides in the fight for a kingdom. What should they see in me but an empty-headed roisterer, frittering away his life in follies? But they will find I am something more. Well, enter there!"

He dropped back among the pillows, striving to look careless, as Maître Menard, the landlord, opened the door and stood shuffling on the threshold.

"Does M. le Comte sleep?" he asked me deferentially, though I think he could not but have heard M. Étienne's tirading halfway down the passage.

"Not yet," I answered. "What is it?"

"Why, a man came with a billet for M. le Comte and insisted it be sent in. I told him Monsieur was not to be disturbed; he had been wounded and was sleeping; I said it was not sense to wake him for a letter that would keep till morning. But he would have it 'twas of instant import, and so –"

"Oh, he is not asleep," I declared, eagerly ushering the maître in, my mind leaping to the conclusion, for no reason save my ardent wish, that Vigo had discovered our whereabouts.

"I dared not deny him further," added Maître Menard. "He wore the liveries of M. de Mayenne."

"Of Mayenne," I echoed, thinking of what M. Étienne had said. "Pardieu, it may be Lucas himself!" And snatching up my master's sword I dashed out of the door and was in the cabaret in three steps.

The room contained some score of men, but I, peering about by the uncertain candlelight, could find no one who in any wise resembled Lucas. A young gamester seated near the door, whom my sudden entrance had jostled, rose, demanding in the name of his outraged dignity to cross swords with me. On any other day I had deemed it impossible to say him nay, but now with a real vengeance, a quarrel à outrance on my hands, he seemed of no consequence at all. I brushed him aside as I demanded M. de Mayenne's man. They said he was gone. I ran out into the dark court and the darker street.

A tapster, lounging in the courtyard, had seen my man pass out, and he opined with much reason that I should not catch him. Yet I ran a hundred yards up street and a hundred yards down street, shouting on the name of Lucas, calling him coward and skulker, bidding him come forth and fight me. The whole neighborhood became aware than I wanted one Lucas to fight: lights twinkled in windows; men, women, and children poured out of doors. But Lucas, if it were he, had for the second time vanished soft-footed into the night.

I returned with drooping tail to M. Étienne. He was alone, sitting up in bed awaiting me, his cheeks scarlet, his eyes blazing.

"He is gone," I panted. "I looked everywhere, but he was gone. Oh, if I caught Lucas –"

"You little fool!" he exclaimed. "This was not Lucas. Had you waited long enough to hear your name called, I had told you. This is no errand of Lucas but a very different matter."

He sat a moment, thinking, still with that glitter of excitement in his eyes. The next instant he threw off the bedclothes and started to rise.

"Get my clothes, Félix. I must go to the Hôtel de Lorraine."

But I flung myself upon him, pushing him back into bed and dragging the cover over him by main force.

"You can go nowhere, M. Étienne; it is madness. The surgeon said you must lie here for three days. You will get a fever in your wounds; you shall not go."

"Get off me, 'od rot you; you're smothering me," he gasped. Cautiously I relaxed my grip, still holding him down. He appealed: "Félix,

I must go. So long as there is a spark of life left in me, I have no choice but to go."

"Monsieur, you said you were done with the Leaguers – with M. de Mayenne."

"Aye, so I did," he cried. "But this – but this is Lorance."

Then, at my look of mystification, he suddenly opened his hand and tossed me the letter he had held close in his palm.

I read:

> *M. de Mar appears to consider himself of very little consequence, or of very great, since he is absent a whole month from the Hôtel de Lorraine. Does he think he is not missed? Or is he so sure of his standing that he fears no supplanting? In either case he is wrong. He is missed but he will not be missed forever. He may, if he will, be forgiven; or he may, if he will, be forgotten. If he would escape oblivion, let him come tonight, at the eleventh hour, to lay his apologies at the feet of*
>
> LORANCE DE MONTLUC

"And she –"

"Is cousin and ward to the Duke of Mayenne. Yes, and my heart's desire."

"Monsieur –"

"Aye, you begin to see it now," he cried vehemently. "You see why I have stuck to Paris these three years, why I could not follow my father into exile. It was more than a handful of pistoles caused the breach with Monsieur; more than a quarrel over Gervais de Grammont. That was the spark kindled the powder, but the train was laid."

"Then you, monsieur, were a Leaguer?"

"Nay, I was not!" he cried. "To my credit, – or my shame, as you choose, – I was not. I was neither one nor the other, neither fish nor flesh. My father thought me a Leaguer, but I was not. I was not disloyal, in deed at least, to the house that bore me. Monsieur reviled me for a skulker, a fainéant; nom de diable, he might have remembered his own three years of idleness!"

"Monsieur held out for his religion –"

"Mademoiselle is my religion," he cried, and then laughed, not merrily.

"Pardieu! for all my pains I have not won her. I have skulked and evaded and temporized – for nothing. I would not join the League and break my father's heart; would not stand out against it and lose Lorance. I have been trying these three years to please both the goat and the cabbage – with the usual ending. I have pleased nobody. I am out of

Mayenne's books: he made me overtures and I refused him. I am out of my father's books: he thinks me a traitor and parricide. And I am out of mademoiselle's: she despises me for a laggard. Had I gone in with Mayenne I had won her. Had I gone with Monsieur I was sure of a command in King Henry's army. But I, wanting both, get neither. Between two stools, I fall miserably to the ground. I am but a dawdler, a do-nothing, the butt and laughingstock of all brave men.

"But I am done with shilly-shally!" he added, catching his breath. "For once I shall do something. Mlle. de Montluc has given me a last chance. She has sent for me, and I go. If I fall dead on her threshold, I at least die looking at her."

"Monsieur, monsieur," I cried in despair, "you will not die looking at her, for you will die out here in the street, and that will profit neither you nor her, but only Lucas and his crew."

"That is as may be. At least I make the attempt. A month back I sent her a letter. I found it tonight in Lucas's doublet. She thinks me careless of her. I must go."

"Monsieur, you are mad," I cried. "You have said yourself Mayenne is likely to be behind Lucas. If you go you do but walk into the enemies' very jaws. It is a trap, a lure."

"Félix, beware what you say!" he interrupted with quick-blazing ire. "I do not permit such words to be spoken in connection with Mlle. de Montluc."

"But, monsieur –"

"Silence!" he commanded in a voice as sharp as crack of pistolet. The St. Quentins had ever the most abundant faith in those they loved. I remembered how Monsieur in just such a blaze of resentment had forbidden me to speak ill of his son. And I remembered, too, that Monsieur's faith had been justified and that my accusations were lies. Natheless, I liked not the look of this affair, and I attempted further warnings.

"Monsieur, in my opinion –"

"You are not here to hold opinions, Félix, but your tongue."

I did, at that, and stood back from the bed to let him do as it liked him. He rose and went over to the chair where his clothes lay, only to drop into it half swooning. I ran to the ewer and dashed half the water in it into his face.

"Peste, you need not drown me!" he cried testily. "I am well; it was but a moment's dizziness." He got up again at once, but was forced to seize my shoulder to keep from falling.

"It was that damnable potion he made me drink," he muttered. "I am all well else; I am not weak. Curse the room; it reels about like a ship at sea."

I put my arm about him and led him back to bed; nor did he argue about it but lay back with his eyes shut, so white against the white bed-linen I thought him fainted for sure. But before I could drench him again he raised his lids.

"Félix, will you go get a shutter? For I see clearly that I shall reach Mlle. de Montluc this night in no other way."

"Monsieur," I said, "I can go. I can tell your mistress you cannot walk across this room tonight. I can do my best for you, M. Étienne."

"My faith! I think I must e'en let you try. But what to bid you say to her – pardieu! I scarce know what I could say to her myself."

"I can tell her how sorely you are hurt – how you would come, but cannot."

"And make her believe it," he cried eagerly. "Do not let her think it a flimsy excuse. And yet I do think she will believe you," he added, with half a laugh. "There is something very trust-compelling about you, Félix. And assure her of my lifelong, never-failing service."

"But I thought monsieur was going to take service with Henry of Navarre."

"I was!" he cried. "I am! Oh, Félix, was ever a poor wight so harried and torn betwixt two as I? Whom Jupiter would destroy he first makes mad. I shall be gibbering in a cage before I have done with it."

"Monsieur will be gibbering in his bed unless he sleeps soon. I go now, monsieur."

"And good luck to you! Félix, I offer you no reward for this midnight journey into the house of our enemies. For recompense you will see her."

XIII

Mademoiselle.

I went to find Maître Menard, to urge upon him that someone should stay with M. Étienne while I was gone, lest he swooned or became lightheaded. But the surgeon himself was present, having returned from bandaging up some common skull to see how his noble patient rested. He promised that he would stay the night with M. le Comte; so, eased of that care, I set out for the Hôtel de Lorraine, one of the inn-servants with a flambeau coming along to guide and guard me. M. Étienne was a favorite in this inn of Maître Menard's; they did not stop to ask whether he had money in his purse before falling over one another in their eagerness to serve him. It is my opinion that one gets more out of the world by dint of fair words than by a long purse or a long sword.

We had not gone a block from the inn before I turned to the right-about, to the impatience of my escort.

"Nay, Jean, I must go back," I said. "I will only delay a moment, but see Maître Menard I must."

He was still in the cabaret where the crowd was thinning.

"Now what brings you back?"

"This, maître," said I, drawing him into a corner. "M. le Comte has been in a fracas tonight, as you perchance may have divined. His arch-enemy gave us the slip. And I am not easy for monsieur while this Lucas is at large. He has the devil's own cunning and malice; he might track him here to the Three Lanterns. Therefore, maître, I beg you to admit no one to M. le Comte – no one on any business whatsoever. Not if he comes from the Duke of Mayenne himself."

"I won't admit the Sixteen themselves," the maître declared.

"There is one man you may admit," I conceded. "Vigo, M. de St. Quentin's equery. You will know him for the biggest man in France."

"Good. And this other; what is he like?"

"He is young," I said, "not above four or five and twenty. Tall and slim, – oh, without doubt, a gentleman. He has light-brown hair and thin, aquiline face. His tongue is unbound, too."

"His tongue shall not get around me," Maître Menard promised. "The host of the Three Lanterns was not born yesterday let me tell you."

With this comforting assurance I set out once more on my expedition with, to tell truth, no very keen enthusiasm for the business. It was all very well for M. Étienne to declare grandly that as recompense for my trouble I should see Mlle. de Montluc. But I was not her lover and I thought I could get along very comfortably without seeing her. I knew not how to bear myself before a splendid young noblewoman. When I had dashed across Paris to slay the traitor in the Rue Coupejarrets I had not been afraid; but now, going with a love-message to a girl, I was scared.

And there was more than the fear of her bright eyes to give me pause. I was afraid of Mlle. de Montluc, but more afraid of M. de Mayenne's cousin. What mocking devil had driven Étienne de Mar, out of a whole France full of lovely women, to fix his unturnable desire on this Ligueuse of Mayenne's own brood? Had his father's friends no daughters, that he must seek a mistress from the black duke's household? Were there no families of clean hands and honest speech, that he must ally himself with the treacherous blood of Lorraine?

I had seen a sample of the League's work today, and I liked it not. If Mayenne were, as Yeux-gris surmised, Lucas's backer, I marveled that my master cared to enter his house; I marveled that he cared to send his servant there. Yet I went nonetheless readily for that; I was here to do his bidding. Nor was I greatly alarmed for my own skin; I thought myself too small to be worth my Lord Mayenne's powder. And I had, I do confess, a lively curiosity to behold the interior of the greatest house in Paris, the very core and center of the League. Belike if it had not been for terror of this young demoiselle I had stepped along cheerfully enough.

Though the hour was late, many people still loitered in the streets, the clear summer night, and all of them were talking politics. As Jean and I passed at a rapid pace the groups under the wine-shop lanterns, we caught always the names of Mayenne and Navarre. Everywhere they asked the same two questions: Was it true that Henry was coming into the Church? And if so, what would Mayenne do next? I perceived that old Maître Jacques of the Amour de Dieu knew what he was talking about: the people of Paris were sick to death of the Leagues and their intriguery, galled to desperation under the yoke of the Sixteen.

Mayenne's fine new hôtel in the Rue St. Antoine was lighted as for a fête. From its open windows came sounds of gay laughter and rattling dice. You might have thought them keeping carnival in the midst of a happy and loyal city. If the Lieutenant-General found anything to vex him in the present situation, he did not let the commonalty know it.

The Duke of Mayenne's house, like my duke's, was guarded by men-at-arms; but his grilles were thrown back while his soldiers lounged on the stone benches in the archway. Some of them were talking to a little knot of street idlers who had gathered about the entrance, while others, with the aid of a torch and a greasy pack of cards, were playing lansquenet.

I knew no way to do but to ask openly for Mlle. de Montluc, declaring that I came on behalf of the Comte de Mar.

"That is right; you are to enter," the captain of the guard replied at once. "But you are not the Comte de Mar yourself? Nay, no need to ask," he added with a laugh. "A pretty count you would make."

"I am his servant," I said. "I am charged with a message for mademoiselle."

"Well, my orders were to admit the count, but I suppose you may go in. If mademoiselle cannot land her lover it were cruel to deny her the consolation of a message."

A laugh went up and one of the gamblers looked round to say:

"It has gone hard with mademoiselle lately, sangdieu! Here's the Comte de Mar has not set foot in the house for a month or more, and M. Paul for a quarter of a year is vanished off the face of the earth. It seemed as if she must take the little cheese or nothing. But now things are looking up with her. M. Paul has walked calmly in, and here is a messenger at least from the other."

"But M. Paul has walked calmly out again," a third soldier took up the tale. "He did not stay very long, for all mademoiselle's graces."

"Then I warrant 'twas mademoiselle sent him off with a flea in his ear," another cried. "She looks higher than a bastard, even Le Balafré's own."

"She had better take care how she flouts Paul de Lorraine," came the retort, but the captain bade me march along. I followed him into the house, leaving Jean to be edified, no doubt, by a whole history, false and true, concerning Mlle. de Montluc. We bow down before the lofty of the earth, we underlings, but behind their backs there is none with whose names we make so free. And there we have the advantage of our masters; for they know little of our private matters while we know everything of theirs.

In the hall the captain turned me over to a lackey who conducted me through a couple of antechambers to a curtained doorway whence issued a merry confusion of voices and laughter. He passed in while I remained to undergo the scrutiny of the pair of flunkies whose repose we had invaded. But in a moment my guide appeared again, lifting the curtain for me to enter.

The big room was ablaze with candles set in mirrored sconces along the walls, set also in silver candelabra on the tables. There was a crowd of people in the place, a hundred it seemed to my dazzled eyes; grouped, most of them, about the tables set up and down, either taking hands themselves at cards or dice or betting on those who did. Bluff soldiers in breastplate and jack-boots were not wanting in the throng, but the larger number of the gallants were brave in silken doublets and spotless ruffs, as became a noble's drawing room. And the ladies! mordieu, what am I to say of them? Tricked out in every gay color under the sun, agleam with jewels – eh bien, the ladies of St. Quentin, that I had thought so fine, were but serving-maids to these.

I stood blinking, dazed by the lights and the crowd and the chatter, unable in the first moment to note clearly any face in the congregation of strange countenances. Nor would it have helped me if I could, for here close about were a dozen fair women, anyone of whom might be Mlle. de Montluc. My heart hammered in my throat. I knew not whom to address. But a young noble near by, dazzling in a suit of pink, took the burden on himself.

"I heard Mar's name; yet you are not M. de Mar, I think."

He spoke with a languid but nonetheless teasing derision. In truth, I must have resembled a little brown hare suddenly turned out of a bag in the midst of that gorgeous company.

"No," I stammered; "I am his servant. I seek Mlle. de Montluc."

"I have wondered what has become of Étienne de Mar this last month," spoke a second young gentleman, advancing from his place behind a fair one's chair. He was neither so pretty nor so fine as the other, but in his short, stocky figure and square face there was a force which his comrade lacked. He regarded me with a far keener glance as he asked:

"Peste! he must be in low water if this is the best he can do for a lackey."

"Perhaps the fellow's errand is to beg an advance from Mlle. de Montluc," suggested the pink youth.

"Who speaks my name?" a clear voice called; and a lady, laying down her hand at cards, rose and came toward me.

She was clad in amber satin. She was tall, and she carried herself with stately grace. Her black hair shadowed a cheek as purely white and pink as that of any yellow-locked Frisian girl, while her eyes, under their sooty lashes, shone blue as corn-flowers.

I began to understand M. Étienne.

"Who is it wants me?" she repeated, and catching sight of me stood regarding me in some surprise, not unfriendly, waiting for me to explain myself. But before I could find my tongue the man in pink answered her with his soft drawl:

"Mademoiselle, this is a minister plenipotentiary and envoy extraordinary – most extraordinary – from the court of his Highness the Comte de Mar."

"Oh, that is it!" she cried with a little laugh, but not, I think, at my uncouthness, though she looked me over curiously.

"He has not come himself, M. de Mar?"

"It appears not, mademoiselle."

She did not seem vastly disconcerted for all she cried in doleful tones:

"Alack! alack! I have lost. And Paul is not present to enjoy his triumph. He wagered me a pair of pearl-broidered gloves that I could not produce M. de Mar."

"But it is not his fault," I answered her, eagerly. "It is not M. de Mar's fault, mademoiselle. He has been hurt today, and he could not come. He is in bed of his wounds; he could not walk across his room. He tried. He bade me lay at mademoiselle's feet his lifelong services."

"Ah, Lorance!" cried a young demoiselle in a sky-colored gown, "methinks you have indeed lost M. de Mar if he sends you no better messenger of his regrets than this horse-boy."

"I have lost the gloves, that is certain and sad," Mlle. de Montluc replied, as if the loss of the wager were all her care. "I am punished for my vanity, mesdames et messieurs. I undertook to produce my recreant squire and I have failed. Alas!" And she put up her white hands before her face with a pretty imitation of despair, save that her eyes sparkled from between her fingers.

By this time the gamesters about us had stopped their play, in a general interest in the affair. An older lady coming forward with an air of authority demanded:

"What is this disturbance, Lorance?"

"A wager between me and my cousin Paul, madame," she answered with instant gravity and respect.

"Paul de Lorraine! Is he here?" the other asked, unpleased, I thought.

"Yes, madame. He dropped from the skies on us this afternoon. He is out of the house again now."

"But while he was in the house," quoth she in sky-color, "though he did not find time to pay his respects to Mme. la Duchesse, he had the leisure for considerable conversation with Mlle. de Montluc."

The other lady, whom I now guessed to be the Duchesse de Mayenne herself, turned somewhat sharply on her cousin of Montluc.

"I do not yet hear your excuses, mademoiselle, for the introduction of a stable boy into my salon."

"I beg you to believe, madame, I am not responsible for it," she protested. "Paul, when he was here, saw fit to rally me concerning M. de Mar. Mlle. de Tavanne informed him of the count's defection and they were pleased to be merry with me over it. I vowed I could get him back if I wished. The end of the matter was that I wrote a letter which my cousin promised to have conveyed to M. le Comte's old lodgings. This is the answer," mademoiselle cried, with a wave of her hand toward me. "But I did not expect it in this guise, madame. Blame your lackeys who know not their duties, not me."

"I blame you, mademoiselle," Mme. de Mayenne answered her, tartly. "I consider my salon no place for intrigues with horse-boys. If you must hold colloquy with this fellow, take him whither he belongs – to the stables."

A laugh went up among those who laugh at whatever a duchess says.

"Come, mesdames, we will resume our play," she added to the ladies who had followed her on the scene, and turned her back in lofty disdain on Mlle. de Montluc and her concerns. But though some of the company obeyed her, a curious circle still surrounded us.

"Dame! if you must be banished to the stables, we all will go, mademoiselle," declared the pink gallant. "We all want news of the vanished Mar."

"Indeed we do. We have missed him sorely. And I dare swear this messenger's account will prove diverting," lisped the sky-colored demoiselle.

I was not enjoying myself. I had given all my hopes of glory to be out in the street again. I wished Mlle. de Montluc would take me to the stables – anywhere out of this laughing company. But she had no such intent.

"I think madame does not mean her sentence," she rejoined. "I would not for the world frustrate your curiosity, Blanche; nor yours, M. de Champfleury. Tell us what has befallen your master, Sir Courier."

"He has been in a duel, mademoiselle."

"Whom was he fighting?"

"And for what lady's favor?"

"Is it a pretty Huguenot this time?"

"Does she make him read his Bible?"

"Or did her big brother set on him for a wicked papist?"

The questions chorused upon me; I saw they were framed to tease mademoiselle. I answered as best I might:

"He thinks of no lady but Mlle. de Montluc. The fight was over other matters. I am only told to say M. le Comte regrets most heartily that his wound prevents his coming, and to assure mademoiselle that he is too weak and faint to walk across the floor."

"Then exceed your instructions a little. Tell us what monsieur has been about these four weeks that he could not take time to visit us."

I was in a dilemma. I knew she was M. Étienne's chosen lady and therefore deserving of all fealty from me; yet at the same time I could not answer her question. It was sheer embarrassment and no intent of rudeness that caused my short answer:

"About his own concerns, mademoiselle."

"The young puppy begins to growl!" exclaimed the thickset soldierly fellow who had bespoken me before, whose hostile gaze had never left my face. "I'll have him flogged, mademoiselle, for this insolence."

"M. de Brie –" she began at the same moment that I cried out to her:

"I meant no insolence; I crave mademoiselle's pardon." I added, in my haste floundering deeper into the mire: "Mademoiselle sees for herself that I cannot tell about M. le Comte's affairs in this house."

Brie had me by the collar.

"So that is what has become of Mar!" he cried triumphantly. "I thought as much. If Mar's affairs are to be a secret from this house, then, nom de dieu, they are no secret."

He shook me back and forth as if to shake the truth out of me, till my teeth rattled together; I could not have spoken if I would. But he cried on, his voice rising with excitement:

"It has been no secret where St. Quentin stands and what he has been about. He came into Paris, smooth and smiling, his own man, forsooth – neither ours nor the heretic's! Mordieu! he was Henry's, fast and sure, save that he was not man enough to say so. I told Mayenne last month we ought to settle with M. de St. Quentin; I asked nothing better than to attend to him. But the general would not, but let him alone, free and unmolested in his work of stirring up sedition. And Mar, too –"

He stopped in the middle of a word. All the company who had been pressing around us halted still. I knew that behind me someone had entered the room.

M. de Brie dragged me back from where we were blocking the passage. I turned in his grasp to face the newcomer.

He was a tall, stout man, deep-chested, thick-necked, heavy-jowled. His wavy hair, brushed up from a high forehead, was lightest brown, while his brows, mustachios, and beard were dark. His eyes were dark also, his full lips red and smiling. He had the beauty and presence of all the Guises; it needed not the star on his breast to tell me that this was Mayenne himself.

He advanced into the room returning the salutes of the company, but his glance traveling straight to me and my captor.

"What have we here, François?"

"This is a fellow of Étienne de Mar's, M. le Duc," Brie answered. "He came here with messages for Mlle. de Montluc. I am getting out of him what Mar has been up to since he disappeared a month back."

"You are at unnecessary pains, my dear François; I already know Mar's whereabouts and doings rather better than he knows them himself."

Brie dropped his hand from my collar, looking by no means at ease. I perceived that this was the way with Mayenne: you knew what he said but you did not know what he thought. His somewhat heavy face varied little; what went on in his mind behind the smiling mask was matter for anxiety. If he asked pleasantly after your health, you fancied he might be thinking how well you would grace the gallows.

M. de Brie said nothing and the duke continued:

"Yes, I have kept watch over him these five weeks. You are late, François. You little boys are fools; you think because you do not know a thing I do not know it. Was I cruel to keep my information from you, ma belle Lorance?"

The attack was absolutely sudden; he had not seemed to observe her. Mademoiselle colored and made no instant reply. His voice was neither loud nor rough; he was smiling upon her.

"Or did you need no information, mademoiselle?"

She met his look unflinching.

"I have not been sighing for tidings of the Comte de Mar, monsieur."

"Because you have had tidings, mademoiselle?"

"No, monsieur, I have had no communication with M. de Mar since May – until tonight."

"And what has happened tonight?"

"Tonight – Paul appeared."

"Paul!" ejaculated the duke, startled momentarily out of his phlegm. "Paul here?"

"He was, monsieur, an hour ago. He has since gone forth again, I know not whither or for what."

Mayenne ruminated over this, pulling off his gloves slowly.

"Well? What has this to do with Mar?"

She had no choice, though in evident fear of his displeasure, but to go through again the tale of the wager and letter. She was moistening her dry lips as she finished, her eyes on his face wide with apprehension. But he answered amiably, half absently, as if the whole affair were a triviality:

"Never mind; I will give you a pair of gloves, Lorance."

He stood smiling upon us as if amused for an idle moment over our childish games. The color came back to her cheeks; she made him a curtsey, laughing lightly.

"Then my grief is indeed cured, monsieur. A new bit of finery is the best of balms for wounded self-esteem, is it not, Blanche? I confess I am piqued; I had dared to imagine that my squire might remember me still after a month of absence. I should have known it too much to ask of mortal man. Not till the rivers run up-hill will you keep our memories green for more than a week, messieurs."

"She turns it off well," cried the little demoiselle in blue, Mlle. Blanche de Tavanne; "you would not guess that she will be awake the night long, weeping over M. de Mar's defection."

"I!" exclaimed Mlle. de Montluc; "I weep over his recreancy? It is a far-fetched jest, my Blanche; can you invent no better? The Comte de Mar – behold him!"

She snatched a card from a tossed-down hand, holding it up aloft for us all to see. It was by chance the knave of diamonds; the pictured face with its yellow hair bore, in my fancy at least, a suggestion of M. Étienne.

"Behold M. de Mar – behold his fate!" With a twinkling of her white fingers she had torn the luckless knave into a dozen pieces and sent them whirling over her head to fall far and wide among the company.

"Summary measures, mademoiselle!" quoth a grizzled warrior, with a laugh. "Mordieu! have we your good permission to deal likewise with the flesh-and-blood Mar, when we go to arrest him for conspiring against the Holy League?"

But Mlle. de Tavanne's quick tongue robbed him of his answer.

"Marry, you are severe on him, Lorance. To be sure he does not come himself, but he sends so gallant a messenger!"

Mademoiselle glanced at me with hard blue eyes.

"That is the greatest insult of all," she said. "I could forgive – and forget – his absence; but I do not forgive his dispatching me his horse-boy."

Thus far I had choked down my swelling rage at her faithlessness, her vanity, her despiteful entreatment of my master's plight. I knew it was sheer madness for me to attempt his defense before this hostile company; nay, there was no object in defending him; there was not one here who cared to hear good of him. But at her last insult to him my blood boiled so hot that I lost all command of myself, and I burst out:

"If I were a horse-boy, – which I am not, – I were twenty times too good to be carrying messages hither. You need not rail at his poverty, mademoiselle; it was you brought him to it. It was for you he was turned out of his father's house. But for you he would not now be lying in a garret, penniless and dishonored. Whatever ills he suffers, it is you and your false house have brought them."

Brie had me by the throat. Mayenne interfered without excitement.

"Don't strangle him, François; I may need him later. Let him be flogged and locked in the oratory."

He turned away as one bored over a trifling matter. And as the lackeys dragged me back to the door, I heard Mlle. de Montluc saying:

"Oh, M. de Latour, what have I done in destroying your knave of diamonds! Ma foi, you had a quatorze!"

XIV

In the oratory.

"Here, Pierre!" M. de Brie called to the head lackey, "here's a candidate for a hiding. This is a cub of that fellow Mar's. He reckoned wrong when he brought his insolence into this house. Lay on well, boys; make him howl."

Brie would have liked well enough, I fancy, to come along and see the fun, but he conceived that his duty lay in the salon. Pierre, the same who had conducted me to Mlle. de Montluc, now led the way into a long oak-paneled parlor. Opposite the entrance was a huge chimney carved with the arms of Lorraine; at one end a door led into a little oratory where tapers burned before the image of the Virgin; at the other, before the two narrow windows, stood a long table with writing-materials. Chests and cupboards nearly filled the walls. I took this to be a sort of council-room of my Lord Mayenne.

Pierre sent one of his men for a cane and to the other suggested that he should quench the Virgin's candles.

"For I don't see why this rascal should have the comfort of a light in there," he said. "As for Madonna Mary, she will not mind; she has a million others to see by."

I was left alone with him and I promised myself the joy of one good blow at his face, no matter how deep they flayed me for it. But as I gathered myself for the rush he spoke to me low and cautiously:

"Now howl your loudest, lad; and I'll not lay on too hard."

My clinched fist dropped to my side.

"You never did me any harm," he muttered. "Howl till they think you half killed, and I'll manage."

I gaped at him, not knowing what to make of it. But this is the way of the world; if there is much cruelty in it, there is much kindness, too.

"Here's the cane, nom d'un chien!" Pierre exclaimed boisterously. "Give it here, Jean; there'll not be much of it left when I get through."

"You'll strip his coat off?" said the second lackey, from the oratory.

"My faith! no; I should kill him if I did, and the duke wants him," Pierre retorted. So without more ado the two men tied my wrists in front of me, and Jean held me by the knot while Pierre laid on. And he, good fellow, grasping my collar, contrived to pull my loose jerkin away from my back, so that he dusted it down without greatly incommoding me. Some hard whacks I did get, but they were nothing to what a strong man could have given in grim earnest.

I trust I could have taken a real flogging with as close lips as anybody, but if my kind succorer wanted howls, howls he should have. I yelled and cowered and dodged about, to the roaring delight of Jean and his mate. Indeed, I had drawn a crowd of grinning varlets to the door before my performance was over. But at length, when I thought I had done enough for their pleasure and that of the nobles in the salon, I dropped down on the floor and lay quiet, with shut eyes.

"He has had his fill, I trow; we must not spoil him for the master," Pierre said.

"Oh, he'll come to in a minute," another answered. "Why, you have not even drawn blood, Pierre!" He laid his hand on my back, whereat I groaned my hollowest.

"It will be many a day before he cares to have his back touched," laughed Pierre. "Here, men, lend a hand. Pardieu! I wonder what Our Lady thinks of some of the devotees we bring her."

As they lifted me he took my hand with an inquiring squeeze; and I squeezed back, grateful, if ever a boy was. They flung me down on the oratory floor and left me there a prisoner.

I spent the next hour or so trying to undo the knot of my handcuff with my teeth; and failing that, to chew the stout rope in two. I was minded as I worked of Lucas and his bonds, and wondered whether he had managed to rid himself of their inconvenience. He went straightway, doubtless, to some confederate who cut them for him, and even now was planning fresh evil against the St. Quentins. I remembered his face as he cried to M. le Comte that they should meet again; and I thought that M. Étienne was likely to have his hands full with Lucas, without this unlucky tanglement with Mlle. de Montluc. In the darkness and solitude I called down a murrain on his folly. Why could he not leave the girl alone? There were other blue eyes in the world. And it would be hard on humanity if there were none kindlier.

He had been at it three years, too. For three long years this girl's fair face had stood between him and his home, between him and action, between him and happiness. It was a fair face, truly; yet, in my opinion, neither it nor any maid's was worth such pains. If she had loved him it had not been worth it, but this girl spurned and flouted him. Why, in the name of Heaven, could he not put the jade out of his mind and turn merrily to St. Denis and the road to glory? When I got back to him and told him how she had mocked him, hang me but he should, though!

Ah, but when was I to get back to him? That rested not with me but with my dangerous host, the League's Lieutenant-General, dark-minded Mayenne. What he wanted with me he had not revealed; nor was it a pleasant subject for speculation. He meant me, of course, to tell him all I knew of the St. Quentins; well, that was soon done; belike he understood more than I of the day's work. But after he had questioned me, what?

Would he consider, with his servant Pierre, that I had never done him any harm? Or would he – I wondered, if they flung me out stark into some alley's gutter, whether M. le Comte would search for me and claim my carcass? Or would he, too, have fallen by the blades of the League?

I was shuddering as I waited there in the darkness. Never, not even this morning in the closet of the Rue Coupejarrets, had I been in such mortal dread. I had walked out of that closet to find M. Étienne; but I was not likely to happen on succor here. Pierre, for all his kind heart, could not save me from the Duke of Mayenne.

Then, when my hope was at its nadir, I remembered who was with me in the little room. I groped my way to Our Lady's feet and prayed her to save me, and if she might not, then to stand by me during the hard moment of dying and receive my seeking soul. Comforted now and deeming I could pass, if it came to that, with a steady face, I laid me down, my head on the prie-dieu cushion, and presently went to sleep.

I was waked by a light in my face, and, all a-quiver, sprang up to meet my doom. But it was not the duke or any of his hirelings who bent over me, candle in hand; it was Mlle. de Montluc.

"Oh, my boy, my poor boy!" she cried pitifully, "I could not save you the flogging; on my honor, I could not. It would have availed you nothing had I pleaded for you on my bended knees."

With bewilderment I observed that the tears were brimming over her lashes and splashing down into the candle-flame. I stared, too confused for speech, while she, putting down the shaking candlestick on the altar, as she crossed herself, covered her face with her hands, sobbing.

"Mademoiselle," I stammered, "it is not worth mademoiselle's tears! The man, Pierre, he told me to scream, so they would think he was half flaying me. But in truth he did not strike very hard. He did not hurt so much."

She struggled to check the rising tempest of her tears, and presently dropped her hands and looked at me earnestly from out her shining wet eyes. "Is that true? Are you not flayed?" And to make sure, she laid her hand delicately on my back.

"They have whacked your coat to ribbons, but, thank St. Généviève, they have not brought the blood. I saw a man flogged once –" she shut her eyes, shuddering, and her mouth quivered anew. "But I am not much hurt, mademoiselle," I answered her.

She took out her film of a handkerchief to wipe her wet cheeks, her hand still trembling. I could think of nothing but to repeat:

"I am not in the least hurt, mademoiselle."

"Ah, but if they have spared you the flogging to take your life!" she breathed.

It was not a heartening suggestion. To my astonishment, suddenly I found myself, frightened victim, striving to comfort this noblewoman for my death.

"Nay, I am not afraid. Since mademoiselle weeps over me, I can die happily."

She sprang toward me as if to protect me with her body from some menacing thrust.

"They shall not kill you!" she cried, her eyes flashing blue fire. "They shall not! Mon dieu! is Lorance de Montluc so feeble a thing that she cannot save a serving-boy?"

She fell back a pace, pressing her hands to her temples as if to stifle their throbbing.

"It was my fault," she cried – "it was all my fault. It was my vanity and silliness brought you to this. I should never have written that letter – a three years' child would have known better. But I had not seen M. de Mar for five weeks – I did not know, what I readily guess now, that he had taken sides against us. M. de Lorraine played on my pique."

"Mademoiselle," I said, "the worst has not followed, since M. Étienne did not come himself."

"You are glad for that?"

"Why, of course, mademoiselle. Was it not a trap for him?"

She caught her breath as if in pain.

"I knew that as soon as I saw that my cousin Mayenne was not angry. When I told what I had done and he smiled at me and said I should have my gloves, why, then I thought my heart would stop beating. I saw what I had accomplished – mon dieu, I was sick with repentance of it!"

I had to tell her I had not thought it.

"No," she answered; "I had got you into this by my foolishness; I must needs try to get you out by my wits. Brie, the one who took you by the throat – there has been bad blood between him and your lord this twelvemonth; only last May M. le Comte ran him through the wrist. Had I interfered for you," she said, coloring a little, "M. de Brie would have inferred interest in the master from that in the man, and he had seen to your beating himself."

It suddenly dawned on me that this M. de Brie was the "little cheese" of guardroom gossip. And I thought that the gentleman would hardly display so much venom against M. Étienne unless he were a serious obstacle to his hopes. Nor would mademoiselle be here at midnight, weeping over a serving-lad, if she cared nothing for the master. If she had not worn her heart on her sleeve before the laughing salon, mayhap she would show it to me.

"Mademoiselle," I cried, "when the billet was brought him M. Étienne rose from his bed at once to come. But he was faint from fatigue and loss of blood; he could not walk across the room. But he bade me try to make mademoiselle believe his absence was no fault of his. He wrote her a month ago; he found today the letter was never delivered."

"Is he hurt dangerously?"

"No," I admitted reluctantly; "no, I think not. He was wounded in the right forearm, and again pinked in the shoulder; but he will recover."

"You said," she went on, the tears standing in her eyes, "that he was penniless. I have not much, but what I have is freely his."

She advanced upon me holding out her silken purse which she had taken from her bosom; but I retreated.

"No, no, mademoiselle," I cried, ashamed of my hot words; "we are not penniless – or if we are, we get on very well sans le sou. They do everything for monsieur at the Trois Lanternes, and he has only to return to the Hôtel St. Quentin to get all the gold pieces he can spend. Oh, no; we are in no want, mademoiselle. I was angry when I said it; I did not mean it. I cry mademoiselle's pardon."

She looked at me a little hesitatingly.

"You are telling me true?"

"Why, yes, mademoiselle; if my monsieur needed money, indeed, indeed, I would not refuse it."

"Then if you cannot take it for him, you can take it for yourself. It will be strange if in all Paris you cannot find something you like as a token from me." With her own white fingers she slipped some tinkling coins into my pouch, and cut short my thanks with the little wailing cry:

"Oh, your poor, bound hands! I have my poniard in my dress. I could free them in a second. But if they knew I had been here with you they never will let you go."

"If mademoiselle is running into danger staying here, I pray her to go back to bed. M. Étienne did not send me hither to bring her grief and trouble."

"Who are you?" she asked me abruptly. "You have never been here before on monsieur's errands?"

"No, mademoiselle; I came up only yesterday from Picardie. I belong on the St. Quentin estate. My name is Félix Broux."

"Alack, you have chosen a bad time to visit Paris!"

"I came up to see life," I said, "and mordieu! I am seeing it."

"I pray God you may not see death, too," she answered soberly.

She stood looking at me helplessly.

"I am in my lord's black books," she said slowly, as if to herself; "but I might weep François de Brie's rough heart to softness. Then it is a question whether he could turn Mayenne. I wish I knew whether the duke himself or only Paul de Lorraine has planned this move tonight. That is," she added, blushing, but speaking out candidly, "whether they attack M. de Mar as the League's enemy or as my lover."

"This M. Paul de Lorraine," said I, speaking as respectfully as I knew how, but eager to find out all I could for M. Étienne – "this M. de Lorraine is mademoiselle's lover, too?"

She shrugged her shoulders, neither assenting nor denying. "We are all pawns in the game for M. de Mayenne to push about as he chooses. For a time M. de Mar was high in his favor. Then my cousin Paul came back after a two years' disappearance, and straightway he was up and

M. de Mar was down. And then Paul vanished again as suddenly as he had come, and it became the turn of M. de Brie. Now tonight Paul walked in as suddenly as he had left and at once played on me to write that unlucky letter. And what it bodes for *him* I know not."

She spoke with amazing frankness; yet, much as she had told me, the fact of her telling it told me even more. I saw that she was as lonely in this great house as I had been at St. Quentin. She would have talked delightedly to M. le Comte's dog.

"Mademoiselle," I said, "I would like well to tell you what has been happening to my M. Étienne this last month, if you are not afraid to stay long enough to hear it."

"Oh, everyone is asleep long ago; it is past two o'clock. Yes, you may tell me if you wish."

She sat down on a praying-cushion, motioning me to the other, and I began my tale. At first she listened with a little air of languor, as if the whole were of slight consequence and she really did not care at all what M. le Comte had been about these five weeks. But as I got into the affair of the Rue Coupejarrets she forgot her indifference and leaned forward with burning cheeks, hanging on my words with eager questions. And when I told her how Lucas had evaded us in the darkness, she cried:

"Blessed Virgin! M. de Mar has enough to contend with in this Lucas, without Paul de Lorraine, and Brie, and the Duke of Mayenne himself."

I was silent, being of her opinion. Presently she asked reluctantly:

"Does your master think this Lucas a tool of M. de Mayenne's?"

"Yes, mademoiselle. He says secretaries do not plot against dukedoms for their own pleasure."

"Assassination was not wont to be my cousin Mayenne's way," she said with an accent of confidence that rang as false as a counterfeit coin. I saw well enough that mademoiselle did fear, at least, Mayenne's guilt. I thought I might tell her a little more.

"M. le Comte told me that since his father's coming to Paris M. de Mayenne made him offers to join the League, and he refused them. So then M. de Mayenne, seeing himself losing the whole house of St. Quentin, invented this."

"But it failed. Thank God, it failed! And now he will leave Paris. He will – he must!"

"He did mean to seek Navarre's camp tomorrow," I answered; "but –"

"But what?"

"But then the letter came."

"But that makes no difference! He must go for all that. The time is over for trimming. He must stand on one side or the other. I am a

Ligueuse born and bred, and I tell him to go to King Henry. It is his father's side; it is his side. He cannot stay in Paris another day."

"I do not think he will go, mademoiselle."

"But he must!" she cried with vehemence. "Paris is not safe for him. If he cannot stand for his wound, he must go. I will send him a letter myself to tell him he must."

"Then he will never go."

"Félix!"

"He will not. He was going because he thought his lady flouted him; when he finds she does not – well, if he budges a step out of Paris, I do not know him. When he thought himself despised –"

"And why did I turn his suit into laughter in the salon if I did not mean that I despised him? I did it for you to tell him how I made a mock of him, that he might hate me and keep away from me."

"Oh," I said, "mademoiselle is beyond me; I cannot keep up with her."

"And you believed it! But you must needs spoil all by flaring out with impudent speech."

"I crave mademoiselle's pardon. I was wrong and insolent. But she played too well."

"And if it was not play?" she cried, rising. "If I do – well, I will not say despise him – but care nothing for him? Will he then go to St. Denis? Then tell him from me that he has my pity as one cruelly cozened, and my esteem as a one-time servant of mine, but never my love. Tell him I would willingly save him alive, for the sake of the love he once bore me. But as for any answering love in my bosom, I have not one spark. Tell him to go find a new mistress at St. Denis. He might as well cry for the moon as seek to win Lorance de Montluc."

"That may be true," I said; "but all the same he will try. Can mademoiselle suppose he will go out of Paris now, and leave her to marry Brie and Lorraine?"

"Only one," she protested with the shadow of a smile; and then a sudden rush of tears blinded her. "I am a very miserable girl," she said woefully, "for I bring nothing but danger to those that love me."

I dropped on my knees before her and kissed the hem of her dress.

"Ah, Félix," she said, "if you really pitied me, you would get him out of Paris!" And she fell to weeping as if her heart would break.

I had no skill to comfort her. I bent my head before her, silent. At length she sobbed out:

"It boots little for us to quarrel over what you shall say to M. de Mar, when we know not that you will ever speak to him again. And it was all my fault."

"Mademoiselle, it was the fault of my hasty tongue."

But she shook her head.

"I maintained that to you, but it was not true. Mayenne had something in his mind before. A general holds his schemes so dear and lives so cheap. But I will do my utmost, Félix, lad. It is not long to daylight now. I will go to François de Brie and we'll believe I shall prevail."

She took up her candle and said good night to me very gently and quietly, and gave me her hand to kiss. She opened the door, – with my fettered wrists I could not do the office for her, – and on the threshold turned to smile on me, wistfully, hopefully. In the next second, with a gasp that was half a cry, she blew out the light and pushed the door shut again.

XV

My Lord Mayenne.

I knew she was shutting the door by the click of the latch; in the next second I made the discovery that she was still on my side of it. "What –" I was beginning, when she laid her hand over my mouth. A line of light showed through the crack. She had not quite closed the door on account of the noise of the latch. She tried again; again it rattled and she desisted. I heard her fluttered breathing and I heard something else – a rapid, heavy tread in the corridor without. Into the council-room came a man carrying a lighted taper. It was Mayenne.

Mademoiselle, with a whispered "God save us!" sank in a heap at my feet.

I bent over her to find if she had swooned, when she seized my hand in a sharp grip that told me plain as words to be quiet.

Mayenne was yawning; he had a rumpled and disheveled look like one just roused from sleep. He crossed over to the table, lighted the three-branched candlestick standing there, and seated himself with his back to us, pulling about some papers. I hardly dared glance at him, for fear my eyes should draw his; the crack of our door seemed to call aloud to him to mark it; but the candlelight scarcely pierced the shadows of the long room.

More quick footsteps in the corridor. Mayenne hitched his chair about, sidewise to the table and to us, facing the outer door. A tall man in black entered, saluting the general from the threshold.

"So you have come back?" spoke the duke in his even tones. It was impossible to tell whether the words were a welcome or a sentence.

"Yes," answered the other, in a voice as noncommittal as Mayenne's own. He shut the door after him and walked over to the table.

"And how goes it?"

"Badly."

The newcomer threw his hat aside and sat down without waiting for an invitation.

"What! Badly, sirrah!" Mayenne exclaimed sharply. "You come to me with that report?"

"I do, monsieur," answered the other with cool insolence, leaning back in his chair. The light fell directly on his face and proved to me what I had guessed at his first word. The duke's night visitor was Lucas. "Yes," he repeated indifferently, "it has gone badly. In fact, your game is up."

Mayenne jumped to his feet, bringing his fist down on the table.

"You tell me this?"

Lucas regarded him with an easy smile.

"Unfortunately, monsieur, I do."

Mayenne turned on him, cursing. Lucas with the quickness of a cat sprang a yard aside, dagger unsheathed.

"Put up that knife!" shouted Mayenne.

"When you put up yours, monsieur."

"I have drawn none!"

"In your sleeve, monsieur."

"Liar!" cried Mayenne.

I know not who was lying, for I could not tell whether the blade that flashed now in the duke's hand came from his sleeve or from his belt. But if he had not drawn before he had drawn now and rushed at Lucas. He dodged and they circled round each other, wary as two matched cocks. Lucas was strictly on the defensive; Mayenne, the less agile by reason of his weight, could make no chance to strike. He drew off presently.

"I'll have your neck wrung for this," he panted.

"For what, monsieur?" asked Lucas, imperturbably. "For defending myself?"

Mayenne let the charge go by default.

"For coming to me with the tale of your failures. Nom de dieu, do I employ you to fail?"

"We are none of us gods, monsieur. You yourself lost Ivry."

Mayenne backed over to his chair and seated himself, laying his knife on the table in front of him. His face smoothed out to good humor – no mean tribute to his power of self-control. For the written words can convey no notion of the maddening insolence of Lucas's bearing – an insolence so studied that it almost seemed unconscious and was thereby well-nigh impossible to silence.

"Sit down," bade the duke, "and tell me."

Lucas, standing at the foot of the table, observed:

"They turned you out of your bed, monsieur, to see me. It was unnecessary severity. My tale will keep till morning."

"By Heaven, it shall not!" Mayenne shouted. "Beware how much further you dare anger me, you Satan's cub!"

He was fingering the dagger again as if he longed to plunge it into Lucas's gullet, and I rather marveled that he did not, or summon his guard to do it. For I could well understand how infuriating was Lucas. He carried himself with an air of easy equality insufferable to the first noble in the land. Mayenne's chosen rôle was the unmoved, the inscrutable, but Lucas beat him at his own game and drove him out into the open of passion and violence. It was a miracle to me that the man lived – unless, indeed, he were a prince in disguise.

"Satan's cub!" Lucas repeated, laughing. "Our late king had called me that, pardieu! But I knew not you acknowledged Satan in the family."

"I ordered Antoine to wake me if you returned in the night," Mayenne went on gruffly. "When I heard you had been here I knew something was wrong – unless the thing were done."

"It is not done. The whole plot is ruined."

"Nom de dieu! If it is by your bungling –"

"It was not by my bungling," Lucas answered with the first touch of heat he had shown. "It was fate – and that fool Grammont."

"Explain then, and quickly, or it will be the worse for you."

Lucas sat down, the table between them.

"Look here," he said abruptly, leaning forward over the board. "Have you Mar's boy?"

"What boy?"

"A young Picard from the St. Quentin estate, whom the devil prompted to come up to town today. Mar sent him here tonight with a love-message to Lorance."

"Oh," said Mayenne, slowly, "if it is a question of mademoiselle's love-affairs, it may be put off till tomorrow. It is plain to the very lackeys that you are jealous of Mar. But at present we are discussing l'affaire St. Quentin."

"It is all one," Lucas answered quickly. "You know what is to be the reward of my success."

"I thought you told me you had failed."

Lucas's hand moved instinctively to his belt; then he thought better of it and laid both hands, empty, on the table.

"Our plot has failed; but that does not mean that St. Quentin is immortal."

"You may be very sure of one thing, my friend," the duke observed. "I shall never give Lorance de Montluc to a white-livered flincher."

"The Duke of St. Quentin is not immortal," Lucas repeated. "I have missed him once, but I shall get him in spite of all."

"I am not sure about Lorance even then," said Mayenne, reflectively. "François de Brie is agitating himself about that young mistress. And he has not made any failures – as yet."

Lucas sprang to his feet.

"You swore to me I should have her."

"Permit me to remind you again that you have not brought me the price."

"I will bring you the price."

"E'en then," spoke Mayenne, with the smile of the cat standing over the mouse – "e'en then I might change my mind."

"Then," said Lucas, roundly, "there will be more than one dead duke in France."

Mayenne looked up at him as unmoved as if it were not in the power of mortal man to make him lose his temper. In stirring him to draw dagger, Lucas had achieved an extraordinary triumph. Yet I somehow thought that the man who had shown hot anger was the real man; the man who sat there quiet was the party leader.

He said now, evenly:

"That is a silly way to talk to me, Paul."

"It is the truth for once," Lucas made sullen answer.

So long as he could prick and irritate Mayenne he preserved an air of unshakable composure; but when Mayenne recovered patience and himself began to prick, Lucas's guard broke down. His voice rose a key, as it had done when I called him fool; and he burst out violently:

"Mort de dieu! monsieur, what am I doing your dirty work for? For love of my affectionate uncle?"

"It might well be for that. I have been your affectionate uncle, as you say."

"My affectionate uncle, you say? My hirer, my suborner! I was a Protestant; I was bred up by the Huguenot Lucases when my father cast off my mother and me to starve. I had no love for the League or the Lorraines. I was fighting in Navarre's ranks when I was made prisoner at Ivry."

"You were spying for Navarre. It was before the fight we caught you. You had been hanged and quartered in that grey dawn had I not recognized you, after twelve years, as my brother's son. I cut the rope from you and embraced you for your father's sake. You rode forth a cornet in my army, instead of dying like a felon on the gallows."

"You had your ends to serve," Lucas muttered.

"I took you into my household," Mayenne went on. "I let you wear the name of Lorraine. I did not deny you the hand of my cousin and ward, Lorance de Montluc."

"Deny me! No, you did not. Neither did you grant it me, but put me off with lying promises. You thought then you could win back the faltering house of St. Quentin by a marriage between your cousin and the Comte de Mar. Afterward, when my brother Charles dashed into Paris, and the people clamored for his marriage with the Infanta, you conceived the scheme of forcing Lorance on him. But it would not do, and again you promised her to me if I could get you certain information from the royalist army. I returned in the guise of an escaped prisoner to Henry's camp to steal you secrets; and the moment my back was turned you listened to proposals from Mar again."

"Mar is not in the race now. You need not speak of him, nor of your brother Charles, either."

"No; I can well understand that my brother's is not a pleasant name in your ears," Lucas agreed. "You acknowledged one King Charles X; you would like well to see another Charles X, but it is not Charles of Guise you mean."

"I have no desire to be King of France," Mayenne began angrily.

"Have you not? That is well, for you will never feel the crown on your brows, good uncle! You are ground between the Spanish hammer and the Béarnais anvil; there will soon be nothing left of you but powder."

"Nom de dieu, Paul —" Mayenne cried, half rising; but Lucas, leaning forward on the table, riveting him with his keen eyes, went on:

"Do not mistake me, monsieur uncle. I think you in bad case, but I am ready to sink or swim with you. So long as the hand of Lorance is in your bestowing I am your faithful servant. I have not hesitated to risk the gallows to serve you. Last March I made my way here, disguised, to tell you of the king's coming change of faith and of St. Quentin's certain defection. I demanded then my price, my marriage with mademoiselle. But you put me off again. You sent me back to Mantes to kill you St. Quentin."

"Aye. And you have been about it these four months, and you have not killed him."

Lucas reddened with ire.

"I am no Jacques Clément to stab and be massacred. You cannot buy such a service of me, M. de Mayenne. If I do bravo's work for you I choose my own time and way. I brought the duke to Paris, delivered him up to you to deal with as it liked you. But you with your army at your back were afraid to kill him. You flinched and waited. You dared not shoulder the onus of his death. Then I, to help you out of your strait, planned to make his own son's the hand that should do the deed; to kill the duke and ruin his heir; to put not only St. Quentin but Mar out of your way –"

"Let us be accurate, Paul," Mayenne said. "Mar was not in my way; he was of no consequence to me. You mean, put him out of your way."

"He was in your way, too. Since he would not join the Cause he was a hindrance to it. You had as much to gain as I by his ruin."

"Something – not as much. I did not want him killed – I preferred him to Valère."

"Nor did I want him killed; so our views jibed well."

"Why not, then? Did you prefer him as your wife's lover to some other who might appear?"

"I do not intend that my wife shall have lovers," Lucas answered.

Mayenne broke into laughter.

"Nom d'un chien, where will you keep her? In the Bastille? Lorance and no lovers! Ho, ho!"

"I mean none whom she favors."

"Then why do you leave Mar alive? She adores the fellow," Mayenne said. I had no idea whether he really thought it or only said it to annoy Lucas. At any rate it had its effect. Lucas's brows were knotted; he spoke with an effort, like a man under stress of physical pain.

"I know she loves him now, and she would love him dead; but she would not love him a parricide."

"Is that your creed? Pardieu! you don't know women. The blacker the villain the more they adore him."

"I know it is true, monsieur," Lucas said smoothly, "that you have had successes."

Mayenne started forward with half an oath, changing to a laugh.

"So it is not enough for you to possess the fair body of Lorance; you must also have her love?"

"She will love me," Lucas answered uneasily. "She must."

"It is not worth your fret," Mayenne declared. "If she did, how long would it last? *Souvent femme varie* – that is the only fixed fact about her. If Lorance loves Mar today, she will love someone else tomorrow, and someone else still the day after tomorrow. It is not worth while disturbing yourself about it."

"She will not love anyone else," Lucas said hoarsely.

Mayenne laughed.

"You are very young, Paul."

"She shall not love anyone else! By the throne of heaven, she shall not!"

Mayenne went on laughing. If Lucas had for the moment teased him out of his equanimity, the duke had paid back the score a hundredfold. Lucas's face was seared with his passions as with the torture-iron; he clinched his hands together, breathing hard. On my side of the door I heard a sharp little sound in the darkness; mademoiselle had gritted her teeth.

"It is a little early to sweat over the matter," Mayenne said, "since mademoiselle is not your wife nor ever likely to become so."

"You refuse her to me?" Lucas cried, livid. I thought he would leap over the table at one bound on Mayenne. It occurred to the duke to take up his dagger.

"I promise her to you when you kill me St. Quentin. And you have not killed me St. Quentin but instead come airily to tell me the scheme – my scheme – is wrecked. Pardieu! it was never my scheme. I never advocated stolen pistoles and suborned witnesses and angered nephews and deceived sons and the rest of your cumbrous machinery. I would have had you stab him as he bent over his papers, and walk out of the house before they discovered him. But you had not the pluck for that; you must needs plot and replot to make someone else do your work. Now, after months of intriguing and waiting, you come to me to tell me you have failed. Morbleu! is there any reason why I should not have you kicked into the gutter, as no true son of the valorous Le Balafré?"

Lucas's hand went to his belt again; he made one step as if to come around the table. Mayenne's angry eye was on him but he did not move; and Lucas made no more steps. Controlling himself with an effort, he said:

"It was not my fault, monsieur. No man could have labored harder or planned better than I. I have been diligent, I have been clever. I have made my worst enemy my willing tool – I have made Monsieur's own son my cat's-paw. I have left no end loose, no contingency unprovided for – and I am ruined by a freak of fate."

"I never knew a failure yet but what the fault was fate's," Mayenne returned.

"Call it accident, then, call it the devil, call it what you like!" Lucas cried. "I still maintain it was not my fault. Listen, monsieur."

He sat down again and began his story, striving as he talked to reconquer something of his old coolness.

"The thing was ruined by the advent of this boy, Mar's lackey I spoke of. You said he had not been here?"

"You may go to Lorance with that question," Mayenne answered; "I have something else to attend to than the intrigues of my wife's maids."

"He started hither; I thought someone would have the sense to keep him. Mordieu! I will find from Lorance whether she saw him."

He fell silent, gnawing his lip; I could see that his thought had traveled away from the plot to the sore subject of mademoiselle's affections.

"Well," said Mayenne, sharply, "what about your boy?"

It was a moment before Lucas answered. When he did he spoke low and hurriedly, so that I could scarce catch the words. I knew it was no fear of listeners that kept his voice down – they had shouted at each other as if there was no one within a mile. I guessed that Lucas, for all his bravado, took little pride in his tale, nor felt happy about its reception. I could catch names now and then, Monsieur's, M. Étienne's, Grammont's, but the hero of the tale was myself.

"You let him to the duke?" Mayenne cried presently.

At the harsh censure of his voice, Lucas's rang out with the old defiance:

"With Vigo at his back I did. Sangdieu! you have yet to make the acquaintance of St. Quentin's equery. A regiment of your lansquenets couldn't keep him out."

"Does he never take wine?" Mayenne asked, lifting his hand with shut fingers over the table and then opening them.

"That is easy to say, monsieur, sitting here in your own hôtel stuffed with your soldiers. But it was not so easy to do, alone in my enemy's house, when at the least suspicion of me they had broken me on the wheel."

"That is the rub!" Mayenne cried violently. "That is the trouble with all of you. You think more of the safety of your own skins than of accomplishing your work. Mordieu! where should I be today – where would the Cause be – if my first care was my own peril?"

"Then that is where we differ, uncle," Lucas answered with a cold sneer. "You are, it is well known, a patriot, toiling for the Church and the King of Spain, with never a thought for the welfare of Charles of Lorraine, Lord of Mayenne. But I, Paul of Lorraine, your humble nephew, lord of my brain and hands, freely admit that I am toiling for no one but the aforesaid Paul of Lorraine. I should find it most inconvenient to get on without a head on my shoulders, and I shall do my best to keep it there."

"You need not tell me that; I know it well enough," Mayenne answered. "You are each for himself, none for me. At the same time, Paul, you will do well to remember that your interest is to forward my interest."

"To the full, monsieur. And I shall kill you St. Quentin yet. You need not call me coward; I am working for a dearer stake than any man in your ranks."

"Well," Mayenne rejoined, "get on with your tale."

Lucas went on, Mayenne listening quietly, with no further word of blame. He moved not so much as an eyelid till Lucas told of M. le Duc's departure, when he flung himself forward in his chair with a sharp oath.

"What! by daylight?"

"Aye. He was afraid, after this discovery, of being set on at night."

"He went out in broad day?"

"So Vigo said. I saw him not," Lucas answered with something of his old nonchalance.

"Mille tonnerres du diable!" Mayenne shouted. "If this is true, if he got out in broad day, I'll have the head of the traitor that let him. I'll nail it over his own gate."

"It is not worth your fret, monsieur," Lucas said lightly. "If you did, how long would it avail? *Souvent homme trahie*; that is the only fixed fact about him. If they pass St. Quentin today, they will pass someone else tomorrow, and someone else still the day after."

Mayenne looked at him, half angry, half startled into some deeper emotion at this deft twisting of his own words.

"Souvent homme trahie,
Mal habile qui s'y fie,"

he repeated musingly. He might have been saying over the motto of the house of Lorraine. For the Guises believed in no man's good faith, as no man believed in theirs.

"Souvent homme trahie," Mayenne said again, as if in the words he recognized a bitter verity. "And that is as true as King Francis's version. I suppose you will be the next, Paul."

"When I give up hope of Lorance," Lucas said bluntly.

I caught myself suddenly pitying the two of them: Mayenne, because, for all his power and splendor and rank next to a king's and ability second to none, he dared trust no man – not the son of his body, not his brother. He had made his own hell and dwelt in it, and there was no need to wish him any ill. And Lucas, perjured traitor, was farther from the goal of his desire than if we had slain him in the Rue Coupejarrets.

"What next? It appears you escaped the redoubted Vigo," Mayenne went on in his everyday tone; and the vision faded, and I saw him once more as the greatest noble and greatest scoundrel in France, and feared and hated him, and Lucas too, as the betrayer of my dear lord Étienne.

"Trust me for that."

"Then came you here?"

"Not at once. I tracked Mar and this Broux to Mar's old lodgings at the Three Lanterns. When I had dogged them to the door I came here and worked upon Lorance to write Mar a letter commanding his presence. For I thought that the night was yet young and tomorrow he might be out of my reach. Well, it appears he had not the courage to come but he sent the boy. I was not sorry. I thought I could settle him more quietly at the inn. The boy went back once and almost ran into me in the court, but he did not see me. I entered and asked for lodgings; but the fat old fool of a host put me through the catechism like an inquisitor, and finally declared the inn was full. I said I would take a garret; but it was no use. Out I must trudge. I did, and paid two men to get into a brawl in front of the house, that the inn people might run out to look. But instead they locked the gate and put up the shutters in the cabaret."

Mayenne burst out laughing.

"It was not your night, Paul."

"No," said Lucas, shortly.

"And what then? It did not take you till three o'clock to be put out of the inn."

"No," Lucas answered; "I spoke to you of the varlet Pontou with whom Grammont had quarreled. He had shut him up in a closet of the house in the Rue Coupejarrets. After the fight in the court we all went our ways, forgetting him. So I paid the house a visit; I was afraid someone else might find him and he might tell tales."

"And will he tell tales?"

"No," said Lucas, "he will tell no tales."

"How about your spy in the Hôtel St. Quentin?"

"Martin, the clerk? Oh, I warned him off before I left," Lucas said easily. "He will lie perdu till we want him again. And Grammont, you see, is dead too. There is no direct witness to the thing but the boy Broux."

"That's as good as to say there is none," Mayenne answered; "for I have the boy."

XVI

Mayenne's ward.

Lucas sprang up.

"You have him? Where?"

"Yes, I have him," Mayenne answered with his tantalizing slowness.

"Alive?"

"I suppose so. He had his flogging but I told them I was not done with him. I thought we might have a use for him. He is in the oratory there."

"Diable! Listening?" cried Lucas, as if a quick doubt of Mayenne's good faith to him struck his mind.

"Certainly not," Mayenne answered. "The door is bolted; he might be in the street for all he can hear. The wall was built for that."

"What will you do with him, monsieur?"

"We'll have him out," said Mayenne. Lucas, needing no second bidding, hastened down the room.

All this while mademoiselle, on the floor at my feet, had neither stirred nor whispered, as rigid as the statued Virgin herself. But now she rose and for one moment laid her hand on my shoulder with an encouraging pat; the next she flung the door wide just as Lucas reached the threshold.

He recoiled as from a ghost.

"Lorance!" he gasped, "Lorance!"

"Nom de dieu!" came Mayenne's shout from the back of the room. "What! Lorance!"

He caught up the candelabrum and strode over to us.

Mademoiselle stepped out into the council-room, I hanging back on the other side of the sill. She was as white as linen, but she lifted her head proudly. She had not the courage that knows no fear, but she had the courage that rises to the need. Crouching on the oratory floor she had been in a panic lest they find her. But in the moment of discovery she faced them unflinching.

"You spying here, Lorance!" Mayenne stormed at her.

"I did not come here to spy, monsieur," she answered. "I was here first, as you see. Your presence was as unlooked for by me as mine by you."

His next accusation brought the blood in scarlet flags to her pale cheeks; she made him no answer but burned him with her indignant eyes.

"Mordieu, monsieur!" Lucas cried. "This is Mlle. de Montluc."

"Then why did you come?" demanded Mayenne.

"Because I had done harm to the lad and was sorry," she said. "You defend me now, Paul, but you did not hesitate to make a tool of me in your cowardly schemes."

"It was kindly meant, mademoiselle," Lucas retorted. "Since I shall kill M. le Comte de Mar in any case, I thought it would pleasure you to have a word with him first."

I think it did not need the look she gave him to make him regret the speech. This Lucas was an extraordinary compound of shrewdness and recklessness, one separating from the other like oil and vinegar in a sloven's salad. He could plan and toil and wait, to an end, with skill and fortitude and patience; but he could not govern his own gusty tempers.

"You have been crying, Lorance," Mayenne said in a softer tone.

"For my sins, monsieur," she answered quickly. "I am grieved most bitterly to have been the means of bringing this lad into danger. Since Paul cozened me into doing what I did not understand, and since this is not the man you wanted but only his servant, will you not let him go free?"

"Why, my pretty Lorance, I did not mean to harm him," Mayenne protested, smiling. "I had him flogged for his insolence to you; I thought you would thank me for it."

"I am never glad over a flogging, monsieur."

"Then why not speak? A word from you and it had stopped."

She flushed red for very shame.

"I was afraid – I knew you vexed with me," she faltered. "Oh, I have done ill!" She turned to me, silently imploring forgiveness. There was no need to ask.

"Then you will let him go, monsieur? Alack that I did not speak before! Thank you, my cousin!"

"Of what did you suspect me? The boy was whipped for a bit of impertinence to you; I had no cause against him."

My heart leaped up; at the same time I scorned myself for a craven that I had been overcome by groundless terror.

"Then I have been a goose so to disturb myself," mademoiselle laughed out in relief. "You do well to rebuke me, cousin. I shall never meddle in your affairs again."

"That will be wise of you," Mayenne returned. "For I did mean to let the boy go. But since you have opened his door and let him hear what he should not, I have no choice but to silence him."

"Monsieur!" she gasped, cowering as from a blow.

"Aye," he said quietly. "I would have let him go. But you have made it impossible."

Never have I seen so piteous a sight as her face of misery. Had my hands been free, Mayenne had been startled to find a knife in his heart.

"Never mind, mademoiselle," I cried to her. "You came and wept over me, and that is worth dying for."

"Monsieur," she cried, recovering herself after the first instant of consternation, "you are degrading the greatest noble in the land! You, the head of the house of Lorraine, the chief of the League, the commander of the allied armies, debase yourself in stooping to take vengeance on a stable boy."

"It is no question of vengeance; it is a question of safety," he answered impatiently. Yet I marveled that he answered at all, since absolute power is not obliged to give an account of itself.

"Is your estate then so tottering that a stable boy can overturn it? In that case be advised. Go hang yourself, monsieur, while there is yet time."

He flushed with anger, and this time he offered no justification. He advanced on the girl with outstretched hand.

"Mademoiselle, it is not my habit to take advice from the damsels of my household. Nor do I admit them to my council-room. Permit me then to conduct you to the staircase."

She retreated toward the threshold where I stood, still covering me as with a shield.

"Monsieur, you are very cruel to me."

"Your hand, mademoiselle."

She did not yield it to him but held out both hands, clasped in appeal.

"Monsieur, you have always been my loving kinsman. I have always tried to do your pleasure. I thought you meant harm to the boy because he was a servant to M. de Mar, and I knew that M. de St. Quentin, at least, had gone over to the other side. I did not know what you would do with him, and I could not rest in my bed because it was through me he came here. Monsieur, if I was foolish and frightened and indiscreet, do not punish the lad for my wrong-doing."

Mayenne was still holding out his hand for her.

"I wish you sweet dreams, my cousin Lorance."

"Monsieur," she cried, shrinking back till she stood against the door-jamb, "will you not let the boy go?"

"How will you look tomorrow," he said with his unchanged smile, "if you lose all your sleep tonight, my pretty Lorance?"

"A reproach to you," she answered quickly. "You will mark my white cheeks and my red eyes, and you will say, 'Now, there is my little cousin Lorance, my good ally Montluc's daughter, and I have made her cry her eyes blind over my cruelty. Her father, dying, gave her to me to guard and cherish, and I have made her miserable. I am sorry. I wish I had not done it.'"

"Mademoiselle," the duke repeated, "will you get to your bed?"

She did not stir, but, fixing him with her brilliant eyes, went on as if thinking aloud.

"I remember when I was a tiny maid of five or six, and you and your brother Guise (whom God rest!) would come to our house. You would ask my father to send for me as you sat over your wine, and I would run in to kiss you and be fed comfits from your pockets. I thought you the handsomest and gallantest gentleman in France, as indeed you were."

"You were the prettiest little creature ever was," Mayenne said abruptly.

"And my little heart was bursting with love and admiration of you," she returned. "When I first could lisp, I learned to pray for my cousin Henri and my cousin Charles. I have never forgotten them one night in all these years. 'God receive and bless the soul of Henri de Guise; God guard and prosper Charles de Mayenne.' But you make it hard for me to ask it for my cousin Charles."

"This is a great coil over a horse-boy," Mayenne said curtly.

"Life is as dear to a horse-boy as to M. le Duc de Mayenne."

"I tell you I did not mean to kill the boy," Mayenne said. "With the door shut he could hear nothing. I meant to question him and let him go. But you have seen fit to meddle in what is no maid's business, mademoiselle. You have unlocked the door and let him listen to my concerns. Dead men, mademoiselle, tell no tales."

"M. de Mayenne," she said, "I cannot see that you need trouble for the tales of boys – you, the lord of half France. But if you must needs fear his tongue, why, even then you should set him free. He is but a serving-boy sent here with a message. It is wanton murder to take his life; it is like killing a child."

"He is not so harmless as you would lead one to suppose, mademoiselle," the duke retorted. "Since you have been eavesdropping, you have heard how he upset your cousin Paul's arrangements."

"For that you should be thankful to him, monsieur. He has saved you the stain of a cowardly crime."

"Mordieu!" Mayenne exclaimed, "who foully murdered my brother?"

"The Valois."

"And his henchman, St. Quentin."

"Not so," she cried. "He was here in Paris when it happened. He was revolted at the deed."

"Did they teach you that at the convent?"

"No, but it is true. M. de St. Quentin warned my cousin Henri not to go to Blois."

"Pardieu, you think them angels, these St. Quentins."

"I think them brave and honest gentlemen, as I think you, Cousin Charles."

"That sounds ill on the lips that have but now called me villain and murderer," Mayenne returned.

"I have not called you that, monsieur; I said you had been saved from the guilt of murder, and I knew one day you would be glad."

He kept silence, eying her in a puzzled way. After a moment she went on:

"Cousin Charles, it is our lot to live in such days of blood and turmoil that we know not any other way to do but injure and kill. I think you are more harassed and troubled than any man in France. You have Henry of Navarre and the Huguenots and half the provinces to fight in the field, and your own League to combat at home. You must make favor with each of a dozen quarreling factions, must strive and strive to placate and loyalize them all. The leaders work each for his own end, each against the others and against you; and the truth is not in one of them, and their pledges are ropes of straw. They intrigue and rebel and betray till you know not which way to turn, and you curse the day that made you head of the League."

"I do curse the day Henri was killed," Mayenne said soberly. "And that is true, Lorance. But I am head of the League, and I must do my all to lead it to success."

"But not by the path of shame!" she cried quickly. "Success never yet lay that way. Henri de Valois slew our Henri, and see how God dealt with him!"

He looked at her fixedly; I think he heeded her words less than her shining, earnest eyes. And he said at last:

"Well, you shall have your boy, Lorance."

"Ah, monsieur!"

With tears dimming the brightness of those sweet eyes she dropped on her knees before him, kissing his hand.

Lucas, since his one unlucky outburst, had said never a word but stood looking on with a ruefulness of visage that it warmed the cockles of my heart to see.

Certes, he was in no very pleasant corner, this dear M. Paul. His mistress had heard his own lips describe his plot against the St. Quentins; there was no possibility of lying himself clear of it. Out of his own mouth he was convicted of spycraft, treachery, and cowardly murder. And in the Hôtel de Lorraine, as in the Hôtel de St. Quentin, his betrayal had come about through me. I was unwitting agent in both cases; but that did not make him love me the more. Could eyes slay, I had fallen of the glance he shot me over mademoiselle's bowed head; but when she rose he said to her:

"Mademoiselle, the boy is as much my prisoner as M. le Duc's, since I got him here. But I, too, freely give him up to you."

She swept him a curtsey, silently, without looking at him. He made an eager pace nearer her.

"Lorance," he cried in a low, rapid voice, "I see I am out of your graces. Now, by Our Lady, what's life worth to me if you will not take me back again? I admit I have tried to ruin the Comte de Mar. Is that any marvel, since he is my rival with you? Last March, when I was hiding here and watched from my window the gay M. de Mar come airily in, day after day, to see and make love to you, was it any marvel that I swore to bring his proud head to the dust?"

Now she turned to him and met his gaze squarely.

"The means you employed was the marvel," she said. "If you did not approve of his visits, you had only to tell him so. He had been ready to defend to you his right to make them. But you never showed him your face; of course, had you, you could not have become his father's housemate and Judas. Oh, I blush to know that the same blood runs in your veins and mine!"

"You speak hard words, mademoiselle," Lucas returned, keeping his temper with a stern effort. "You forget that we live in France in war-time, and not in the kingdom of heaven. I was toiling for more than my own revenges. I was working at your cousin Mayenne's commands, to aid our holy cause, for the preservation of the Catholic Church and the Catholic kingdom of France."

"Your conversion is sudden, then; only an hour ago you were working for nothing and no one but Paul de Lorraine."

"Come, come, Lorance," Mayenne interposed, his caution setting him ever on the side of compromise. "Paul is no worse than the rest of us. He hates his enemies, and so do we all; he works against them to the best of his power, and so do we all. They are Kingsmen, we are Leaguers; they fight for their side, and we fight for ours. If we plot against them, they plot against us; we murder lest we be murdered. We cannot scruple over our means. Nom de dieu, mademoiselle, what do you expect? Civil war is not a dancing-school."

"Mademoiselle is right," Lucas said humbly, refusing any defense. "We have been using cowardly means, weapons unworthy of Christian gentlemen. And I, at least, cannot plead M. le Duc's excuse that I was blinded in my zeal for the Cause. For I know and you know there is but one cause with me. I went to kill St. Quentin because I was promised you for it, as I would have gone to kill the Pope himself. This is my excuse; I did it to win you. There is no crime in God's calendar I would not commit for that."

He had possessed himself of her hand and was bending over her, burning her with his hot eyes. Mass of lies as the man was, in this last sentence I knew he spoke the truth.

She strove to free herself from him with none of the flattered pride in his declaration which he had perhaps looked for. Instead, she eyed him with positive fear, as if she saw no way of escape from his rampant desire.

"I wish rather you would practice a little virtue to win me," she said.

"So I will if you ask it," he returned, unabashed. "Lorance, I love you so there is no depth to which I could not stoop to gain you; there is no height to which I cannot rise. There is no shame so bitter, no danger so awful, that I would not face it for you. Nor is there any sacrifice I will not make to gain your good will. I hate M. de Mar above any living man because you have smiled on him; but I will let him go for your sake. I swear to you before the figure of Our Blessed Lady there that I will drop all enmity to Étienne de Mar. From this time forward I will neither move against him nor cause others to move against him in any shape or manner, so help me God!"

He dropped her hand to kiss the cross of his sword. She retreated from him, her face very pale, her breast heaving.

"You make it hard for me to know when you are speaking the truth," she said.

"May the lightning strike me if I am lying!" Lucas cried. "May my tongue rot at the root if ever I lie to you, Lorance!"

"Then I am very grateful and glad," she said gravely, and again curtsied to him.

"Yes, I give you my word for that, too, Lorance," Mayenne added. "I have no quarrel with young Mar. His father has stirred up more trouble for me than any dozen of Huguenots; I have my score to settle with St. Quentin. But I have no quarrel with the son. I will not molest him."

"Grand'merci, monsieur," she said, sweeping him another of her graceful obeisances.

"Understand me, mademoiselle," Mayenne went on. "I pardon him, but not that he may be anything to you. That time is past. The St. Quentins are Navarre's men now, and our enemies. For your sake I will let Mar alone; but if he come near you again, I will crush him as I would a buzzing fly."

"That I understand, monsieur," she answered in a low tone. "While I live under your roof, I shall not be treacherous to you. I am a Ligueuse and he is a Kingsman, and there can be nothing between us. There shall be nothing, monsieur. I do not swear it, as Paul needs, because I have never lied to you."

She did not once look at Lucas, yet I think she saw him wince under her stab. The Duke of Mayenne was right; not even Mlle. de Montluc loved her enemies.

"You are a good girl, Lorance," Mayenne said.

"Will you let the boy go now, Cousin Charles?" she asked.

"Yes, I will let your boy go," he made answer. "But if I do this for you, I shall expect you henceforth to do my bidding."

"You have called me a good girl, cousin."

"Aye, so you are. And there is small need to look so Friday-faced about it. If I have denied you one lover, I will give you another just as good."

"Am I Friday-faced?" she said, summoning up a smile. "Then my looks belie me. For since you free this poor boy whom I was like to have ruined I take a grateful and happy heart to bed."

"Aye, and you must stay happy. Pardieu, what does it matter whether your husband have yellow hair or brown? My brother Henri was for getting himself into a monastery because he could not have his Margot.

Yet in less than a year he is as merry as a fiddler with the Duchesse Katharine."

"You have made me happy, tonight at least, monsieur," she answered gently, if not merrily.

"It is the most foolish act of my life," Mayenne answered. "But it is for you, Lorance. If ill comes to me by it, yours is the credit."

"You can swear him to silence, monsieur," she cried quickly.

"What use? He would not keep silence."

"He will if I ask it," she returned, flinging me a look of bright confidence that made the blood dance in my veins. But Mayenne laughed.

"When you have lived in the world as long as I have, you will not so flatter yourself, Lorance."

Thus it happened that I was not bound to silence concerning what I had seen and heard in the house of Lorraine.

Mayenne took out his dagger.

"What I do I do thoroughly. I said I'd set you free. Free you shall be."

Mademoiselle sprang forward with pleading hand.

"Let me cut the cords, Cousin Charles."

He recoiled a bare second, the habit of a lifetime prompting him against the putting of a weapon in anyone's hand. Then, ashamed of the suspicion, which indeed was not of her, he yielded the knife and she cut my bonds. She looked straight into my eyes, with a glance earnest, beseeching, loving; I could not begin to read all she meant by it. The next moment she was making her deep curtsey before the duke.

"Monsieur, I shall never cease to love you for this. And now I thank you for your long patience, and bid you good night."

With a bare inclination of the head to Lucas, she turned to go. But Mayenne bade her pause.

"Do I get but a curtsey for my courtesy? No warmer thanks, Lorance?"

He held out his arms to her, and she let him kiss both her cheeks.

"I will conduct you to the staircase, mademoiselle," he said, and taking her hand with stately politeness led her from the room. The light seemed to go from it with the gleam of her yellow gown.

"Lorance!" Lucas cried to her, but she never turned her head. He stood glowering, grinding his teeth together, his glib tongue finding for once no way to better his sorry case. He was the picture of trickery rewarded; I could not repress a grin at him. Marking which, he burst out at me, vehemently, yet in a low tone, for Mayenne had not closed the door:

"You think I am bested, do you, you devil's brat? Let him laugh that wins; I shall have her yet."

"I will tell M. le Comte so," I answered with all the impudence I could muster.

"By Heaven, you will tell him nothing," he cried. "You will never see daylight again."

"I have Mayenne's word," I began, but his retort was to draw dagger. I deemed it time to stop parleying, and I did what the best of soldiers must do sometimes: I ran. I bounded into the oratory, flinging the door to after me. He was upon it before I could get it shut, and the heavy oak was swung this way and that between us, till it seemed as if we must tear it off the hinges. I contrived not to let him push it open wide enough to enter; meantime, as I was unarmed, I thought it no shame to shriek for succor. I heard an answering cry and hurrying footsteps. Then Lucas took his weight from the door so suddenly that mine banged it shut. The next minute it flew open again, mademoiselle, frightened and panting, on the threshold.

A tall soldier with a musket stood at her back; at one side Lucas lounged by the cabinet where the duke had set down the light. His right hand he held behind his back, while with his left he poked his dagger into the candle-flame.

Mayenne, red and puffing, hurried into the room.

"What is the pother?" he demanded. "What devilment now, Paul?"

"Mademoiselle's protégé is nervous," Lucas answered with a fine sneer. "When I drew out my knife to get the thief from the candle he screamed to wake the dead and took sanctuary in the oratory."

I had given him the lie then and there, but as I emerged from the darkness Mayenne commanded:

"Take him out to the street, d'Auvray."

The tall musketeer, saluting, motioned me to precede him. For a moment I hesitated, burning to defend my valor before mademoiselle. Then, reflecting how much harm my hasty tongue had previously done me, and that the path to freedom was now open before me, I said nothing. Nor had I need. For as I turned she flashed over to Lucas and said straight in his face:

"When you marry me, Paul de Lorraine, you will marry a dead wife."

XVII

"I'll win my lady!"

Lucas's prophecy came to grief within five minutes of the making. For when the musketeer unbarred the house door for me, the first thing I saw was the morning sun.

My spirits danced at sight of him, as he himself might dance on Easter day. Within the close, candle-lit room I had had no thought but that it was still black midnight; and now at one step I passed from the gloomy house into the heartening sunshine of a new clean day. I ran along as joyously as if I had left the last of my troubles behind me, forgotten in some dark corner of the Hôtel de Lorraine. Always my heart lifts when, after hours within walls, I find myself in the open again. I am afraid in houses, but out of doors I have no fear of harm from any man or any thing.

Though Sir Sun was risen this half-hour, and at home we should all have been about our business, these lazy Paris folk were still snoring. They liked well to turn night into day and lie long abed of a morning. Although here a shopkeeper took down shutters, and there a brisk servant-lass swept the doorstep, yet I walked through a sleeping city, quiet as our St. Quentin woods, save that here my footsteps echoed in the emptiness. At length, with the knack I have, whatever my stupidities, of finding my way in a strange place, I arrived before the courtyard of the Trois Lanternes. The big wooden doors were indeed shut, but when I had pounded lustily awhile a young tapster, half clad and cross as a bear, opened to me. I vouchsafed him scant apology, but, dropping on a heap of hay under a shed in the court, passed straightway into dreamless slumber.

When I awoke my good friend the sun was looking down at me from near his zenith, and my first happy thought was that I was just in time for dinner. Then I discovered that I had been prodded out of my rest by the pitchfork of a hostler.

"Sorry to disturb monsieur, but the horses must be fed."

"Oh, I am obliged to you," I said, rubbing my eyes. "I must go up to M. le Comte."

"He has been himself to look at you, and gave orders you were not to be disturbed. But that was last week. Dame! you slept like a sabot."

It did not take me long to brush the straw off me, wash my face at the trough, and present myself before monsieur. He was dressed and sitting at table in his bedchamber, while a drawer served him with dinner.

"You are out of bed, monsieur," I cried.

"But yes," he answered, springing up, "I am as well as ever I was. Félix, what has happened to you?"

I glanced at the serving-man; M. Étienne ordered him at once from the room.

"Now tell me quickly," he cried, as I faltered, tongue-tied from very richness of matter. "Mademoiselle?"

"Ah, mademoiselle!" I exclaimed. "Mademoiselle is –" I paused in a dearth of words worthy of her.

"She is, she is!" he agreed, laughing. "Oh, go on, you little slow-poke! You saw her? And she said –"

He was near to laying hands on me, to hurry my tale.

"I saw her and Mayenne and Lucas and ever so many things," I told him. "And they had me flogged, and mademoiselle loves you."

"She does!" he cried, flushing. "Félix, does she? You cannot know."

"But I do know it," I answered, not very lucidly. "You see, she wouldn't have wept so much, just over me."

"Did she weep? Lorance?" he exclaimed.

"They flogged me," I said. "They didn't hurt me much. But she came down in the night with a candle and cried over me."

"And what said she? Now I am sorry they beat you. Who did that? Mayenne? What said she, Félix?"

"And then," I went on, not heeding his questions in sudden remembrance of my crowning news, "Mayenne and Lucas came in. And here is something you do not know, monsieur. Lucas is Paul de Lorraine, Henri de Guise's son."

"Mille tonnerres du ciel! But he is a Huguenot, a Rochelais!"

"Yes, but he is a son of Henri le Balafré. His mother was Rochelaise, I think. He was a spy for Navarre and captured at Ivry. They were going to hang him when Mayenne, worse luck, recognized him for a nephew. Since then he has been spying for them. Because Mayenne promised him Mlle. de Montluc in marriage."

He stared at me with dropped jaw, absolutely too startled to swear.

"He has not got her yet!" I cried. "Mayenne told him he should have her when he had killed St. Quentin. And St. Quentin is alive."

"Great God!" said M. Étienne, only half aloud, dropping down on the arm of his chair, overcome to realize the issue that had hung on a paltry handful of pistoles. Then, recovering, himself a little, he cried:

"But she – mademoiselle?"

"You need give yourself no uneasiness there," I said. "Mademoiselle hates him."

"Does she know –"

"I think she understands quite well what Lucas is," I made answer. "Monsieur, I must tell you everything that happened from the beginning, or I shall never make it clear to you."

"Yes, yes, go on," he cried.

He sat down at table again, with the intention of eating his dinner as I talked, but precious few mouthfuls he took. At every word I spoke he got deeper into the interest of my tale. I never talked so much in my life, me, as I did those few days. I was always relating a history, to Monsieur, to mademoiselle, to M. Étienne, to – well, you shall know.

I had finished at length, and he burst out at me:

"You little scamp, you have all the luck! I never saw such a boy! Well do they call you Félix! Mordieu, here I lie lapped in bed like a baby, while you go forth knight-erranting. I must lie here with old Galen for all company, while you bandy words with the Generalissimo himself! And make faces at Lucas, and kiss the hands of mademoiselle! But I'll stand it no longer. I'm done with lying abed and letting you have all the fun. No; today I shall take part myself."

"But monsieur's arm –"

"Pshaw, it is well!" he cried. "It is a scratch – it is nothing. Pardieu, it takes more than that to put a St. Quentin out of the reckoning. Today is no time for sloth; I must act."

"Monsieur –" I began, but he broke in on me:

"Nom de dieu, Félix, are we to sit idle while mademoiselle is carried off by that beast Lucas?"

"Of course not," I said. "I was only trying to ask what monsieur meant to do."

"To take the moon in my teeth," he cried.

"Yes, monsieur, but how?"

"Ah, if I knew!"

He stared at me as if he would read the answer in my face, but he found it as blank as the wall. He flung away and made a turn down the room, and came back to seize me by the arm.

"How are we to do it, Félix?" he demanded.

But I could only shrug my shoulders and answer:

"Sais pas."

He paced the floor once more, and presently faced me again with the declaration:

"Lucas shall have her only over my dead body."

"He will only have her own dead body," I said.

He turned away abruptly and stood at the window, looking out with unseeing eyes. "Lorance – Lorance," he murmured to himself. I think he did not know he spoke aloud.

"If I could get word to her –" he went on presently. "But I can't send you again. Should I write a letter – But letters are mischievous. They fall into the wrong hands, and then where are we?"

"Monsieur," I suggested, "if I could get a letter into the hands of Pierre, that lackey who befriended me –" But he shook his head.

"They know you about the place. It were safer to dispatch one of these inn-men – if any had the sense to go rein in hand. Hang me if I don't think I'll go myself!"

"Monsieur," I said, "Lucas swore by all things sacred that he would never molest you more. Therefore you will do well to keep out of his way."

"My faith, Félix," he laughed, "you take a black view of mankind."

"Not of mankind, M. Étienne. Only of Lucas. Not of Monsieur, or you, or Vigo."

"And of Mayenne?"

"I don't make out Mayenne," I answered. "I thought he was the worst of the crew. But he let me go. He said he would, and he did."

"Think you he meant to let you go from the first?"

"Who knows?" I said, shrugging. "Lucas is always lying. But Mayenne – sometimes he lies and sometimes not. He's base, and then again he's kind. You can't make out Mayenne."

"He does not mean you shall," M. Étienne returned. "Yet the key is not buried. He is made up, like all the rest of us, of good and bad."

"Monsieur," I said, "if there is any bad in the St. Quentins I, for one, do not know it."

"Ah, Félix," he cried, "you may believe that till doomsday – you will – of Monsieur."

His face clouded a little, and he fell silent. I knew that, besides his thoughts of his lady, came other thoughts of his father. He sat gravely silent. But of last night's bitter distress he showed no trace. Last night he had not been able to take his eyes from the miserable past; but today he saw the future. A future not altogether flowery, perhaps, but one which, however it turned out, should not repeat the old mistakes and shames.

"Félix," he said at length, "I see nothing for it but to eat my pride."

I kept still in the happy hope that I should hear just what I longed to; he went on:

"I swore then that I would never darken his doors again; I was mad with anger; so was he. He said if I went with Gervais I went forever."

"Monsieur, if you repent your hot words, so does he."

"I must e'en give him the chance. If he do repent them, it were churlish to deny him the opportunity to tell me so. If he still maintain them, it were cowardly to shrink from hearing it. No, whatever Monsieur replies, I must go tell him I repent."

I came forward to kiss his hand, I was so pleased.

"Oh, you look very smiling over it," he cried. "Think you I like sneaking back home again like a whipped hound to his kennel?"

"But," I protested, indignant, "monsieur is not a whipped hound."

"Well, a prodigal son, as Lucas named me yesterday. It is the same thing."

"I have heard M. l'Abbé read the story of the prodigal son," I said. "And he was a vaurien, if you like – no more monsieur's sort than Lucas himself. But it says that when his father saw him coming a long way off, he ran out to meet him and fell on his neck."

M. Étienne looked not altogether convinced.

"Well, however it turns out, it must be gone through with. It is only decent to go to Monsieur. But even at that, I think I should not go if it were not for mademoiselle."

"You will beg his aid, monsieur?"

"I will beg his advice at least. For how you and I are to carry off mademoiselle under Mayenne's hand – well, I confess for the nonce that beats me."

"We must do it, monsieur," I cried.

"Aye, and we will! Come, Félix, you may put your knife in my dish. We must eat and be off. The meats have got cold and the wine warm, but never mind."

I did not mind, but was indeed thankful to get any dinner at all. Once resolved on the move, he was in a fever to be off; it was not long before we were in the streets, bound for the Hôtel St. Quentin. He said no more of Monsieur as we walked, but plied me with questions about Mlle. de Montluc – not only as to every word she said, but as to every turn of her head and flicker of her eyelids; and he called me a dull oaf when I could not answer. But as we entered the Quartier Marais he fell silent, more Friday-faced than ever his lady looked. He had his fair allowance of pride, this M. Étienne; he found his own words no palatable meal.

However, when we came within a dozen paces of the gate he dropped, as one drops a cloak, all signs of gloom or discomposure, and approached the entrance with the easy swagger of the gay young gallant who had lived there. As if returning from a morning stroll he called to the sentry:

"Holà, squinting Charlot! Open now!"

"Morbleu, M. le Comte!" the fellow exclaimed, running to draw the bolts. "Well, this is a sight for sore eyes, anyway."

M. Étienne laughed out in pleasure. It put heart into him, I could see, that his first greeting should be thus friendly.

"Vigo didn't know what had become of you, monsieur," Chariot volunteered. "The old man wasn't in the best of tempers last night, after Lucas got away and you gave us the slip, too. He called us all blockheads and cursed idiots. Things were lively for a time, nom d'un chien!"

"Eh bien, I am found," M. Étienne returned. "In time we'll get Lucas, too. Is Monsieur back?"

"No, M. Étienne, not yet."

I think he was half sorry, half glad.

"Where's Vigo?" he demanded.

"Somewhere about. I'll find him for monsieur."

"No, stay at your post. I'll find him."

He went straight across the court and in at the door he had sworn never again to darken. Humility and repentance might have brought him there, but it was the hand of mademoiselle drew him over the threshold without a falter.

Alone in the hall was my little friend Marcel, throwing dice against himself to while the time away. He sprang up at sight of us, agleam with excitement.

"Well, Marcel," my master said, "and where is M. l'Écuyer?"

"I think in the stables, monsieur."

"Bid him come to me in the small cabinet."

He turned with accustomed feet into the room at the end of the hall where Vigo kept the rolls of the guard. I, knowing it to be my duty to keep close at hand lest I be wanted, followed. Soon Marcel came flying back to say Vigo was on his way. M. Étienne thanked him, and he hung about, longing to pump me, and, in my lord's presence, not quite daring, till I took him by the shoulders and turned him out. I hate curiosity.

M. Étienne stood behind the table, looking his haughtiest. He was unsure of a welcome from the contumacious Vigo; I read in his eyes a stern determination to set this insolent servant in his place.

The big man entered, saluted, came straight over to his young lord's side, no whit hesitating, and said, as heartily as if there had never been a hard word between them:

"M. Étienne, I had liefer see you stand here than the king himself."

M. Étienne displayed the funniest face of bafflement. He had been prepared to lash rudeness or sullenness, to accept, de haut en bas, shamed contrition. But this easy cordiality took the wind out of his sails. He stared, and then flushed, and then laughed. And then he held out his hand, saying simply:

"Thank you, Vigo."

Vigo bent over to kiss it in cheerful ignorance of how that hand had itched to box his ears.

"What became of you last night, M. Étienne?" he inquired.

"I was hunting Lucas. When does Monsieur return, Vigo?"

"He thought he might be back today. But he could not tell."

"Have you sent to tell him about me?" he asked, coloring.

"No, I couldn't do that," Vigo said. "You see, it is quite on the cards that the Spanish gang may come hither to clean us out. I want every man I have if they do."

"I understand that," M. Étienne said, "but –"

"So long as you are innocent a day or two matters not," Vigo pronounced. "He will presently turn up here or send word that he will not return till the king comes in. But since you are impatient, M. le Comte, you can go to him at St. Denis. If *he* can get through the gates *you* can."

"Aye, but I have business in Paris. I mean to join King Henry, Vigo. There's glory going begging out there at St. Denis. It would like me well to bear away my share. But –"

He broke off, to begin again abruptly:

"Ah, Vigo, that still tongue of yours! You knew, then, that there was more cause of trouble between my father and me than the pistoles?"

"I knew he suspected you of a kindness for the League, monsieur. But you are cured of that."

"There you are wrong. For I never had it, and I am not cured of it. If I hung around the Hôtel de Lorraine, it was not for politics; it was for petticoats."

Vigo made no answer, but the corners of his grim mouth twitched.

"That's no news, either? Well, then, since you know so much, you may as well know more. Step up, Félix, and tell your tale."

I did as I was bid, M. Étienne now and then taking the words out of my mouth in his eagerness, Vigo listening to us both with grave attention. I had for the second time in my career the pleasure of startling him out of his iron composure when I told him the true name and condition of Lucas. But at the end of the adventure all the comment he made was:

"A fool for luck."

"Well," said M. Étienne, impatiently, "is that all you have to say? What are we to do about it?"

"Do? Why, nothing."

"Nothing?" he cried, with his hand on his sword. "Nothing? And let that scoundrel have her?"

"That is M. de Mayenne's affair," Vigo said. "We can't help it."

"I will help it!" M. Étienne declared. "Mordieu! Am I to let that traitor, that spy, that soul of dirt, marry Mlle. de Montluc?"

"What Mayenne wishes he'll have," Vigo said. "Some day you will surely get a chance to fight Lucas, monsieur."

"And meantime he is to enjoy her?"

"It is a pity," Vigo admitted. "But there is Mayenne. Can we storm the Hôtel de Lorraine? No one can drink up the sea."

"One could if he wanted to as much as I want mademoiselle," my lord declared.

But Vigo shook his head.

"Monsieur," he said gravely, "monsieur, you have a great chance. You have a sword and a good cause to draw it in. What more should a man ask in the world than that? Your father has been without it these three years, and for want of it he has eaten his heart out. You have been without it, and you have got yourself into all sorts of mischief. But now all that is coming straight. King Henry is turning Catholic, so that a man may follow him without offence to God. He is a good fellow and a first-rate general. He's just out there, at St. Denis. There's your place, M. Étienne."

"Not today, Vigo."

"Yes, M. Étienne, today. Be advised, monsieur," Vigo said with his steady persistence. "There is nothing to gain by staying here to drink up the sea. Mayenne will no more give your lady to you now than he would give her to Félix. And you can no more carry her off than could Félix. Mayenne will have you killed and flung into the Seine, as easy as eat breakfast."

"And you bid me grudge my life? Strange counsel from you, Vigo."

"No, monsieur, but I bid you not throw it away. We all hope to die afield, but we have a preference how and where. If you fell fighting for Navarre, I should be sorry; Monsieur would grieve deep. But we should say it was well; we grudged not your life to the country and the king. While, if you fall in this fool affair —"

"I fall for my lady," M. Étienne finished. "The bravest captain of them all does no better than that."

"M. Étienne, she is no wife for you. You cannot get her. And if you could 'twere pity. She is a Ligueuse, and you from now on are a staunch Kingsman. Give her up, monsieur. You have had this maggot in your brain this four years. Once for all, get it out. Go to St. Denis; take your troop among Biron's horse. That is the place for you. You will marry a maid of honor and die a marshal of France."

M. Étienne laid his arm around Vigo's shoulder with a smile.

"Good old Vigo! Vigo, tell me this; if you saw a marshal's baton waiting you in the field, and at home your dearest friend were alone and in peril, would you go off after glory?"

"Aye, if 'twas a hopeless business to stay, certes I would go."

"Oh, tell that in Bedlam!" M. Étienne cried. "You would do nothing of the sort. Was it to win glory you stayed three years in that hole, St. Quentin?"

"I had no choice, monsieur. My master was there."

"And my mistress is here! You may save your breath, Vigo; I know what I shall do. The eloquence of monk Christin wouldn't change me."

"What is your purpose, M. Étienne?" Vigo asked.

Indeed, there was a vagueness about his scheme as revealed to us.

"It is quite simple. I purpose to get speech with mademoiselle if I can contrive it, and I think I can. I purpose to smuggle her out of the Hôtel de Lorraine – such feats have been accomplished before and may be again. Then I shall bring her here and hold her against all comers."

"No," Vigo said, "no, monsieur. You may not do that."

"Ventre bleu, Vigo!" his young lord cried.

"No," said Vigo. "I can't have her here, and Mayenne's army after her."

"Coward!" shouted M. Étienne.

I thought Vigo would take us both by the scruff of our necks and throw us out of the place. But he answered undisturbed:

"No, that is not the reason, monsieur. If M. le Duc told me to hold this house against the armies of France and Spain, I'd hold it till the last man of us was dead. But I am here in his absence to guard his hôtel, his moneys, and his papers. I don't call it guarding to throw a firebrand among them. Bringing Mayenne's niece here would be worse than that."

"Monsieur would never hesitate! Monsieur is no chicken-heart!" M. Étienne cried. "If he were here, he'd say, 'We'll defend the lady if every stone in this house is pulled from its fellow!'"

A twinkle came into Vigo's eyes.

"I think that is likely true," he said. "Monsieur opposed the marriage as long as Mayenne desired it; but now that Mayenne forbids it, stealing the demoiselle is another pair of sleeves."

"Well, then," cried M. Étienne, all good humor in a moment, "what more do you want? We'll divert ourselves pouring pitch out of the windows on Mayenne's ruffians."

"No, M. Étienne, it can't be done. If M. le Duc were here and gave the command to receive her, that would be one thing. No one would obey with a readier heart than I. Mordieu, monsieur, I have no objection to succoring a damsel in distress; I have been in the business before now."

"Then why not now? Death of my life, Vigo! When I know, and you know, Monsieur would approve."

"I don't know it, monsieur," Vigo said. "I only think it. And I cannot move by my own guesswork. I am in charge of the house till Monsieur returns. I purpose to do nothing to jeopard it. But I interfere in no way with your liberty to proceed as you please."

"I should think not, forsooth!" M. Étienne blazed out furiously.

"I could," rejoined Vigo, with his maddening tranquility. "I could order the guard – and they would obey – to lock you up in your chamber. I believe Monsieur would thank me for it. But I don't do it. I leave you free to act as it likes you."

My lord was white with ire.

"Who is master here, you or I?"

"Neither of us, M. le Comte. But Monsieur, leaving, put the keys in my hand, and I am head of the house till he returns. You are very angry, M. Étienne, but my shoulders are broad enough to bear it. Your madness will get no countenance from me."

"Hang you for an obstinate pig!" M. Étienne cried.

Vigo said no more. He had made plain his position; he had naught to add or retract. Yeux-gris's face cleared. After all, there was no use being angry with Vigo; one might as well make fists at the flow of the Seine.

"Very well." M. Étienne swallowed his wrath. "It is understood that I get no aid from you. Then I have nobody in the world with me save Félix here. But for all that I'll win my lady!"

XVIII

To the Bastille.

But Vigo proved better than his word. If he would give us no countenance, he gave freely good broad gold pieces. He himself suggested M. Étienne's need of the sinews of war, not in the least embarrassed or offended because he knew M. le Comte to be angry with him. He was no feather ruffled, serene in the consciousness that he was absolutely in the right. His position was impregnable; neither persuasion, ridicule, nor abuse moved him one whit. He had but a single purpose in life; he was born to forward the interests of the Duke of St. Quentin. He would forward them, if need were, over our bleeding corpses.

On top of all his disobedience and disrespect he was most amiable to M. Étienne, treating him with a calm assumption of friendliness that would have maddened a saint. Yet it was not hypocrisy; he liked his young lord, as we all did. He would not let him imperil Monsieur, but aside from that he wished him every good fortune in the world.

M. Étienne argued no more. He was wroth and sore over Vigo's attitude, but he said little. He accepted the advance of money – "Of course Monsieur would say, What coin is his is yours," Vigo explained – and dispatched me to settle his score at the Three Lanterns.

I set out on my errand rather down in the mouth. We had accomplished nothing by our return to the hôtel. Nay, rather had we lost, for we were both of us, I thought, disheartened by the cold water flung on our ambitions. I took the liberty of doubting whether perfect loyalty to Monsieur included thwarting and disobeying his heir. It was all very well for Monsieur to spoil Vigo and let him speak his mind as became not his station, for Vigo never disobeyed *him,* but stood by him in all things. But I imagined that, were M. Étienne master, Vigo, for all his years of service, would be packed off the premises in short order.

I walked along in a brown study, wondering how M. Étienne did purpose to rescue mademoiselle. His scheme, so far as vouchsafed to me, was somewhat in the air. I could only hope he had more in his mind than he had let me know. It seemed to me a pity not to be doing something in the matter, and though I had no particular liking for Hôtel de Lorraine hospitality, I had very willingly been bound thither at this moment to try to get a letter to mademoiselle. But he would not send me.

"No," he had said, "it won't do. Think of something better, Félix."

But I could not, and so was taking my dull way to the inn of the Trois Lanternes.

The city wore a sleepy afternoon look. It was very hot, and few cared to be stirring. I saw nothing worth my notice until, only a stone's throw from the Three Lanterns, I came upon a big black coach standing at the door of a rival auberge, L'Oie d'Or. It aroused my interest at once, for a traveling-coach was a rare sight in the beleaguered city. As my master had said, this was not a time of pleasure-trips to Paris. I readily imagined that the owner of this chariot came on weighty business indeed. He might be an ambassador from Spain, a legate from Rome.

I paused by the group of street urchins who were stroking the horses and clambering on the back of the coach, to wonder whether it would be worth while to wait and see the dignitary come out. I was just going to ask the coachman a question or two concerning his journey, when he began to snap his whip about the bare legs of the little whelps. The street was so narrow that he could hardly chastise them without danger to me, so it seemed best to saunter off. The screaming urchins stopped just out of the reach of his lash and set to pelting mud at him with a right good will, but I was too old for that game. I reflected that I was charged with business for my master, and that it was nothing to me what envoys might come to Mayenne. I went on into the Three Lanterns.

The cabaret was absolutely deserted; one might have walked all about and carried off what he pleased, as from the sleeping palace in the tale. "This is a pretty way to keep an inn," I thought. "Where have all the lazy rascals got to?" Then I heard a confused murmur of voices and shuffle of feet from the back, and I went through into the passage where the staircase was.

Here were gathered, in a huddle, like scared sheep, some dozen of the serving-folk, men and maids, the lasses most of them in tears, the men looking scarce less terrified. Their gaze was fixed on the closed door of Maître Menard's little counting-room, whence issued the shrill cry:

"Spare me, noble gentlemen! Spare a poor innkeeper! I swear I know nothing of his whereabouts."

As my footsteps sounded on the threshold, one and all spun round to look at me in fresh dread.

"Mon dieu, it is his lackey!" a chambermaid cried. In the next second a little wiry dame, her eyes blazing with fury, darted out of the group and seized me by the arm with a grip of her nails that made me think a panther had got me.

"So here you are," she screamed. I declare I thought she was going to bite me. "Oh-h-h, you and your fine master, that come here and devour our substance and never pay one sou, but bring ruin to the house! Now, go you straight in there and let them squeeze your throat awhile, and see how you like it yourself!"

She swept me across the passage like a whirlwind, opened the door, shoved me in, and banged it after me before I could collect my senses.

The room was small; it was very well filled up by a bureau, a strongbox, a table, two chairs, three soldiers, one innkeeper, and myself.

The bureau stood by the window, with Maître Menard's account-books on it. Opposite was the table, with a captain of dragoons on it. Of his two men, one took the middle of the room, amusing himself with the windpipe of Maître Menard; the other was posted at the door. I was shot out of Mme. Menard's grasp into his, and I found his the gentler of the two.

"I say I know not where he went," Maître Menard was gasping, black in the face from the dragoon's attentions. "He did not tell – I have no notion. Ah –" The breath failed him utterly, but his eyes, bloodshot and bulging, rolled toward me.

"What now?" the captain cried, springing to his feet. "Who are you?"

He wore under his breastplate what I took to be the uniform of the city guards. I had seen the like on the officer of the gate the night I entered Paris. He was a young man of a decidedly bourgeois appearance, as if he were not much, outside of his uniform.

"My name is Félix Broux," I said. "I came to pay a bill –"

"His servant," Maître Menard contrived to murmur, the dragoon allowing him a breath.

"Oh, you are the Comte de Mar's servant, are you? Where have you left your master?"

"What do you want of him?" I asked in turn.

"Never you mind. I want him."

"But Mayenne said he should not be touched," I cried. "The Duke of Mayenne said himself he should not be touched."

"I know nothing about that," he returned, a trifle more civilly than he had spoken. "I have naught to do with the Duke of Mayenne. If he is friends with your master, M. de Mar may not stay behind bars very long. But I have the governor's warrant for his arrest."

"On what charge?"

"A trifle. Merely murder."

"Murder?"

"Yes, the murder of a lackey, one Pontou."

"But that is ridiculous!" I cried. "M. le Comte did not –"

I came to a halt, not knowing what to say. "Lucas – Paul de Lorraine killed him," was on the tip of my tongue, but I choked it down. To fling wild accusations against a great man's man were no wisdom. By accident I had given the officer the impression that we were friends of Mayenne. I should do ill to imperil the delusion. "M. le Comte –" I began again, and again stopped. I meant to say that monsieur had never left the inn last night; he could have had no hand in the crime. Then I bethought me that I had better not know the hour of the murder. "M. le Comte is a very grand gentleman; he would not murder a lackey," I got out at last.

"You can tell that to the judges," the captain rejoined.

At this I felt ice sliding down my spine. To be arrested as a witness was the last thing I desired.

"I know nothing whatever about it," I cried. "He seemed to me a very fine gentleman. But you can't always tell about these nobles. The Comte de Mar, I've only known him twenty-four hours. Until he engaged me as lackey, yesterday afternoon, I had never laid eyes on him. I know not what he has been about. He engaged me yesterday to carry a message for him to the Hôtel St. Quentin. I came into Paris but night before last, and put up at the Amour de Dieu in the Rue Coupejarrets. Yesterday he employed me to run his errands, and last night brought me here with him. But I had never seen him till this time yesterday. I know nothing about him save that he seemed a very free-handed, easy master."

To a nice ear I might have seemed a little too voluble, but the captain only laughed at my patent fright.

"Oh, you need not look so whey-faced; I have no warrant for your arrest. I dare say you are as great a rogue as he, but the order says nothing about you. Don't swoon away; you are in no peril."

I was stung to be thought such a craven, but I pocketed the insult, and merely answered:

"I assure you, monsieur, I know naught of the matter." Yesterday I would have blurted out to him the whole truth; decidedly my experiences were teaching me something.

"Come now, I can't fool about here all day," he said impatiently. "Tell me where that precious master of yours is now. And be quicker about it than this old mule."

Maître Menard, then, had told them nothing – staunch old loyalist. He knew perfectly that M. le Comte had gone home, and they had throttled him, and yet he had not told. Well, he should not lose by it.

"Monsieur is about the streets somewhere. On my life, I know not where. But I know he will be back here to supper."

"Oh, you don't know, don't you? Then perhaps Gaspard can quicken your memory."

At the word the soldier who had attended to Maître Menard came over to me and taught me how it feels to be hanged. I said to myself that if I had talked like a dastard I was not one, and every time he let me speak I gasped, "I don't know." The room was black to me, and the sea roared in my ears, and I wondered whether I had done well to tell the lie. For had I said that my master was in the Hôtel St Quentin, still those fellows would have found it no easy job to take him. Vigo might not be ready to defend Mlle. de Montluc, but he would defend Monsieur's heir to the last gasp. Yet I would not yield before the choking Maître Menard had withstood, and I stuck to my lie.

Then I bethought me, while the room reeled about me and my head seemed like to burst, that perchance if they should keep me here a captive for M. le Comte's arrival he might really follow to see what had become of me. I turned sick with the fear of it, and resolved on the truth. But Gaspard's last gullet-gripe had robbed me of the power to speak. I could only pant and choke. As I struggled painfully for wind, the door was flung open before a tall young man in black. Through the haze that hung before my vision I saw the soldier seize him as he crossed the threshold. Through the noise of waters I heard the captain's cry of triumph.

"Oh, M. Étienne!" I gasped, in agony that my pain had been for nothing. Now all was lost. Then the blur lifted, and my amazed eyes beheld not my master, but – Lucas!

"How now, sirrah?" he cried to the dragoon. "Hands off me, knaves!" For the second soldier had seized his other arm.

"I regret to inconvenience monsieur," the captain answered, "but he is wanted at the Bastille."

"Wanted? I?" Lucas cried, fear flashing into his eyes.

He felt an instant's terror, I deem, lest Mayenne had betrayed him. Quick as he was, he did not see that he had been taken for another man.

"You, monsieur. You are wanted for the murder of your man, Pontou."

He grew white, looking instinctively at me, remembering where I had been at three o'clock this morning.

"It is a lie! He left my service a month back and I have never seen him since."

"Tell that to the judges," the captain said, as he had said to me. "I am not trying you. The handcuffs, men."

One of them produced a pair. Lucas struggled frantically in his captors' grasp. He dragged them from one end of the room to the other, calling down all the curses of Heaven upon them; but they snapped the handcuffs on for all that.

"If this is Mayenne's work –" he panted.

The officer caught nothing but the name Mayenne.

"The boy said you were a friend to his Grace, monsieur, but orders are orders. I have the warrant for your arrest from M. de Belin."

"At whose instigation?"

"How should I know'? I am a soldier of the guard. I have naught to do with it but to arrest you."

"Let me see the warrant."

"I am not obliged to. But I will, though. It may quiet your bluster."

He took out the warrant and held it at a safe distance before Lucas's eyes. A great light broke in on that personage.

"Mille tonnerres! I am not the Comte de Mar!"

"Oh, you say that now, do you? Pity you had not thought of it sooner."

"But I am not the Comte de Mar! I am Paul de Lorraine, nephew to my Lord Mayenne."

"Why don't you say straight out that you're the Duc de Guise?"

"I am not the Due de Guise," Lucas returned with dignity. He must have been cursing himself that he had not given his name sooner. "But I am his brother."

"You take me for a fool."

"Aye, who shall hang for his folly!"

"You must think me a fool," the captain repeated. "The Duke of Guise's eldest brother is but seventeen –"

"I did not say I was legitimate."

"Oh, you did not say that? You did not know, then, that I could reel off the ages of every Lorraine of them all. No, M. de Mar, I am not so simple as you think. You will come along with me to the Bastille."

"Blockhead! I'll have you broken on the wheel for this," Lucas stormed. "I am no more Count of Mar than I am King of Spain. Speak up, you old turnspit," he shouted to Maître Menard. "Am I he?"

Poor Maître Menard had dropped down on his iron box, too limp and sick to know what was going on. He only stared helplessly.

"Speak, rascal," Lucas cried. "Am I Comte de Mar?"

"No," the maître answered in low, faltering tones. He was at the last point of pain and fear. "No, monsieur officer, it is as he says. He is not the Comte de Mar."

"Who is he, then?"

"I know not," the maître stammered. "He came here last night. But it is as he says – he is not the Comte de Mar."

"Take care, mine host," the officer returned; "you're lying."

I could not wonder at him; if I had not been in a position to know otherwise, I had thought myself the maître was lying.

"If you had spoken at first I might have believed you," the captain said, bestowing a kick on him. "Get out of here, old ass, before I cram your lie down your throat. And clear your people away from this door. I'll not walk through a mob. Send every man Jack about his business, or it will be the worse for him. And every woman Jill, too."

"M. le Capitaine," Maître Menard quavered, rising unsteadily to his feet, "you make a mistake. On my sacred word, you mistake; this is not –"

"Get out!" cried the captain, helping him along with his boot. Maître Menard fell rather than walked out of the door.

A grey hue came over Lucas's face. His first fright had given way to fury at perceiving himself the victim of a mistake, but now alarm was born in his eyes again. Was it, after all, a mistake? This obstinate disbelief in his assertion, this ordering away of all who could swear to his identity – was it not rather a plot for his ruin? He swallowed hard once or twice, fear gripping his throat harder than ever the dragoon's fingers had gripped mine. Certainly he was not the Comte de Mar; but then he was the man who had killed Pontou.

"If this is a plot against me, say so!" he cried. "If you have orders to arrest me, do so. But arrest me by the name of Paul de Lorraine, not of Étienne de Mar."

"The name of Étienne de Mar will do," the captain returned; "we have no fancy for aliases at the Bastille."

"It is a plot!" Lucas cried.

"It is a warrant; that is all I know about it"

"But I am not Comte de Mar," Lucas repeated.

His uneasy conscience had numbed his wits. In his dread of a plot he had done little to dissipate an error. But now he pulled himself together; error or intention, he would act as if he knew it must be error.

"My captain, you have made a mistake likely to cost you your shoulder-straps. I tell you I am not Mar; the landlord, who knows him well, tells you I am not Mar. Ask those who know M. de Mar; ask these inn people. They will one and all tell you I am not he. Ask that boy there; even he dares not say to my face that I am."

His eyes met mine, and I could see that, even in the moment of challenging me, he repented. He believed that I would give the lie. But the dragoon who was bending over him, relieving him of his sword-belt, spared me the necessity.

"Captain, you need give yourself no uneasiness; this is the Comte right enough. I live in the Quartier Marais, and I have seen this gentleman a score of times riding with M. de St. Quentin."

Lucas, at this unexpected testimony, looked so taken aback that the captain burst out laughing.

"Yes, my dear monsieur, it is a little hard for M. de Mayenne's nephew – you are a nephew, are you not? – to explain how he comes to ride with the Duc de St. Quentin."

It was awkward to explain. Lucas, knowing well that there was no future for him who betrayed the Generalissimo's secrets, cried out angrily:

"He lies! I never rode out with M. de St. Quentin."

"Oh, come now. Really you waste a great deal of breath," the captain said. "I regret the cruel necessity of arresting you, M. de Mar; but there is nothing gained by blustering about it. I usually know what I am about."

"You do not know! Nom de dieu, you do not know. Félix Broux, speak up there. If you have told him behind my back that I am Étienne de Mar, I defy you to say it to my face."

"I know nothing about it, messieurs." I repeated my little refrain. "Monsieur captain, remember, if you please, I never saw him till yesterday; he may be Paul de Lorraine for all I know. But he did not call himself that yesterday."

"You hell-hound!" Lucas cried.

"Go tell Louis to drive up to the cabaret door, Gaspard," bade the captain.

Lucas gazed at him as if to tear out of him the truth of the matter. I think he was still a prey to suspicion of a plot in this, and it paralyzed his tongue. He so reeked with intrigue that he smelled one wherever he went. He was much too clever to believe that this arresting officer was simply thick-witted.

"I say no more," he cried. "You may spare yourself your lies, the whole crew of you. I go as your prisoner, but I go as Paul of Lorraine, son of Henry, Duke of Guise."

He said it with a certain superbness; but the young captain, bourgeois of the bourgeois, did not mean to let himself be put down by any sprig of the noblesse.

"Certainly, if it is any comfort to you," he retorted. "But you are very dull, monsieur, not to be aware that your identity is known perfectly to others besides your lackey here and my man. I did not come to arrest you without a minute description of you from M. de Belin himself."

"Ventre bleu!" Lucas shouted. "I wrote the description. I myself lodged information against Mar. I came here to make sure you took him. Carry me before Belin; he will know me."

I trembled lest the officer could not but see that the man spoke truth. But I had no need to fear; there is a combination of stupidity and vanity which nothing can move.

"I have no orders to take you to M. de Belin," he returned calmly. "So you wrote the description, did you? Perhaps you will deny that it fits you?"

He read from the paper:

"'Charles-André-Étienne-Marie de St. Quentin, Comte de Mar. Age, three-and-twenty; figure, tall and slender; was dressed yesterday in black with a plain falling-band; carries his right arm in a sling –'"

"Is my arm in a sling?" Lucas demanded.

"No, in a handcuff," the captain laughed, at the same moment that his dragoon exclaimed, "His right wrist is bandaged, though."

"That is nothing! It is a mere scratch. I did it myself last night by accident," Lucas shouted, striving with his hampered left hand to pull the folds apart to show it. But he could not, and fell silent, wide-eyed, like one who sees the net of fate drawing in about him. The captain went on reading from his little paper:

"'Fair hair, grey eyes, aquiline nose' – I suppose you will still tell us, monsieur, that you are not the man?"

"I am not he. The Comte de Mar and I are nothing alike. We are both young, tall, yes; but that is all. He is slashed all up the forearm; my wrist is but scratched with a knife-edge. He has yellow hair; mine is brown. His eyes –"

"It is plain to me, monsieur," the officer interrupted, "that the description fits you in every particular." And so it did.

I, who had heard M. Étienne described twenty times, had yesterday mistaken Lucas for him; the same items served for both. It was the more remarkable because they actually looked no more alike than chalk and cheese. Lucas had set down his catalogue without a thought that he was drawing his own picture. If ever hunter was caught in his own gin, Lucas was!

"You lie!" he cried furiously. "You know I am not Mar. You lie, the whole pack of you!"

"Gag him, Ravelle," the captain commanded with an angry flush.

"I demand to be taken before M. de Belin!" Lucas shouted.

The next moment the soldier had twisted a handkerchief about his mouth.

"Ready?" the captain asked of Gaspard, who had come back just in time to aid in the throttling. "Move on, then."

He led the way out, the two dragoons following with their prisoner. And this time Lucas's fertile wits failed him. He did not slip from his captors' fingers between the room and the street. He was deposited in the big black coach that had aroused my wonder. Louis cracked his whip and off they rumbled.

I laughed all the way back to the Hôtel St. Quentin.

XIX

To the Hôtel de Lorraine.

I found M. Étienne sitting on the steps before the house. He had doffed his rusty black for a suit of azure and silver; his sword and poniard were heavy with silver chasings. His blue hat, its white plume pinned in a silver buckle, lay on the stone beside him. He had discarded his sling and was engaged in tuning a lute.

Evidently he was struck by some change in my appearance; for he asked at once:

"What has happened, Félix?"

"Such a lark!" I cried.

"What! did old Menard share the crowns with you for your trouble?"

"No; he pocketed them all. That was not it."

I was so choked with laughter as to make it hard work to explain what was it, while his first bewilderment changed to an amazed interest, which in its turn gave way, not to delight, but to distress.

"Mordieu!" he cried, starting up, his face ablaze, "if I resemble that dirt –"

"As chalk and cheese," I said. "No one seeing you both could possibly mistake you for two of the same race. But there was nothing in his catalogue that did not fit him. It mentioned, to be sure, the right arm in a sling; his was not, but he had his wrist bandaged. I think he cut himself last night when he was after me and I flung the door in his face, for afterward he held his hand behind his back. At any rate, there was the bandage; that was enough to satisfy the captain."

"And they took him off?"

"Truly. They gagged him because he protested so much, and lugged him off."

"To the Bastille?" he demanded, as if he could scarcely realize the event.

"To the Bastille. In a big traveling-coach, between the officer and his men. He may be there by this time."

He looked at me as if he were still not quite able to believe the thing.

"It is true, monsieur. If I were inventing it I could not invent anything better; but it is true."

"Certes, you could not invent anything better! Nor anything half so good. If ever there was a case of the biter bit –" he broke off, laughing.

"Monsieur, you know not half how funny it was. Had you seen their faces – the more Lucas swore he was not Comte de Mar, the more the officer was sure he was."

"Félix, you have all the luck. I said this morning you should go about no more without me. Then I send you off on a stupid errand, and see what you get into!"

"Monsieur, I put it to you: Had you been there, how could Lucas have been arrested for Comte de Mar?"

"He won't stay arrested long – more's the pity."

"No," I said regretfully; "but they may keep him overnight."

"Aye, he may be out of mischief overnight. I am happy to say that my face is not known at the Bastille."

"Nor his, I take it. I thought from what I heard last night that he had never been in Paris save for a while in the spring, when he lay perdu. At the Bastille they may know nothing of the existence of a Paul de Lorraine. But, monsieur, if Mayenne has broken his word already, if they are arresting you on this trumped-up charge, you must get out of the gates tonight."

"Impossible," he answered, smiling; "I have an engagement in Paris."

"But monsieur may not keep it. He must go to St. Denis."

"I must go nowhere but to the Hôtel Lorraine."

"Monsieur!"

"Why, look you, Félix; it is the safest spot for me in all Paris; it is the last place where they will look for me. Besides, now that they think me behind bars, they will not be looking for me at all. I shall be as safe as the hottest Leaguer in the camp."

"But in the hôtel –"

"Be comforted; I shall not enter the hôtel. There is a limit to my madness. No; I shall go softly around to a window in the side street under which I have often stood in the old days. She used to contrive to be in her chamber after supper."

"But, monsieur, how long is it since you were there last?"

"I think it must be two months. I had little heart for it after my father – So, you see, no one will be on the lookout for me tonight."

"Neither will mademoiselle," I made my point.

"I hope she may," he answered. "She will know I must see her tonight. And I think she will be at the window."

The reasoning seemed satisfactory to him. And I thought one wet blanket in the house was enough.

"Very well, monsieur. I am ready for anything you propose."

"Then I propose supper."

Afterward we played shovel-board, I risking the pistoles mademoiselle had given me. I won five more, for he paid little heed to what he was about, but was ever fidgeting over to the window to see if it was dark enough to start. At length, when it was still between dog and wolf, he announced that he would delay no longer.

"Very well, monsieur," I said with all alacrity.

"But you are not to come!"

"Monsieur!"

"Certainly not. I must go alone tonight."

"But, monsieur, you will need me. You will need someone to watch the street while you speak with mademoiselle."

"I can have no listener tonight," he replied immovably.

"But I will not listen, monsieur! I shall stand out of ear-shot. But you must have someone to give you warning should the guard set on you."

"I can manage my own affairs," he retorted haughtily; "I desire neither your advice nor your company."

"Monsieur!" I cried, almost in tears.

"Enough!" he bade sharply. "Go send me Vigo."

I went like one in whose face the doors of heaven had shut.

Vigo came at once from the guardroom at my summons. It was on my tongue to tell him of M. le Comte's mad resolve to fare forth alone; to beg him to stop it. But I remembered how blameworthy I myself had held the equery for interfering with M. Étienne, and I made up my mind that no word of cavil at my lord should ever pass my lips. I lagged across the court at Vigo's heels, silent.

M. Étienne was standing in the doorway.

"Vigo," he said, without a change of countenance, "get Félix a rapier, which he can use prettily enough. I cannot take him out tonight unarmed."

Vigo hesitated a moment, saluted, and went.

"Monsieur," I cried out, "you meant all the time to take me!"

He gazed down on my heated visage and laughed and laughed.

"Félix," he gasped, "you had your sport over there at the inn. But I have seen nothing this summer as funny as *your* face."

Vigo came back with a sword and baldric for me, and a horse-pistol besides, but M. Étienne would not let me have it.

"Circumstances are such, Vigo, that I want no noisy weapons."

The equery regarded him with a troubled countenance.

"I wish I knew, monsieur, whether I do right to let you go."

"We will not discuss that, an it please you."

"I do not, monsieur. I have no right to curtail M. le Comte's liberties. But I let you go with a heavy heart."

He looked after us with foreboding eyes as we went out of the great gate, alone, with not so much as a linkboy. But if his heart was heavy, our hearts were light. We paced along as merrily as though to a feast. M. Étienne hung his lute over his neck and strummed it; and whenever we passed under a window whence leaned a pretty head, he sang snatches of love songs. We were alone in the dark streets of a hostile city, bound for the house of a mighty foe; and one of us was wounded and one a tyro. Yet we laughed as we went; for there was Lucas languishing in prison, and here were we, free as air, steering our course for mademoiselle's window. One of us was in love, and the other wore a sword for the first time, and all the power of Mayenne daunted us not.

We came at length within bow-shot of the Hôtel de Lorraine, where M. Étienne was willing to abate somewhat his swagger. We left the Rue St. Antoine, creeping around behind the house through a narrow and twisting alley – it was pitch-black, but he knew the way well – into a little street dim-lighted from the windows of the houses upon it. It was only a few rods long, running from the open square in front of the hôtel to the network of unpaved alleys behind. On the farther side stood a row of high-gabled houses, their doors opening directly on the pavement; on this side was but one big pile, the Hôtel de Lorraine. The wall was broken by few windows, most of them dark; this was not the gay side of the house. The overhanging turret on the low second story, under which M. Étienne halted, was as dark as the rest, nor, though the casement was open wide, could we tell whether anyone was in the room. We could hear nothing but the breeze crackling in the silken curtains.

"Take your station at the corner there," he bade, "and shout if they seem to be coming for us. But I think we shall not be molested. My fingers are so stiff they will hardly recognize my hand on the strings."

I went to my post, and he began singing, scarce loud enough for any but his lady above to mark him:

Fairest blossom ever grew
Once she loosened from her breast.
This I say, her eyes are blue.

From her breast the rose she drew,
Dole for me, her servant blest,
Fairest blossom ever grew.

The music paused, and I turned from my watch of the shadowy figures crossing the square, in instant alarm lest something was wrong. But whatever startled him ceased, for in a moment he went on again, and as he sang his voice rang fuller:

Of my love the guerdon true,
'Tis my bosom's only guest.
This I say, her eyes are blue.

Still to me 'tis bright of hue
As when first my kisses prest
Fairest blossom ever grew.

Sweeter than when gathered new
'Twas the sign her love confest.
This I say, her eyes are blue.

He stopped again and stood gazing up into the window, but whether he saw something or heard something I could not tell. Apparently he was not sure himself, for presently, a little tremulous, he added the four verses:

Askest thou of me a clue
To that lady I love best?
Fairest blossom ever grew!
This I say, her eyes are blue.

He doffed his hat, pushing back the hair from his brow, and waited, eager, hopeful. There was a little stir in the room that one thought was not the wind.

I had come unconsciously halfway up the street to him in the ardor of my interest; but now I was startled back to my duty by the sound of men running round the corner behind me. One glance was enough; two abreast, swords in hand, they were charging us. I ran before them, drawing blade as I went and shouting to M. Étienne. But even as I called an answering shout came from the alley; two men of the Spanish guards shot out of the darkness and at us.

M. Étienne, with his extraordinary quickness, had got the lute off his neck, and now, for want of a better use of it, flung it at the head of his nearest assailant, who received it full in the face, stopped, hesitated a moment, and ran back the way he had come. But three foes remained, with the whole Hôtel de Lorraine behind them.

We put our backs to the wall and set to. The remaining Spaniard engaged me; M. Étienne, protected somewhat in the embrasure of a doorway, held at bay with his good left arm a pair of attackers. These were in the dress of gentlemen, and wore masks as if their cheeks blushed (well they might) for the deeds of their hands.

A broad window in the Hôtel de Lorraine was flung open; a man leaned far out with a torch. The bright glare in our faces bewildered our gloom-accustomed eyes; I could not see what I was about, and rammed my point against my Spaniard's hilt, snapping my blade.

The sudden impact sent him stumbling back a pace, and M. Étienne, who, with the quick eye of the born fencer, saw everything, cried to me, "Here!"

I darted back into the doorway beside him. His two assailants finding that they gained nothing by their joint attack, but rather hampered each other, one dropped back to watch his comrade, the cleverer swordsman. This was decidedly a man of talent, but he was shorter in the arm than my master and had the disadvantage of standing on the ground, whereas M. Étienne was up one step. He could not force home any of his shrewd-planned thrusts; nor could he drive M. Étienne out of his coign to where in the open the two could make short work of him. The rapiers clashed and parted and twisted about each other and flew apart again;

and then before I could see who was touched the attacker fell to his knees, with M. Étienne's sword in his breast.

M. Étienne wrenched the blade out; the wounded man sank backward, his mask-string breaking. He was the one whom I had thought him – François de Brie.

M. Étienne was ready for the second gentleman, but neither he nor the soldier attacked. The torch-bearer in the window, with a shout, waved his arm toward the square. A mob of armed men hurled itself around the corner, a pikeman with lowered point in the van.

This was not combat; it was butchery. M. Étienne, with a little moan, lifted his eyes for the first time from his assailant to the turret window. In the same instant I felt the door behind us give. Throwing my whole weight upon it, I seized M. Étienne and pulled him over the threshold. Someone inside slammed the door to, just as the Spaniard hurled himself against it.

XX

"On guard, monsieur."

We found ourselves in a narrow paneled passageway, lighted by a flickering oil-lamp pendent from a bracket. Confronting us was our preserver – a little old lady in black velvet, leaning back in chuckling triumph against the shot bolts.

She was very small and very old. Her figure was bent and shrunken, a pitiful little bag of bones in a rich dress; her hair was as white as her ruff; her skin as yellow and dry as parchment, furrowed with a thousand wrinkles; but her black eyes sparkled like a girl's.

"I did not mean to let my nightingale's throat be slit," she cried in a shrill voice quavering like a young child's. "I have listened to your singing many a night, monsieur; I was glad tonight to find the nightingale back again. When I saw that crew rush at you, I said I would save you if only you would put your back to my door. Monsieur, you are a young man of intelligence."

"I am a young man of amazing good fortune, madame," M. Étienne replied, with his handsomest bow, sheathing his wet blade. "I owe you a debt of gratitude which is ill repaid in the base coin of bringing trouble to this house."

"Not at all – not at all!" she protested with animation. "No one is likely to molest this house. It is the dwelling of M. Ferou."

"Of the Sixteen?"

"Of the Sixteen," she nodded, her shrewd face agleam with mischief. "In truth, if my son were within, you were little likely to find harborage here. But, as it is, he and his wife are supping with his Grace of Lyons. And the servants are one and all gone to mass, leaving madame grand'mère to shift for herself. No, no, my good friends; you may knock till you drop, but you won't get in."

The attacking party was indeed hammering energetically on the door, shouting to us to open, to deny them at our peril. The eyes of the old lady glittered with new delight at every rap.

"I fancy they will think twice before they batter down M. Ferou's door! Ma foi! I fancy they are a little mystified at finding you sanctuaried in this house. Was it not my Lord Mayenne's jackal, François de Brie?"

"Yes; and Marc Latour."

"I thought I knew them," she cried in evident pride at her sharpness. "It was dark, and they were masked, and my eyes are old, but I knew them! And which of the ladies is it?"

He could do no less than answer his savior.

"Ah, well," she said, with a little sigh, "I too once – but that is a long time ago." Then her eyes twinkled again; I trow she was not much given to sighing. "That is a long time ago," she repeated briskly, "and now they think I am too old to do aught but tell my beads and wait for death. But I like to have a hand in the game."

"I will come to take a hand with you anytime, madame," M. Étienne assured her. "I like the way you play."

She broke into shrill, delighted laughter.

"I'll warrant you do! And I don't mean to do the thing by halves. No; I shall save you, hide and hair. Be so kind, my lad, as to lift the lantern from the hook."

I did as she bade me, and we followed her down the passage like spaniels. She was so entirely equal to the situation that we made no protests and asked no questions. At the end of the hall she paused, opening neither the door on the right nor the door on the left, but, passing her hand up one of the panels of the wainscot, suddenly she flung it wide.

"You are not so small as I," she chuckled, "yet I think you can make shift to get through. You, monsieur lantern-bearer, go first."

I doubled myself up and scrambled through. The old lady, gathering her petticoats daintily, followed me without difficulty, but M. Étienne was put to some trouble to bow his tall head low enough. We stood at the top of a flight of stone steps descending into blackness. The old lady unhesitatingly tripped down before us.

At the foot of the stairs was a vaulted stone passageway, slippery with lichen, the dampness hanging in beads on the wall. Turning two corners, we brought up at a narrow, nail-studded door.

"Here I bid you farewell," quoth the little old lady. "You have only to walk on till you get to the end. At the steps, pull the rope once and wait. When he opens to you, say, 'For the Cause,' and draw a crown with your finger in the air."

"Madame," M. Étienne cried, "I hope the day may come when I shall make you suitable acknowledgements. My name –"

"I prefer not to know it," she interrupted, glancing up at him. "I will call you M. Yeux-gris; that is enough. As for acknowledgments – pooh! I am overpaid in the sport it has been."

"But, madame, when monsieur your son discovers –"

"Mon dieu! I am not afraid of my son or of any other woman's son!" she cried, with cackling laughter. And I warrant she was not.

"Madame," M. Étienne said, "I trust we shall meet again when I shall have time to tell you what I think of you." He dropped on his knees before her, kissing both her hands.

"Yes, yes, of course you are grateful," she said, somewhat bored apparently by his demonstration. "Naturally one does not like to die at your age. I wish you a pleasant journey, M. Yeux-gris, and you too, you fresh-faced boy. Give me back my lantern and fare you well."

"You will let us see you safe back in your hall."

"I will do nothing of the sort! I am not so decrepit, thank you, that I cannot get up my own stairs. No, no; no more gallantries, but get on your way! Begone with you! I must be back in my chamber working my altar-cloth when my daughter-in-law comes home."

Crowing her elfin laugh, she pulled the door open and fairly hustled us through.

"Good-bye – you are fine boys"; and she slammed the door upon us. We were in absolute darkness. As we took our first breath of the dank, foul air, we heard bolts snap into place.

"Well, since we cannot go back, let us go forward," said M. Étienne, cheerfully. "I am glad she has bolted the door; it is to throw them off the scent should they track us."

I knew very well that he was not at all glad; that the same thought which chilled my blood had come to him. This little beldam, with her beady eyes and her laughter, was the wicked witch of our childhood days; she had shut us up in a charnel-house to die.

I heard him tapping the pavement before him with his scabbard, using it as a blind man's staff. And so we advanced through the fetid gloom, the passage being only wide enough to let us walk shoulder to shoulder. There was a whirring of wings about us, and a squeaking; once something swooped square into my face, knocking a cry of terror from me, and a laugh from him.

"What was it? a bat? Cheer up, Félix; they don't bite." But I would not go on till I had made sure, as well as I could without seeing, that the cursed thing was not clinging on me somewhere.

We walked on then in silence, the stone walls vibrant with our tread. We went on till it seemed we had traversed the width of Paris; and I wondered who were sleeping and feasting and scheming and loving over our heads. M. Étienne said at length:

"Mordieu! I hope this snake-hole does not empty us out into the Seine." But I thought that as long as it emptied us out somewhere, I should not greatly mind the Seine.

At this very moment M. Étienne clutched my arm, jerking me to a halt. I bounded backward, trying in the blackness to discern a precipice yawning at my feet. "Look!" he cried in a low, tense voice. I perceived, far before us in the gloom, a point of light, which, as we watched it, grew bigger and bigger, till it became an approaching lantern.

"This is like to be awkward," murmured M. Étienne.

The man carrying the light came on with firm, heavy tread; naturally he did not see us as soon as we saw him. I thought him alone, but it was hard to tell in this dark, echoy place.

He might easily have approached within touch of my sad clothing without becoming aware of me, but M. Étienne's azure and white caught the lantern rays a rod away. The newcomer stopped short, holding up the light between us and his face. We could make nothing of him, save that he was a large man, soberly clad.

"Who is it?" he demanded, his voice ringing out loud and steady. "Is it you, Ferou?"

M. Étienne hooked his scabbard in place, and went forward into the clear circle of light.

"No, M. de Mayenne; it is Étienne de Mar."

"Ventre bleu!" Mayenne ejaculated, changing his lantern with comical alacrity to his left hand, and whipping out his sword. My master's came bare, too, at that. They confronted each other in silence, till Mayenne's ever-increasing astonishment forced the cry from him:

"How the devil come you here?"

"Evidently by way of M. Ferou's house," M. Étienne answered. Mayenne still stared in thick amazement; after a moment my master added: "I must in justice say that M. Ferou is not aware that I am using this passage; he is, with madame his wife, supping with the Archbishop of Lyons."

M. Étienne leaned his shoulder against the wall, smiling pleasantly, and waiting for the duke to make the next move. Mayenne kept a nonplussed silence. The situation was indeed somewhat awkward. He could not come forward without encountering an agile opponent, whose exceeding skill with the sword was probably known to him. He could not turn tail, had his dignity allowed the course, without exposing himself to be spitted. He was in the predicament of the goat on the bridge. Yet was he gaping at us less in fear, I think, than in bewilderment. This Ferou, as I learned later, was one of his right-hand men, years-long supporter. Mayenne had as soon expected to meet a lion in the tunnel as to meet a foe. He cried out again upon us, with an instinctive certainty that a great prince's question must be answered:

"How came you here?"

"I don't ask," said M. Étienne, "how it happens that M. le Duc is walking through this rat-hole. Nor do I feel disposed to make any explanation to him."

"Very well, then," said Mayenne; "our swords, if you are ready, will make adequate explanation."

"Now, that is gallant of you," returned M. Étienne, "as it is evident that the closeness of these walls will inconvenience your Grace more than it will me."

The walls of the passage were roughly laid. Mayenne perched his lantern on a projecting stone.

"On guard, sir," he answered.

The silence was profound. Mayenne had no companion following him. He was alone with his sword. He was not now head of the state, but only a man with a sword, standing opposite another man with a sword. Nor was he in the pink of form. Though he gave the effect, from his clear color and proud bearing, perhaps also from his masterful energy, of tremendous force and strength, his body was in truth but a poor machine, his great corpulence making him clumsy and scant of breath. He must have known, as he eyed his supple antagonist, what the end would be. Yet he merely said:

"On guard, monsieur."

M. Étienne did not raise his weapon. I retreated a pace, that I might not be in the way of his jump, should Mayenne spring on him. M. Étienne said slowly:

"M. de Mayenne, this encounter was none of my contriving. Nor have I any wish to cross swords with you. Family quarrels are to be deprecated. Since I still intend to become your cousin, I must respectfully beg to be released from the obligation of fighting you."

A man knowing himself overmatched cannot refuse combat. He may, even as Mayenne had done, think himself compelled to offer it. But if he insists on forcing battle with a reluctant adversary, he must be a hothead indeed. And Mayenne was no hothead. He stood hesitant, feeling that he was made ridiculous in accepting the clemency and should be still more ridiculous to refuse it. He half lifted his sword, only to lower it again, till at last his good sense came to his relief in a laugh.

"M. de Mar, it appears that, after all, some explanations are necessary. You think that in declining to fight you put me in your debt. Possibly you are right. But if you expect that in gratitude I shall hand over Lorance de Montluc, you were never more mistaken. Never, while I live, shall she marry into the king's camp. Now, monsieur, that we understand each other, I abide by your decision whether we fight or not."

For answer, M. Étienne put up his blade. The Duke of Mayenne, saluting with his, did the like. "Mar," he said, "you stood off from us, like a coquetting girl, for three years. At length, last May, you refused point-blank to join us. I do not often ask a man twice, but I ask you. Will you join the League tonight, and marry Lorance tomorrow?"

No man could have spoken with a franker grace. I believe then, I believe now, he meant it. M. Étienne believed he meant it.

"Monsieur," he answered, "I have shilly-shallied long; but I am planted squarely at last with my father on the king's side. You put your interesting nephew into my father's house to kill him; I shall not sign myself with the League."

"In that case," returned Mayenne, "perhaps we might each continue on his way."

"With all my heart, monsieur."

Each drew back against the wall to let the other pass, with a wary eye for daggers. Then M. Étienne, laughing a little, but watching Mayenne like a lynx, started to go by. The duke, seeing the look, suddenly raised his hands over his head, holding them there while both of us squeezed past him.

"Cousin Charles," said M. Étienne, "I see that when I have married Lorance you and I shall get on capitally. Till then, God have you ever in guard."

"I thank you, monsieur. You make me immortal."

"I have no need to make you witty. M. de Mayenne, when you have submitted to the king, as you will one of these days, I shall have as delightful a kinsman as heart of man could wish. You and I will yet drink a loving-cup together. Till that happy hour, I am your good enemy. Fare you well, monsieur."

He bowed; the duke, half laughing despite a considerable ire, returned the obeisance with all pomp. M. Étienne took me by the arm and departed. Mayenne stood still for a space; then we heard his retreating footsteps, and the glimmer of his light slowly faded away.

"It wasn't necessary to tell him the door is bolted," M. Étienne muttered.

We hurried along now without precaution, knowing that the floor which had supported Mayenne would support us. The consequence was that we stumbled abruptly against a step, and fell with a force like to break our kneecaps. I picked myself up at once, and ran headlong up the stairs, to hit my crown on the ceiling and reel back on M. Étienne, sweeping him off his feet, so that we rolled in a struggling heap on the stones of the passage. And for the minute the place was no longer dark; I saw more lightning than even flashed in the Rue Coupejarrets.

"Are you hurt, Félix?" cried M. Étienne, the first to disentangle himself.

"No," I said, groaning; "but I banged my head. She did not say it was a trapdoor."

We ascended the stairs a second time – this time most cautiously on our hands and knees. Above us, at the end, we could feel, with upleaping of spirit, a wooden ceiling.

"Ah, I have the cord!" he exclaimed.

The next instant we heard a faint but most comforting tinkle somewhere above us. Before we had time to wonder whether any marked it but us, we heard steps overhead, and a noise as of a chest being pulled about, and then the trap lifted. We climbed out into a silk-mercer's shop.

"Faith, my man," said M. Étienne to the little bourgeois who had opened to us, "I am glad to see you appear so promptly."

He looked at us, somewhat troubled or alarmed.

"You must have met –" he suggested with hesitancy.

"Yes," said M. Étienne; "but he did not object. We are, of course, of the initiated."

"Of course, of course," the little fellow assented, with a funny assumption of knowing all about it. "Not everyone has the secret of the passage. Well, I can call myself a lucky man. 'Tis mighty few mercers have a duke in their shop as often as I."

We looked curiously about us. The shop was low and dim, with piles of stuff in rolls on the shelves, and other stuffs lying loose on the counter before us, as if the man had just been measuring them – gorgeous brocades and satins. Above us, a bell on the rafter still quivered.

"Yes, that is the bell of the trap," the proprietor said, following our glance. "Customers do not know where it rings from. And if I am not at liberty to open, I drop my brass yardstick on the floor – But they told you that, doubtless, monsieur?" he added, regarding M. Étienne again a little uneasily.

"They told me something else I had near forgotten," M. Étienne answered, and, drawing a crown in the air, gave the password, "For the Cause."

"For the King," the shopkeeper made instant rejoinder, drawing in the air in his turn a letter C and the numeral X.

M. Étienne laid a gold piece on the counter, and if the shopkeeper had felt any doubts of this well-dressed gallant who wore no hat, they vanished in its radiance.

"And now, my friend, let us out into the street and forget our faces."

The man took up his candle to light us to the door.

"Perhaps it would not trouble monsieur to say a word for me over there?" he suggested, pointing in the direction of the tunnel. "M. le Duc has every confidence in me. Still, it would do no harm if monsieur should mention how quickly I let him out."

"When I see him, I will surely mention it," M. Étienne promised him. "Continue to be vigilant tonight, my friend. There is another man to come."

Followed by the little bourgeois's thanks and adieus, we walked out into the sweet open air. As soon as his door was shut again, we took to our heels, nor stopped running till we had put half a dozen streets between us and the mouth of the tunnel. Then we walked along in breathless silence.

Presently M. Étienne cried out:

"Death of my life! Had I fought there in the burrow, I should have changed the history of France!"

XXI

A chance encounter.

The street before us was as orderly as the aisle of Notre Dame. Few way-farers passed us; those there were talked together as placidly as if love-trysts and mêlées existed not, and tunnels and countersigns were but the smoke of a dream. It was a street of shops, all shuttered, while, above, the burghers' families went respectably to bed.

"This is the Rue de la Ferronnerie," my master said, pausing a moment to take his bearings. "See, under the lantern, the sign of the Pierced Heart. The little shop is in the Rue de la Soierie. We are close by the Halles – we must have come half a mile underground. Well, we'll swing about in a circle to get home. For this night I've had enough of the Hôtel de Lorraine."

And I. But I held my tongue about it, as became me.

"They were wider awake than I thought – those Lorrainers. Pardieu! Féix, you and I came closer quarters with death than is entirely amusing."

"If that door had not opened –" I shuddered.

"A new saint in the calendar – la Sainte Ferou! But what a madcap of a saint, then! My faith, she must have led them a dance when Francis I was king!

"Natheless it galls me," he went on, half to himself, "to know that I was lost by my own folly, saved by pure chance. I underrated the enemy – worst mistake in the book of strategy. I came near flinging away two lives and making a most unsightly mess under a lady's window."

"Monsieur made somewhat of a mess as it was."

"Aye. I would I knew whether I killed Brie. We'll go round in the morning and find out."

"I am thankful that monsieur does not mean to go tonight."

"Not tonight, Félix; I've had enough. No; we'll get home without passing near the Hôtel de Lorraine, if we go outside the walls to do it. Tonight I draw my sword no more."

To this day I have no quite clear idea of how we went. A strange city at night – Paris of all cities – is a labyrinth. I know that after a time we came out in some meadows along the river-bank, traversed them, and plunged once more into narrow, high-walled streets. It was very late, and lights were few. We had started in clear starlight, but now a rack of clouds hid even their pale shine.

"The snake-hole over again," said M. Étienne. "But we are almost at our own gates."

But, as in the snake-hole, came light. Turning a sharp corner, we ran straight into a gentleman and his porte-flambeau, swinging along at as smart a pace as we.

"A thousand pardons," M. Étienne cried to his encounterer, the possessor of years and gravity but of no great size, whom he had almost knocked down. "I heard you, but knew not you were so close. We were speeding to get home."

The personage was also of a portliness, and the collision had knocked the wind out of him. He leaned panting against the wall. As he scanned M. Étienne's open countenance and princely dress his alarm vanished.

"It is unseemly to go about on a night like this without a lantern," he said with asperity. "The municipality should forbid it. I shall certainly bring the matter up at the next sitting."

"Monsieur is a member of the Parliament?" M. Étienne asked with immense respect.

"I have that honor, monsieur," the little man replied, delighted to impress us, as he himself was impressed, by the sense of his importance.

"Oh," said M. Étienne, with increasing solemnity, "perhaps monsieur had a hand in a certain decree of the 28th June?"

The little man began to look uneasy.

"There was, as monsieur says, a measure passed that day," he stammered.

"A rebellious and contumacious decree," M. Étienne rejoined, "most offensive to the general-duke." Whereupon he fingered his sword.

"Monsieur," the little deputy cried, "we meant no offence to his Grace, or to any true Frenchman. We but desire peace after all these years of blood. We were informed that his Grace was angry; yet we believed that even he will come to see the matter in a different light –"

"You have acted in a manner insulting to his Grace of Mayenne," M. Étienne repeated inexorably, and he glanced up the street and down the street to make sure the coast was clear. The wretched little deputy's teeth chattered.

The linkman had retreated to the other side of the way, where he seemed on the point of fleeing, leaving his master to his fate. I thought it would be a shame if the badgered deputy had to stumble home in the dark, so I growled out to the fellow:

"Stir one step at your peril!"

I was afraid he would drop the flambeau and run, but he did not; he only sank back against the wall, eyeing my sword with exceeding deference. He knew not that there was but a foot of blade in the scabbard.

The burgher looked up the street and down the street, after M. Étienne's example, but there was no help to be seen or heard. He turned to his tormentor with the valor of a mouse at bay.

"Monsieur, beware what you do. I am Pierre Marceau!"

"Oh, you are Pierre Marceau? And can M. Pierre Marceau explain how he happened to be faring forth from his dwelling at this unholy hour?"

"I am not faring forth; I am faring home. I – we had a little con – that is, not to say a conference, but merely a little discussion on matters of no importance –"

"I have the pleasure," interrupted M. Étienne, sternly, "of knowing where M. Marceau lives. M. Marceau's errand in this direction is not accounted for."

"But I was going home – on my sacred honor I was! Ask Jacques, else. But as we went down the Rue de l'Évêque we saw two men in front of us. As they reached the wall by M. de Mirabeau's garden a gang of footpads fell on them. The two drew blades and defended themselves, but the ruffians were a dozen – a score. We ran for our lives."

M. Étienne wheeled round to me.

"Félix, here is work for us. As I was saying, M. Marceau, your decree is most offensive to the general-duke, and therefore, since he is my particular enemy, most pleasing to me. A beautiful night, is it not, sir? I wish you a delightful walk home."

He seized me by the hand, and we dashed up the street.

At the corner the noise of a fray came faintly but plainly to our ears. M. le Comte without hesitation plunged down a lane in the direction of the sound.

"I said I wanted no more fighting tonight, but two against a mob! We know how it feels."

The clash of steel on steel grew ever louder, and as we wheeled around a jutting garden wall we came full upon the combatants.

"A rescue, a rescue!" cried M. Étienne. "Shout, Félix! Montjoie St. Denis! A rescue, a rescue!"

We charged down the street, drawing our swords and shouting at the top of our lungs.

It was too dark to see much save a mass of struggling figures, with every now and then, as the steel hit, a point of light flashing out, to fade and appear again like a brilliant glow-worm. We could scarce tell which were the attackers, which the two comrades we had come to save.

But if we could not make them out, neither could they us. We shouted as boldly as if we had been a company, and in the clatter of their heels on the stones they could not count our feet. They knew not how many followers the darkness held. The group parted. Two men remained in hot combat close under the left wall. Across the way one sturdy fighter held off two, while a sixth man, crying on his mates to follow, fled down the lane.

M. Étienne knew now what he was about, and at once took sides with the solitary fencer. The combat being made equal, I started in pursuit of the flying figure. I had run but a few yards, however, when I tripped and fell prostrate over the body of a man. I was up in a moment, feeling him to find out if he were dead; my hands over his heart dipped into a pool of something wet and warm like new milk. I wiped them on his sleeve as best I could, and hastily groped about for his sword. He did not need it now, and I did.

When I rose with it my quarry was swallowed up in the shadows. M. Étienne, whose light clothing made a distinguishable spot in the gloom, had driven his opponent, or his opponent had driven him, some rods up the lane the way we had come. I stood perplexed, not knowing where to busy myself. M. Étienne's side I could not reach past the two duels; and of the four men near me, I could by no means tell, as they circled about and about, which were my chosen allies. They were all somberly clad, their faces blurred in the darkness. When one made a clever pass, I knew not whether to rejoice or despair. But at length I picked out one who fenced, though valiantly enough, yet with greater effort than the rest; and I deemed that this had been the hardest pressed of all and must certainly be one of the attacked and the one most deserving of succor. He was plainly losing ground. I darted to his side just as his foe ran him through the arm.

The assailant pulled his blade free and darted back against the wall to face the two of us. But the sword of the wounded man fell from his loose fingers.

"I'm out of it," he cried to me; "I go for aid." And as his late combatant sprang forward to engage me, I heard him running off, stumbling where I had.

There had been little light toward the last in the court of the house in the Rue Coupejarrets, and less under the windows of the Hôtel de Lorraine; but here was none at all, I had to use my sword solely by the feel of his against it, and I underwent chilling qualms lest presently, without in the least knowing how it got there, I should find his point sticking out of my back. I could hardly believe he was not hitting me; I began to prickle in half a dozen places, and knew not whether the stings were real or imaginary. But one was not imaginary; my shoulder which Lucas had pinked and the doctor bandaged was throbbing painfully. I fancied that in my earlier combat the wound had opened again and that I was bleeding to death; and the fear shook me. I lunged wildly, and I had been sent to my account in short order had not at this moment one of the other pair near us, as it afterward appeared, driven his weapon square through his vis-à-vis's breast.

"I am done for. Run who can!" he cried as he fell. The sword snapped in two against the paving-stones; he rolled over and lay still, his face in the dirt.

My encounterer, with a shout to his single remaining comrade, made off down the lane. On my part, I was very willing to let him depart in peace.

The clash of swords up the lane had ceased at the stricken man's cry, and out of the gloom came the sound of footfalls fainter and fainter. I deemed that the battle was over.

The champion came toward me, three white patches visible for his face and hands; the rest of him but darkness moving in darkness. He held a sword rifled from the enemy, and advanced on me hesitatingly, not sure whether friend or foe remained to him. I felt that an explanation was due from me, but in my ignorance as to who he was and who his foes were, and why they had been fighting him and why we had been fighting them, I stood for a moment confused. It is hard to open conversation with a shadow.

He spoke first, in a voice husky from his exertion:

"Who are you?"

"A friend," I said. "My master and I saw two men fighting four – we came to help the weaker side. Your friend was hurt, but he got away safe to fetch aid."

The unknown made a rapid step toward me, crying, "What –"

But at the word M. Étienne emerged from the shadows.

"Who lives?" he called out. "You, Félix?"

"Not hurt, monsieur. And you?"

"Not a scratch. Nor did I scratch my man. Permit me to congratulate you, monsieur l'inconnu, on our coming up when we did."

The unknown said one word:

"Étienne!"

I sprang forward with the impulse to throw my arms about him, in the pure rapture of recognizing his voice. This struggler, whom we had rushed in, blindfold, to save, was Monsieur! If we had been content to mind our own business, had sheered away like the deputy – it turned me faint to think how long we had delayed with old Marceau, we were so nearly too late. I wanted to seize Monsieur, to convince myself that he was all safe, to feel him quick and warm.

I made one pace and stopped; for I remembered what ghastly shape stood between me and Monsieur – that horrible lying story.

"Dieu!" gasped M. Étienne, "Monsieur!"

For a moment we all kept silence, motionless; then Monsieur flung his sword over the wall.

"Do your will, Étienne."

His son darted forward with a cry.

"Monsieur, Monsieur, I am not your assassin! I came to your aid not dreaming who you were; but, had I known, I would have fought a hundred times the harder. I never plotted against you. On the honor of a St. Quentin I swear it."

Monsieur said naught, and we could not see his face; could not know whether he believed or rejected, softened or condemned.

M. Étienne, catching at his breath, went on:

"Monsieur, I know it is hard to credit. I have been a bad son to you, unloving, rebellious, insolent. We quarreled; I spoke bitter words. But I am no ruffian. I am a St. Quentin. Had you had me whipped from the house, still would I never have raised hand against you. I knew nothing of the plot. Félix told you I was in it – small blame to him. But he was wrong. I knew naught of it."

Had he been content to rest his case here, I think Monsieur could not but have believed his innocence on his bare word. The stones in the pavement must have known that he was uttering truth. But he in his eagerness paused for no answer, but went on to stun Monsieur with statements new and amazing to his ear.

"My cousin Grammont – who is dead – was in the plot, and his lackey Pontou, and Martin the clerk; but the contriver was Lucas."

"Lucas?"

"Lucas," continued M. Étienne. "Or, to give him his true title, Paul de Lorraine, son of Henri de Guise."

"But that is impossible" Monsieur cried, stupefied.

"It is impossible, but it is true. He is a Lorraine – Mayenne's nephew, and for years Mayenne's spy. He came to you to kill you – for that object pure and simple. Last spring, before he came to you, he was here in Paris with Mayenne, making terms for your murder. He is no

Huguenot, no Kingsman. He is Mayenne's henchman, son to Guise himself."

"And how long have you known this?" asked Monsieur.

"Since this morning." Then, as the import of the question struck him, he fell back with a groan. "Ah, Monsieur, if you can ask that, I have no more to say. It is useless." He turned away into the darkness.

That they should part thus was too miserable to be endured. I was sure Monsieur's question was no accusation, but the groping of bewilderment.

"M. Étienne, stop!" I commanded. "Monsieur, it is the truth. Indeed it is the truth. He is innocent, and Lucas *is* a Guise. Monsieur, you must listen to me. M. Étienne, you must wait. I stirred up the whole trouble with my story to you, Monsieur, and I take it back. I believed I was telling the truth. I was wrong. When I left you, I went straight back to the Rue Coupejarrets to kill your son – your murderer, I thought. And there I found Grammont and Lucas side by side. We thought them sworn foes: they were hand in glove. They came at me to end me because I had told, and M. Étienne saved me. Lucas mocked him to his face because he had been tricked; Lucas bragged that it was his own scheme – that M. Étienne was his dupe. Vigo will tell you. Vigo heard him. His scheme was to saddle M. Étienne with your murder. He was tricked. He believed what he told me – that the thing was a duel between Lucas and Grammont. You must believe it, Monsieur!"

M. Étienne, who had actually obeyed me, – me, his lackey, – turned to his father once again.

"Monsieur, if you cannot believe me, believe Félix. You believed him when he took away my good name. Believe him now when he restores it."

"Nay," Monsieur cried; "I believe thee, Étienne."

And he took his son in his arms.

XXII

The signet of the king.

Already a wan light was revealing the round tops of the plum trees in M. de Mirabeau's garden, the high grey wall, and the narrow alleyway beneath it. And the two vague shapes by me were no longer vague shapes, but were turning moment by moment, as if coming out of an enchantment, into their true forms. It really was Monsieur in the flesh, with a wet glint in his eyes as he kissed his boy.

Neither thought of me, and it was none of my concern what they said to each other. I went a rod or two down the lane, round a curve in the wall, and watched the bands of light streaking the eastern sky, in utter content. Never before had the world seemed to me so good a place. Since this misery had come right, I knew all the rest would; I should yet dance at M. Étienne's wedding.

I leaned my head back against the wall, and had shut my eyes to consider the matter more quietly, when I heard my name.

"Félix! Félix! Where is the boy got to?"

The sun was clean up over the horizon, and as I blinked and wondered how he had contrived the feat so quickly, my two messieurs came hand in hand round the corner to me, the level rays glittering on Monsieur's burnished breastplate, on M. Étienne's bright head, and on both their shining faces. Now that for the first time I saw them together, I found them, despite the dark hair and the yellow, the brown eyes and the grey, wonderfully alike. There was the same carriage, the same cock of the head, the same smile. If I had not known before, I knew now, the instant I looked at them, that the quarrel was over. Save as it gave them a deeper love of each other, it might never have been.

I sprang up, and Monsieur, my duke, embraced me.

"Lucky we came up the lane when we did, eh, Félix?" M. Étienne said. "But, Monsieur, I have not asked you yet what madness sent you traversing this back passage at two in the morning."

"I might ask you that, Étienne."

The young man hesitated a bare moment before he answered:

"I am just come from serenading Mlle. de Montluc."

A shade fell over Monsieur's radiance. At his look, M. Étienne cried out:

"I've told you I'm no Leaguer! Mayenne offered me mademoiselle if I would come over. I refused. Last night he sent me word that he would kill me as a common nuisance if I sought to see her. That was why I tried."

"Monsieur," I cried, curiosity mastering me, "was she in the window?"

He shook his head, his eyes on his father' face.

"Étienne," Monsieur said slowly, "can't you see that Mlle. de Montluc is not for you?"

"I shall never see it, Monsieur. The first article in my creed says she is for me. And I'll have her yet, for all Mayenne."

"Then, mordieu, we'll steal her together!"

"You! You'll help me?"

"Why, dear son," Monsieur explained, "it broke my heart to think of you in the League. I could not bear that my son should help a Spaniard to the throne of France, or a Lorrainer either. But if it is a question of stealing the lady – well, I never prosed about prudence yet, thank God!"

M. Étienne, wet-eyed, laughing, hugged Monsieur.

"By St. Quentin, we'll get you your lady! I hated the marriage while I thought it would make you a Leaguer. I could not see you sacrifice your honor to a girl's bright eyes. But your life – that is different."

"My life is a little thing."

"No," Monsieur said; "it is a good deal – one's life. But one is not to guard one's life at the cost of all that makes life sweet."

"Ah, you know how I love her!"

"They call me a fool," Monsieur went on musingly, "because I risk my life in wild errands. But, mordieu! I am the wise man. For they who think ever of safety, and crouch and scheme and shuffle to procure it, why, look you, they destroy their own ends. For, when all is done, they have never really lived. And that is why they hate death so, these worthies. While I, who have never cringed to fear, I live like a king. I go my ways without any man's leave; and if death comes to me a little sooner for that, I am a poor creature if I do not meet him smiling. If I may live as I please, I am content to die when I must."

"Aye," said M. Étienne, "and if we live as we do not please, still we must die presently. Therefore do I purpose never to give over striving after my lady."

"Oh, we'll win her by noon. But first we'll sleep. There's Félix yawning his head off. Come, come."

We set off along the alley, the St. Quentins arm in arm, I at their heels. Monsieur looked over his shoulder with a sudden anxiety.

"Félix, you said Huguet had run for aid?"

"Yes, Monsieur; Vigo should have been here before now," I answered, remembering Vigo's promptitude yesterday.

"Everyone was asleep; he has been hammering this half-hour to get in," M. Étienne said easily.

But Monsieur asked of me:

"Was he much hurt, Félix?"

"No; I am sure not, Monsieur. He was run through the arm; I am sure he was not hurt otherwise."

We came to where the two slain men lay across the way. M. Étienne exclaimed:

"If you do not hold your life dear, you sell it dear, Monsieur! How many of the rascals were there?"

"It was hard to tell in the dark. Five, I think."

"Now, Monsieur, how came you to be in this place in the dark?"

"Why, what to do, Étienne? I came in at the gate just after midnight. I could not leave St. Denis earlier, and night is my time to enter Paris. The inns were shut –"

"But some friend near the gate? Tarigny would have sheltered you."

"Aye, and got into trouble for it, had it leaked out to the Sixteen."

"Tarigny is no craven."

"But neither am I," said Monsieur, smiling.

"Oh, I give you up! Go your ways. But I will not come to save you next time."

"No, lad; you will be at my side hereafter."

M. Étienne laughed and said no more.

"But in truth," Monsieur added, "I did not expect waylaying. If these fellows watched by the gate, they hid cleverly. I never saw a fingertip of them till they sprang upon us by the corner here, when we were almost home."

M. Étienne bent over and turned face up the man whom Monsieur had run through the heart. He was an ugly enough fellow, one eye entirely closed by a great scar that ran from his forehead nearly to his grizzled mustache.

"This is Bernet le Borgne," he said. "Have you encountered him before, Monsieur? He was a soldier under Guise once, they say, but he has done naught but hang about Paris taverns this many a year. We used to wonder how he lived; we knew he did somebody's dirty work. Clisson employed him once, so I know something of him. With his one eye he could fence better than most folks with two. My congratulations to you, Monsieur."

But Monsieur, not heeding, was bending over the other man.

"Your acquaintance is wider than mine. Do you know this one?"

M. Étienne shook his head over this other man, who lay face up, staring with wide dark eyes into the sky. His hair curled in little rings about his forehead, and his cheeks were smooth; he looked no older than I.

"He dashed at me the first of all," Monsieur said in a low voice. "I ran him through before the others came up. Mordieu! I am glad it was dark. A boy like that!"

"He had good mettle to run up first," M. Étienne said. "And it is no disgrace to fall to your sword, Monsieur. Come, let us go."

But Monsieur looked back again at the dead lad, and then at his son and at me, and came with us heavy of countenance.

On the stones before us lay a trail of blood-drops.

"Now, that is where Huguet ran with his wounded arm," I said to M. Étienne.

"Aye, and if we did not know the way home we could find it by this red track."

But the trail did not reach the door; for when we turned into the little street where the arch is, where I had waited for Martin, as we turned the familiar corner under the walls of the house itself, we came suddenly on the body of a man. Monsieur ran forward with a cry, for it was the squire Huguet.

He wore a leather jerkin lined with steel rings, mail as stout as any forged. Someone had stabbed once and again at the coat without avail, and had then torn it open and stabbed his defenseless breast. Though we had killed two of their men, they had rained blows enough on this man of ours to kill twenty.

Monsieur knelt on the ground beside him, but he was quite cold.

"The man who fled when we charged them must have lurked about," I said. "Huguet's sword-arm was useless; he could not defend himself."

"Or else he fainted from his wound, he bled so," M. Étienne answered. "And one of those who fled last came upon him helpless and did this."

"Why didn't I follow him instead of sitting down, a John o'dreams?" I cried. "But I was thinking of you and Monsieur; I forgot Huguet."

"I forgot him, too," Monsieur sorrowed. "Shame to me; he would not have forgotten me."

"Monsieur," his son said, "it was no negligence of yours. You could have saved him only by following when he ran. And that was impossible."

"In sight of the door," Monsieur said sadly. "In sight of his own door."

We held silent. Monsieur got soberly to his feet.

"I never lost a better man."

"Monsieur," I cried, "he asks no better epitaph. If you will say that of me when I die, I shall not have lived in vain."

He smiled at the outburst, but I did not care; if he would only smile, I was content it should be at me.

"Nay, Félix," he said. "I hope it will not be I who compose your epitaph. Come, we must get to the house and send after poor Huguet."

"Félix and I will carry him," M. Étienne said, and we lifted him between us – no easy task, for he was a heavy fellow. But it was little enough to do for him.

We bore him along slowly, Monsieur striding ahead. But of a sudden he turned back to us, laying quick fingers on the poor torn breast.

"What is it, Monsieur?" cried his son.

"My papers."

We set him down, and the three of us examined him from top to toe, stripping off his steel coat, pulling apart his blood-clotted linen, prying into his very boots. But no papers revealed themselves.

"What were they, Monsieur?"

A drawn look had come over Monsieur's face.

"Papers which the king gave me, and which I, fool and traitor, have lost."

I ran back to the spot where we had found Huguet; there was his hat on the ground, but no papers. I followed up the red trail to its beginning, looking behind every stone, every bunch of grass; but no papers. In my desperation I even pulled about the dead man, lest the packet had been covered, falling from Huguet in the fray. The two gentlemen joined me in the search, and we went over every inch of the ground, but to no purpose.

"I thought them safer with Huguet than with me," Monsieur groaned. "I knew we ran the risk of ambush. Myself would be the object of attack; I bade Huguet, were we waylaid, to run with the papers."

"And of course he would not."

"He should; it was my command. He stayed and saved my life perhaps, and lost me what is dearer than life – my honor."

"He could not leave you to be killed, Monsieur; that were asking the impossible."

"Aye, but I am saved at the ruin of a hundred others!" Monsieur cried. "The papers contained certain lists of names of Mayenne's officers pledged to support the king if he turn Catholic. I had them for Lemaître. But at this date, in Mayenne's hands, they spell the men's destruction. Huguet should have known that if I told him to desert me, I meant it."

M. Étienne ventured no word, understanding well enough that in such bitter moments no consolation consoles. M. le Duc added after a moment:

"Mordieu! I am ashamed of myself. I might be better occupied than in blaming the dead – the brave and faithful dead. Belike he could not run, they set on us so suddenly. When he could, he did go, and he went to his death. They were my charge, the papers. I had no right to put the responsibility on any other. I should have kept them myself. I should have gone to Tarigny. I should never have ventured myself through these black lanes. Fool! traitorous fool!"

"Nay, Monsieur, the mischance might have befallen anyone."

"It would not have befallen Villeroi! It would not have befallen Rosny!" Monsieur exclaimed bitterly. "It befalls me because I am a lack-wit who rushes into affairs for which he is not fit. I can handle a sword, but I have no business to meddle in statecraft."

"Then have those wiseheads out at St. Denis no business to employ you," M. Étienne said. "He is not unknown to fame, this Duke of St. Quentin; everybody knows how he goes about things. Monsieur, they gave you the papers because no one else would carry them into Paris. They knew you had no fear in you; and it is because of that that the papers are lacking. But take heart, Monsieur. We'll get them back."

"When? How?"

"Soon," M. Étienne answered, "and easily, if you will tell me what they are like. Are they open?"

"I fear by now they may be. There are three sheets of names, and a fourth sheet, a letter – all in cipher."

"Ah, but in that case –"

Monsieur cut short his son's jubilation.

"But – Lucas."

"Of course – I forgot him. He knows your ciphers, then?"

"Dolt that I was, he knows everything."

"Then must we lay hands on the papers before they reach Mayenne, and all is saved," M. Étienne declared cheerfully. "These fellows can't read a cipher. If the packet be not open, Monsieur?"

"It was a span long, and half as wide; for all address, the letters *St. Q.* in the corner. It was tied with red cord and bore the seal of a flying falcon, and the motto, *Je reviendrai.*"

"What! the king's seal? That's serious. Expect, then, Monsieur, to see the papers in an hour's time."

"Étienne, Étienne," Monsieur cried, "are you mad?"

"No madder than is proper for a St. Quentin. It's simple enough. I told you I recognized that worthy back there for one Bernet, who lodged at an inn I wot of over beyond the markets. Do we betake ourselves thither, we may easily fall in with some comrades of his bosom who have not the misfortune to be lying dead in a back lane, who will know something of your loss. Bernet's sort are no bigots; while they work for the League, they will lend a kindly ear to the chink of Kingsmen's florins."

"Ah," cried Monsieur, "then let us go." But M. Étienne laid a restraining hand on his shoulder.

"Not you. I. They will kill you in the Halles just as cheerfully as in the Quartier Marais. This is my affair."

He looked at Monsieur with kindling eyes, seeing his chance to prove his devotion. The duke yielded to his eagerness.

"But," M. Étienne added generously, "you may have the honor of paying the piper."

"I give you carte blanche, my son. Étienne, if you put that packet into my hand, it is more than if you brought the scepter of France."

"Then go practice, Monsieur, at feeling more than king."

He embraced his father, and we turned off down the street.

The sun was well up by this time, and the city rousing to the labors of the day. Half was I glad of the lateness of the hour, for we ran no risk now of cutthroats; and half was I sorry, for it behooves not a man supposed to be in the Bastille to show himself too liberally to the broad eye of the streets. Every time – and it was often – that we approached a person who to my nervous imagination looked official, I shook in my shoes. The way seemed fairly to bristle with soldiers, officers, judges; for aught I knew, members of the Sixteen, Governor Belin himself. It was a great surprise to me when at length we arrived without let or hindrance before the door of a mean little drinking-place, our goal.

We went in, and M. Étienne ordered wine, much to my satisfaction. My stomach was beginning to remind me that I had given it nothing for twelve hours or so, while I had worked my legs hard.

"Does M. Bernet lodge with you?" my master asked of the landlord. We were his only patrons at the moment.

"M. Bernet? Him with the eye out?"

"The same."

"Why, no, monsieur. I don't let lodgings. The building is not mine. I but rent the ground floor for my purposes."

"But M. Bernet lodges in the house, then?"

"No, he doesn't. He lodges round the corner, in the court off the Rue Clichet."

"But he comes here often?"

"Oh, aye. Every morning for his glass. And most evenings, too."

M. Étienne laid down the drink-money, and something more.

"Sometimes he has a friend with him, eh?"

The man laughed.

"No, monsieur; he comes in here alone. Many's the time I'll standing in my door when he'll go by with some gallant, and he never chances to see me or my shop. While if he's alone it's 'Good morning, Jean. Anything in the casks today?' He can no more get by my door than he'll get by Death's when the time comes."

"No," agreed M. Étienne; "we all stop there, soon or late. Those friends of M. Bernet, then – there is none you could put a name to?"

"Why, no, monsieur, more's the pity. He has none lives in this quarter. M. Bernet's in low water, you understand, monsieur. If he lives here, it is because he can't help it. But he goes elsewhere for his friends."

"Then you can tell us, my man, where he lodges?"

"Aye, that can I," mine host answered, bustling out from behind the bar, eager in the interest of the pleasant-spoken, open-handed gallant. "Just round the corner of the Rue Clichet, in the court. The first house on the left, that is his. I would go with monsieur, only I cannot leave the shop alone, and the wife not back from market. But monsieur cannot miss it. The first house in the court. Thank you, monsieur. Au revoir, monsieur."

In the doorway of the first house on the left in the little court stood an old man with a wooden leg, sweeping heaps of refuse out of the passage.

"It appears that everyone on this stair lacks something," M. Étienne murmured to me. "It is the livery of the house. Can you tell me, friend, where I may find M. Bernet?"

The concierge regarded us without cordiality, while by no means ceasing his endeavors to cover our shoes with his sweepings.

"Third story back," he said.

"Does M. Bernet lodge alone?"

"One of him's enough," the old fellow growled, whacking out his dirty broom on the doorpost, powdering us with dust. M. Étienne, coughing, pursued his inquiries:

"Ah, I understood he shared his lodgings with a comrade. He has a friend, then, in the building?"

"Aye, I suppose so," the old chap grinned, "when monsieur walks in."

"But he has another friend besides me, has he not?" M. Étienne persisted. "One who, if he does not live here, comes often to see M. Bernet?"

"You seem to know all about it. Better see Bernet himself, instead of chattering here all day."

"Good advice, and I'll take it," said M. Étienne, lightly setting foot on the stair, muttering to himself as he mounted, "and come back to break your head, mon vieillard."

We went up the three flights and along the passage to the door at the back, whereon M. Étienne pounded loudly. I could not see his reason, and heartily I wished he would not. It seemed to me a creepy thing to be knocking on a man's door when we knew very well he would never open it again. We knocked as if we fully thought him within, when all the while we knew he was lying a stone on the stones under M. de Mirabeau's garden wall. Perhaps by this time he had been found; perhaps one of the marquis's liveried lackeys, or a passing idler, or a woman with a market basket had come upon him; perhaps even now he was being borne away on a plank to be identified. And here were we, knocking, knocking, as if we innocently expected him to open to us. I had a chill dread that suddenly he would open to us. The door would swing wide and show him pale and bloody, with the broken sword in his heart. At the real creaking of a hinge I could scarce swallow a cry.

It was not Bernet's door, but the door at the front which opened, letting a stream of sunlight into the dark passage. In the doorway stood a woman, with two bare-legged babies clinging to her skirts.

"Madame," M. Étienne addressed her, with the courtesy due to a duchess, "I have been knocking at M. Bernet's door without result. Perhaps you could give me some hint as to his whereabouts?"

"Ah, I am sorry. I know nothing to tell monsieur," she cried regretfully, impressed, as the concierge had not been, by his look and manner. "But this I can say: he went out last night, and I do not believe he has been in since. He went out about nine – or it may have been later than that. Because I did not put the children to bed till after dark; they enjoy running about in the cool of the evening as much as anybody else, the little dears. And they were cross last night, the day was so hot, and I was a long time hushing them to sleep. Yes, it must have been after ten, because they were asleep, and the man stumbling on the stairs woke Pierre. And he cried for an hour. Didn't you, my angel?"

She picked one of the brats up in her arms to display him to us. M. Étienne asked:

"What man?"

"Why, the one that came for him. The one he went out with."

"And what sort of person was this?"

"Nay, how was I to see? Would I be out walking the common passage with a child to hush? I was rocking the cradle."

"But who does come here to visit M. Bernet?"

"I've never seen anyone, monsieur. I've never laid eyes on M. Bernet but twice. I keep in my apartment. And besides, we have only been here a week."

"I thank you, madame," M. Étienne said, turning to the stairs.

She ran out to the rail, babies and all.

"But I could take a message for him, monsieur. I will make a point of seeing him when he comes in."

"I will not burden you, madame," M. Étienne answered from the story below. But she was loath to stop talking, and hung over the railing to call:

"Beware of your footing, monsieur. Those second-floor people are not so tidy as they might be; one stumbles over all sorts of their rubbish out in the public way."

The door in front of us opened with a startling suddenness, and a big, brawny wench bounced out to demand of us:

"What is that she says? What are you saying of us, you slut?"

We had no mind to be mixed in the quarrel. We fled for our lives down the stair.

The old carl, though his sweeping was done, leaned on his broom on the outer step.

"So you didn't find M. Bernet at home? I could have told you as much had you been civil enough to ask."

I would have kicked the old curmudgeon, but M. Étienne drew two gold pieces from his pouch.

"Perchance if I ask you civilly, you will tell me with whom M. Bernet went out last night?"

"Who says he went out with anybody?"

"I do," and M. Étienne made a motion to return the coins to their place.

"Since you know so much, it's strange you don't know a little more," the old chap growled. "Well, Lord knows if it is really his, but he goes by the name of Peyrot."

"And where does he lodge?"

"How should I know? I have trouble enough keeping track of my own lodgers, without bothering my head about other people's."

"Now rack your brains, my friend, over this fellow," M. Étienne said patiently, with a persuasive chink of his pouch. "Recollect now; you have been sent to this monsieur with a message."

"Well, Rue des Tournelles, sign of the Gilded Shears," the old carl spat out at last.

"You are sure?"

"Hang me else."

"If you are lying to me, I will come back and beat you to a jelly with your own broom."

"It's the truth, monsieur," he said, with some proper show of respect at last. "Peyrot, at the Gilded Shears, Rue des Tournelles. You may beat me to a jelly if I lie."

"It would do you good in any event," M. Étienne told him, but flinging him his pistoles, nevertheless. The old fellow swooped upon them, gathered them up, and was behind the closed door all in one movement. But as we walked away, he opened a little wicket in the upper panel, and stuck out his ugly head to yell after us:

"If M. Bernet's not at home yet, neither will his friend be. I've told you what will profit you none."

"You mistake, Sir Gargoyle," M. Étienne called over his shoulder. "Your information is entirely to my needs."

XXIII

The Chevalier of the Tournelles.

It was a long walk to the Rue des Tournelles, which lay in our own quarter, not a dozen streets from the Hôtel St. Quentin itself. We found the Gilded Shears hung before a tailor's shop in the cellar of a tall, cramped structure, only one window wide. Its narrow door was inhospitably shut, but at our summons the concierge appeared to inform us that M. Peyrot did truly live here and, moreover, was at home, having arrived but half an hour earlier than we. He would go up and find out whether monsieur could see us.

But M. Étienne thought that formality unnecessary, and was able, at small expense, to convince the concierge of it. We went alone up the stairs and crept very quietly along the passage toward the door of M. Peyrot. But our shoes made some noise on the flags; had he been listening, he might have heard us as easily as we heard him. Peyrot had not yet gone to bed after the night's exertion; a certain clatter and gurgle convinced us that he was refreshing himself with supper, or breakfast, before reposing.

M. Étienne stood still, his hand on the door-knob, eager, hesitating. Here was the man; were the papers here? If they were, should we secure them? A single false step, a single wrong word, might foil us.

The sound of a chair pushed back came from within, and a young man's quick, firm step passed across to the far side of the room. We heard a box shut and locked. M. Étienne nipped my arm; we thought we knew what went in. Then came steps again and a loud yawn, and presently two whacks on the floor. We knew as well as if we could see that Peyrot had thrown his boots across the room. Next a clash and jangle of metal, that meant his sword-belt with its accoutrements flung on the table. M. Étienne, with the rapid murmur, "If I look at you, nab him," turned the door-handle.

But M. Peyrot had prepared against surprise by the simple expedient of locking his door. He heard us, too, for he stopped in the very middle of a prolonged yawn and held himself absolutely still. M. Étienne called out softly:

"Peyrot!"

"Who is it?"

"I want to speak with you about something important."

"Who are you, then?"

"I'll tell you when you let me in."

"I'll let you in when you tell me."

"My name's Martin. I'm a friend of Bernet. I want to speak to you quietly about a matter of importance."

"A friend of Bernet. Hmm! Well, friend of Bernet, it appears to me you speak very well through the door."

"I want to speak with you about the affair of tonight."

"What affair?"

"Tonight's affair."

"Tonight? I go to a supper-party at St. Germain. What have you to say about that?"

"Last night, then," M. Étienne amended, with rising temper. "If you want me to shout it out on your stairs, the St. Quentin affair."

"Now, what may you mean by that?" called the voice from within. If Peyrot was startled by the name, he carried it off well.

"You know what I mean. Shall I take the house into our confidence?"

"The house knows as much of your meaning as I. See here, friend of Bernet, if you are that gentleman's mate, perhaps you have a password about you."

"Aye," said M. Étienne, readily. "This is it: twenty pistoles."

No answer came immediately; I could guess Peyrot puzzled. Presently he called to us:

"By the bones of St. Anne, I don't believe a word you've been saying. But I'll have you in and see what you look like."

We heard him getting into his boots again and buckling on his baldric. Then we listened to the turning of a key; a lid was raised and banged down again, and the lock refastened. It was the box once more. M. Étienne and I looked at each other.

At length Peyrot opened the door and surveyed us.

"What, two friends of Bernet, ventre bleu!" But he allowed us to enter.

He drew back before us with a flourishing bow, his hand resting lightly on his belt, in which was stuck a brace of pistols. Any idea of doing violence on the person of M. Peyrot we dismissed for the present.

Our eyes traveled from his pistols over the rest of him. He was small, lean, and wiry, with dark, sharp face and deep-set twinkling eyes. One moment's glance gave us to know that Peyrot was no fool.

My lord closed the door after him and went straight to the point.

"M. Peyrot, you were engaged last night in an attack on the Duke of St. Quentin. You did not succeed in slaying him, but you did kill his man, and you took from him a packet. I come to buy it."

He looked at us a little dazed, not understanding, I deem, how we knew this. Certes, it had been too dark in the lane for his face to be seen, and he had doubtless made sure that he was not followed home. He said directly:

"You are the Comte de Mar."

"Even so, M. Peyrot. I did not care to have the whole stair know it, but to you I have no hesitation in confiding that I am M. de Mar."

M. Peyrot swept a bow till his head almost touched the floor.

"My poor apartment is honored."

As he louted low, I made a spring forward; I thought to pin him before he could rise. But he was up with the lightness of a bird from the bough and standing three yards away from me, where I crouched on the spring like a foiled cat. He grinned at me in open enjoyment.

"Monsieur desired?" he asked sympathetically.

"No, it is I who desire," said M. Étienne, clearing himself a place to sit on the corner of the table. "I desire that packet, monsieur. You know this little expedition of yours tonight was something of a failure. When you report to the general-duke, he will not be in the best of humors. He does not like failures, the general; he will not incline to reward you dear. While I am in the very best humor in the world."

He smiled to prove it. Nor do I think his complaisance altogether feigned. The temper of our host amused him.

As for friend Peyrot, he still looked dazed. I thought it was because he had not yet made up his mind what line to take; but had I viewed him with neutral eyes I might easily have deemed his bewilderment genuine.

"Perhaps we should get on better if I could understand what monsieur is driving at?" he suggested. "Monsieur's remarks about his noble father and the general-duke are interesting, but humble Jean Peyrot, who does not move in court circles, is at a loss to translate them. In other words, I have no notion what you are talking about."

"Oh, come," M. Étienne cried, "no shuffling, Peyrot. We know as well as you where you were before dawn."

"Before dawn? Marry, I was sleeping the sleep of the virtuous."

M. Étienne slipped across the room as quickly as Peyrot's self might have done, lifted up a heavy curtain hanging before an alcove, and disclosed the bed folded smooth, the pillow undisturbed. He turned with a triumphant grin on the owner, who showed all his teeth pleasantly in answer, no whit abashed.

"For all you are a count, monsieur, you have the worst manners ever came inside these walls."

M. le Comte, with no attempt at mending them, went on a tour about the room, examining with sniffing interest all its furniture, even to the dishes and tankards on the table. Peyrot, leaning against the wall by the window, regarded him steadily, with impassive face. At length M. Étienne walked over to the chest by the chimneypiece and deliberately put his hand on the key.

Instantly Peyrot's voice rang out, "Stop!" M. Étienne, turning, looked into his pistol-barrel.

My lord stood exactly as he was, bent over the chest, his fingers on the key, looking over his shoulder at the bravo with raised, protesting eyebrows and laughing mouth. But though he laughed, he stood still.

"If you make a movement I do not like, M. de Mar, I will shoot you as I would a rat. Your side is down and mine is up; I have no fear to kill you. It will be painful to me, but if necessary I shall do it."

M. Étienne sat down on the chest and smiled more amiably than ever.

"Why – have I never known you before, Peyrot?"

"One moment, monsieur." The nose of the pistol pointed around to me. "Go over there to the door, you."

I retreated, covered by the shining muzzle, to a spot that pleased him.

"Now are we more comfortable," Peyrot observed, pulling a chair over against the wall and seating him, the pistol on his knee. "Monsieur was saying?"

Monsieur crossed his legs, as if of all seats in the world he liked his present one the best. He had brought none of the airs of the noble into this business, realizing shrewdly that they would but hamper him, as lace ruffles hamper a duelist. Peyrot, treeless adventurer, living by his sharp sword and sharp wits, reverenced a count no more than a hod-carrier. His occasional mocking deference was more insulting than outright rudeness; but M. Étienne bore it unruffled. Possibly he schooled himself so to bear it, but I think rather that he felt so easily secure on the height of his gentlehood that Peyrot's impudence merely tickled him.

"I was wondering," he answered pleasantly, "how long you have dwelt in this town and I not known it. You are from Guienne, methinks."

"Carcassonne way," the other said indifferently. Then memory bringing a deep twinkle to his eye, he added: "What think you, monsieur? I was left a week-old babe on the monastery step; was reared up in holiness within its sacred walls; chorister at ten, novice at eighteen, full-fledged friar, fasting, praying, and singing misereres, exhorting dying saints and living sinners, at twenty."

"A very pretty brotherhood, you for sample."

"Nay, I am none. Else I might have stayed. But one night I took leg-bail, lived in the woods till my hair grew, and struck out for Paris. And never regretted it, neither."

He leaned his head back, his eyes fixed contemplatively on the ceiling, and burst into song, in voice as melodious as a lark's:

Piety and Grace and Gloom,
For such like guests I have no room!
Piety and Gloom and Grace,
I bang my door shut in your face!
Gloom and Grace and Piety,
I set my dog on such as ye!

Finishing his stave, he continued to beat time with his heel on the floor and to gaze upon the ceiling. But I think we could not have twitched a finger without his noting it. M. Étienne rose and leaned across the table toward him.

"M. Peyrot has made his fortune in Paris? Monsieur rolls in wealth, of course?"

Peyrot shrugged his shoulders, his eyes leaving the ceiling and making a mocking pilgrimage of the room, resting finally on his own rusty clothing.

"Do I look it?" he answered.

"Oh," said M. Étienne, slowly, as one who digests an entirely new idea, "I supposed monsieur must be as rich as a Lombard, he is so cold on the subject of turning an honest penny."

Peyrot's roving eye condescended to meet his visitor's.

"Say on," he permitted lazily.

"I offer twenty pistoles for a packet, seal unbroken, taken at dawn from the person of M. de St. Quentin's squire."

"Now you are talking sensibly," the scamp said, as if M. Étienne had been the shuffler. "That is a fair offer and demands a fair answer. Moreover, such zeal as you display deserves success. I will look about a bit this morning among my friends and see if I can get wind of your packet. I will meet you at dinner-time at the inn of the Bonne Femme."

"Dinner-time is far hence. You forget, M. Peyrot, that you are risen earlier than usual. I will go out and sit on the stair for five minutes while you consult your friends."

Peyrot grinned cheerfully.

"M. de Mar doesn't seem able to get it through his head that I know nothing whatever of this affair."

"No, I certainly don't get that through my head."

Peyrot regarded him with an air ill-used yet compassionate, such as he might in his monkish days have employed toward one who could not be convinced, for instance, of the efficacy of prayer.

"M. de Mar," quoth he, plaintively, in pity half for himself so misunderstood, half for his interlocutor so willfully blind, "I do solemnly assure you, once and for all, that I know nothing of this affair of yours. Till you so asserted, I had no knowledge that Monsieur, your honored father, had been set on, and deeply am I pained to hear it. These be evil days when such things can happen. As for your packet, I learn of it only through your word, having no more to do with this deplorable business than a babe unborn."

I declare I was almost shaken, almost thought we had wronged him. But M. Étienne gauged him otherwise.

"Your words please me," he began.

"The contemplation of virtue," the rascal droned with down-drawn lips, in pulpit tone, "is always uplifting to the spirit."

"You have boasted," M. Étienne went on, "that your side was up and mine down. Did you not reflect that soon my side may be up and yours down, you would hardly be at such pains to deny that you ever bared blade against the Duke of St. Quentin."

"I have made my declaration in the presence of two witnesses, far too honorable to falsify, that I know nothing of the attack on the duke," Peyrot repeated with apparent satisfaction. "But of course it is possible that by scouring Paris I might get on the scent of your packet. Twenty pistoles, though. That is not much."

M. Étienne stood silent, drumming tattoos on the table, not pleased with the turn of the matter, not seeing how to better it. Had we been sure of our suspicions, we would have charged him, pistol or no pistol, trusting that our quickness would prevent his shooting, or that the powder would miss fire, or that the ball would fly wide, or that we should be hit in no vital part; trusting, in short, that God was with us and would in some fashion save us. But we could not be sure that the packet was with Peyrot. What we had heard him lock in the chest might have been these very pistols that he had afterward taken out again. Three men had fled from M. de Mirabeau's alley; we had no means of knowing whether this Peyrot were he who ran as we came up, he whom I had encountered, or he who had engaged M. Étienne. And did we know, that would not tell us which of the three had stabbed and plundered Huguet. Peyrot might have the packet, or he might know who had it, or he might be in honest ignorance of its existence. If he had it, it were a crying shame to pay out honest money for what we might take by force; to buy your own goods from a thief were a sin. But supposing he had it not? If we could seize upon him, disarm him, bind him, threaten him, beat him, rack him, would he – granted he knew – reveal its whereabouts? Writ large in his face was every manner of roguery, but not one iota of cowardice. He might very well hold us baffled, hour on hour, while the papers went to Mayenne. Even should he tell, we had the business to begin again from the very beginning, with some other knave mayhap worse than this.

Plainly the game was in Peyrot's hands; we could play only to his lead.

"If you will put the packet into my hands, seal unbroken, this day at eleven, I engage to meet you with twenty pistoles," M. Étienne said.

"Twenty pistoles were a fair price for the packet. But monsieur forgets the wear and tear on my conscience incurred for him. I must be reimbursed for that."

"Conscience, quotha!"

"Certainly, monsieur. I am in my way as honest a man as you in yours. I have never been false to the hand that fed me. If, therefore, I divert to you a certain packet which of rights goes elsewhere, my sin must be made worth my while. My conscience will sting me sorely, but with the aid of a glass and a lass I may contrive to forget the pain.

Mirth, my love, and Folly dear,
Baggages, you're welcome here!

I fix the injury to my conscience at thirty pistoles, M. le Comte. Fifty in all will bring the packet to your hand."

It had been a pleasure to M. le Comte to fling a tankard in the fellow's face. But the steadfast determination to win the papers for Monsieur, and, possibly, respect for Peyrot's weapon, withheld him.

"Very well, then. In the cabaret of the Bonne Femme, at eleven. You may do as you like about appearing; I shall be there with my fifty pistoles."

"What guaranty have I that you will deal fairly with me?"

"The word of a St. Quentin."

"Sufficient, of course."

The scamp rose with a bow.

"Well, I have not the word of a gentleman to offer you, but I give you the opinion of Jean Peyrot, sometime Father Ambrosius, that he and the packet will be there. This has been a delightful call, monsieur, and I am loath to let you go. But it is time I was free to look for that packet."

M. Étienne's eyes went over to the chest.

"I wish you all success in your arduous search."

"It is like to be, in truth, a long and weary search," Peyrot sighed. "My ignorance of the perpetrators of the outrage makes my task difficult indeed. But rest assured, monsieur, that I shall question every man in Paris, if need be. I shall leave no stone unturned."

M. Étienne still pensively regarded the chest.

"If you leave no key unturned, 'twill be more to the purpose."

"You appear yet to nurse the belief that I have the packet. But as a matter of fact, monsieur, I have not."

I studied his grave face, and could not for the life of me make out whether he were lying. M. Étienne said merely:

"Come, Félix."

"You'll drink a glass before you go?" Peyrot cried hospitably, running to fill a goblet muddy with his last pouring. But M. Étienne drew back.

"Well, I don't blame you. I wouldn't drink it myself if I were a count," Peyrot said, setting the draft to his own lips. "After this noon I shall drink it no more all summer. I shall live like a king.

Kiss me, Folly; hug me, Mirth:
Life without you's nothing worth!

Monsieur, can I lend you a hat?"

I had already opened the door and was holding it for my master to pass, when Peyrot picked up from the floor and held out to him a battered and dirty toque, with its draggled feather hanging forlornly over the side. Chafed as he was, M. Étienne could not deny a laugh to the rascal's impudence.

"I cannot rob monsieur," he said.

"M. le Comte need have no scruple. I shall buy me better out of his fifty pistoles."

But M. Étienne was out in the passage, I following, banging the door after me. We went down the stair in time to Peyrot's lusty caroling:

Mirth I'll keep, though riches fly,
While Folly's sure to linger by!

"Think you we'll get the packet?" I asked.

"Aye. I think he wants his fifty pistoles. Mordieu! it's galling to let this dog set the terms."

"Monsieur," I cried, "perhaps he'll not stir out at once. I'll run home for Vigo and his men, and we'll make the rascal disgorge."

"Now are you more zealous than honest, boy."

I was silent, abashed, and he added:

"I had not been afraid to try conclusions with him, pistols or not, were I sure that he had the packet. I believe he has, yet there is the chance that, after all, in this one particular he speaks truth. I cannot take any chances; I must get those papers for Monsieur."

"Yes, we could not have done otherwise, M. Étienne. But, monsieur, will you dare go to this inn? M. le Comte is a man in jeopardy; he may not keep rendezvous of the enemy's choosing."

"I might not keep one of Lucas's choosing. Though," he added, with a smile, "natheless, I think I should. But it is not likely this fellow knows of the warrant against me. Paris is a big place; news does not travel all over town as quickly as at St. Quentin. I think friend Peyrot has more to gain by playing fair than playing false, and appointing the cabaret of the Bonne Femme has a very open, pleasing sound. Did he mean to brain me he would scarce have set that place."

"It was not Peyrot alone I meant. But monsieur is so well known. In the streets, or at the dinner-hour, someone may see you who knows Mayenne is after you."

"Oh, of that I must take my chance," he made answer, no whit troubled by the warning. "I go home now for the ransom, and I will e'en be at the pains to doff this gear for something darker."

"Monsieur," I pleaded, "why not stay at home to get your dues of sleep? Vigo will bring the gold; he and I will put the matter through."

"I ask not your advice," he cried haughtily; then with instant softening: "Nay, this is my affair, Félix. I have taken it upon myself to recover Monsieur his papers. I must carry it through myself to the very omega."

I said no more, partly because it would have done no good, partly because, in spite of the strange word, I understood how he felt.

"Perhaps you should go home and sleep," he suggested tenderly.

"Nay," cried I. "I had a cat-nap in the lane; I'm game to see it through."

"Then," he commanded, "you may stay hereabouts and watch that door. For I have some curiosity to know whether he will need to fare forth after the treasure. If he do as I guess, he will spend the next hours as you counsel me, making up arrears of sleep, and you'll not see him till a quarter or so before eleven. But whenever he comes out, follow him. Keep your safe distance and dog him if you can."

"And if I lose him?"

"Come back home. Station yourself now where he won't notice you. That arch there should serve."

We had been standing at the street corner, sheltered by a balcony over our heads from the view of Peyrot's window.

"Monsieur," I said, "I do wish you would bring Vigo back with you."

"Félix," he laughed, "you are the worst courtier I ever saw."

I crossed the street as he told me, glancing up at the third story of the house of the Gilded Shears. No watcher was visible. From the archway, which was entrance to a court of tall houses, I could well command Peyrot's door, myself in deep shadow M. Étienne nodded to me and walked off whistling, staring full in the face everyone he met.

I would fain have occupied myself as we guessed the knave Peyrot to be doing, and shut mine aching eyes in sleep. But I was sternly determined to be faithful to my trust, and though for my greater comfort – cold enough comfort it was – I sat me down on the paving-stones, yet

I kept my eyelids propped open, my eyes on Peyrot's door. I was helped in carrying out my virtuous resolve by the fact that the court was populous and my carcass in the entrance much in the way of the busy passers-by, so that full half of them swore at me, and the half of that half kicked me. The hard part was that I could not fight them because of keeping my eyes on Peyrot's door.

He delayed so long and so long that I feared with shamed misgiving I must have let him slip, when at length, on the very stroke of eleven, he sauntered forth. He was yawning prodigiously, but set off past my lair at a smart pace. I followed at goodly distance, but never once did he glance around. He led the way straight to the sign of the Bonne Femme.

I entered two minutes after him, passing from the cabaret, where my men were not, to the dining-hall, where, to my relief, they were. At two huge fireplaces savory soups bubbled, juicy rabbits simmered, fat capons roasted; the smell brought the tears to my eyes. A concourse of people was about: gentles and burghers seated at table, or passing in and out; waiters running back and forth from the fires, drawers from the cabaret. I paused to scan the throng, jostled by one and another, before I descried my master and my knave. M. Étienne, the prompter at the rendezvous, had, like a philosopher, ordered dinner, but he had deserted it now and stood with Peyrot, their backs to the company, their elbows on the deep window-ledge, their heads close together. I came up suddenly to Peyrot's side, making him jump.

"Oh, it's you, my little gentleman!" he exclaimed, smiling to show all his firm teeth, as white and even as a court beauty's. He looked in the best of humors, as was not wonderful, considering that he was engaged in fastening up in the breast of his doublet something hard and lumpy. M. Étienne held up a packet for me to see, before Peyrot's shielding body; it was tied with red cord and sealed with a spread falcon over the tiny letters, *Je reviendrai.* In the corner was written very small, *St. Q.* Smiling, he put it into the breast of his doublet.

"Monsieur," my scamp said to him with close lips that the room might not hear, "you are a gentleman. If there ever comes a day when You-know-who is down and you are up, I shall be pleased to serve you as well as I have served him."

"I hanker not for such service as you have given him," M. Étienne answered. Peyrot's eyes twinkled brighter than ever.

"I have said it. I will serve you as vigorously as I have served him. Bear me in mind, monsieur."

"Come, Félix," was all my lord's answer.

Peyrot sprang forward to detain us.

"Monsieur, will you not dine with me? Both of you, I beg. I will have every wine the cellar affords."

"No," said M. Étienne, carelessly, not deigning to anger; "but there is my dinner for you, an you like. I have paid for it, but I have other business than to eat it."

Bidding a waiter serve M. Peyrot, he walked from the room without other glance at him. A slight shade fell over the reckless, scampish face; he was a moment vexed that we scorned him. Merely vexed, I think; shamed not at all; he knew not the feel of it. Even in the brief space I watched him, as I passed to the door, his visage cleared, and he sat him down contentedly to finish M. Étienne's veal broth.

My lord paced along rapidly and gladly, on fire to be before Monsieur with the packet. But one little cloud, transient as Peyrot's, passed across his lightsome countenance.

"I would that knave were of my rank," he said. "I had not left him without slapping a glove in his face."

That Peyrot had come off scot-free put me out of patience, too, but I regretted the gold we had given him more than the wounds we had not. The money, on the contrary, troubled M. Étienne no whit; what he had never toiled for he parted with lightly.

We came to our gates and went straightway up the stairs to Monsieur's cabinet. He sprang to meet us at the door, snatching the packet from his son's eager hand.

"Well done, Étienne, my champion! An you brought me the crown of France I were not so pleased!"

The flush of joy at generous praise of good work kindled on M. Étienne's cheek; it were hard to say which of the two messieurs beamed the more delightedly on the other.

"My son, you have brought me back my honor," spoke Monsieur, more quietly, the exuberance of his delight abating, but leaving him nonetheless happy. "If you had sinned against me – which I do not admit, dear lad – it were more than made up for now."

"Ah, Monsieur, I have often asked myself of late what I was born for. Now I know it was for this morning."

"For this and many more mornings, Étienne," Monsieur made gay answer, laying a hand on his son's shoulder. "Courage, comrade. We'll have our lady yet."

He smiled at him hearteningly and turned away to his writing-table. For all his sympathy, he was, as was natural, more interested in his papers than in Mlle. de Montluc.

"I'll get this off my hands at once," he went on, with the effect of talking to himself rather than to us. "It shall go straight off to Lemaître.

You'd better go to bed, both of you. My faith, you've made a night of it!"

"Won't you take me for your messenger, Monsieur? You need a trusty one."

"A kindly offer, Étienne. But you have earned your rest. And you, true as you are, are yet not the only staunch servant I have, God be thanked. Gilles will take this straight from my hand to Lemaître's."

He had enclosed the packet in a clean wrapper, but now, a thought striking him, he took it out again.

"I'd best break off the royal seal, lest it be spied among the president's papers. I'll scratch out my initial, too. The cipher tells nothing."

"He is not likely to leave it about, Monsieur."

"No, but this time we'll provide for every chance. We'll take all the precautions ingenuity can devise or patience execute."

He crushed the seal in his fingers, and took the knife-point to scrape the wax away. It slipped and severed the cords. Of its own accord the stiff paper of the flap unfolded.

"The cipher seems as determined to show itself to me again as if I were in danger of forgetting it," Monsieur said idly. "The truth is –"

He stopped in the middle of a word, snatching up the packet, slapping it wide open, tearing it sheet from sheet. Each was absolutely blank!

XXIV

The Florentines.

M. Étienne, forgetting his manners, snatched the papers from his father's hand, turning them about and about, not able to believe his senses. A man hurled over a cliff, plunging in one moment from flowery lawns into a turbulent sea, might feel as he did.

"But the seal!" he stammered.

"The seal was genuine," Monsieur answered, startled as he. "How your fellow could have the king's signet –"

"See," M. Étienne cried, scratching at the fragments. "This is it. Dunce that I am not to have guessed it! Look, there is a layer of paper embedded in the wax. Look, he cut the seal out, smeared hot wax on the false packet, pressed in the seal, and curled the new wax over the edge. It was cleverly done; the seal is but little thicker, little larger than before. It did not look tampered with. Would you have suspected it, Monsieur?" he demanded piteously.

"I had no thought of it. But this Peyrot – it may not yet be too late –"

"I will go back," M. Étienne cried, darting to the door. But Monsieur laid forcible hands on him.

"Not you, Étienne. You were hurt yesterday; you have not closed your eyes for twenty-four hours. I don't want a dead son. I blame you not for the failure; not another man of us all would have come so near success."

"Dolt! I should have known he could not deal honestly," M. Étienne cried. "I should have known he would trick me. But I did not think to doubt the crest. I should have opened it there in the inn, but it was Lemaître's sealed packet. However, Peyrot sat down to my dinner: I can be back before he has finished his three kinds of wine."

"Stop, Étienne," Monsieur commanded. "I forbid you. You are grey with fatigue. Vigo shall go."

M. Étienne turned on him in fiery protest; then the blaze in his eyes flickered out, and he made obedient salute.

"So be it. Let him go. I am no use; I bungle everything I touch. But he may accomplish something."

He flung himself down on the bench in the corner, burying his face in his hands, weary, chagrined, disheartened. A statue-maker might have copied him for a figure of Defeat.

"Go find Vigo," Monsieur bade me, "and then get you to bed."

I obeyed both orders with all alacrity.

I too smarted, but mine was the private's disappointment, not the general's who had planned the campaign. The credit of the rescue was none of mine; no more was the blame of failure. I need not rack myself with questioning, Had I in this or that done differently, should I not have triumphed? I had done only what I was told. Yet I was part of the expedition; I could not but share the grief. If I did not wet my pillow with my tears, it was because I could not keep awake long enough. Whatever my sorrows, speedily they slipped from me.

I roused with a start from deep, dreamless sleep, and then wondered whether, after all, I had waked. Here, to be sure, was Marcel's bed, on which I had lain down; there was the high gable-window, through which the westering sun now poured. There was the wardrobe open, with Marcel's Sunday suit hanging on the peg; here were the two stools, the little image of the Virgin on the wall. But here was also something else, so out of place in the chamber of a page that I pinched myself to make sure it was real. At my elbow on the pallet lay a box of some fine foreign wood, beautifully grained by God and polished by grateful man. It was about as large as my lord's dispatch-box, bound at the edges with shining brass and having long brass hinges wrought in a design of leaves and flowers. Beside the box were set three shallow trays, lined with blue velvet, and filled full of goldsmith's work-glittering chains, linked or twisted, bracelets in the form of yellow snakes with green eyes, buckles with ivory teeth, glove-clasps thick with pearls, earrings and finger-rings with precious stones.

I stared bedazzled from the display to him who stood as showman. This was a handsome lad, seemingly no older than I, though taller, with a shock of black hair, rough and curly, and dark, smooth face, very boyish and pleasant. He was dressed well, in bourgeois fashion; yet there was about him and his apparel something, I could not tell what, unfamiliar, different from us others.

He, meeting my eye, smiled in the friendliest way, like a child, and said, in Italian:

"Good day to you, my little gentleman."

I had still the uncertain feeling that I must be in a dream, for why should an Italian jeweler be displaying his treasures to me, a penniless page? But the dream was amusing; I was in no haste to wake.

I knew my Italian well enough, for Monsieur's confessor, the Father Francesco, who had followed him into exile, was Florentine; and as he always spoke his own tongue to Monsieur, and I was always at the duke's heels, I picked up a deal of it. After Monsieur's going, the father, already a victim, poor man, to the falling-sickness, of which he died, stayed behind with us, and I found a pricking pleasure in talking with him in the speech he loved, of Monsieur's Roman journey, of his exploits in the war of the Three Henrys. Therefore the words came easily to my lips to answer this lad from over the Alps:

"I give you good day, friend."

He looked somewhat surprised and more than pleased, breaking at once into voluble speech:

"The best of greetings to you, young sir. Now, what can I sell you this fine day? I have not been half a week in this big city of yours, yet already I have but one boxful of trinkets left. They are noble, open-handed customers, these gallants of Paris. I have not to show them my wares twice, I can tell you. They know what key will unlock their fair mistresses' hearts. And now, what can I sell you, my little gentleman, to buy your sweetheart's kisses?"

"Nay, I have no sweetheart," I said, "and if I had, she would not wear these gauds."

"She would if she could get them, then," he retorted. "Now, let me give you a bit of advice, my friend, for I see you are but young: buy this gold chain of me, or this ring with this little dove on it, – see, how cunningly wrought, – and you'll not lack long for a sweetheart."

His words huffed me a bit, for he spoke as if he were vastly my senior.

"I want no sweetheart," I returned with dignity, "to be bought with gold."

"Nay," he cried quickly, "but when your own valor and prowess have inflamed her with passion, you should be willing to reward her devotion and set at rest her suspense by a suitable gift."

I looked at him uneasily, for I had a suspicion that he might be making fun of me. But his countenance was as guileless as a kitten's.

"Well, I tell you again I have no sweetheart and I want no sweetheart," I said; "I have no time to bother with girls."

At once he abandoned the subject, seeing that he was making naught by it.

"The messer is very much occupied?" he asked with exceeding deference. "The messer has no leisure for trifling in boudoirs; he is occupied with great matters? Oh, that can I well believe, and I cry the messer's pardon. For when the mind is taken up with affairs of state, it is distasteful to listen even for a moment to light talk of maids and jewels."

Again I eyed him challengingly; but he, with face utterly unconscious, was sorting over his treasures. I made up my mind his queer talk was but the outlandish way of a foreigner. He looked at me again, serious and respectful.

"The messer must often be engaged in great risks, in perilous encounters. Is it not so? Then he will do well to carry ever over his heart the sacred image of our Lord."

He held up to my inspection a silver rosary from which depended a crucifix of ivory, the sad image of the dying Christ carved upon it. Even in Monsieur's chapel, even in the church at St. Quentin, was nothing so masterfully wrought as this figurine to be held in the palm of the hand. The tears started in my eyes to look at it, and I crossed myself in reverence. I bethought me how I had trampled on my crucifix; the stranger all unwittingly had struck a bull's-eye. I had committed grave offence against God, but perhaps if, putting gewgaws aside, I should give my all for this cross, he would call the account even. I knew nothing of the value of a carving such as this, but I remembered I was not moneyless, and I said, albeit somewhat shyly:

"I cannot take the rosary. But I should like well the crucifix. But then, I have only ten pistoles."

"Ten pistoles!" he repeated contemptuously. "Corpo di Bacco! The workmanship alone is worth twenty." Then, viewing my fallen visage, he added: "However, I have received fair treatment in this house, beshrew me but I have! I have made good sales to your young count. What sort of master is he, this M. le Comte de Mar?"

"Oh, there's nobody like him," I answered, "except, of course, M. le Duc."

"Ah, then you have two masters?" he inquired curiously, yet with a certain careless air. It struck me suddenly, overwhelmingly, that he was a spy, come here under the guise of an honest tradesman. But he should gain nothing from me.

"This is the house of the Duke of St. Quentin," I said. "Surely you could not come in at the gate without discovering that?"

"He is a very grand seigneur, then, this duke?"

"Assuredly," I replied cautiously.

"More of a man than the Comte de Mar?"

I would have told him to mind his own business, had it not been for my hopes of the crucifix. If he planned to sell it to me cheap, thereby hoping to gain information, marry, I saw no reason why I should not buy it at his price – and withhold the information. So I made civil answer:

"They are both as gallant gentlemen as any living. About this cross, now –"

"Oh, yes," he answered at once, accepting with willingness – well feigned, I thought – the change of topic. "You can give me ten pistoles, say you? 'Tis making you a present of the treasure. Yet, since I have received good treatment at the hands of your master, I will e'en give it to you. You shall have your cross."

With suspicions now at point of certainty, I drew out my pouch from under my pillow, and counted into his hand the ten pieces which were my store. My rosary I drew out likewise; I had broken it when I shattered the cross, but one of the inn-maids had tied it together for me with a thread, and it served very well. The Italian unhooked the delicate carving from the silver chain and hung it on my wooden one, which I threw over my neck, vastly pleased with my new possession. Marcel's Virgin was a botch compared with it. I remembered that mademoiselle, who had given me half my wealth, the half that won me the rest, had bidden me buy something in the marts of Paris; and I told myself with pride that she could not fail to hold me high did she know how, passing by all vanities, I had spent my whole store for a holy image. Few boys of my age would be capable of the like. Certes, I had done piously, and should now take a further pious joy, my purchase safe on my neck, in thwarting the wiles of this serpent. I would play with him awhile, tease and baffle him, before handing him over in triumph to Vigo.

Sure enough, he began as I had expected:

"This M. de Mar downstairs, he is a very good master, I suppose?"

"Yes," I said, without enthusiasm.

"He has always treated you well?"

I bethought myself of the trick I had played successfully with the officer of the burgess guard.

"Why, yes, I suppose so. I have only known him two days."

"But you have known him well? You have seen much of him?" he demanded with ill-concealed eagerness.

"But not so very much," I made tepid answer. "I have not been with him all the time of these two days. I have seen really very little of him."

"And you know not whether or no he be a good master?"

"Oh, pretty good. So-so."

He sprang forward to deal me a stinging box on the ear.

I was out of bed at one bound, scattering the trinkets in a golden rain and rushing for him. He retreated before me. It was to save his jewels, but I, fool that I was, thought it pure fear of me. I dashed at him, all headlong confidence; the next I knew he had somehow twisted his foot between mine, and tripped me before I could grapple. Never was wight more confounded to find himself on the floor.

I was starting up again unhurt when I saw something that made me to forget my purpose. I sat still where I was, with dropped jaw and bulging eyes. For his hair, that had been black, was golden.

"Ventre bleu!" I said.

"And so you know not you little villain, whether you have a good master or not?"

"But how was I to dream it was monsieur?" I cried, confounded. "I knew there was something queer about him – about you, I mean – about the person I took you for, that is. I knew there was something wrong about you – that is to say, I mean, I thought there was; I mean I knew he wasn't what he seemed – you were not. And Peyrot fooled us, and I didn't want to be fooled again."

"Then I am a good master?" he demanded truculently, advancing upon me.

I put up my hands to my ears.

"The best, monsieur. And monsieur wrestled well, too."

"I can't prove that by you, Félix," he retorted, and laughed in my nettled face. "Well, if you've not trampled on my jewels, I forgive your contumacy."

If I had, my bare toes had done them no harm. I crawled about the floor, gathering them all up and putting them on the bed, where I presently sat down myself to stare at him, trying to realize him for M. le Comte. He had seated himself, too, and was dusting his trampled wig and clapping it on again.

He had shaved off his mustaches and the tuft on his chin, and the whole look of him was changed. A year had gone for every stroke of the razor; he seemed such a boy, so particularly guileless! He had stained his face so well that it looked for all the world as though the Southern sun had done it for him; his eyebrows and, lashes were dark by nature. His wig came much lower over his forehead than did his own hair, and altered the upper part of his face as much as the shaving of the lower. Only his eyes were the same. He had had his back to the window at first, and I had not noted them; but now that he had turned, his eyes gleamed so light as to be fairly startling in his dark face – like stars in a stormy sky.

"Well, then, how do you like me?"

"Monsieur confounds me. It's witchery. I cannot get used to him."

"That's as I would have it," he returned, coming over to the bedside to arrange his treasures. "For if I look new to you, I think I may look so to the Hôtel de Lorraine."

"Monsieur goes to the Hôtel de Lorraine as a jeweler?" I cried, enlightened.

"Aye. And if the ladies do not crowd about me –" he broke off with a gesture, and put his trays back in his box.

"Well, I wondered, monsieur. I wondered if we were going to sell ornaments to Peyrot."

He locked the box and proceeded solemnly and thoroughly to damn Peyrot. He cursed him waking, cursed him sleeping; cursed him eating, cursed him drinking; cursed him walking, riding, sitting; cursed him summer, cursed him winter; cursed him young, cursed him old; living, dying, and dead. I inferred that the packet had not been recovered.

"No, pardieu! Vigo went straight on horseback to the Bonne Femme, but Peyrot had vanished. So he galloped round to the Rue Tournelles, whither he had sent two of our men before him, but the bird was flown.

He had been home half an hour before, – he left the inn just after us, – had paid his arrears of rent, surrendered his key, and taken away his chest, with all his worldly goods in it, on the shoulders of two porters, bound for parts unknown. Gilles is scouring Paris for him. Mordieu, I wish him luck!"

His face betokened little hope of Gilles. We both kept chagrined silence.

"And we thought him sleeping!" presently cried he.

"Well," he added, rising, "that milk's spilt; no use crying over it. Plan a better venture; that's the only course. Monsieur is gone back to St. Denis to report to the king. Marry, he makes as little of these gates as if he were a tennis-ball and they the net. Time was when he thought he must plan and prepare, and know the captain of the watch, and go masked at midnight. He has got bravely over that now; he bounces in and out as easily as kiss my hand. I pray he may not try it once too often."

"Mayenne dare not touch him."

"What Mayenne may dare is not good betting. Monsieur thinks he dares not. Monsieur has come through so many perils of late, he is happily convinced he bears a charmed life. Félix, do you come with me to the Hôtel de Lorraine?"

"Ah, monsieur!" I cried, bethinking myself that I had forgotten to dress.

"Nay, you need not don these clothes," he interposed, with a look of wickedness which I could not interpret. "Wait; I'm back anon."

He darted out of the room, to return speedily with an armful of apparel, which he threw on the bed.

"Monsieur," I gasped in horror, "it's woman's gear!"

"Verily."

"Monsieur! you cannot mean me to wear this!"

"I mean it precisely."

"Monsieur!"

"Why, look you, Félix," he laughed, "how else am I to take you? You were at pains to make yourself conspicuous in M. de Mayenne's salon; they will recognize you as quickly as me."

"Oh, monsieur, put me in a wig, in cap and bells, an you like! I will be monsieur's clown, anything, only not this!"

"I never heard of a jeweler accompanied by his clown. Nor have I any party-color in my armoires. But since I have exerted myself to borrow this toggery, – and a fine, big lass is the owner, so I think it will fit, – you must wear it."

I was like to burst with mortification; I stood there in dumb, agonized appeal.

"Oh, well, then you need not go at all. If you go, you go as Félicie. But you may stay at home, if it likes you better."

That settled me. I would have gone in my grave-clothes sooner than not go at all, and belike he knew it. I began arraying myself sullenly and clumsily in the murrain petticoats.

There was a full kirtle of grey wool, falling to my ankles, and a white apron. There was a white blouse with a wide, turned-back collar, and a scarlet bodice, laced with black cords over a green tongue. I was soon in such a desperate tangle over these divers garments, so utterly muddled as to which to put on first, and which side forward, and which end up, and where and how by the grace of God to fasten them, that M. Étienne, with roars of laughter, came unsteadily to my aid. He insisted on stuffing the whole of my jerkin under my blouse to give my figure the proper curves, and to make me a waist he drew the lacing-cords till I was like to suffocate. His mirth had by this time got me to laughing so that every time he pulled me in, a fit of merriment would jerk the laces from his fingers before he could tie them. This happened once and again, and the more it happened the more we laughed and the less he could dress me. I ached in every rib, and the tears were running down his cheeks, washing little clean channels in the stain.

"Félix, this will never do," he gasped when at length he could speak. "Never after a carouse have I been so maudlin. Compose yourself, for the love of Heaven. Think of something serious; think of me! Think of Peyrot, think of Mayenne, think of Lucas. Think of what will happen to us now if Mayenne know us for ourselves."

"Enough, monsieur," I said. "I am sobered."

But even now that I held still we could not draw the last holes in the bodice-point nearly together.

"Nay, monsieur, I can never wear it like this," I panted, when he had tied it as tight as he could. "I shall die, or I shall burst the seams." He had perforce to give me more room; he pulled the apron higher to cover gaps, and fastened a bunch of keys and a pocket at my waist. He set a brown wig on my head, nearly covered by a black mortier, with its wide scarf hanging down my back.

"Hang me, but you make a fine, strapping grisette," he cried, proud of me as if I were a picture, he the painter. "Félix, you've no notion how handsome you look. Dame! you defrauded the world when you contrived to be born a boy."

"I thank my stars I was born a boy," I declared. "I wouldn't get into this toggery for anyone else on earth. I tell monsieur that, flat."

"You must change your shoes," he cried eagerly. "Your hobnails spoil all."

I put one of his gossip's shoes on the floor beside my foot.

"Now, monsieur, I ask you, how am I to get into that?"

"Shall I fetch you Vigo's?" he grinned.

"No, Constant's," I said instantly, thinking how it would make him writhe to lend them.

"Constant's best," he promised, disappearing. It was as good as a play to see my lord running errands for me. Perhaps he forgot, after a month in the Rue Coupejarrets, that such things as pages existed; or, more likely, he did not care to take the household into his confidence. He was back soon, with a pair of scarlet hose, and shoes of red morocco, the gayest affairs you ever saw. Also he brought a hand-mirror, for me to look on my beauty.

"Nay, monsieur," I said with a sulk that started anew his laughter. "I'll not take it; I want not to see myself. But monsieur will do well to examine his own countenance."

"Pardieu! I should say so," he cried. "I must e'en go repair myself; and you, Félix, – Félicie, – must be fed."

I was in truth as hollow as a drum, yet I cried out that I had rather starve than venture into the kitchen.

"You flatter yourself," he retorted. "You'd not be known. Old Jumel will give you the pick of the larder for a kiss," he roared in my sullen face, and added, relenting: "Well, then, I will send one of the lackeys up with a salver. The lazy beggars have naught else to do."

I bolted the door after him, and when the man brought my tray, bade him set it down outside. He informed me through the panels that he would go drown himself before he would be content to lie slugabed the livelong day while his betters waited on him. I trembled for fear in his virtuous scorn he should take his fardel away again. But he had had his orders. When, after listening to his footsteps descending the stairs, I reached out a cautious arm, the tray was on the floor. The generous meat and wine put new heart into me; by the time my lord returned I was eager for the enterprise.

"Have you finished?" he demanded. "Faith, I see you have. Then let us start; it grows late. The shadows, like good Mussulmans, are stretching to the east. I must catch the ladies in their chambers before supper. Come, we'll take the box between us."

"Why, monsieur, I carry that on my shoulders."

"What, my lass, on your dainty shoulders? Nay, 'twould make the townsfolk stare."

I gnawed my lip in silence; he exclaimed:

"Now, never have I seen a maid fresh from the convent blush so prettily. I'd give my right hand to walk you out past the guardroom."

I shrank as a snail when you touch its horns. He cried:

"Marry, but I will, though!"

Now I, unlike Sir Snail, had no snug little fortress to take refuge in; I might writhe, but I could not defend myself.

"As you will, monsieur," I said, setting my teeth hard.

"Nay, I dare not. Those fellows would follow us laughing to the doors of Lorraine House itself. I've told none of this prank; I have even contrived to send all the lackeys out of doors on fools' errands. We'll sneak out like thieves by the postern. Come, tread your wariest."

On tiptoe, with the caution of malefactors, we crept from stair to stair, giggling under our breath like the callow lad and saucy lass we looked to be. We won in safety to the postern, and came out to face the terrible eye of the world.

XXV

A double masquerade.

"Félix, we are speaking in our own tongue. It is such lapses as these bring men to the gallows. Italian from this word, my girl."

"Monsieur, I have no notion how to bear myself, what to say," I answered uneasily.

"Say as little as you can. For, I confess, your voice and your hands give me pause; otherwise I would take you anywhere for a lass. Your part must be the shy maiden. My faith, you look the rôle; your cheeks are poppies! You will follow docile at my heels while I tell lies for two. I have the hope that the ladies will heed me and my jewels more than you."

"Monsieur, could we not go safelier at night?"

"I have thought of that. But at night the household gathers in the salon; we should run the gantlet of a hundred looks and tongues. While now, if we have luck, we may win to mademoiselle's own chamber –" He broke off abruptly, and walked along in a daydream.

"Well," he resumed presently, coming back to the needs of the moment, "let us know our names and station. I am Giovanni Rossini, son of the famous goldsmith of Florence; you, Giulietta, my sister. We came to Paris in the legate's train, trade being dull at home, the gentry having fled to the hills for the hot month. Of course you've never set foot out of France, Fé – Giulietta?"

"Never out of St. Quentin till I came hither. But Father Francesco has talked to me much of his city of Florence."

"Good; you can then make shift to answer a question or two if put to it. Your Italian, I swear, is of excellent quality. You speak French like the Picard you are, but Italian like a gentleman – that is to say, like a lady."

"Monsieur," I bemoaned miserably, "I shall never come through it alive, never in the world. They will know me in the flick of an eye for a boy; I know they will. Why, the folk we are passing can see something wrong; they all are staring at me."

"Of course they stare," he answered tranquilly. "I should think some wrong if they did not. Can your modesty never understand, my Giulietta, what a pretty lass you are?"

He fell to laughing at my discomfort, and thus, he full of gay confidence, I full of misgiving, we came before the doors of the Hôtel de Lorraine.

"Courage," he whispered to me. "Courage will conquer the devil himself. Put a good face on it and take the plunge." The next moment he was in the archway, deluging the sentry with his rapid Italian.

"Nom d'un chien! What's all this? What are you after?" the man shouted at us, to make us understand the better. "Haven't you a word of honest French in your head?"

M. Étienne, tapping his box, very brokenly, very laboriously stammered forth something about jewels for the ladies.

"Get in with you, then."

We were not slow to obey.

The courtyard was deserted, nor did we see anyone in the windows of the house, against which the afternoon sun struck hotly. To keep out his unwelcome rays, the house door was pushed almost shut. We paused a moment on the step, to listen to the voices of gossiping lackeys within, and then M. Étienne boldly knocked.

There was a scurrying in the hall, as if half a dozen idlers were plunging into their doublets and running to their places. Then my good friend Pierre opened the door. In the row of underlings at his back I recognized the two who had taken part in my flogging. The cold sweat broke out upon me lest they in their turn should know me.

M. Étienne looked from one to another with the childlike smile of his bare lips, demanding if any here spoke Italian.

"I," answered Pierre himself. "Now, what may your errand be?"

"Oh, it's soon told," M. Étienne cried volubly, as one delighted to find himself understood. "I am a jeweler from Florence; I am selling my wares in your great houses. I have but just sold a necklace to the Duchesse de Joyeuse; I crave permission to show my trinkets to the fair ladies here. But take me up to them, and they'll not make you repent it."

"Go tell madame," Pierre bade one of his men, and turning again to us gave us kindly permission to set down our burden and wait.

For incredible good luck, the heavy hangings were drawn over the sunny windows, making a soft twilight in the room. I sidled over to a bench in the far corner and was feeling almost safe, when Pierre – beshrew him! – called attention to me.

"Now, that is a heavy box for a maid to help lug. Do you make the lasses do porters' work, you Florentines?"

"But I am a stranger here," M. Étienne explained. "Did I hire a porter, how am I to tell an honest one? Belike he might run off with all my treasures, and where is poor Giovanni then? Besides, it were cruel to leave my little sister in our lodging, not a soul to speak to, the long day through. There is none where we lodge knows Italian, as you do so like an angel, Sir Master of the Household."

Now, Pierre was no more maître d'hôtel than I was, but that did not dampen his pleasure to be called so. He sat down on the bench by M. Étienne.

"How came you two to be in Paris?" he asked.

My lord proceeded to tell him I know not what glib and convincing farrago, with every excellence, I made no doubt, of accent and gesture. But I could not listen; I had affairs of my own by this time. The lackeys had come up close round me, more interested in me than in my brother, and the same Jean who had held me for my beating, who had wanted my coat stripped off me that I might be whacked to bleed, now said:

"I'll warrant you're hot and tired and thirsty, mademoiselle, for all you look as fresh as cress. Will you drink a cup of wine if I fetch it?"

I had kept my eyes on the ground from the first moment of encounter, in mortal dread to look these men in the face; but now, gaining courage,

I raised my glance and smiled at him bashfully, and faltered that I did not understand.

He understood the sense, if not the words, of my answer, and repeated his offer, slowly, loudly. I strove to look as blank as the wall, and shook my head gently and helplessly, and turned an inquiring gaze to the others, as if beseeching them to interpret. One of the fellows clapped Jean on the shoulder with a roar of laughter.

"A fall, a fall!" he shouted. "Here's the all-conquering Jean Marchand tripped up for once. He thinks nothing that wears petticoats can withstand him, but here's a maid that hasn't a word to throw at him."

"Pshaw! she doesn't understand me," Jean returned, undaunted, and promptly pointed a finger at my mouth and then raised his fist to his own, with sucks and gulps. I allowed myself to comprehend then. I smiled in as coquettish a fashion as I could contrive, and glanced on the ground, and slowly looked up again and nodded.

The men burst into loud applause.

"Good old Jean! Jean wins. Well played, Jean! Vive Jean!"

Jean, flushed with triumph, ran off on his errand, while I thought of Margot, the steward's daughter, at home, and tried to recollect every air and grace I had ever seen her flaunt before us lads. It was not bad fun, this. I hid my hands under my apron and spoke not at all, but sighed and smiled and blushed under their stares like any fine lady. Once in one's life, for one hour, it is rather amusing to be a girl. But that is quite long enough, say I.

Jean came again directly with a great silver tankard.

"Burgundy, pardieu!" cried one of his mates, sticking his nose into the pot as it passed him, "and full! Ciel, you must think your lass has a head."

"Oh, I shall drink with her," Jean answered.

I put out my hand for the tankard, running the risk of my big paw's betraying me, resolved that he should not drink with me of that draft, when of a sudden he leaned over to snatch a kiss. I dodged him, more frightened than the shyest maid. Though in this half-light I might perfectly look a girl, I could not believe I should kiss like one. In a panic, I fled from Jean to my master's side.

M. Étienne, wheeling about, came near to laughing out in my face, when he remembered his part and played it with a zeal that was like to undo us. He sprang to his feet, drawing his dagger.

"Who insults my sister?" he shouted. "Who is the dog does this!"

They were on him, wrenching the knife from his hand, wrenching his lame arm at the same time so painfully that he gasped. I was scared chill; I knew if they mishandled him they would brush the wig off.

"Mind your manners, sirrah!" Jean cried.

Monsieur's ardor vanished; a gentle, appealing smile spread over his face.

"I cry your pardon, sir," he said to Jean; then turning to Pierre, "This messer does not understand me. But tell him, I beg you, I crave his good pardon. I was but angered for a moment that any should think to touch my little sister. I meant no harm."

"Nor he," Pierre retorted. "A kiss, forsooth! What do you expect with a handsome lass like that? If you will take her about –"

"Madame says the jeweler fellow is to come up," our messenger announced, returning.

My lord besought Pierre:

"My knife? I may have my knife? By the beard of St. Peter, I swear to you, I meant no harm with it. I drew it in jest."

Now, this, which was the sole true statement he had made since our arrival, was the only one Pierre did not quite believe. He took the knife from Jean, but he hesitated to hand it over to its owner.

"No," he said; "you were angry enough. I know your Italian temper. I'm thinking I'll keep this little toy of yours till you come down."

"Very well, Sir Majordomo," M. Étienne rejoined indifferently, "so be it you give it to me when I go." He grasped the handle of the box, and we followed our guide up the stair, my master offering me the comforting assurance:

"It really matters not in the least, for if we be caught the dagger's not yet forged can save us."

We were ushered into a large, fair chamber hung with arras, the carpet under our feet deep and soft as moss. At one side stood the bed, raised on its dais; opposite were the windows, the dressing-table between them, covered with scent-bottles and boxes, brushes and combs, very glittering and grand. Fluttering about the room were some half-dozen fine dames and demoiselles, brave in silks and jewels. Among them I was quick to recognize Mme. de Mayenne, and I thought I knew vaguely one or two other faces as those I had seen before about her. I started presently to discover the little Mlle. de Tavanne: that night she had worn sky-color and now she wore rose, but there was no mistaking her saucy face.

We set our box on a table, as the duchess bade us, and I helped M. Étienne to lay out its contents, which done, I retired to the background, well content to leave the brunt of the business to him. It was as he prophesied: they paid me no heed whatever. He was smoothly launched on the third relating of his tale; I trow by this time he almost believed it himself. Certes, he never faltered, but rattled on as if he had two tongues, telling in confidential tone of our father and mother, our little brothers and sisters at home in Florence; our journey with the legate, his kindness and care of us (I hoped that dignitary would not walk in just now to pay his respects to madame la générale); of our arrival in Paris, and our wonder and delight at the city's grandeur, the like of which was not to be found in Italy; and, last, but not least, he had much to say, with an innocent, wide-eyed gravity, in praise of the ladies of Paris, so beautiful, so witty, so generous! They were all crowding around him, calling him pretty boy, laughing at his compliments, handling and exclaiming over his trinkets, trying the effect of a buckle or a bracelet, preening and cooing like bright-breasted pigeons about the corn-thrower. It was as pretty a sight as ever I beheld, but it was not to smile at such that we had risked our heads. Of Mlle. de Montluc there was no sign.

No one was marking me, and I wondered if I might not slip out unseen and make my way to mademoiselle's chamber. I knew she lodged on this story, near the back of the house, in a room overlooking the little street and having a turret-window. But I was somewhat doubtful of my skill to find it through the winding corridors of a great palace. I was more than likely to meet someone who would question my purpose, and what answer could I make? I scarce dared say I was seeking mademoiselle. I am not ready at explanations, like M. le Comte.

Yet here were the golden moments flying and our cause no further advanced. Should I leave it all to M. Étienne, trusting that when he had made his sales here he would be permitted to seek out the other ladies of the house? Or should I strive to aid him? Could I win in safety to mademoiselle's chamber, what a feat!

It so irked me to be doing nothing that I was on the very point of gingerly disappearing when one of the ladies, she with the yellow curls, the prettiest of them all, turned suddenly from the group, calling clearly:

"Lorance!"

Our hearts stood still – mine did, and I can vouch for his – as the heavy window-curtain swayed aside and she came forth.

She came listlessly. Her hair sweeping against her cheek was ebony on snow, so white she was; while under her blue eyes were dark rings, like the smears of an inky finger. M. Étienne let fall the bracelet he was holding, staring at her oblivious of aught else, his brows knotted in distress, his face afire with love and sympathy. He made a step forward; I thought him about to catch her in his arms, when he recollected himself and dropped on his knees to grope for the fallen trinket.

"You wanted me, madame?" she asked Mme. de Mayenne.

"No," said the duchess, with a tartness of voice she seemed to reserve for Mlle. de Montluc; "'twas Mme. de Montpensier."

"It was I," the fair-haired beauty answered in the same breath. "I want you to stop moping over there in the corner. Come look at these baubles and see if they cannot bring a sparkle to your eye. Fie, Lorance! The having too many lovers is nothing to cry about. It is an affliction many and many a lady would give her ears to undergo."

"Take heart o' grace, Lorance!" cried Mlle. de Tavanne. "If you go on looking as you look today, you'll not long be troubled by lovers."

She made no answer to either, but stood there passively till it might be their pleasure to have done with her, with a patient weariness that it wrung the heart to see.

"Here's a chain would become you vastly, Lorance," Mme. de Montpensier went on, friendlily enough, in her brisk and careless voice. "Let me try it on your neck. You can easily coax Paul or someone to buy it for you."

She fumbled over the clasp. M. Étienne, with a "Permit me, madame," took it boldly from her hand and hooked it himself about mademoiselle's neck. He delayed longer than he need over the fastening of it, looking with burning intentness straight into her face. She lifted her eyes to his with a quick frown of displeasure, drawing herself back; then all at once the color waved across her face like the dawn flush over a grey sky. She blushed to her very hair, to her very ruff. Then the red vanished as quickly as it had come; she clutched at her bosom, on the verge of a swoon.

He threw out his arms to catch her. Instantly she stepped aside, and, turning with a little unsteady laugh to the lady at whose elbow she found herself, asked:

"Does it become me, madame?"

The little scene had passed so quickly that it seemed none had marked it. Mademoiselle had stood a little out of the group, monsieur with his back to it, and the ladies were busy over the jewels. She whom mademoiselle had addressed, a big-nosed, loud-voiced lady, older than any of the others, answered her bluntly:

"You look a shade too green-faced today, mademoiselle, for anything to become you."

"What can you expect, Mme. de Brie?" Mlle. Blanche promptly demanded. "Mlle. de Montluc is weary and worn from her vigils at your son's bedside."

Mme. de Montpensier had the temerity to laugh; but for the rest, a sort of little groan ran through the company. Mme. de Mayenne bade sharply, "Peace, Blanche!" Mme. de Brie, red with anger, flamed out on her and Mlle. de Montluc equally:

"You impudent minxes! 'Tis enough that one of you should bring my son to his death, without the other making a mock of it."

"He's not dying," began the irrepressible Blanche de Tavanne, her eyes twinkling with mischief; but whatever naughty answer was on her tongue, our mademoiselle's deeper voice overbore her:

"I am guiltless of the charge, madame. It was through no wish of mine that your son, with half the guard at his back, set on one wounded man."

"I'll warrant it was not," muttered Mlle. Blanche.

"Mar has turned traitor, and deserves nothing so well as to be spitted in the dark," Mme. de Brie cried out.

Mademoiselle waited an instant, with flashing eyes meeting madame's. She had spoken hotly before, but now, in the face of the other's passion, she held herself steady.

"Your charge is as false, madame, as your wish is cruel. Do you go to vespers and come home to say such things? M. de Mar is no traitor; he was never pledged to us, and may go over to Navarre when he will."

It was quietly spoken, but the blue lightning of her eyes was too much for Mme. de Brie. She opened her mouth to retort, faltered, dropped her eyes, and finally turned away, yet seething, to feign interest in the trinkets. It was a rout.

"Then you are the traitor, Lorance," chimed the silvery tones of Mme. de Montpensier. "It is not denied that M. de Mar has gone over to the enemy; therefore are you the traitor to have intercourse with him."

She spoke without heat, without any appearance of ill feeling. Hers was merely the desire, for the fun of it, to keep the flurry going. But mademoiselle answered seriously, with the fleetingest glance at M. le Comte, where he, forgetting he knew no French, feasted his eyes recklessly on her, pitying, applauding, adoring her. I went softly around the group to pull his sleeve; we were lost if any turned to see him.

"Madame," mademoiselle addressed her cousin of Montpensier, speaking particularly clearly and distinctly, "I mean ever to be loyal to my house. I came here a penniless orphan to the care of my kinsman Mayenne; and he has always been to me generous and loving –"

"If not madame," murmured Mile. Blanche to herself.

"– as I in my turn have been loving and obedient. It was only two nights ago he told me M. de Mar must be as dead to me. Since then I have held no intercourse with him. Last night he came under my window; I was not in my chamber, as you know. I knew naught of the affair till M. de Brie was brought in bleeding. It was not by my will M. de Mar came here – it was a misery to me. I sent him word by his boy that other night to leave Paris; I implored him to leave Paris. If, instead, he comes here, he racks my heart. It is no joy to me, no triumph to me, but a bitter distress, that any honest gentleman should risk his life in a vain and empty quest. M. de Mar must go his ways, as I must go mine. Should he ever make attempt to reach me again, and could I speak to him, I should tell him just what I have said now to you."

I pressed monsieur's hand in the endeavor to bring him back to sense; he seemed about to cry out on her. But mademoiselle's earnestness had drawn all eyes.

"Pshaw, Lorance! banish these tragedy airs!" Mme. de Montpensier rejoined, her lightness little touched. A wounded bird falls by the rippling water, but the ripples tinkle on. "M. de Mar is not likely ever to venture here again; he had too warm a welcome last night. My faith, he may be dead by this time – dead to all as well as to you. After he vanished into Ferou's house, no one seems to know what happened. Has Charles told you, my sister?"

"Ferou gave him up, of course," Mme. de Mayenne answered. "Monsieur has done what seemed to him proper."

"You are darkly mysterious, sister."

Mme. de Mayenne raised her eyebrows and smiled, as one solemnly pledged to say no more. She could not, indeed, say more, knowing nothing whatever about it. Our mademoiselle spoke in a low voice, looking straight before her:

"If Heaven willed that he escaped last night, I pray he may leave the city. I pray he may never try to see me more. I pray he may depart instantly – at once."

"I pray your prayers may be answered, so be it we hear no more of him," Mme. de Montpensier retorted, tired of the subject she herself had started. "He was never tedious himself, M. de Mar, but all this solemn prating about him is duller than a sermon." She raised a dainty hand behind which to yawn audibly. "Come, mesdames, let us get back to our purchases. Ma foi! it's lucky these jeweler folk know no French."

M. Étienne was himself again, all smiles and quick pleasantries. I slipped off to my post in the background, trying to get out of the eye of Mlle. de Tavanne, who had been staring at me the last five minutes in a way that made my goose-flesh rise, so suspicious, so probing, was it. On my retreat she did indeed move her gaze from me, but only to watch M. le Comte as a hound watches a thicket. It was a miracle that none had pounced on him before, so reckless had he been. I perceived with sickening certainty that Mlle. de Tavanne had guessed something amiss. She fairly bristled with suspicion, with knowledge. I waited from breathless moment to moment for announcement. There was nothing to be done; she held us in the hollow of her hand. We could not flee, we could not fight. We could do nothing but wait quietly till she spoke, and then submit quietly to arrest; later, most like, to death.

Minute followed minute, and still she did not speak. Hope flowed back to me again; perhaps, after all, we might escape. I wondered how high were the windows from the ground.

As I stole across the room to see, Mlle. de Tavanne detached herself from the group and glided unnoticed out of the door.

It was thirty feet to the stones below – sure death that way. But she had given us a respite; something might yet be done. I seized M. Étienne's arm in a grip that should tell him how serious was our pass. Remembering, for a marvel, my foreign tongue, I bespoke him:

"Brother, it grows late. We must go. It will soon be dark. We must go now – now!"

He turned on me with an impatient frown, but before he could answer, Mme. de Montpensier cried, with a laugh:

"And do you fear the dark, wench? Marry, you look as if you could take care of yourself."

"Nay, madame," I protested, "but the box. Come, Giovanni. If we linger, we may be robbed in the dark streets."

"Why, my sister, where are your manners?" he retorted, striving to shake me off. "The ladies have not yet dismissed me."

"We shall be robbed of the box," I persisted; "and the night air is bad for your health, my Nino. If you stay longer you will have trouble in the throat."

He looked at me hard. I tried to make my eyes tell him that my fear was no vague one of the streets, that his throat was in peril here and now. He understood; he cried with merry laughter to Mme. de Montpensier:

"Pray excuse her lack of manners, duchessa. I know what moves the maid. I must tell you that in the house where we lodge dwells also a beautiful young captain – beautiful as the day. It's little of his time he spends at home, but we have observed that he comes every evening to array himself grandly for supper at someone's palace. We count our day lost an we cannot meet him, by accident, on the stairs."

They all laughed. I, with my cheeks burning like any silly maid's, set to work to put up our scattered wares. But despair weighed me down; if we had to remember ceremony we were lost. The ladies were protesting, declaring they had not made their bargains, and monsieur was smirking and bowing, as if he had the whole night before him. Our one chance was to bolt; to charge past the sentry and flee as from the devil. I pulled monsieur's arm again, and muttered in his ear:

"She knows us; she's gone to tell. We must run for it."

At this moment there arose from down the corridor piercing shriek on shriek, the howls of a young child frantic with rage and terror. At the same time sounded other different cries, wild, outlandish chattering.

"The baby! It's Toto! Oh, ciel!" Mme. de Mayenne gasped. "Help, mesdames!" She rushed from the room, Mme. de Montpensier at her heels, all the rest following after.

All, that is, but one. Mlle. de Montluc started as the rest, but at the threshold paused to let them pass. She flung the door to behind them, and ran back to monsieur, her face drawn with terror, her hand outstretched.

"Monsieur, monsieur!" she panted. "Go! you must go!"

He seized her hand in both of his.

"O Lorance! Lorance!"

She laid her left hand on his for emphasis.

"Go! go! An you love me, go!"

For answer he fell on his knees before her, covering those sweet hands with kisses.

The door was flung open; Mlle. de Tavanne stood on the threshold. They started apart, monsieur leaping to his feet, mademoiselle springing back with choking cry. But it was too late; she had seen us.

She was rosy with running, her little face brimming over with mischief. She flitted into the room, crying:

"I knew it! I knew it was M. de Mar! The grey eyes! M. le Duc has done with him as he thought proper, forsooth! Well, I have done as I thought proper. I unchained Mme. de Montpensier's monkey and threw him into the nursery, where he's scared the baby nearly into spasms. Toto carried the cloth-of-gold coverlet up on top of the tester, where he's picking it to pieces, the darling! They won't be back – you're safe for a while, my children. I'll keep watch for you. Make good use of your time. Kiss her well, monsieur."

"Mademoiselle, you are an angel."

"No, she is the angel," Mlle. Blanche laughed back at him. "I'm but your warder. Have no fear; I'll keep good watch. Here, you in the petticoats, that were a boy the other night, go to the farther door. Mme. de Nemours takes her nap in the second room beyond. You watch that door; I'll watch the corridor. Farewell, my children! Peste! think you Blanche de Tavanne is so badly off for lovers that she need grudge you yours, Lorance?"

She danced out of the door, while I ran across to my station, Mlle. de Montluc standing bewildered, ardent, grateful, half laughing, half in tears.

"Lorance, Lorance!" M. Étienne murmured tremulously. "She said I should kiss you –"

I put my fingers in my ears and then took them out again, for if my ears were sealed, how was I to hear Mme. de Nemours approaching? But I admit I should have kept my eyes glued to the crack of the door; that I ever turned them is my shame. I have no business to know that mademoiselle bowed her face upon her lover's shoulder, her hand clasping his neck, silent, motionless. He pressed his cheek against her hair, holding her close; neither had any will to move or speak. It seemed they were well content to stand so the rest of their lives.

Mademoiselle was the first to stir; she raised her head and strove to break away from his locked arms.

"Monsieur! monsieur! This is madness! You must go!"

"Are you sorry I came?" he demanded vibrantly. "Are you sorry, Lorance?"

His eyes held hers; she threw pretence to the winds.

"No, monsieur; I am glad. For if we never meet again, we have had this."

"Aye. If I die tonight, I have had today."

Their voices were like the rune of the heart of the forest, like the music of deep streams. I turned away my head ashamed, and strove to think of nothing but the waking of Mme. de Nemours.

"I thought you dead," she moaned, her voice muffled against his cheek. "No one would tell me what happened last night. I could not devise any way of escape for you –"

"There is a tunnel from Ferou's house to the Rue de la Soierie. His mother – merciful angel – let me through."

"And you were not hurt?"

"Not a scratch, ma mie."

"But the wound before? Félix said –"

"I was put out of combat the night I got it," he explained earnestly, troubled even now because he had not obeyed her summons. "I was dizzy; I could not walk."

"But now, monsieur? Does it heal?"

"It is well – almost. 'Twas but a slash on the arm."

"Oh, then have I no anxiety," she murmured, with a smile that twinkled across her lips and was gone. "I cannot perceive you to be disabled, monsieur."

"My sweeting!" he laughed out. "If I cannot hold a sword yet, I can hold my love."

"But you must not, monsieur," she cried, fear, that had slept a moment, springing on her again. "You must go, and this instant, while the others are yet away. I knew you, Blanche knew you; some other will. Oh, go, go, I implore you!"

"If you will come with me."

She made no answer, save to look at him as at a madman.

"Nay, I mean not now, past the sentry. I am not so crazy as that. But you will slip out, you will find a way, and come to me."

Silently, sadly, she shook her head. His arms loosened, and she freed herself from him. But instantly he was close on her again.

"But you must! you will, you must! Ah, Lorance, my father is won over. He bids me win you. He has sworn to welcome you; when he sees you he will be your slave."

"But my cousin Mayenne is not won over."

"Devil fly away with your cousin Mayenne!" M. Étienne retorted with a vehemence that made me shudder, lest the walls have ears.

"Ah, you are free to say that, monsieur, but I am not. I am of his blood, and dwell in his house, and eat at his board."

He was looking at her with a passionate ardor, grasping her actual words less than their import of refusal.

"Are you afraid?" he cried. "Are you frightened, heart-root of mine? You need not be, mignonne. You can contrive to slip from the house – Mlle. de Tavanne will help you. Once in the street, I will meet you; I will carry you home to hold you against all the world."

"It is not that," she answered.

"Am I your fear?" he cried quickly. "Ah, Lorance, my Lorance, you need not. I love you as I love the Queen of Heaven."

"Ah, hush!"

"As I love the Queen of Heaven. I will as soon do sacrilege toward her as ill to you."

He dropped on his knees before her, kissing the hem of her gown. She stood looking down on his bowed head with a tenderness that seemed to infold him as with a mantle.

He raised his eyes to hers, still kneeling at her feet.

"Lorance, will you come with me?"

She was silent a moment, with heaving breast and face a-quiver.

"Monsieur, I am sworn. That night when Félix came, when I was in deadly terror for him and for you, Étienne, I promised my lord, an he would lift his hand from you, to obey him in all things. He bade me never again to hold intercourse with you – alack, I am already forsworn! But I cannot –"

He leaped to his feet, crying out:

"Lorance, he was the first forsworn! For he did move against me –"

"He told you – the warning went through Félix – that if you tried to reach me he would crush you as a buzzing fly. Oh, monsieur, I implored you to leave Paris! You are not kind to me, you are cruel, when you venture here."

"You are cruel to me, Lorance."

Sighing, she turned from him, hiding her face in her hands.

"Mayenne has not kept faith with you!" monsieur went on vehemently. "He has broken his oath. I mean not last night. I had my warning; the attack was provoked. But yesterday in the afternoon, before I made the attempt to see you, he sent to arrest me for the murder of the lackey Pontou."

"Paul's deed!" she cried in white surprise. "He spoke of it – we heard, Félix and I. What, monsieur! sent to arrest you? But you are here."

"They missed me. They took by mistake Paul de Lorraine."

"He was not here last night!" she cried. "Mayenne was demanding him of me."

"Then he slept pleasantly in the Bastille. May he never look on the outside of its walls again!"

"But he will, he does. He must be free by this time; they cannot keep Mayenne's nephew in the Bastille. And oh, if he hated you before, how he will hate you now! Oh, Étienne, if you love me, go! Go to your own camp, your own side, at St. Denis. There are you safe. Here in Paris you may not draw a tranquil breath."

"And shall I flee my dangers? Shall I run, in the face of my peril?"

"Ah, monsieur, perhaps your life is nothing to you. But it is more to me than tongue can tell."

"My love, my love!" He snatched her into his arms; she held away from him to look him beseechingly in the face, her little clutching hands on his shoulders.

"Oh, you will go! you will go!"

"Only if you come with me. Lorance, it is such a little way! Only to meet me in the next square. We will slip out of the gates together – leave Paris and all its plots and murders, and at St. Denis keep our honeymoon."

"Monsieur," she said slowly, "I am told that my cousin Mayenne offered a month ago to give me to you for your name on the roster of the League. Is that true?"

"It is true. But you cannot think, Lorance, it was for any lack of love for you. I swear to you –"

"Nay, you need not. I have it by heart that you love me."

"Lorance!"

"But when you could not take me with honor you would not take me. Your house stands against us; you would not desert your house. Am I then to be false to mine?"

"A woman belongs to her husband's house."

"Aye, but she does not wed the enemy of her own. Monsieur, you are full of loyalty; shall I have none? I was born, my father before me, in the shadow of the house of Lorraine; the Lorraine princes our kinsmen, our masters, our friends. When I was orphaned young, and penniless because King Henry's Huguenots had wrenched our lands away, I came here to my cousin Mayenne, to dwell here in kindness and love as a daughter of the house. Am I to turn traitor now?"

"Lorance," he was fiercely beginning, when Mlle. de Tavanne bounded in.

"On guard!" she hissed at us. "They come!"

She looked behind her into the corridor. Mademoiselle gave her lips to monsieur in one last kiss, and slipped like water from his arms. I was at his side, and we busied ourselves over the trinkets, he with shaking fingers, cheeks burning through the stain.

The ladies streamed into the room, the lovely Mme. de Montpensier alone conspicuous by her absence. Mme. de Mayenne's face was hot and angry, and bore marks of tears. Not in this room only had a combat raged.

"Never shall he come into this house again," madame was crying vigorously. "I had had him strangled, the vile little beast, an she had not seized him. I will now, if she ever dares bring him hither again."

"You certainly should, madame," replied the nearest of the ladies. "You have been, in the goodness of your heart, far too forbearing, too patient under many presumptions. One would suppose the mistress here to be Mme. de Montpensier."

"I will show who is mistress here," the Duchesse de Mayenne retorted. Then her eye fell on Mlle. de Montluc, making her way softly to the door, and the vials of her wrath overflowed upon her:

"What, Lorance, you could not be at the pains to follow me to the rescue of my child! Your little cousin, poor innocent, may be eaten by the beasts for aught you care, while you prink over trinkets."

Mademoiselle faced her blankly, scarce understanding, midst the whirl of her own thoughts, of what she was accused. The little Tavanne came gallantly to the rescue:

"I did not follow you either, madame. We thought it scarcely safe; Lorance could not bear to leave this fellow alone."

Mme. de Mayenne glanced instinctively at her dressing-table's rich accoutrements, touched in spite of herself by such care of her belongings.

"I had not suspected you maids of such fore-thought," she said with relenting. "I vow for once I am beholden to you. You did quite right, Lorance."

XXVI

Within the spider's web.

Mademoiselle slipped softly out of the room, taking our hearts with her. Our one desire now was to be gone; but it was easier wished than accomplished, for there remained the dreary process of bargaining. Mme. de Mayenne had set her heart on a pearl bracelet, Mme. de Brie wanted a vinaigrette, a third lady a pair of shoe-buckles. M. Étienne developed a recklessness about prices that would have whitened the hair of a goldsmith father; I thought the ladies could not fail to be suspicious of such prodigality, to imagine we carried stolen goods. But no; the quick settlements defeated their own ends: they fired our customers with longing to purchase further. I was despairing, when at length Mme. de Mayenne bethought herself that supper-time was at hand, and that no one was yet dressed. To my eyes the company already looked fine enough for a coronation; but I rejoiced to hear them thanking madame for her reminder, with the gratitude of victims snatched from an awful fate. We were commanded to bundle out, which with all alacrity we did.

Freedom was in sight. I was not so nervous on this journey as I had been coming in. As we passed, lackey-led, through the long corridors, I had ease enough of mind to enable me to take my bearings, and to whisper to my master, "That door yonder is the door of the council-room, where I was." Even as I spoke the door opened, two gentlemen appearing at the threshold. One was a stranger; the other was Mayenne.

Our guide held back in deference. The duke and his friend stood a moment or two in low-voiced converse; then the visitor made his farewells, and went off down the staircase.

Mayenne had not appeared aware of our existence, thirty feet up the passage, but now he inquired, as if we had been pieces of merchandise:

"What have you there, Louis?"

"An Italian goldsmith, so please your Grace. Madame has just dismissed him."

He led us forward. Mayenne surveyed us deliberately, and at length said to M. le Comte:

"I will look at your wares."

M. Étienne smiled his eager, deprecating smile, informing his Highness that we, poor creatures, spoke no French.

"How came you in Paris, then?"

M. Étienne for the fourth time went through with his tale. I think this time he must have trembled over it. My Lord Mayenne had not the reputation of being easily gulled. For aught we knew, he might be informed of the name and condition of every person who had entered Paris this year. He might, as he listened stolid-faced, be checking off to himself the number of monsieur's lies. But if M. Étienne trembled in his soul, his words never faltered; he knew his history well, by this. At its finish Mayenne said:

"Come in here."

The lackey was ordered to wait outside, while we followed his Grace of Mayenne across the council-room to that table by the window where he had sat with Lucas night before last. I clinched my teeth to keep them from chattering together. Not Grammont's brutality, not Lucas's venom, not Mlle. de Tavanne's rampant suspicion, had ever frightened me so horribly as did Mayenne's amiable composure. He made me feel as I had felt when I entered the tunnel, helpless in the dark, unable to cope with dangers I could not see. Mayenne was a well, the light shining down its sides a way, and far below the still surface of the water. You hang over the edge and peer till your eyes drop out; you can as easily look through iron as discern how deep the water is. I seemed to see clearly that Mayenne suspected us not in the least. He was as placid as a summer day, turning over the contents of the box, showing little interest in us, much in our wares, every now and then speaking a generous word of praise or asking a friendly question. He was the very model of the gracious prince; the humble tradesmen whom we feigned to be must needs have worshipfully loved him. Yet withal I believed that all the time he knew us; that he was amusing himself with us. Presently, when he tired, he would walk casually out of the room and send in his creatures to stab us.

Had I known this for a truth, that he had discovered us, I should have braced myself, I trow, to meet it. The certainty would have been bearable; I had courage to face ruin. It was the uncertainty that was so heart-shaking – like crossing a morass in the dark. We might be on the safe path; we might with every step be wandering away farther and farther into the treacherous bog; there was no way to tell. Mayenne was quite the man to be kindly patron of the crafts, to pick out a rich present for a friend. He was also the man to sit in the presence of his enemy, unbetraying, tranquil, assured, waiting. It seemed to me that in a few minutes more of this I should go mad; I should scream out: "Yes, I am Félix Broux, and he is M. le Comte de Mar!"

But before I had verily come to this, something happened to change the situation. Entered like a young tempest, slamming the door after him, Lucas.

M. Étienne clutched me by the arm, drawing me back into the embrasure of the window, where we stood in plain sight but with our faces blotted out against the light. Mayenne looked up from two rings he was comparing, one in each hand. Lucas, hat on head, came rapidly across the room.

"So you have appeared again," Mayenne said. "I could almost believe myself back in night before last."

"Aye; at last I have." Lucas was all hot and ruffled, panting half from hurry, half from wrath.

"You saw fit to be absent last night," Mayenne went on indifferently, his eyes on the ring. "I trust, for your sake, you have used your time profitably."

"I have been about my own concerns," Lucas answered lightly, arming himself with his insolence against the other's disdain. In a moment he had mastered the excitement that brought him so stormily into the room. He was once more the Lucas who had entered that other night, nonchalant, mocking.

"Pretty trinkets," he observed, sitting down and lifting a bracelet from the tray.

The close kinship of these men betrayed itself in nothing so sharply as in their unerring instinct for annoying each other. Had Lucas volunteered explanation for his absence, Mayenne would not have listened to it; but as he withheld it, the duke demanded brusquely:

"Well, do you give an account of yourself? You had better."

Lucas repeated the tactics which he had found such good entertainment before. He looked with raised eyebrows toward us.

"You would not have me speak before these vermin, uncle?"

"These vermin understand no French," Mayenne made answer. "But do as it likes you. It is nothing to me."

My master pinched my hand. Mayenne did not know us! After all, he was what M. Étienne had called him – a man, neither god nor devil. He could make mistakes like the rest of us. For once he had been caught napping.

Lucas leaned back in his chair with a meditative air, as if idly wondering whether to speak or not. In his place I should not have wondered one moment. Had Mayenne assured me in that quiet tone that he cared nothing whether I spoke, I should scarce have been able to utter my words fast enough. But there was so strange a twist in Lucas's nature that he must sometimes thwart his own interests, value his caprice above his prosperity. Also, in this case his story was no triumphant one. But at length he did begin it:

"I went to Belin to inform him that day before yesterday Étienne de Mar murdered his lackey, Pontou, in Mar's house in the Rue Coupejarrets."

"Was that your errand?" Mayenne said, looking up in slow surprise. "My faith! your oaths to Lorance trouble you little."

Lucas started forward sharply. "Do you tell me you did not know my purpose?"

"I knew, of course, that you were up to some warlockry," Mayenne answered; "I did not concern myself to discover what."

"There speaks the general! There speaks the gentleman!" Lucas cried out. "A general hangs a spy, yet he profits by spying. The spy runs the risks, incurs the shames; the general sits in his tent, his honor untarnished, pocketing all the glory. Faugh, you gentlemen! You will not do dirty work, but you will have it done for you. You sit at home with clean hands and eyes that see not, while we go forth to serve you. You are the Duke of Mayenne. I am your bastard nephew, living on your favor. But you go too far when you sneer at my smirches."

He was on his feet, standing over Mayenne, his face blazing. M. Étienne made an instinctive step forward, thinking him about to knife the duke. But Mayenne, as we well knew, was no craven.

"Be a little quieter, Paul," he said, unmoved. "You will have the guard in, in a moment."

Lucas held absolutely still for a second. So did Mayenne. He knew that Lucas, standing, could stab quicker than he defend. He sat there with both hands on the table, looking composedly up at his nephew. Lucas flung away across the room.

"I shall have dismissed these people directly," Mayenne continued. "Then you can tell me your tale."

"I can tell it now in two words," Lucas answered, coming abruptly back. "Belin signed the warrant, and sent a young ass of the burgher guard after Mar. I attended to some affairs of my own. Then after a time I went round to the Trois Lanternes to see if they had got him. He was not there – only that cub of a boy of his. When I came in, he swore, the innkeeper swore, the whole crew swore, I was Mar. The fool of an officer arrested me."

I expected Mayenne to burst out laughing in Lucas's chagrined face. But instead he seemed less struck with his nephew's misfortunes than with some other aspect of the affair. He said slowly:

"You told Belin this arrest was my desire?"

"I may have implied something of the sort."

"You repeated it to the arresting officer before Mar's boy!"

"I had no time to say anything before they hustled me off," Lucas exclaimed. "Mille tonnerres! Never had any man such luck as I. It's enough to make me sign papers with the devil."

"Mar would believe I had broken faith with him?"

"I dare say. One isn't responsible for what Mar believes," Lucas answered carelessly.

Mayenne was silent, with knit brows, drumming his hand on the table. Lucas went on with the tale of his woes:

"At the Bastille, I ordered the commissary to send to you. He did not; he sent to Belin. Belin was busy, didn't understand the message, wouldn't be bothered. I lay in my cell like a mouse in a trap till an hour agone, when at last he saw fit to appear – damn him!"

Mayenne fell to laughing. Lucas cried out:

"When they arrested me my first thought was that this was your work."

"In that case, how should you be free now?"

"You found you needed me."

"You are twice wrong, Paul. For I knew nothing of your arrest. Nor do I think I need you. Pardieu! you succeed too badly to give me confidence."

Lucas stood glowering, gnawing his lip, picturing the chagrin, the angry reproaches, the justifications he did not utter. I am certain he pitied himself as the sport of fate and of tyrants, the most shamefully used of mortal men. And so long as he aspired to the hand of Mayenne's ward, so long was he helpless under Mayenne's will.

"'Twas pity," Mayenne said reflectively, "that you thought best to be absent last night. Had you been here, you had had sport. Your young friend Mar came to sing under his lady's window."

"Saw she him?" Lucas cried sharply.

"How should I know? She does not confide in me."

"You took care to find out!" Lucas cried, knowing he was being badgered, yet powerless to keep himself from writhing.

"I may have."

"Did she see him?" Lucas demanded again, the heavy lines of hatred and jealousy searing his face.

"No credit to you if she did not. You accomplish singularly little to harass M. de Mar in his love-making. You deserve that she should have seen him. But, as a matter of fact, she did not. She was in the chapel with madame."

"What happened?"

"François de Brie – now there is a youngster, Paul," Mayenne interrupted himself to point out, "who has not a tithe of your cleverness; but he has the advantage of being on the spot when needed. Desiring a word with mademoiselle, he betook himself to her chamber. She was not there, but Mar was warbling under the window."

"Brie?"

"Brie bestirred himself. He sent two of the guard round behind the house to cut off the retreat, while he and Latour attacked from the front."

"Mar's killed?" Lucas cried. "He's killed!"

"By no means," answered Mayenne. "He got away."

Before he could explain further, – if he meant to, – the door opened, and Mlle. de Montluc came in.

Her eyes traveled first to us, in anxiety; then with relief to Mayenne, sitting over the jewels; last, to Lucas, with startlement. She advanced without hesitation to the duke.

"I am come, monsieur, to fetch you to supper."

"Pardieu, Lorance!" Mayenne exclaimed, "you show me a different face from that of dinner-time." Indeed, so she did, for her eyes were shining with excitement, while the color that M. Étienne had kissed into them still flushed her cheeks.

"If I do," she made quick answer, "it is because, the more I think on it, the surer I grow that my loving cousin will not break my heart."

"I want a word with you, Lorance," Mayenne said quietly.

"As many as you like, monsieur," she replied promptly. "But will you not send these creatures from the room first?"

"Do you include your cousin Paul in that term?"

"I meant these jewelers. But since you suggest it, perhaps it would be as well for Paul to go."

"You hear your orders, Paul."

"Aye, I hear and I disobey," Lucas retorted. "Mademoiselle, I take too much joy in your presence to be willing to leave it."

"Monsieur," she said to the duke, ignoring her cousin Paul with a coolness that must have maddened him, "will you not dismiss your tradespeople? Then can we talk comfortably."

"Aye," answered Mayenne, "I will. I am more gallant than Paul. If you command it, out they go, though I have not half had time to look their wares over. Here, master jeweler," he addressed M. Étienne, slipping easily into Italian, "pack up your wares and depart."

M. Étienne, bursting into rapid thanks to his Highness for his condescension in noticing the dirt of the way, set about his packing. Mayenne turned to his lovely cousin.

"Now for my word to you, mademoiselle. You wept so last night, it was impossible to discuss the subject properly. But now I rejoice to see you more tranquil. Here is the beginning and the middle and the end of the matter: your marriage is my affair, and I shall do as I like about it."

She searched his face; before his steady look her color slowly died. M. Étienne, whether by accident or design, knocked his tray of jewels off the table. Murmuring profuse apologies, he dropped on his knees to grope for them. Neither of the men heeded him, but kept their eyes steadily on the lady.

"Mademoiselle," Mayenne deliberately went on, "I have been over-fond with you. Had I followed my own interests instead of bowing to your whims, you had been a wife these two years. I have indulged you, mademoiselle, because you were my ally Montluc's daughter, because you came to me a lonely orphan, because you were my little cousin whose baby mouth I kissed. I have let you cavil at this suitor and that, pout that one was too tall and one too short, and a third too bold and a fourth not bold enough. I have been pleased to let you cajole me. But now, mademoiselle, I am at the end of my patience."

"Monsieur," she cried, "I never meant to abuse your kindness. You let me cajole you, as you say, else I could not have done it. You treated my whims as a jest. You let me air them. But when you frowned, I have put them by. I have always done your will."

"Then do it now, mademoiselle. Be faithful to me and to your birth. Cease sighing for the enemy of our house."

"Monsieur," she said, "when you first brought him to me, he was not the enemy of our house. When he came here, day after day, season after season, he was not our enemy. When I wrote that letter, at Paul's dictation, I did not know he was our enemy. You told me that night that I was not for him. I promised you obedience. Did he come here to me and implore me to wed with him, I would send him away."

Mayenne little imagined how truly she spoke; but he could not look in her eyes and doubt her honesty.

"You are a good child, Lorance," he said. "I could wish your lover as docile."

"He will not come here again," she cried. "He knows I am not for him. He gives it up, monsieur – he takes himself out of Paris. I promise you it is over. He gives me up."

"I have not his promise for that," Mayenne said dryly; "but the next time he comes after you, he may settle with your husband."

She uttered a little gasp, but scarce of surprise – almost of relief that the blow, so long expected, had at last been dealt.

"You will marry me, monsieur?" she murmured. "To M. de Brie?"

"You are shrewd, mademoiselle. You know that it will be a good three months before François de Brie can stand up to be wed. You say to yourself that much may happen in three months. So it may. Therefore will your bridegroom be at hand tomorrow morning."

She made no rejoinder, but her eyes, wide like a hunted animal's, moved fearsomely, loathingly, to Lucas. Mayenne uttered an abrupt laugh.

"No; Paul is not the happy man. Besides bungling the St. Quentin affair, he has seen fit to make free with my name in an enterprise of his own. Therefore, Paul, you will dance at Lorance's wedding a bachelor. Mademoiselle, you marry in the morning Señor el Conde del Rondelar y Saragossa of his Majesty King Philip's court. After dinner you will depart with your husband for Spain."

Lucas sprang forward, hand on sword, face ablaze with furious protest. Mayenne, heeding him no more than if he had not been there, rose and went to Mlle de Montluc.

"Have I your obedience, cousin?"

"You know it, monsieur."

She was curtseying to him when he folded her in his arms, kissing both her cheeks.

"You are as good as you are lovely, and that says much, ma mie. We will talk a little more about this after supper. Permit me, mademoiselle."

He took her hand and led her in leisurely fashion out of the room.

It wondered me that Lucas had not killed him. He looked murder. Haply had the duke disclosed by so much as a quivering eyelid a consciousness of Lucas's rage, of danger to himself, Lucas had struck him down. But he walked straight past, clad in his composure as in armor, and Lucas made no move. I think to stab was the impulse of a moment, gone in a moment. Instantly he was glad he had not killed the Duke of Mayenne, to be cut himself into dice by the guard. After the duke was gone, Lucas stood still a long time, no less furious, but cogitating deeply.

We had gathered up our jewels and locked our box, and stood holding it between us, waiting our chance to depart. We might have gone a dozen times during the talking, for none marked us; but M. Étienne, despite my tuggings, refused to budge so long as mademoiselle was in the room. Now was he ready enough to go, but hesitated to see if Lucas would not leave first. That worthy, however, showed no intention of stirring, but remained in his pose, buried in thought, unaware of our presence. To get out, we had to walk round one end or the other of the table, passing either before or behind him. M. le Comte was for marching carelessly before his face, but I pulled so violently in the other direction that he gave way to me. I think now that had we passed in front of him, Lucas would have let us go by without a look. As it was, hearing steps at his back, he wheeled about to confront us. If the eye of love is quick, so is the eye of hate. He cried out instantly:

"Mar!"

We dropped the box, and sprang at him. But he was too quick for us. He leaped back, whipping out his sword.

"I have you now, Mar!" he cried.

M. Étienne grabbed up the heavy box in both hands to brain him. Lucas retreated. He might run through M. Étienne, but only at the risk of having his head split. After all, it suited his book as well to take us alive. Shouting for the guards, he retreated toward the door.

But I was there before him. As he ran at M. Étienne, I had dashed by, slammed the door shut, and bolted it. If we were caught, we would make a fight for it. I snatched up a stool for weapon.

He halted. Then he darted over to the chimney, and pulled violently the bell-rope hanging near. We heard through the closed door two loud peals somewhere in the corridor.

We both ran for him. Even as he pulled the rope, M. Étienne struck the box over his sword, snapping it. I dropped my stool, as he his box, and we pinned Lucas in our arms.

"The oratory!" I gasped. With a strength born of our desperation, we dragged him kicking and cursing across the room, heaved him with all our force into the oratory, and bolted the door on him.

"Your wig!" cried M. Étienne, running to recover his box. While I picked it up and endeavored with clumsy fingers to put it on properly, he set on its legs the stool I had flung down, threw the pieces of Lucas's sword into the fireplace, seized his box, dashed to me and set my wig straight, dashed to the outer door, and opened it just as Pierre came up the corridor.

"Well, what do you want?" the lackey demanded. "You ring as if it was a question of life and death."

"I want to be shown out, if the messer will be so kind. His Highness the duke, when he went to supper, left me here to put up my wares, but I know not my way to the door."

It was after sunset, and the room, back from the windows, was dusky. The lackey seemed not to mark our flushed and rumpled looks, and to be quite satisfied with M. Étienne's explanation, when of a sudden Lucas, who had been stunned for the moment by the violent meeting of his head and the tiles, began to pound and kick on the oratory door.

He was shouting as well. But the door closed with absolute tightness; it had not even a keyhole. His cries came to us muffled and inarticulate.

"Corpo di Bacco!" M. Étienne exclaimed, with a face of childlike surprise. "Someone is in a fine hurry to enter! Do you not let him in, Sir Master of the Household?"

"I wonder who he's got there now," Pierre muttered to himself in French, staring in puzzled wise at the door. Then he answered M. Étienne with a laugh:

"No, my innocent; I do not let him in. It might cost me my neck to open that door. Come along now. I must see you out and get back to my trenchers."

We met not a soul on the stairs, everyone, served or servants, being in the supper-room. We passed the sentry without question, and round the corner without hindrance. M. Étienne stopped to heave a sigh of thanksgiving.

"I thought we were done for that time!" he panted. "Mordieu! another scored off Lucas! Come, let us make good time home! 'Twere wise to be inside our gates when he gets out of that closet."

We made good time, ever listening for the haro after us. But we heard it not. We came unmolested up the street at the back, of the Hôtel St. Quentin, on our way to the postern. Monsieur took the key out of his doublet, saying as we walked around the corner tower:

"Well, it appears we are safe at home."

"Yes, M. Étienne."

Even as I uttered the words, three men from the shadow of the wall sprang out and seized us.

"This is he!" one cried. "M. le Comte de Mar, I have the pleasure of taking you to the Bastille."

XXVII

The countersign.

Instantly two more men came running from the postern arch. The five were upon us like an avalanche. One pinned my arms while another gagged me. Two held M. Étienne, a third stopping his mouth.

"Prettily done," quoth the leader. "Not a squeal! Morbleu! I wasn't anxious to have old Vigo out disputing my rights."

M. Étienne's wrists were neatly trussed by this time. At a word from the leader, our captors turned us about and marched us up the lane by Mirabeau's garden, where Bernet's blood lay rusty on the stones. We offered no resistance whatever; we should only have been prodded with a sword-point for our pains. I made out, despite the thickening twilight, the familiar uniform of the burgher guard; M. de Belin, having bagged the wrong bird once, had now caught the right one.

The captain bade one of the fellows go call the others off; I could guess that the job had been done thoroughly, every approach to the house guarded. I gnashed my teeth over the gag, that I had not suspected the danger. The truth was, both of us had our heads so full of mademoiselle, of Mayenne, and of Lucas, that we had forgotten the governor and his preposterous warrant.

They led us into the Rue de l'Évêque, where was waiting the same black coach that had stood before the Oie d'Or, the same Louis on the box. Its lamps were lighted; by their glimmer our captors for the first time saw us fairly.

"Why, captain," cried the man at M. Étienne's elbow, "this is no Comte de Mar! The Comte de Mar is fair-haired; I've seen him scores of times."

"The Comte de Mar answers to the name of Étienne, and so does this fellow," the captain answered. He took the candle from one of the lamps and held it in M. Étienne's face. Then he put out a sudden hand, and pulled the wig off.

"Good for you, captain!" cried the men. We were indeed unfortunate to encounter an officer with brains.

"We'll take your gag off too, M. le Comte, in the coach," the captain told him.

"Will you bring the lass along, captain?"

"Not exactly," the leader laughed. "A fine prison it would be, could a felon have his bonnibel at his side. No, I'll leave the maid; but she needn't give the alarm yet. Do you stay awhile with her, L'Estrange; you'll not mind the job. Keep her a quarter of an hour, and then let her go her ways."

They bundled my lord into the coach, box and all, the captain and two men with him. The fourth clambered up beside Louis as he cracked his whip and rattled smartly down the street.

My guardian stole a loving arm around my waist and marched me down the quiet lane between the garden walls. He was clutching my right wrist, but my left hand was free, and I fumbled at my gag. In the middle of the deserted lane he halted.

"Now, my beauty, if you'll be good I'll take that stopper off. But if you make a scream, by Heaven, it'll be your last!"

I shook my head and squeezed his hand imploringly, while he, holding me tight in one sinewy arm, plucked left-handedly at the knot. I waited, meek as Griselda, till the gag was off, and then I let him have it. Volleying curses, I hammered him square in the eye.

It was a mad course, for he was armed, I not. But instead of stabbing, he dropped me like a hot coal, gasping in the blankest consternation:

"Thousand devils! It's a boy!"

A second later, when he recollected himself, I was tearing down the lane.

I am a good runner, and then, anyone can run well when he runs for his life. Despite the wretched kirtle tying up my legs, I gained on him, and when I had reached the corner of our house, he dropped the pursuit and made off in the darkness. I ran full tilt round to the great gate, bellowing for the sentry to open. He came at once, with a dripping torch, to burst into roars of laughter at the sight of me. My wig was somewhere in the lane behind me; he knew me perfectly in my silly toggery. He leaned against the wall, helpless with laughing, shouting feebly to his comrades to come share the jest. I, you may well imagine, saw nothing funny about it, but kicked and shook the grilles in my rage and impatience. He did open to me at length, and in I dashed, clamoring for Vigo. He had appeared in the court by this, as also half a dozen of the guard, who surrounded me with shouts of astonished mockery; but I, little heeding, cried to the equery:

"Vigo, M. le Comte is arrested! He's in the Bastille!"

Vigo grasped my arm, and lifted rather than led me in at the guard-room door, slamming it in the soldiers' faces.

"Now, Félix."

"M. Étienne!" I gasped – "M. Étienne is arrested! They were lying in wait for him at the back of the house, by the tower. They've taken him off in a coach to the Bastille."

"Who have?"

"The governor's guard. You'll saddle and pursue? You'll rescue him?"

"How long ago?"

"About ten minutes. The coach was standing in the Rue de l'Évêque. They left a man guarding me, but I broke away."

"It can't be done," Vigo said. "They'll be out of the quarter by now. If I could catch them at all, it would be close by the Bastille. No good in that; no use fighting four regiments. What the devil are they arresting him for, Félix? I understand Mayenne wants his blood, but what has the city guard to do with it?"

"It's Lucas's game," I said. Then I remembered that we had not confided to him the tale of the first arrest. I went on to tell of the adventure of the Trois Lanternes, and, reflecting that he might better know just how the land lay with us, I made a clean breast of everything – the fight before Ferou's house, the rescue, the reencounter in the tunnel, today's excursion, and all that befell in the council-room. I wound up with a second full account of our capture under the very walls of the house, our garroting before we could cry on the guards to save us. Vigo said nothing for some time; at length he delivered himself:

"Monsieur wouldn't have a patrol about the house. He wouldn't publish to the mob that he feared any danger whatever. Of course no one foresaw this. However, the arrest is the best thing could have happened."

"Vigo!" I gasped in horror. Was Vigo turned traitor? The solid earth reeled beneath my feet.

"He'd never rest till he got himself killed," Vigo went on. "Monsieur's hot enough, but M. Étienne's mad to bind. If they hadn't caught him tonight he'd have been in some worse pickle tomorrow; while, as it is, he's safe from swords at least."

"But they can murder as well in the Bastille as elsewhere!" I cried.

Vigo shook his head.

"No; had they meant murder, they'd have settled him here in the alley. Since they lugged him off unhurt, they don't mean it. I know not what the devil they are up to, but it isn't that."

"It was Lucas's game in the first place," I repeated. "He's too prudent to come out in the open and fight M. Étienne. He never strikes with his own hand; his way is to make someone else strike for him. So he gets M. Étienne into the Bastille. That's the first step. I suppose he thinks Mayenne will attend to the second."

"Mayenne dares not take the boy's life," Vigo answered. "He could have killed him, an he chose, in the streets, and nobody the wiser. But now that monsieur's taken publicly to the Bastille, Mayenne dares not kill him there, by foul play or by law – the Duke of St. Quentin's son. No; all Mayenne can do is to confine him at his good pleasure. Whence presently we will pluck him out at King Henry's good pleasure."

"And meantime is he to rot behind bars?"

"Unless Monsieur can get him out. But then," Vigo went on, "a month or two in a cell won't be a bad thing for him, neither. His head will have a chance to cool. After a dose of Mayenne's purge he may recover of his fever for Mayenne's ward."

"Monsieur! You will send to Monsieur?"

"Of course. You will go. And Gilles with you to keep you out of mischief."

"When? Now?"

"No," said Vigo. "You will go clothe yourself in breeches first, else are you not likely to arrive anywhere but at the mad-house. And then eat your supper. It's a long road to St. Denis."

I ran at once, through a fusillade of jeers from soldiers, grooms, and house-men, across the court, through the hall, and up the stairs to Marcel's chamber. Never was I gladder of anything in my life than to doff those swaddling petticoats. Two minutes, and I was a man again. I found it in my heart to pity the poor things who must wear the trappings their lives long.

But for all my joy in my freedom, I choked over my supper and pushed it away half tasted, in misery over M. Étienne. Vigo might say comfortably that Mayenne dared not kill him, but I thought there were few things that gentleman dared not do. Then there was Lucas to be reckoned with. He had caught his fly in the web; he was not likely to let him go long undevoured. At best, if M. Étienne's life were safe, yet was he helpless, while tomorrow our mademoiselle was to marry. Vigo seemed to think that a blessing, but I was nigh to weeping into my soup. The one ray of light was that she was not to marry Lucas. That was something. Still, when M. Étienne came out of prison, if ever he did, – I could scarce bring myself to believe it, – he would find his dear vanished over the rocky Pyrenees.

Vigo would not even let me start when I was ready. Since we were too late to find the gates open, we must wait till ten of the clock, at which hour the St. Denis gate would be in the hands of a certain Brissac, who would pass us with a wink at the word St. Quentin.

I was so wroth with Vigo that I would not stay with him, but went upstairs into M. Étienne's silent chamber, and flung myself down on the window-bench his head might never touch again, and wondered how he was faring in prison. I wished I were there with him. I cared not much what the place was, so long as we were together. I had gone down the mouth of hell smiling, so be it I went at his heels. Mayhap if I had struggled harder with my captors, shown my sex earlier, they had taken me too. Heartily I wished they had; I trow I am the only wight ever did wish himself behind bars. And promptly I repented me, for if Vigo had proved but a broken reed, there was Monsieur. Monsieur was not likely to sit smug and declare prison the best place for his son.

The slow twilight faded altogether, and the dark came. The city was very still. Once in a while a shout or a sound of bell was borne over the roofs, or infrequent voices and footsteps sounded in the street beyond our gate. The men in the court under my window were quiet too, talking among themselves without much raillery or laughter; I knew they discussed the unhappy plight of the heir of St. Quentin. The chimes had rung some time ago the half-hour after nine, and I was fidgeting to be off, but huffed as I was with him, I could not lower myself to go ask Vigo's leave to start. He might come after me when he wanted me.

"Félix! Félix!" Marcel shouted down the corridor. I sprang up; then, remembering my dignity, moved no further, but bade him come in to me.

"Where are you mooning in the dark?" he demanded, stumbling over the threshold. "Oh, there you are. Dame! you'd come downstairs mighty quick if you knew what was there for you?"

"What?" I cried, divided between the wild hope that it was Monsieur and the wilder one that it was M. Étienne.

"Don't you wish I'd tell you? Well, you're a good boy, and I will. It's the prettiest lass I've seen in a month of Sundays – you in your petticoats don't come near her."

"For me?" I stuttered.

"Aye; she asked for M. le Duc, and when he wasn't here, for you. I suppose it's some friend of M. Étienne's."

I supposed so, indeed; I supposed it was the owner of my borrowed plumage come to claim her own, angry perhaps because I had not returned it to her. I wondered whether she would scratch my eyes out because I had lost the cap – whether I could find it if I went to look with a light. None too eagerly I descended to her.

She was standing against the wall in the archway. Two or three of the guardsmen were about her, one with a flambeau, by which they were all surveying her. She wore the coif and blouse, the black bodice and short striped skirt, of the country peasant girl, and, like a country girl, she showed a face flushed and downcast under the soldiers' bold scrutiny. She looked up at me as at a rescuing angel. It was Mlle. de Montluc!

I dashed past the torch-bearer, nearly upsetting him in my haste, and snatched her hand.

"Mademoiselle! Come into the house!"

She clutched me with fingers as cold as marble, which trembled on mine.

"Where is M. de St. Quentin?"

"At St. Denis."

"You must take me there tonight."

"I was going," I stammered, bewildered; "but you, mademoiselle –"

"You knew of M. de Mar's arrest?"

"Aye."

"What coil is this, Félix?" demanded Vigo, coming up. He took the torch from his man, and held it in mademoiselle's face, whereupon an amazing change came over his own. He lowered the light, shielding it with his hand, as if it were an impertinent eye.

"You are Vigo," she said at once.

"Yes; and I know not what noble lady mademoiselle can be, save – will it please her to come into the house?"

He led the way with his torch, not suffering himself to look at her again. He had his foot on the staircase, when she called to him, as if she had been accustomed to addressing him all her life:

"Vigo, this will do. I will speak to you here."

"As mademoiselle wishes. I thought the salon fitter. My cabinet here will be quieter than the hall, mademoiselle."

He opened the door, and she entered. He pushed me in next, giving me the torch and saying:

"Ask mademoiselle, Félix, whether she wants me." He amazed me – he who always ordered.

"I want you, Vigo," mademoiselle answered him herself. "I want you to send two men with me to St. Denis."

"Tomorrow?"

"No; tonight."

"But mademoiselle cannot go to St. Denis."

"I can, and I must."

"They will not let a horse-party through the gate at night," Vigo began.

"We will go on foot."

"Mademoiselle," Vigo answered, as if she had proposed flying to the moon, "you cannot walk to St. Denis."

"I must!" she cried.

I had put the flambeau in a socket on the wall. Now that the light shone on her steadily, I saw for the first time, though I might have known it from her presence here, how rent with emotion she was, white to the lips, with gleaming eyes and stormy breast. She had spoken low and quietly, but it was a main-force composure, liable to snap like glass. I thought her on the very verge of passionate tears. Vigo looked at her, puzzled, troubled, pitying, as on some beautiful, mad creature. She cried out on him suddenly, her rich voice going up a key:

"You need not say 'cannot' to me, Vigo! You know not how I came here. I was locked in my chamber. I changed clothes with my Norman maid. There was a sentry at each end of the street. I slid down a rope of my bedclothes; it was dark – they did not see me. I knocked at Ferou's door – thank the saints, it opened to me quickly! I told M. Ferou – God forgive me! – I had business for the duke at the other end of the tunnel. He took me through, and I came here."

"But, mademoiselle, the bats!" I cried.

"Yes, the bats," she returned, with a little smile. "And my hands on the ropes!" She turned them over; the skin was torn cruelly from her delicate palms and the inside of her fingers. Little threads of blood marked the scores. "Then I came here," she repeated. "In all my life I have never been in the streets alone – not even for one step at noonday. Now will you tell me, M. Vigo, that I cannot go to St. Denis?"

"Mademoiselle, it is yours to say what you can do."

As for me, I dropped on my knees and laid my lips to her fingers, softly, for fear even their pressure might hurt her tenderness.

"Mademoiselle!" I cried in pure delight. "Mademoiselle, that you are here!"

She flushed under my words.

"Ah, it is no little thing brought me. You knew M. de Mar was arrested?"

We assented; she went on, more to me than to Vigo, as if in telling me she was telling M. Étienne. She spoke low, as if in pain.

"After supper M. de Mayenne went back to his cabinet and let out Paul de Lorraine."

"I wish we had killed him," I muttered. "We had no time or weapons."

"M. de Mayenne sent for me then," she went on, wetting her lips. "I have never seen him so angry. He was furious because M. de Mar had been before his face and he had not known it. He felt he had been made a mock of. He raged against me – I never knew he could be so angry. He said the Spanish envoy was too good for me; I should marry Paul de Lorraine tomorrow."

"Mordieu, mademoiselle!"

"That was not it. I had borne that!" she cried. "Mayhap I deserved it. But while my lord thundered at me, word came that M. de Mar was taken. My lord swore he should die. He swore no man ever set him at naught and lived to boast of it."

"Will –"

She swept on unheeding:

"He said he should be tried for the murder of Pontou – he should be tortured to make him confess it."

She dropped down on her knees, hiding her face in her arms on the table, shaking from head to foot as in an ague. Vigo swore to himself, loudly, violently: "If Mayenne do that, by the throne of Heaven, I'll kill him!"

She sprang to her feet, dry-eyed, fierce as a young lioness.

"Is that all you can say? Mayenne may torture him and be killed for it?"

"I shall send to the duke –" Vigo began.

"Aye! I shall go to the duke! I can say who killed Pontou. I know much besides to tell the king. I was Mayenne's cousin, but if he would save his secrets he must give up M. de Mar. Mother of God! I have been his obedient child; I have let him do so with me as he would. I sent my lover away. I consented to the Spanish marriage. But to this I will not submit. He shall not torture and kill Étienne de Mar!"

Vigo took her hand and kissed it.

"Shall we start, Vigo? Once at St. Denis, I am hostage for his safety. The king can tell Mayenne that if Mar is tortured he will torture me! Mayenne may not tender me greatly, but he will not relish his cousin's breaking on the wheel."

"Mayenne won't torture M. Étienne," Vigo said, patting her hand in both of his, forgetting she was a great lady, he an equery. "Fear not! you will save him, mademoiselle."

"Let us go!" she cried feverishly. "Let us go!"

Gilles was in the court waiting, stripped of his livery, dressed peaceably as a porter, but with a mallet in his hand that I should not like to receive on my crown. I thought we were ready, but Vigo bade us wait. I stood on the house-steps with mademoiselle, while he took aside Squinting Charlot for a low-voiced, emphatic interview.

"Must we wait?" mademoiselle urged me, quivering like the arrow on the bow-string. "They may discover I am gone. Need we wait?"

"Aye," I answered; "if Vigo bids us. He knows."

We waited then. Vigo disappeared presently. Mademoiselle and I stood patient, with, oh! what impatience in our hearts, wondering how he could so hinder us. Not till he came back did it dawn on me for what we had stayed. He was dressed as an under-groom, not a tag of St. Quentin colors on him.

"I beg a thousand pardons, mademoiselle. I had to give my lieutenant his orders. Now, if you will give the word, we go."

"Do you go, M. Vigo?" She breathed deep. It was easy to see she looked upon him as a regiment.

"Of course," Vigo answered, as if there could be no other way.

I said in pure devilry, to try to ruffle him:

"Vigo, you said you were here to guard Monsieur's interests-his house, his goods, his moneys. Do you desert your trust?"

Mademoiselle turned quickly to him:

"Vigo, you must not let me take you from your rightful post. Félix and your man here will care for me –"

"The boy talks silliness, mademoiselle," Vigo returned tranquilly. "Mademoiselle is worth a dozen hôtels. I go with her."

He walked beside her across the court, I following with Gilles, laughing to myself. Only yesterday had Vigo declared that never would he give aid and comfort to Mlle. de Montluc. It was no marvel she had conquered M. Étienne, for he must needs have been in love with someone, but in bringing Vigo to her feet she had won a triumph indeed.

We had to go out by the great gate, because the key of the postern was in the Bastille. But as if by magic every guardsman and hanger-about had disappeared – there was not one to stare at the lady; though when we had passed someone locked the gates behind us. Vigo called me up to mademoiselle's left. Gilles was to loiter behind, far enough to seem not to belong to us, near enough to come up at need. Thus, at a good pace, mademoiselle stepping out as brave as any of us, we set out across the city for the Porte St. Denis.

Our quarter was very quiet; we scarce met a soul. But afterward, as we reached the neighborhood of the markets, the streets grew livelier. Now were we gladder than ever of Vigo's escort; for whenever we approached a band of roisterers or of gentlemen with lights, mademoiselle sheltered herself behind the equerry's broad back, hidden as behind a tower. Once the gallant M. de Champfleury, he who in pink silk had adorned Mme. de Mayenne's salon, passed close enough to touch her. She heaved a sigh of relief when he was by. For her own sake she had no fear; the midnight streets, the open road to St. Denis, had no power to daunt her: but the dread of being recognized and turned back rode her like a nightmare.

Close by the gate, Vigo bade us pause in the door of a shop while he went forward to reconnoiter. Before long he returned.

"Bad luck, mademoiselle. Brissac's not on. I don't know the officer, but he knows me, that's the worst of it. He told me this was not St. Quentin night. Well, we must try the Porte Neuve."

But mademoiselle demurred:

"That will be out of our way, will it not, Vigo? It is a longer road from the Porte Neuve to St. Denis?"

"Yes; but what to do? We must get through the walls."

"Suppose we fare no better at the Porte Neuve? If your Brissac is suspected, he'll not be on at night. Vigo, I propose that we part company here. They will not know Gilles and Félix at the gate, will they?"

"No," Vigo said doubtfully; "but –"

"Then can we get through!" she cried. "They will not stop us, such humble folk! We are going to the bedside of our dying mother at St. Denis. Your name, Gilles?"

"Forestier, mademoiselle," he stammered, startled.

"Then are we all Forestiers – Gilles, Félix, and Jeanne. We can pass out, Vigo; I am sure we can pass out. I am loath to part with you, but I fear to go through the city to the Porte Neuve. My absence may be discovered – I must place myself without the walls speedily.

"Well, mademoiselle may try it," Vigo gave reluctant consent. "If you are refused, we can fall back on the Porte Neuve. If you succeed – Listen to me, you fellows. You will deliver mademoiselle into Monsieur's hands, or answer to me for it. If anyone touches her little finger – well, trust me!"

"That's understood," we answered, saluting together.

"Mademoiselle need have no doubts of them," Vigo said. "Félix is M. le Comte's own henchman. And Gilles is the best man in the household, next to me. God speed you, my lady. I am here, if they turn you back."

We went boldly round the corner and up the street to the gate. The sentry walking his beat ordered us away without so much as looking at us. Then Gilles, appointed our spokesman, demanded to see the captain of the watch. His errand was urgent.

But the sentry showed no disposition to budge. Had we a passport? No, we had no passport. Then we could go about our business. There was no leaving Paris tonight for us. Call the captain? No; he would do nothing of the kind. Be off, then!

But at this moment, hearing the altercation, the officer himself came out of the guardroom in the tower, and to him Gilles at once began his story. Our mother at St. Denis had sent for us to come to her dying bed. He was a street-porter; the messenger had had trouble to find him. His young brother and sister were in service, kept to their duties till late. Our mother might even now be yielding up the ghost! It was a pitiful case, M. le Capitaine; might we not be permitted to pass?

The young officer appeared less interested in this moving tale than in the face of mademoiselle, lighted up by the flambeau on the tower wall.

"I should be glad to oblige your charming sister," he returned, smiling, "but none goes out of the city without a passport. Perhaps you have one, though, from my Lord Mayenne?"

"Would our kind be carrying a passport from the Duke of Mayenne?" quoth Gilles.

"It seems improbable," the officer smiled, pleased with his wit. "Sorry to discommode you, my dear. But perhaps, lacking a passport, you can yet oblige me with the countersign, which does as well. Just one little word, now, and I'll let you through."

"If monsieur will tell me the little word?" she asked innocently.

He burst into laughter.

"No, no; I am not to be caught so easy as that, my girl."

"Oh, come, monsieur captain," Gilles urged, "many and many a fellow goes in and out of Paris without a passport. The rules are a net to stop big fish and let the small fry go. What harm will it do to my Lord Mayenne, or you, or anybody, if you have the gentleness to let three poor servants through to their dying mother?"

"It desolates me to hear of her extremity," the captain answered, with a fine irony, "but I am here to do my duty. I am thinking, my dear, that you are some great lady's maid?"

He was eying her sharply, suspiciously; she made haste to protest:

"Oh, no, monsieur; I am servant to Mme. Mesnier, the grocer's wife."

"And perhaps you serve in the shop?"

"No, monsieur," she said, not seeing his drift, but on guard against a trap. "No, monsieur; I am never in the shop. I am far too busy with my work. Monsieur does not seem to understand what a servant-lass has to do."

For answer, he took her hand and lifted it to the light, revealing all its smooth whiteness, its dainty, polished nails.

"I think mademoiselle does not understand it, either."

With a little cry, she snatched her hand from him, hiding it in the folds of her kirtle, regarding him with open terror. He softened somewhat at sight of her distress.

"Well, it's none of my business if a lady chooses to be masquerading round the streets at night with a porter and a lackey. I don't know what your purpose is – I don't ask to know. But I'm here to keep my gate, and I'll keep it. Go try to wheedle the officer at the Porte Neuve."

In helpless obedience, glad of even so much leniency, we turned away – to face a tall, grizzled veteran in a colonel's shoulder-straps. With a dragoon at his back, he had come so softly out of a side alley that not even the captain had marked him.

"What's this, Guilbert?" he demanded.

"Some folks seeking to get through the gates, sir. I've just turned them away."

"What were you saying about the Porte Neuve?"

"I said they could go see how that gate is kept. I showed them how this is."

"Why must you pass through at this time of night?" said the commanding officer, civilly. Gilles once again bemoaned the dying mother. The young captain, eager to prove his fidelity, interrupted him:

"I believe that's a fairy-tale, sir. There's something queer about these people. The girl says she is a grocer's servant, and has hands like a duchess's."

The colonel looked at us sharply, neither friendly nor unfriendly. He said in a perfectly neutral manner:

"It is of no consequence whether she be a servant or a duchess – has a mother or not. The point is whether these people have the countersign. If they have it, they can pass, whoever they are."

"They have not," the captain answered at once. "I think you would do well, sir, to demand the lady's name."

Mademoiselle started forward for a bold stroke just as the superior officer demanded of her, "The countersign?" As he said the word, she pronounced distinctly her name:

"Lorance –"

"Enough!" the colonel said instantly. "Pass them through, Guilbert."

The young captain stood in a mull, but no more bewildered than we.

"Mighty queer!" he muttered. "Why didn't she give it to me?"

"Stir yourself, sir!" his superior gave sharp command. "They have the countersign; pass them through."

XXVIII

St. Denis — and Navarre!

As the gates clanged into place behind us, Gilles stopped short in his tracks to say, as if addressing the darkness before him:

"Am I, Gilles, awake or asleep? Are we in Paris, or are we on the St. Denis road?"

"Oh, come, come!" Mademoiselle hastened us on, murmuring half to herself as we went: "O you kind saints! I saw he could not make us out for friends or foes; I thought my name might turn the scale. Mayenne always gives a name for a countersign; tonight, by a marvel, it was mine!"

I like not to think often of that five-mile tramp to St. Denis. The road was dark, rutty, and in places still miry from Monday night's rain. Strange shadows dogged us all the way. Sometimes they were only bushes or wayside shrines, but sometimes they moved. This was not now a wolf country, but two-footed wolves were plenty, and as dangerous. The hangers-on of the army – beggars, feagues, and footpads – hovered, like the cowardly beasts of prey they were, about the outskirts of the city. Did a leaf rustle, we started; did a shambling shape in the gloom whine for alms, we made ready for onset. Gilles produced from some place of concealment – his jerkin, or his leggings, or somewhere – a brace of pistols, and we walked with finger on trigger, taking care, whenever a rustle in the grass, a shadow in the bushes, seemed to follow us, to talk loud and cheerfully of common things, the little interests of a humble station. Thanks to this diplomacy, or the pistol-barrels shining in the faint starlight, none molested us, though we encountered more than one mysterious company. We never passed into the gloom under an arch of trees without the resolution to fight for our lives. We never came out again into the faint light of the open road without wondering thanks to the saints – silent thanks, for we never spoke a word of any fear, Gilles and I. I trow mademoiselle knew well enough, but she spoke no word either. She never faltered, never showed by so much as the turn of her head that she suspected any danger, but, eyes on the distant lights of St. Denis, walked straight along, half a step ahead of us all the way. Stride as we might, we two strong fellows could never quite keep up with her.

The journey could not at such pace stretch out forever. Presently the distant lights were no longer distant, but near, nearer, close at hand – the lights of the outposts of the camp. A sentinel started out from the quoin of a wall to stop us, but when we had told our errand he became as friendly as a brother. He went across the road into a neighboring tournebride to report to the officer of the guard, and came back presently with a torch and the order to take us to the Duke of St. Quentin's lodging.

It was near an hour after midnight, and St. Denis was in bed. Save for a drowsy patrol here and there, we met no one. Fewer than the patrols were the lanterns hung on ropes across the streets; these were the only lights, for the houses were one and all as dark as tombs. Not till we had reached the middle of the town did we see, in the second story of a house in the square, a beam of light shining through the shutter-chink.

"Someone in mischief." Gilles pointed.

"Aye," laughed the sentry, "your duke. This is where he lodges, over the saddler's."

He knocked with the butt of his musket on the door. The shutter above creaked open, and a voice – Monsieur's voice – asked, "Who's there?"

Mademoiselle was concealed in the embrasure of the doorway; Gilles and I stepped back into the street where Monsieur could see us.

"Gilles Forestier and Félix Broux, Monsieur, just from Paris, with news."

"Wait."

"Is it all right, M. le Duc?" the sentry asked, saluting.

"Yes," Monsieur answered, closing the shutter.

The soldier, with another salute to the blank window, and a nod of "Good-bye, then," to us, went back to his post. Left in darkness, we presently heard Monsieur's quick step on the flags of the hall, and the clatter of the bolts. He opened to us, standing there fully dressed, with a guttering candle.

"My son?" he said instantly.

Mademoiselle, crouching in the shadow of the doorpost, pushed me forward. I saw I was to tell him.

"Monsieur, he was arrested and driven to the Bastille tonight between seven and eight. Lucas – Paul de Lorraine – went to the governor and swore that M. Étienne killed the lackey Pontou in the house in the Rue

Coupejarrets. It was Lucas killed him – Lucas told Mayenne so. Mlle. de Montluc heard him, too. And here is mademoiselle."

At the word she came out of the shadow and slowly over the threshold.

Her alarm and passion had swept her to the door of the Hôtel St. Quentin as a whirlwind sweeps a leaf. She had come without thought of herself, without pause, without fear. But now the first heat of her impulse was gone. Her long tramp had left her faint and weary, and here she had to face not an equery and a page, hers to command, but a great duke, the enemy of her house. She came blushfully in her peasant dress, shoes dirty from the common road, hair ruffled by the night winds, to show herself for the first time to her lover's father, opposer of her hopes, thwarter of her marriage. Proud and shy, she drifted over the door-sill and stood a moment, neither lifting her eyes nor speaking, like a bird whom the least movement would startle into flight.

But Monsieur made none. He kept as still, as tongue-tied, as she, looking at her as if he could hardly believe her presence real. Then as the silence prolonged itself, it seemed to frighten her more than the harsh speech she may have feared; with a desperate courage she raised her eyes to his face.

The spell was broken. Monsieur stepped forward at once to her.

"Mademoiselle, you have come a journey. You are tired. Let me give you some refreshment; then will you tell me the story."

It was an unlucky speech, for she had been on the very point of unburdening herself; but now, without a word, she accepted his escort down the passage. But as she went, she flung me an imploring glance; I was to come too. Gilles bolted the door again, and sat down to wait on the staircase; but I, though my lord had not bidden me, followed him and mademoiselle. It troubled me that she should so dread him – him, the warmest-hearted of all men. But if she needed me to give her confidence, here I was.

Monsieur led her into a little square parlor at the end of the passage. It was just behind the shop, I knew, it smelt so of leather. It was doubtless the sitting-and eating-room of the saddler's family. Monsieur set his candle down on the big table in the middle; then, on second thought, took it up again and lighted two iron sconces on the wall.

"Pray sit, mademoiselle, and rest," he bade, for she was starting up in nervousness from the chair where he had put her. "I will return in a moment."

When he had gone from the room, I said to her, half hesitating, yet eagerly:

"Mademoiselle, you were never afraid on the way, where there was good cause for fear. But now there is nothing to dread."

She rose and fluttered round the walls of the room, looking for something. I thought it was for a way of escape, but it was not, for she passed the three doors and came back to her place with an air of disappointment, smoothing the loose strands of her hair.

"I never before went anywhere unmasked," she murmured.

Monsieur entered with a salver containing a silver cup of wine and some Rheims biscuit. He offered it to her formally; she accepted with scarcely audible thanks, and sat, barely touching the wine to her lips, crumbling the biscuit into bits with restless fingers, making the pretence of a meal serve as excuse for her silence. Monsieur glanced at her, puzzled-wise, waiting for her to speak. Had the Infanta Isabella come to visit him, he could not have been more surprised. It seemed to him discourteous to press her; he waited for her to explain her presence.

I wanted to shake mademoiselle. With a dozen swift words, with a glance of her blue eyes, she could sweep Monsieur off his feet as she had swept Vigo. And instead, she sat there, not daring to look at him, like a child caught stealing sweets. She had found words to defend herself from the teasing tongues at the Hôtel de Lorraine, to plead for me, to lash Lucas, to move Mayenne himself; but she could not find one syllable for the Duke of St. Quentin. She had been to admiration the laughing coquette, the stout champion, the haughty great lady, the frank lover; but now she was the shy child, blushing, stammering, constrained.

Had Monsieur attacked her with blunt questions, had he demanded of her up and down what had brought her this strange road at such amazing hour and in such unfitting company, she must needs have answered, and, once started, she would quickly have kindled her fire again. Had he, on other part, with a smile, an encouraging word, given her ever so little a push, she had gone on easily enough. But he did neither. He was courteous and cold. Partly was his coldness real; he could not look on her as other than the daughter of his enemy's house, ward of the man who had schemed to kill him, will-o'-the-wisp who had lured his son to disaster. Partly was it mere absence; M. Étienne's plight was more to him than mademoiselle's. When she spoke not, he turned impatiently to me.

"Tell me, Félix, all about it."

Before I could answer him the door behind us opened to admit two gentlemen, shoulder to shoulder. They were dressed much alike, plainly, in black. One was about thirty years of age, tall, thin-faced, and dark, and of a gravity and dignity beyond his years. Living was serious business to him; his eyes were thoughtful, steady, and a little cold. His companion was some ten years older; his beard and curling hair, worn away from his forehead by the helmet's chafing, were already sprinkled with grey. He had a great beak of a nose and dark-grey eyes, as keen as a hawk's, and a look of amazing life and vim. The air about him seemed to tingle with it. We had all done something, we others; we were no shirks or sluggards: but the force in him put us out, penny candles before the sun. I deem not Jeanne the Maid did any marvel when she recognized King Charles at Chinon. Here was I, a common lout, never heard a heavenly voice in all my days, yet I knew in the flick of an eye that this was Henri Quatre.

I was hot and cold and trembling, my heart pounding till it was like to choke me. I had never dreamed of finding myself in the presence. I had never thought to face any man greater than my duke. For the moment I was utterly discomfited. Then I bethought me that not for God alone were knees given to man, and I slid down quietly to the floor, hoping I did right, but reflecting for my comfort that in any case I was too small to give great offence.

Mademoiselle started out of her chair and swept a curtsey almost to the ground, holding the lowly pose like a lady of marble. Only Monsieur remained standing as he was, as if a king was an everyday affair with him. I always thought Monsieur a great man, but now I knew it.

The king, leaving his companion to close the door, was across the room in three strides.

"I am come to look after you, St. Quentin," he cried, laughing. "I cannot have my council broken up by pretty grisettes. The precedent is dangerous."

With the liveliest curiosity and amusement he surveyed the top of mademoiselle's bent head, and Monsieur's puzzled, troubled countenance.

"This is no grisette, Sire," Monsieur answered, "but a very highborn demoiselle indeed – cousin to my Lord Mayenne."

Astonishment flashed over the king's mobile face; his manner changed in an instant to one of utmost deference.

"Rise, mademoiselle," he begged, as if her appearance were the most natural and desirable thing in the world. "I could wish it were my good adversary Mayenne himself who was come to treat with us; but be assured his cousin shall lack no courtesy."

She swayed lightly to her feet, raising her face to the king's. Into his countenance, which mirrored his emotions like a glass, came a quick delight at the sight of her. The color waxed and waned in her cheeks; her breath fluttered uncertainly; her eyes, anxious, eager, searched his face.

"I cry your Majesty's good pardon," she faltered. "I had urgent business with M. de St. Quentin – I did not guess he was with your Majesty –"

"The king's business is glad to step aside for yours, mademoiselle."

She curtseyed, blushing, hiding her eyes under their sooty lashes; thinking as I did, I made no doubt, here was a king indeed. His Majesty went on:

"I can well believe, mademoiselle, 'tis no trifling matter brings you at midnight to our rough camp. We will not delay you further, but be at pains to remember that if in anything Henry of France can aid you he stands at your command."

He made her a noble bow and took her hand to kiss, when she, like a child that sees itself losing a protector, clutched his hand in her little trembling fingers, her wet eyes fixed imploringly on his face. He beamed upon her; he felt no desire whatever to be gone.

"Am I to stay?" he asked radiantly; then with grave gentleness he added: "Mademoiselle is in trouble. Will she bring her trouble to the king? That is what a king is for – to ease his subjects' burdens."

She could not speak; she made him her obeisance with a look out of the depths of her soul.

"Then are you my subject, mademoiselle?" he demanded slyly.

She shook the tears from her lashes, and found her voice and her smile to answer his:

"Sire, I was a true Ligueuse this morning. But I came here half Navarraise, and now I swear I am wholly one."

"Now, that is good hearing!" the king cried. "Such a recruit from Mayenne! Also is it heartening to discover that my conversion is not the only sudden one in the world. It has taken me five months to turn my coat, but here is mademoiselle turns hers in a day."

He had glanced over his shoulder to point this out to his gentleman, but now he faced about in time to catch his recruit looking triste again.

"Mademoiselle," he said, "you are beautiful, grave; but, as you had the graciousness to show me just now, still more beautiful, smiling. Now we are going to arrange matters so that you will smile always. Will you tell me what is the trouble, my child?"

"Gladly, Sire," she answered, and dropped down a moment on her knees before him, to kiss his hand.

I marveled that Mayenne and all his armies had been able to keep this man off his throne and in his saddle four long years. It was plain why his power grew stronger every day, why every hour brought him new allies from the ranks of the League. You had only to see him to adore him. Once get him into Paris, the struggle would be over. They would put up with no other for king.

"Sire," mademoiselle said with hesitancy, "I shall tire you with my story."

"I am greatly in dread of it," the king answered, ceremoniously placing her in a chair before seating himself to listen. Then, to give her a moment, I think, to collect herself, he turned to his companion:

"Here, Rosny, if you ache to be grubbing over your papers, do not let us delay you."

"I am in no haste, Sire," his gentleman answered, unmoving.

"Which is to say, you dare not leave me alone," the king laughed out. "I tell you, St. Quentin, if I am not dragooned into a staid, discreet, steady-paced monarch, 'twill be no lapse of Whip-King Rosny's. I am listening, mademoiselle."

She began at once, eager and unfaltering. All her confusion was gone. It had been well-nigh impossible to tell the story to M. de St. Quentin, impossible to tell it to this impassive M. de Rosny. But to the King of France and Navarre it was as easy to talk as to one's playfellow.

"Sire, I am Lorance de Montluc. My grandfather was the Marshal Montluc."

"Were today next Monday, I could pray, 'God rest his soul,'" the king rejoined. "But even a heretic may say that he was a gallant general, an honor to France. He married a sister of François le Balafré? And mademoiselle is orphaned now, and my friend Mayenne's ward?"

"Yes, Sire. I came here, Sire, to tell M. de St. Quentin concerning his son. And though I am talking of myself, it is all the same story. Three years ago, after the king died, M. de Mayenne was endeavoring with all his might to bring the Duke of St. Quentin into the League. He offered me to him for his son, M. de Mar."

"And you are still Mlle. de Montluc?"

She turned to Monsieur with the prettiest smile in the world.

"M. de St. Quentin, though he has not fought for you, Sire, has ever been whole-heartedly loyal."

"Ventre-saint-gris!" the king exclaimed. "He is either an incredible loyalist or an incredible ass!"

Even the grave Rosny smiled, and the victim laughed as he defended himself.

"That my loyalty may be credible, Sire, I make haste to say that I had never seen mademoiselle till this hour."

"I know not whether to think better of you for that, or worse," the king retorted. "Had I been in your place, beshrew me but I should have seen her."

Monsieur smiled and was silent, with anxious eyes on mademoiselle.

"M. de St. Quentin withdrew to Picardie, Sire, but M. de Mar stayed in Paris. And my cousin Mayenne never gave up entirely the notion of the marriage. He is very tenacious of his plans."

"Aye," said the king, with a grimace. "Well I know."

"He blew hot and cold with M. de Mar. He favored the marriage on Sunday and scouted it on Wednesday and discussed it again on Friday."

"And what were M. de Mar's opinions?"

She met his probing gaze blushing but candid.

"M. de Mar, Sire, favored it every day in the week."

"I'll swear he did!" the king cried.

"When M. le Duc came back to Paris," mademoiselle went on, "and it was known he had espoused your cause, Sire, Mayenne was so loath to lose the whole house of St. Quentin to you that he offered to marry me out of hand to M. de Mar. And he refused."

"Ventre-saint-gris!" Henry cried. "We will marry you to a king's son. On my honor, mademoiselle –"

"Sire," she pleaded, "you promised to hear me."

"That I will, then. But I warn you I am out of patience with these St. Quentins."

"Then you are out of patience with devotion to your cause, Sire."

"What! you speak for the recreants?"

"I assure you, Sire, you have no more loyal servant than M. de Mar."

"Strange I cannot recollect the face of my so loyal servant," the king said dryly.

But she, with a fine scorn of argument, made the audacious answer: "When you see it, you will like it, Sire."

"Not half so well as I like yours, mademoiselle, I promise you! But he comes to me well commended, since you vouch for him. Or rather, he does not come. What is this ardent follower doing so long away from me? Where the devil does this eager partisan keep himself? St. Quentin, where is your son?"

"He had been with you long ago, Sire, but for the bright eyes of a lady of the League. And now she comes to tell me – my page tells me – he is in the Bastille."

"Ventre-saint-gris! And how has that calamity befallen?"

She hesitated a moment, embarrassed by her very wealth of matter, confused between her longing to set the whole case before the king, and her fear of wearying his patience. But his glance told her she need have no misgiving. Had she come to present him Paris, he could not have been more interested.

In the little silence Monsieur found his moment and his words.

"Sire, may I interrupt mademoiselle? Last night, for the first time in a month, I saw my son. He was just returned from an adventure under her window. Mayenne's guard had set on him, and he was escaped by the skin of his teeth. He declared to me that never till he was slain should he cease endeavor to win Mlle. de Montluc. And I? Marry, I ate my words in humblest fashion. After three years I made my surrender. Since you are his one desire, mademoiselle, then are you my one desire. I bade him God-speed."

She gave her hand to Monsieur, sudden tears welling over her lashes.

"Monsieur, I thought tonight I had no friends. And I have so many!"

"Mademoiselle," the king cried in the same breath, "fear not. I will get you your lover if I sell France for him."

She brushed the tears away and smiled on him.

"I have no fear, Sire. With you and M. de St. Quentin to save him, I can have no fear. But he is in desperate case. Has M. de St. Quentin told you of his secretary Lucas, my cousin Paul de Lorraine?"

"Aye," said the king, "it is a dolorous topic – very painful! Eh, Rosny?"

"I do not shrink from my pains, Sire," M. de Rosny answered quietly. "I hold myself much to blame in this matter. I thought I knew the Lucases root and branch – I did not discover that a daughter of the house had ever been a friend to Henri de Guise."

"And how should you discover it?" the king demanded. He had made the attack; now, since Rosny would not resent it, he rushed himself to the defense. "How were you to dream it? Henri de Guise's side was the last place to look for a girl of the Religion. But I forgive him. If he stole a Rochelaise, we have avenged it deep: we have stolen the flower of Lorraine."

"Paul Lucas – Paul de Lorraine," she went on eagerly, "was put into M. le Duc's house to kill him. He went all the more willingly that he believed M. de Mar to be my favored suitor. He tried to draw M. de Mar into the scheme, to ruin him. He failed. And the whole plot came to naught."

"I have learned that," the king said. "I have been told how a country boy stripped his mask off."

He glanced around suddenly at me where I stood red and abashed. He was so quick that he grasped everything at half a word. Instantly he had turned to the lady again. "Pray continue, dear mademoiselle."

"Afterward – that is, yesterday – Paul went to M. de Belin and swore against M. de Mar that he had murdered a lackey in his house in the Rue Coupejarrets. The lackey was murdered there, but Paul de Lorraine did it. The man knew the plot; Paul killed him to stop his tongue. I heard him confess it to M. de Mayenne. I and this Félix Broux were in the oratory and heard it."

"Then M. de Mar was arrested?"

"Not then. The officers missed him. Today he came to our house, dressed as an Italian jeweler, with a case of trinkets to sell. Madame admitted him; no one knew him but me and my chamber-*mate. On the way out, Mayenne met him and kept him while he chose a jewel. Paul de Lorraine was there too. I was like to die of fear. I went in to M. de Mayenne; I begged him to come out with me to supper, to dismiss the tradespeople that I might talk with him there – anything. But it availed not. M. de Mayenne spoke freely before them, as one does before common folk. Presently he led me to supper. Paul was left alone with M. de Mar and the boy. He recognized them. He was armed, and they were not, but they overbore him and locked him up in the closet."

"Mordieu, mademϕiselle! I was to rescue M. de Mar for your sake, but now I will do it for his own. I find him much to my liking. He came away clear, mademoiselle?"

"Aye, to be seized in the street by the governor's men. When M. de Mayenne found how he had been tricked, Sire, he blazed with rage."

"I'll warrant he did!" the king answered, suppressing, however, in deference to her distress, his desire to laugh. "Ventre-saint-gris, mademoiselle! forgive me if this amuses me here at St. Denis. I trow it was not amusing in the Hôtel de Lorraine."

"He sent for me, Sire," she went on, blanching at the memory; "he accused me of shielding M. de Mar. It was true. He called me liar, traitor, wanton. He said I was false to my house, to my bread, to my honor. He said I had smiling lips and a Judas-heart – that I had kissed him and betrayed him. I had given him my promise never to hold intercourse with M. de Mar again, I had given my word to be true to my house. M. de Mar came by no will of mine. I had no inkling of such purpose till I beheld him before madame and her ladies. He came to entreat me to fly – to wed him. I denied him, Sire. I sent him away. But was I to say to the guard, 'This way, gentlemen. This is my lover'?"

"Mademoiselle," the king exclaimed, "good hap that you have turned your back on the house of Lorraine. Here, if we are but rough soldiers, we know how to tender you."

"It was not for myself I came," she said more quietly. "My lord had the right to chasten me. I am his ward, and I did deceive him. But while he foamed at me came word of M. de Mar's capture. Then Mayenne swore he should pay for this dear. He said he should be found guilty of the murder. He said plenty of witnesses would swear to it. He said M. de Mar should be tortured to make him confess."

With an oath Monsieur sprang forward.

"Aye," she cried, starting up, "he swore M. de Mar should suffer the preparatory and the previous, the estrapade and the brodekins!"

"He dare not," the king shouted. "Mordieu, he dare not!"

"Sire," she cried, "you can promise him that for every blow he strikes Étienne de Mar you will strike me two. Mar is in his hands, but I am in yours. For M. de Mar, unhurt, you will deliver him me, unhurt. If he torture Mar, you will torture me."

"Mademoiselle," the king cried, "rather shall he torture every chevalier in France than I touch a hair of your head!"

"Sire –" the word died away in a sigh; like a snapped rose she fell at his feet.

The king was quick, but Monsieur quicker. On his knees beside her, raising her head on his arm, he commanded me:

"Upstairs, Félix! The door at the back – bid Dame Verney come instantly."

I flew, and was back to find him risen, holding mademoiselle in his arms. Her hair lay loose over his shoulder like a rippling flag; her lashes clung to her cheeks as they would never lift more.

"St. Quentin," his Majesty was saying, "I would have married her to a prince. But since she wants your son she shall have him, ventre-saint-gris, if I storm Paris tomorrow!" And as Monsieur was carrying her from the room, the king bent over and kissed her.

"Mademoiselle has dropped a packet from her dress," M. de Rosny said. "Will you take it, St. Quentin?"

The king, who was nearest, turned to pass it to him; at the sight of it he uttered his dear "ventre-saint-gris!" It was a flat, oblong packet, tied about with common twine, the seal cut out. The king twitched the string off, and with one rapid glance at the papers put them into Monsieur's hand.

"Take them, St. Quentin; they are yours."

XXIX

The two dukes.

Mademoiselle being given into Dame Verney's motherly hands, Gilles and I were ordered to repose ourselves on the skins in the saddler's shop. Lying there in the malodorous gloom, I could see the crack of light under the door at the back and hear, between Gilles's snores, the murmur of voices. The king and his gentlemen were planning to save my master; I went to sleep in perfect peace.

At daybreak, even before the saddler opened the shop, Monsieur routed us out.

"I'm off for Paris, lads. Félix comes with me. Gilles stays to guard mademoiselle."

I felt not a little injured, deeming that I, whom mademoiselle knew best, should not be the one chosen to stay by her. But the sting passed quickly. After all, Paris was likely to be more exciting than St. Denis.

The day being Friday, we delayed not to eat, but straightway mounted the two nags that a sunburned Béarn pikeman had brought to the door. As we walked them gently across the square, which at this rath hour we alone shared with the twittering birds, we saw coming down one of the empty streets the hurrying figure of M. de Rosny. My lord drew rein at once.

"You are no slugabed, St. Quentin," the young councilor called. "I deserved to miss you. Fear not! I come not to hinder you, but to wish you God-speed."

"Now, this is kind, Rosny," Monsieur answered, grasping his hand. "The more that you don't approve me."

Rosny smiled, like a sudden burst of sunshine in a December day. Another man's embrace would have meant less.

"I approve you so much, St. Quentin, that I cannot composedly see you putting your head into the lion's jaws."

"My head is used to the pillow. Do the teeth close, I am no worse off than my son."

"Your death makes your son's no easier."

"Why, what else to do, Rosny?" Monsieur exclaimed. "Mishandle the lady? Storm Paris? Sell the Cause?"

"I would we could storm Paris," Rosny sighed. "It would suit me better to seize the prisoner than to sue for him. But Paris is not ripe for us yet. You know my plan – to send to Villeroi. I believe he could manage this thing."

"I am second to none," Monsieur said politely, "in my admiration of M. de Villeroi's abilities. But to reach him is uncertain; what he can or will do, uncertain. Étienne de Mar is not Villeroi's son; he is mine."

"Aye, it is your business," Rosny assented. "It is yours to take your way."

"A mad way, but mine. But come, now, Rosny, you must admit that once or twice, when all your wiseacres were deadlocked, my madness has served."

Rosny took Monsieur's hand in a silent grip.

"Maximilien," the duke said, smiling down on him, "what a pity you are a scamp of a heretic!"

"Henri," Rosny returned gravely, "I would you had had the good fortune to be born in the Religion."

Again he wished us God-speed, and we gathered up our reins. As we turned the corner I glanced back to find him still standing as we had left him, gazing soberly after us.

The man who was going into the lion's den was far less solemn over it. By fits and starts, as he thought on his son's great danger, he contrived a gloomy countenance: but Monsieur had ridden all his life with Hope on the pillion; she did not desert him now. As we cantered steadily along in the fresh, cool morning, he already pictured M. Étienne released. However mad he acknowledged his errand to be, I think he was scarce visited by a doubt of its success. It was impossible to him that his son should not be saved.

We entered with perfect ease the gate of Paris, and took our way without hesitancy through the busiest streets. Nowhere did the guard spring on us, but, instead, more than once, the passers-by gathered in knots, the tradesmen and artisans ran out of their shops to cheer St. Quentin, to cheer France, to cheer peace, to cheer to the echo the Catholic king.

"I hope Mayenne hears them," Monsieur said to me, doffing his hat to a big farrier who had come out of his smithy waving impudently in the eye of all the world the white flag of the king.

We kept a brisk pace alike where they cheered us and where, in other streets, they scowled and hooted at us, so that I looked out for men with pistols in second-story windows. But, friend or foe, none stopped us till at length we drew rein before the grilles of the Hôtel de Lorraine.

They made no demur at admitting us. Monsieur went into the house, while I led the horses to the stables, where three or four grooms at once volunteered to rub them down, in eagerness to pump their guardian. But before the fellows had had time to get much out of me came Jean Marchand, all unrecognizing, to summon me indoors. I followed him in delight, partly for curiosity, partly because it had seemed to me when the doorway swallowed Monsieur that I might never see him more. Jean ushered me into the well-remembered council-room, where Monsieur stood alone, surprised at the sight of me.

"A lackey came for me," I said. "Look, Monsieur, that's where we shut up Lucas."

I ceased hastily, for I knew the step in the corridor.

It was difficult to credit mademoiselle's tale, to believe that Mayenne could ever be in a rage. In he came, big and calm and smiling, whatever emotion he may have felt at Monsieur's arrival not only buried, but with a flower-bed blooming over it. He greeted his guest with all the courteous ease of an unruffled conscience and a kindly heart. Not till his glance fell on me did he show any sign of discomposure.

"What, you!" he exclaimed brusquely.

"Your servant brought him hither," Monsieur said for me.

"I understood that one of your gentlemen had come with you. I sent for him, deeming his presence might conduce to your ease, M. de St. Quentin."

"I am at my ease, M. de Mayenne," my lord answered, with every appearance of truth. "You may go, Félix."

"No," said Mayenne. "Since he is here, he may stay. He serves the purpose as well as another."

He did not say what the purpose was, nor could I see for what he had kept me, unless as a sign to Monsieur that he meant to play fair. I began to feel somewhat heartened.

"You have guessed, M. de Mayenne, my errand?"

"Certainly. You have come to join the League."

Monsieur laughed out.

"On the contrary, M. de Mayenne, I have come to persuade you to join the King."

"That was a waste of horse-flesh."

"My friend, you know as well as we do that before long you will come over."

"I am not there yet, nor are my enemies scattered, nor is the League dead."

"Dying, my lord. It will get its coup de grâce o' Sunday, when the king goes to mass."

"St. Quentin," Mayenne made quiet answer, "when I am in such case that nothing remains to me but to fall on my sword or to kneel to Henry, be assured I shall kneel to Henry. Till then I play my game."

"Play it, then. We have the patience to wait for you, monsieur. Be assured, in your turn, that when you do come on your knees to his Majesty you will do well to have a friend or two at court."

"Morbleu," Mayenne cried, suddenly showing his teeth, "you will never go back to him if I choose to stop you!"

Monsieur raised his eyebrows at him, pained by the unsuavity.

"Of course not, monsieur. I quite understood that when I entered the gate. I shall never leave this house if you will otherwise."

"You will leave the house unharmed," Mayenne said curtly. "I shall not treat you as your late master treated my brother."

"I thank your generosity, monsieur, and commend your good sense."

Mayenne looked for a moment as if he repented of both. Then he broke into a laugh.

"One permits the insolences of the court jester."

Monsieur sprang up, his hand on his sword. But at once the quick flush passed from his face, and he, too, laughed.

Mayenne sat as he was, in somewhat lowering silence. My duke made a step nearer him, and spoke for the first time with perfect seriousness.

"My Lord Mayenne, it was no outrecuidance brought me here this morning. There is the Bastille. There is the axe. I know that my course has been offensive to you – your nephew proved me that. I know also that you do not care to meddle with me openly. At least, you have not meddled. Whether you will change your method – but I venture to believe not. I am popular just now in Paris. I had more cheers as I came in this morning than have met your ears for many a month. You have a great name for prudence, M. de Mayenne; I believe you will not molest me."

I hardly thought my duke was making a great name for prudence. But then, as he said, he had to work in his own way. Mayenne returned, with chilling calm:

"You may find me, St. Quentin, less timid than you suppose."

"Impossible. Mayenne's courage is unquestioned. I rely not on his timidity, but on his judgment."

"You take a great deal upon yourself in supposing that I wanted your death on Tuesday and do not want it on Friday."

"The king is three days nearer the true faith than on Tuesday. His party is three days stronger. On Tuesday it would have been a blunder to kill me; on Friday it is three days worse a blunder."

"But not less a pleasure. I have had something of the kind in mind ever since your master killed my brother."

"You should profit by that murderer's experience before you take a leaf from his book, M. de Mayenne. Henry of Valois gained singularly little when he slew Guise to make you head of the League."

Mayenne started, and then laughed to show his scorn of the flattery. But I think he was, all the same, half pleased, nonetheless because he knew it to be flattery. He said unexpectedly:

"Your son comes honestly by his unbound tongue."

"Ah, my son! Now that you mention him, we shall discuss him a little. You have put my son, monsieur, in the Bastille."

"No; Belin and my nephew Paul, whom you know, have put him there."

"But M. de Mayenne can get him out if he choose."

"If he choose."

Monsieur sat down again, with the air of one preparing for an amiable discussion.

"He is charged with the murder of one Pontou, a lackey. Of course he did not commit it, nor would you care if he had. His real offence is making love to your ward."

"Well, do you deny it?"

"Not the love, but the offence of it. Palpably you might do much worse than dispose of the lady to my heir."

"I might do much better than bestow my time on you if that is all you have to say."

"We have hardly opened the subject, M. de Mayenne –"

"I have no wish to carry it further."

"Monsieur, the king's ranks afford no better match than my heir."

"No maid of mine shall ever marry a Royalist."

"I swore no son of mine should ever marry a Leaguer, but I have come to see the error of my ways, as you will see yours, Mayenne. It is for you to choose where among the king's forces you will marry mademoiselle."

A vague uneasiness, a fear which he would not own a fear, crept into Mayenne's eyes. He studied the face before him, a face of gay challenge, and said, at length, not quite confidently himself:

"You speak with a confidence, St. Quentin."

"Why, to be sure."

Mayenne jumped heavily to his feet.

"What mean you?"

"I mean that mademoiselle's marrying is in my hands. Where is your ward, M. de Mayenne?"

"Mordieu! Have you found her?"

"You speak sooth."

"In your hôtel –"

"No, eager kinsman. In a place whither you cannot follow her."

Mayenne looked about, as if with some instinctive idea of seeking a weapon, of summoning his soldiers.

"By God's throne, you shall tell me where!"

"With pleasure. She is at St. Denis."

Mayenne cried helplessly, as numbed under a blow:

"St. Denis! But how –"

"How came she there? On foot, every step. I suppose she never walked two streets in her life before, has she, M. de Mayenne? But she tramped to St. Denis through the dark, to knock at my door at one in the morning."

Mayenne seized Monsieur's wrist.

"She is safe, St. Quentin? She is safe?"

"As safe, monsieur, as the king's protection can make her."

"Pardieu! Is she with the king?"

"She is at my lodgings, in the care of the saddler's wife who lets them. I left a staunch man in charge – I have no doubt of him."

"You answer for her safety?" Mayenne cried huskily; his breath coming short. He was flushed, the veins in his forehead corded.

"When she came last night, it happened that the king was there," Monsieur went on. "Her loveliness and her misery moved him to the heart."

"Thousand thunders of heaven! You, with your son, shall be hostages for her safe return."

"The king," Monsieur went on, as immovably as Mayenne himself at his best, "with that warm heart of his pitying beauty in distress, is eager for mademoiselle's marriage with her lover Mar. But he did not favor my venture here; he called it a silly business. He said you would clap me in jail, and he told me flat I might rot my life out there before he would give up to you Mlle. de Montluc."

"Well, then, pardieu, we'll try if he means it!"

"He gave me to understand that he meant it. The St. Quentins out of the way, there is Valère, stout Kingsman, to succeed. The king loses little."

"Then are you gone mad that you put yourself in my grasp?"

"I was never saner. I come, my friend, to make you listen to sanity."

I had waited from moment to moment Mayenne's summons to his soldiers. But he had not rung, and now he flung himself down again in his armchair.

"What, to your understanding, is sanity?"

"If you send me to join my son, monsieur, you leave mademoiselle without a protector, friendless, penniless, in the midst of a hostile army cursing the name of Mayenne. Have you reared her delicately, tenderly, for that?"

Mayenne sat silent, his face a mask. It was impossible to tell whether the shot hit. Monsieur went on:

"You can of course hold us in durance, torture us, kill us; but you must answer for it to the people of Paris."

Still was Mayenne silent, drumming on the edge of the table. Finally he said roughly, as if the words were dragged from him against his will:

"I shall not torture you. I never meant to torture Mar. The arrest was not my work. Since it was done, I meant to profit by it to keep him awhile out of my way – only that. I threatened my cousin otherwise in heat of passion. But I shall not torture him. I shall not kill him."

"Monsieur –"

"I put a card in your hand," Mayenne said curtly. His pride ill brooked to concede the point, but he could not have it supposed that he did not see what he was doing. "I give you a card. Do what you can with it."

"Monsieur, you show what little surprises me – knightly generosity. It is to that generosity I appeal."

"Is the horse of that color? But now you were frightening my prudence."

"Ah, but how fortunate the man to whom generosity and prudence point the same path!"

It may have been but pretence, this smiling bonhomie of Monsieur's. Mayenne doubtless gauged it as such, but, at any rate, he suffered it to warm him. He regained of a sudden all the amiability with which he had greeted his guest. Smiling and calm, he answered:

"St. Quentin, I care little for either your threats or your cajoleries. They amuse me alike, and move me not. But I have a care for my sweet cousin. Since you threaten me with her danger, you have the whiphand."

Now it was Monsieur's turn to sit discreetly silent, waiting.

"I went last night to tell the child I would not harm her lover. Lo! she had flown. I had a regiment searching Paris for her. I was in the streets myself till dawn."

"Monsieur, she made her way to us at St. Denis to offer herself to our torture did you torture Mar."

"Morbleu!" Mayenne cried, half rising.

"God's mercy, we're not ruffians out there! I tell it to show you to what the maid was strung."

"I never thought it great matter whom one married," Mayenne said slowly: "one boy is much like another. I should have mated her as befitted her station – I thought she would be happy enough. And she was good about it: I did not see how deep she cared. She was docile till I drove her too hard. She's a loving child. You are fortunate in your daughter, St. Quentin."

Monsieur sprang up radiant, advancing on him open-armed. Mayenne added, with his cool smile:

"You need not flatter yourself, Monsieur, that it is your doing. I laugh at your threats. 'Twere sport to me to clap you behind bars, to say to your king, to the mob you brag of, 'Come, now, get him out.'"

"Then," cried Monsieur, "I must value my sweet daughter more than ever."

He was standing over Mayenne with outstretched hand, but the chief delayed taking it.

"Not quite so fast, my friend. If I yield up the Duc de St. Quentin, the Comte de Mar, and Mlle. Lorance de Montluc, I demand certain little concessions for myself."

"By all means, monsieur. You stamp us churls else."

My duke sat again, his smile a shade uneasy. Which Mayenne perceived with quiet enjoyment, as he went on blandly: "Nothing that I could ask of you, M. de St. Quentin, could equal, could halve, what I give. Still, that the knightliness may not be, to your mortification, all on one side, I have thought of something for you to grant."

"Name it, monsieur."

"Another point in your favor I had forgot," Mayenne observed, with his usual reluctance to show his cards even when the time had come to spread them. "Last night I laid on this table a packet, just arrived, which I was told belonged to you. When I had time to think of it again, it had vanished. I accused my lackeys, but later it occurred to me that Mlle. de Montluc, arming for battle, had purloined it."

"Your shrewdness does you credit."

"You see you have scored a fourth point, though again by no prowess of your own. Therefore am I emboldened to demand what I want."

"Even to half my fortune –"

"No, not your gear. Save that for your Béarnais's itching palm."

"Then what the devil is it you want? You will not get my name in the League."

"I am glad my nephew Paul bungled that affair of his," Mayenne went on at his own pace. "It might have been a blunder to kill you; it had certainly been a pity. Though we Lorraines have two murders to avenge, I have changed my mind about beginning with yours."

"You are wise, monsieur. I am, after all, a harmless creature."

Mayenne laughed.

"Natheless have you done your best here in Paris to undermine me. Did I let you carry on your little works unhindered, they might in time annoy me. Therefore I request that so long as I stay in Paris you stay out."

"Oh, I don't like that!"

The naïveté amazed while it amused Mayenne.

"Possibly not, but you will consent to it. You will ride out of my court, when we have finished some necessary signing of papers, straight to the St. Denis gate. And you will pledge me your honor to make no attempt hereafter to enter so long as the city is mine."

Mayenne was smiling broadly, Monsieur frowning. He relished the condition little. He was enjoying himself much in Paris, his dangers, his successes, his biting his thumb at the power of the League. To be killed at his post was nothing, but to be bundled away from it to inglorious safety, that stuck in his gorge. For a moment he actually hesitated. Then he began to laugh at his own hesitation.

"Well, ma foi! what do I expect? To walk, a rabbit, into the lion's den and make my own terms to Leo? I am happy to accept yours, M. de Mayenne, especially since, do I refuse, you will nonetheless pack me off."

"You mistake, St. Quentin. You are welcome to spend the rest of your days with me."

"In the Bastille?"

"Or in the League."

"The former is preferable."

"You may count yourself thrice fortunate, then, that a third alternative is given you."

"It needs not the reminder. You have treated me as a prince indeed. Be assured the St. Quentins will not forget."

"Everyone forgets."

"Perhaps. But when you need our good offices we shall not have had time to forget."

"Pardieu, St. Quentin, you have good courage to tell me to my head my course is run!"

"My dear Mayenne, none punishes the maunderings of the court jester."

Monsieur laughed out with a gay gusto; after a moment Mayenne laughed too. My duke cried quickly, rising and walking the length of the table to his host:

"You have dealt with me munificently, Mayenne. You have kept back but one thing I want. That is yourself. You know you must come over to us sooner or later. Come now!"

The other did not flame out at Monsieur, but answered coldly:

"I have no taste to be Navarre's vassal."

"Better his than Spain's."

Mayenne shrugged his shoulders, his face at its stolidest.

"Well, I am no astrologer to read the future."

Monsieur laid an emphatic hand on his host's shoulder.

"But I read it, my friend. I see a French land under a French king, a Catholic and a gallant fellow, faithful to old friends, friendly to old foes. I see the dear land at peace at last, the looms humming, the mills clacking, wheat growing thick on the battlefields."

Mayenne looked up with a grim smile.

"I have still a field or two to water for that wheat. My compliments to your new master, St. Quentin; you may tell him from me that when I submit, I submit. When I have made my surrender, from that hour forth am I his hound to lick his hand, to guard and obey him. Till then, let him beware of my teeth! While I have one pikeman to my back, one sou in my pouch, I fight my cause."

"And when you have none, you yet have three pairs of hands at Henry's court to pull you up out of the mire."

"I thank their graciousness, though I shall never need their offices," Mayenne said grandly. He stood there stately and proud and confident, the picture of princeliness and strength. Last night at St. Denis it had seemed to me that no power could defy my king. Now it seemed to me that no king could nick the power of my Lord Mayenne. When suddenly, precisely like a mummer who in his great moment winks at you to let you know it is make-believe, the general-duke's dignity melted into a smile.

"After all," he said, "it's as well to lay an anchor to windward."

XXX

My young lord settles scores with two foes at once.

Occupied in wrangling with the grooms over the merits of our several stables, with the soldiers over politics and the armies, I awaited in a shady corner of the court the conclusion of formalities. I had just declared that King Henry would be in Paris within a week, and was on the point of getting my crown cracked for it, when, as if for the very purpose – save the mark! – of rescuing me, entered from the street Lucas. He approached rapidly, eyes straight in front of him, heeding us no whit; but all the loungers turned to stare at him. Even then he paid no heed, passing us without a glance. But the tall d'Auvray bespoke him.

"M. de Lorraine! Any news?"

He started and turned to us in half-absent surprise, as if he had not known of our presence nor, indeed, quite realized it now. He was both pale and rumpled, like one who has not closed an eye all night.

"Any news here?" he made Norman answer.

"No, monsieur, unless his Grace has information. We have heard nothing."

"And the woman?"

"Sticks to it mademoiselle told her never a word."

Lucas stood still, his eyes traveling dully over the group of us, as if he expected somewhere to find help. At the same time he was not in the least thinking of us. He looked straight at me for a full minute before he awoke to my identity.

"You!"

"Yes, M. de Lorraine," I said, with all the respectfulness I could muster, which may not have been much. Considering our parting, I was ready for any violence. But after the first moment of startlement he regarded me in a singularly lackluster way, while he inquired without apparent resentment how I came there.

"With M. le Duc de St. Quentin," I grinned at him. "We and M. de Mayenne are friends now."

I could not rouse him even to curiosity, it seemed. But he turned abruptly to the men with more life than he had yet shown.

"You've not told this fellow?"

"We understand our orders, monsieur," d'Auvray answered, a bit huffed.

Now this was eminently the place for me to hold my tongue, but of course I could not.

"They had no need to tell me, M. de Lorraine. I know quite well what the trouble is. I know rather more about it than you do yourself."

He confronted me now with all the fire I could ask.

"What mean you, whelp?"

"I mean mademoiselle. What else should I mean?"

"What do you know?"

"Everything."

"Her whereabouts?"

"Her whereabouts."

He had his hand to his knife by this. I abated somewhat of my drawl to say, still airily:

"Go ask M. de St. Quentin. He's here. He'll be so glad to see you."

"Here?"

"Certes. He's closeted now with M. de Mayenne. They're thicker than brothers. Go see for yourself, M. – Lucas."

"Where is mademoiselle?"

"Safe. She's to marry the Comte de Mar tomorrow."

He stared at me for one moment, weighing whether this could be true; then without further parley he shot into the house.

"Is that true?" d'Auvray demanded.

Their tongues loosened now, they flooded me with questions concerning mademoiselle, which I answered warily as I could, heartily repenting me by this of baiting Lucas. No good could come of it. He might even turn Mayenne from his bargain, upset all our triumph. I hardly heard what the soldiers said to me; I was almost nervous enough, wild enough, to dash upstairs after him. But that was no help. I stayed where I was, fevered with anxiety.

At the end of five minutes he came out of the house again, and, without a glance at us, went straight through the gate with the step and air of a man who knows what he is about. I was no easier in my mind though I saw him gone.

Soon on his steps came a lackey to order M. de St. Quentin's horses and two musketeers to mount and ride with him. On reaching the door with the nags, I discovered I was not to be of the party; our second steed must carry gear of mademoiselle's and her handwoman, a hard-faced peasant, silent as a stone. Though the men quizzed her, asking if she were glad to get to her mistress again, whether she had known all this time the lady's whereabouts, she answered no single word, but busied herself seeing the horse loaded to her notion. Presently, in the guidance of Pierre, Monsieur appeared.

"You stay, Félix, and go to the Bastille for your master. Then you will wait at the St. Denis gate for Vigo, with horses."

"Is all right, Monsieur?" I had to ask, as I held his stirrup. "Is all right? Lucas –"

His face had been a little clouded as he came down the stairs, and now it darkened more, but he answered:

"Quite right, Achates. M. de Mayenne stands to his word. Lucas availed nothing."

He stood a moment frowning, then his countenance cleared up.

"My faith! I have enough to gladden me without fretting that Lucas is alive. Fare you well, Félix. You are like to reach St. Denis as soon as I. My son's horse will not lag."

He sprang to the saddle with a smiling salute to his guardians, and the little train clattered off.

Pierre came to my elbow with an open paper – the order signed and sealed for M. de Mar's release.

"Here, my young cockerel, you and d'Auvray are to take this to the Bastille, and it will be strange if your master does not walk free again. His Grace bids you tell M. de Mar he remembers Wednesday night, underground."

"And I remember Tuesday night in the council-room, Pierre," I was beginning, but he cut me short. Even now that I was in favor, he risked no mention of his disobedience. He packed me off with d'Auvray on the instant; I had no chance to ask him whether he suspected us yesterday. Sometimes I have thought he did, but I am bound to say he gave us no look to show it.

D'Auvray and I walked straight across Paris to the many-towered Bastille. It seemed a little way. Before the potent name of Mayenne bars flew open; a sentry on guard in the court led us into a small room all stone, floor, walls, ceiling, where sat at the table some high official, perhaps the governor of the prison himself. He was an old campaigner, grizzled and weather-beaten, his right sleeve hanging empty. An interesting figure, no doubt, but I paid him scant attention, for at his side stood Lucas.

"I come on M. de Mayenne's business," he was expostulating, vehement, yet civil. "I suppose he did not think it necessary to write the order, since you know me."

"The regulations, M. de Lorraine –" The officer broke off to demand of our escort, "Well, what now?"

I went straight up to him, not waiting permission, and held out my paper.

"An order, if it please you, monsieur, for the Comte de Mar's release."

Lucas's hand went out to snatch and crumple it; then his clenched fist dropped to his side. It seemed as if his eyes would blacken the paper with their fire.

"Just that – the requisition for M. de Mar's release," the officer told him, looking up from it. "All perfectly regular and in order. In five minutes, M. de Lorraine, the Comte de Mar shall be before you. You may have all the conversation you wish."

Lucas's face was as blank as the wall.

"I am a soldier, and a soldier's orders must be obeyed," the officer went on to explain, evidently not caring to offend the general's nephew. "Without the written order I could not admit your brother of Guise. But now you can have all the conversation you desire with M. de Mar."

Lucas's face did not change, save to scowl at the very name of his brother Guise. He said curtly, "No, I must get back to his Grace," and, barely bowing, went from the room.

"Now, I don't make that out," the keeper muttered in his beard. That Lucas should be in one moment cured of his urgent need of seeing the Comte de Mar was too much for him, but no riddle to me. I knew he had come to stab M. Étienne in his cell. It was his last chance, and he had missed it. I feared him no longer, for I believed in Mayenne's faith. My master once released, Lucas could not hurt him.

What was as much to the point, the officer had no doubt of Mayenne's good faith. He went with his paper into an inner room, where we caught sight, through the door, of big books with a clerk or two behind them, and in a moment appeared again with a key.

"Since the young gentleman's a count, I'll do turnkey's office myself," he said, his grim old battlement of a face smiling.

This was our day; from Mayenne down, everybody went out of his way to pleasure us. I was suddenly emboldened by his manner.

"Monsieur, perhaps it is preposterous to ask, but might I go with you?"

He looked at me a moment, surprised.

"Well, after all, why not? You too, Sir Musketeer, an you like."

So the three of us, he and d'Auvray and I, went to rescue the Comte de Mar.

We passed through corridor after corridor, row after row of heavy-barred doors. The deeper we penetrated the mighty pile, the fonder I grew of my friend Mayenne, by whose complaisance none of these doors would shut on me. We climbed at last a steep turret stair winding about a huge fir trunk, lighted by slits of windows in the four-foot wall, and at the top turned down a dark passage to a door at the end, the bolts of which, invisible to me in the gloom, the veteran drew back with familiar hand.

The cell was small, with one high window through which I could see naught but the sky. For all furniture it contained a pallet, a stool, a bench that might serve as table. M. Étienne stood at the window, his arm crooked around the iron bars, gazing out over the roofs of Paris.

He wheeled about at the door's creaking.

"I go to trial, monsieur?" he asked quickly, not seeing me behind the keeper.

"No, M. le Comte. The charge is canceled. I come to set you free."

I dashed in past the officer, snatching my lord's hand to kiss.

"It's true, monsieur! You're free! It's all settled with Mayenne. Monsieur's seen him; he sets you free. He said, 'In recognizance of Wednesday night.'"

Incredulous joy flashed over his face, to give way to belief without joy.

"Now I know she's married."

"Nothing of the sort!" I fairly shouted at him, dancing up and down in my eagerness. "She's to marry M. le Comte. She's at St. Denis with Monsieur. She's to marry you. It's all arranged. Mayenne consents – the king – everybody. It's all settled. She marries you."

Preposterous as it seemed, he could not discredit my fervor. He followed us out of the cell and through the fortress in a radiant daze. He half believed himself dreaming, I think, and feared to speak lest his happiness should melt. I fancied even that he walked lightly and gingerly, as if the slightest unwary movement might break the spell. Not till we were actually in the open door of the court, face to face with freedom, did he rouse himself to acknowledge the thing real. With a joyous laugh, he turned to the keeper:

"M. de La Motte, you should employ your leisure in writing down your reflections, like the Chevalier de Montaigne. You could give us a trenchant essay on the Ingratitude of Man. Here are you host of the biggest inn in Paris – a pile more imposing than the Louvre itself. Your hospitality is so eager that you insist on entertaining me, so lavish that you lodge me for nothing, would keep me without a murmur till the end of my life. Yet I, ingrate that I am, depart without a thank you!"

"They don't leave in such case that they can very well thank me, most of my guests," La Motte answered, with a dry smile. "You are a fortunate man, M. de Mar."

"M. le Comte, will you come quietly with me to the St. Denis gate?" d'Auvray asked him. "Or must I borrow a guard from M. de La Motte?"

M. Étienne's whole face was smiling; not his lips alone, but his eyes. Even his skin and hair seemed to have taken on a brighter look. He glanced at d'Auvray in surprise at the absurd question.

"I will come like a lamb, M. le Mousquetaire."

We saluted La Motte and walked merrily out into the Place Bastille. I think I never felt so grand as when I passed through the noble sally-port, the soldiers making no motion to hinder us, but all saluting as if we owned the place. It had its advantage, this making friends with Mayenne.

The first thing my lord did, still in the shadow of the prison, was to come to terms with d'Auvray.

"See here, my friend, why must you put yourself to the fatigue of escorting me to the gate?"

"Orders, monsieur. The general-duke wants to know that you get into no mischief between here and the gate. You are banished, you understand, from Paris."

"I pledge you my word I shall make no attempt to elude my fate. I go straight to the gate. But, with all politeness to you, Sir Musketeer, I could dispense with your company."

"I am a soldier, and a soldier's orders must be obeyed," d'Auvray quoted the keeper's words, which seemed to have impressed him. "However, M. le Comte, if I had something to look at, I could walk ten paces behind you and look at it."

"Oh, if it is a question of something to play with!" M. Étienne laughed.

D'Auvray was provided with toys, and M. Étienne linked arms with me, the soldier out of ear-shot behind us. He followed till we were in the Rue St. Denis, when, waving his hand in farewell, he turned his steps with the pious consciousness of duty done. Only I looked back to see it; monsieur had forgotten his existence.

"I am not proud; I don't mind being marched through the streets by a musketeer," M. Étienne explained as we started; "but I can't talk before him. Tell me, Félix, the story, if you would have me live."

And I told him, till we almost ran blindly into the tower of the St. Denis gate.

We learned of the warder that M. de St. Quentin had recently passed out, but that nothing had been seen of his equery. No steeds were here for us.

"Well, then, we'll go have a glass. But if Vigo doesn't come soon, by my faith, I'll walk to St. Denis!"

But that promised glass was never drunk, nor were we to set out at once for St. Denis; for in the door of the wine-shop we met Lucas.

I had dismissed him from thought, as something out of the reckoning, dead and done with, powerless as yesterday's broken sword. I thought him gone out of our lives when he went out of prison – gone forever, like last year's snow. And here within the hour we encountered him, a naked sword in his hand, a smile on his lips. He said, in the flower of his easy insolence:

"Tuesday I told you our hour would come. It is here."

"At your service," quoth my lord.

"Then it needs not to slap your face?"

"You insult me safely, Lucas. You have but one life. That is forfeit, be you courteous."

"You think so?"

"I know it."

Lucas held out the bare sword, hilt toward us.

"Monsieur had a box for weapon yesterday, but as I prefer to fight in the established way, I ventured to provide him with a sword."

"Thoughtful of you, Lucas. Is this the make of sword you elect to be killed with?"

He was bending the blade to try its temper. Lucas unsheathed his own.

"M. de Mar may have his choice."

M. de Mar professed himself satisfied with the blade given him.

"Have you summoned your seconds, Lucas?"

Lucas raised his eyebrows.

"Is that necessary? I thought we might settle our affairs without delay. I confess myself impatient."

"Your sentiments for once are mine."

"It is understood you bring your spaniel with you. He will watch that I do not spring on you before you are ready," Lucas said, with a fine sneer.

"And who is to watch me?"

"Oh, monsieur's chivalry is notorious. Precautions are unnecessary. It is your privilege, monsieur, to appoint the happy spot."

"The spot is near at hand. Where you slew Pontou is the fitting place for you to die."

"It is fitting for you to die in your own house," Lucas amended.

Without further parley we turned into the Rue des Innocents, on our way to that of the Coupejarrets.

Now, I had been on the watch from the first instant for foul play. I had suspected something wrong with the sword, but my lord, who knew, had accepted it. Then, when Lucas proposed no seconds, I had felt sure of a trap. But his inviting my presence at the place of our choice smelt like honesty.

M. Étienne remarked casually to me:

"Faith, there'll soon be as many ghosts in the house as you thought you saw there – Grammont, Pontou, and now Lucas. What ails you, lad? Footsteps on your grave?"

But it was not thoughts of my grave caused the shudder, but of his. For of the three men of the lightning-flash, the third was not Lucas, but M. Étienne. What if the vision were, after all, the thing I had at first believed it – a portent? An appearance not of those who had died by steel, but of those who must. One, two, and now the third.

Next moment I almost laughed out in relief. It was not Pontou I had seen, but Louis Martin. And he was living. The vision was no omen, but a mere happening. Was I a babe to shiver so?

And yet Martin, if not dead, was like to die. He was in duress as a Leaguer spy, to await King Henry's will. All who entered this house lay under a curse. We should none of us pass out again, save to our tombs.

We entered the well-remembered little passage, the well-remembered court, where shards of glass still strewed the pavement. Someone – the gendarmes, I fancy, when they took away Pontou – had put a heavy padlock on the door Lucas and Grammont left swinging.

"We go in by your postern, Félix," my master said. "M. Lucas, I confess I prefer that you go first."

Lucas put his back to the wall.

"Why go farther, M. le Comte?"

"Do you long for interruption'?"

"We were not noticed coming in. The street was quiet."

He crossed the court abruptly and went down the alley to look into the street.

"Not a soul in sight," he said, coming back. "I think we shall not be interrupted. Still, it is wise to use every care. We will fight, if you like, in the house."

He opened with his knife the fastened shutter, and leaped lightly in. Monsieur followed. I, the last, was for closing the shutter, but he stopped me.

"No; leave it wide. I have no fancy for a walk in pitch-darkness with M. Lucas."

"Do we fight here?" Lucas asked, facing us in the wide, square hall. "We can let in more light."

"You seem anxious, my friend, to call attention to your whereabouts. As I am host, I designate the fighting-ground. Upstairs, if you please."

"I suppose you insist on my walking first," Lucas sneered.

"I request it, monsieur."

"With all the willingness in the world," his rogue-ship answered, setting foot straightway on the stair and mounting steadily, never turning to see how near we followed, or what we did with our hands. His trust made me ashamed of our lack of it. I almost believed we did him injustice. Yet at heart I could not bring myself to credit him with any fair dealing.

We went up one flight, up two. We had left behind us the twilight of the lower story, had not reached dawn again at the top. We walked in blackness. Suddenly I halted.

"Monsieur!"

"What?"

"I heard a noise."

"Of course you did. The place is full of rats."

"It was no rat. It was footsteps."

We all three held still.

"There, monsieur. Don't you hear?"

"Nothing, Félix; your teeth are chattering. Cross yourself and come on."

But I could not stand it.

"I'll go back and see, monsieur."

"No," Lucas said, striding back from the foot of the next flight. "I will go."

We saw a glint in the gloom, monsieur's bared sword.

"You will go neither one of you. Hush! If we show ourselves, there'll be no duel today."

We kept still, all three leaning over the banister, peering down to where the white tiles picked themselves out of the floor of the hall far beneath. We could see them better than we could see one another. All was silent. Not so much as a rustle came up from below. Suddenly Lucas made a step or two, as if to pass us. M. Étienne wheeled about, raising his sword toward the spot where from his footfalls we supposed Lucas to be.

"You show an eagerness to get away from me, M. de Lorraine."

"Not in the least, M. de Mar. This alarm is but Félix's poltroonery, yet it prompts me to go down and close the shutter."

"On the contrary, you will go up with me. Félix will close the shutter."

They confronted each other, vague shapes in the darkness, each with drawn sword. Then Lucas raised his in salute.

"As you will; so be someone sees to it."

"Go, Félix."

Lucas first, they mounted the last flight of stairs, and their footsteps passed along the corridor to the room at the back. I, as I was ordered, set my face down the stairs.

They might mock me as they liked, but I could not get it out of my head that I had heard steps below. Cautiously, with a thumping heart, I stole from stair to stair, pausing at the bottom of the flight. I heard plainly the sound of moving above me, and of voices; but below not a whisper, not a creak. It must have been my silly fears. Resolved to choke them, I planted my feet boldly on the next flight, and descended humming, to prove my ease, the rollicky tune of Peyrot's catch. Suddenly, from not three feet off, came the soft singing:

Mirth, my love, and Folly dear –

My knees knocked together, and the breath fluttered in my throat. It seemed the darkness itself had given tongue. Then came a low laugh and the muttered words:

"Here we are, M. de Lorraine. Are you ready?"

There was a stir of feet on the landing before me, behind the voice. The house, then, was full of Lucas's cutthroats, the first of them Peyrot. In the height of my terror, I remembered that M. Étienne's life, too, depended on my wits, and I kept them. I whispered, for whispering voices are hard to tell apart:

"Not yet. The two of them are up there. Keep quiet, and I'll send the boy down. When you've finished him, come up."

"As you say, monsieur. It is your job."

I turned, scarce able to believe my luck, and, not daring to run, walked upstairs again. Prick my ears as I might, I heard no movement after me. Actually, I had fooled Peyrot. I had gone down to meet my death, and a tune had saved me.

When I reached the uppermost landing, I rushed along the passage and into the room, flinging the door shut, locking and bolting it.

They had not begun to fight, but had busied themselves clearing the space of all obstacles. The table was pushed against the wall in the corner by the door; the chairs were heaped one on another at the end of the room. Both shutters were wide open. M. Étienne, bareheaded, in his shirt, stood at guard. Lucas was kneeling on the floor, picking up with scrupulous care some bits of a broken plate. He sprang to his feet at sight of me.

"What is it?" cried M. Étienne.

"Cutthroats. They'll be here in a minute."

Even as I spoke, I heard tramping on the stairs below. My slam of the door had warned them that something was wrong.

"Was that your delay?" M. Étienne shouted, springing at his foe.

"I play to win!" Lucas answered, smiling.

The blades met; the men circled about and about. Lucas, though he preferred to murder, knew how to duel.

We were doomed. With monsieur's sword for only weapon, we could never hope to pass the gang. In another minute they would be here to batter the door down and end us. Our consolation lay in killing Lucas first. Yet as I watched, I feared that M. Étienne, in the brief moments that remained to him, could not conquer him, so shrewd and strong was Lucas's fence. Must the scoundrel win? I started forward to play Pontou's trick. Lucas sought to murder us. Why not we him?

One flash from my lord's eyes, and I retreated in despair. For I knew that did I touch Lucas, M. Étienne would let fall his sword, let Lucas kill him. And the bravos were on the last flight.

Was there no escape? There were three doors in the room. One led to the passage, one to the closet, the third – I dashed through to find myself in a large empty chamber, a door wide open giving on the passage. Through it I could see the dusky figures of four men running up the stairs.

I was across the room like an arrow, and got the door shut and bolted before they could reach the landing. The next moment someone flung against it. It stood firm. Delaying only a moment to shake it, three of the four I could hear run to the farther door, whence issued the noise of the swords.

I, inside the wall, ran back too. The combat still raged. Neither, that I could see, had gained the least advantage. Outside, the murderers dashed themselves upon the door.

I dragged at the heavy table, and, with a strength that amazed myself, pushed and pulled it before the door. It would make the panels a little firmer.

Was there no escape? None? I ran once more into the second chamber. Its shutters were closed; I threw them open. There was no other door to the room, no hiding place. There was a chimney, but spanned a foot above the fireplace by two iron bars. The thinnest sweep that ever wielded broom could not have squeezed between them.

In despair, I ran to the window again. Top of the house as it was, I thought I would sooner leap than be stabbed to death. I stuck my head out. It was the same window where I had stood when Grammont seized me. There, not ten feet away, eight at the most, but a little above me, was the casement of my garret in the Amour de Dieu. Would it be possible to jump and catch the sill? If I did, I could scarce pull myself in.

I looked below me. There swung the sign of the Amour de Dieu. And there beside it stood a homespun figure surely known to me. There was no mistaking that bald pate. I yelled at the top of my lungs:

"Maître Jacques!"

He looked up, gaping at this voice out of the sky, but, despite his amazement, I saw that he knew me.

"Maître Jacques! We're being murdered! We can't get out! Help us for the love of Christ! Bring a plank, a rope, to the window there!"

For an instant he stood confounded. Then he vanished into the inn.

I waited, on fire. Still from the next room sounded the clash of steel. White shirt and black doublet passed the door in turn, unflagging, ungaining.

Suddenly came a new noise from the passage, of trampling and rending, blows and oaths. My first thought was that they were fighting out there, that rescuers had come. Then, as I listened, I learned better. Despairing of kicking down the door, they were tearing out a piece of stair-rail for a battering-ram. It would not long stand against that.

I ran back to the window. No Jacques appeared. We were lost, lost!

Hark, from the next room a cry, a fall! Well, were it Lucas's victory, he might kill me as well as another. I walked into the back room. But it was Lucas who lay prone.

"Come, come!" I cried, clutching monsieur's wrist. But he would not till with Lucas's own misericorde he had given him coup de grâce.

Crash! Crash! The upper panel shivered in twain. A great splinter six inches wide, hanging from the top, blocked the opening. A hand came through to wrench it away.

M. Étienne, across the room at a leap, drove his knife through the hand, nailing it to the wood. On the instant he recognized its owner.

"Good morning, Peyrot. We've recovered the packet."

Not waiting for further amenities, I seized my lord and dashed him into the front room, only a faint hope to lead me, but the oaths of the bravos a good spur. And, St. Quentin be thanked, there in the garret window were Jacques and his tapsters, pushing a ladder to us.

"Go, monsieur! There are four behind us. Go!"

"You first!"

But I, who had snatched up his sword as he stabbed Lucas, ran back to guard the door. He had the sense to see there was no good arguing. Crying, "Quick after me, Félix!" he crawled out on the ladder.

Peyrot was released. Another blow from the ram, and the door fell to finders. They leaped in over the table like a freshet over a dam. I darted to the window. M. Étienne was in the garret, helping hold the ladder for me. I flung myself upon it all too eagerly. Like a lath it snapped.

XXXI

"The very pattern of a king."

The next world appeared to be strangely like this. I found myself lying on a straw bed in a little low attic, my head resting comfortably on someone's shoulder, while someone else poured wine down my gullet. Presently I discovered that Maître Jacques's was the ministering hand, M. Étienne's the shoulder. After all, this was not heaven, but still Paris.

I had no desire to speak so long as the flow of old Jacques's best Burgundy continued; but when he saw my eyes wide open, he stopped, and I said, my voice, to my surprise, very faint and quavery:

"What happened?"

"Dear, brave lad! You fainted!"

My lord's voice was as unsteady as mine.

"But the ladder?" I murmured.

"The ladder broke. But you had hold beyond the break. You hung on till we seized you. And then you swooned."

"What a baby!" I said, getting to my feet. "But the men, monsieur? Peyrot?"

"I think we've seen the last of those worthies. They took to their heels when you escaped them."

"But, monsieur, they've gone to inform! You'll be taken for killing Lucas."

"I doubt it. Themselves smell too strong of blood to dare bruit the matter. Natheless, if you can walk now, we'll make good time to the gate."

But for all his haste, he would not start till I had had some bread and soup down in the kitchen.

"We must take good care of you, boy Félix," he said. "For where the St. Quentins would be without you, I tremble to think."

I set out a new man. In three steps, it seemed to me, we had reached the city gate, to find the way blocked by a company of twenty or thirty horse, the St. Quentin uniform flaunting gay in the sun. The nearest trooper set up a shout at sight of us, when Vigo, coming out suddenly from behind a nag, took M. le Comte in his big embrace. He released him immediately, looking immensely startled at his own demonstration.

M. Étienne laughed out at him.

"Be more careful, I beg you, Vigo! You will make me imagine myself of some importance."

"I thought you swallowed up," Vigo growled. "You had been here – I couldn't get a trace of you."

"I was killing Lucas."

"Sacré! He's dead?"

"Dead."

"That's the best morning's work ever you did, M. Étienne."

"Have you horse for us, Vigo?"

"Of course. Some of the men will walk. I suppose we're leaving Paris to buy you out of the Bastille?"

"Not worth it, eh, Vigo?"

"Yes," said Vigo, gravely – "yes, M. Étienne. You are worth it."

Vigo's troop was but slow-moving, as some of the horses carried double, some were loaded with chattels. M. Étienne and I, on the duke's blood-chargers, soon left the cavalcade behind us. Before I knew it, we were halted at the outpost of the camp. My lord gave his name.

"To be sure!" cried the sentry. "We've orders about you. You dine with the king, M. de Mar."

"Mordieu! I do?"

"You do. Orders are to take you to him out of hand. Captain!"

The officer lounged out of the tavern door.

"Captain, M. de Mar."

"Oh, aye!" cried the captain, coming forward with brisk interest. "M. de Mar, you're the child of luck. You dine with the king."

"I am the child of bewilderment, captain."

"And you've not too much time to recover from it, M. le Comte. You are to go straight to the king."

"I may go to M. de St. Quentin's lodgings first?"

"No, monsieur; straight to the king."

"What! in my shirt?"

"I can't help it, monsieur," the captain laughed. "I suppose the king did not guess you were coming in your shirt. Anyway, his order was to fetch you direct. And direct you go. But never care. Our king's no stickler for toggery. He's known what it is himself to lack for a coat."

"I might wash my face, then."

"Certainly. No harm in that."

So M. Étienne went into the tournebride and washed his face. And that was all the toilet he made for audience with the greatest king in the world.

"You'll ride to Monsieur's," he commanded me, when the captain answered:

"No; he goes with you, monsieur, if he's the boy Choux, Troux, whatever it is."

"Broux – Félix Broux!" I cried, a-quiver.

"That's it. You go to the king, too. Another luck-child."

I thought so indeed. We followed the sentry through the town in a waking dream, content to let him do with us as he would. He did the talking, explained to the grandees in the king's hall our names and errand. One of them led us up the stairs and knocked at a closed door.

"Enter!"

It was Henry's own voice. I pinched monsieur's hand to tell him. Our guide opened the door a crack.

"M. de Mar, Sire, and his servant."

"Good, La Force. Let them enter."

M. La Force fairly pushed us over the sill, so abashed were we, and shut the door upon us.

The king was alone. But before this simple gentleman in the rusty black, M. Étienne caught his breath as he had not done before a court in full pomp. He had seen courts, but he had never seen the first soldier of Europe. He advanced three steps into the room, and forgot to kneel, forgot to lower his gaze in the presence, but merely stared wide-eyed at majesty, as majesty stared at him. Thus they stood surveying each other from top to toe in the frankest curiosity, till at length the king spoke:

"M. de Mar, you look less like a carpet-knight than I expected."

M. Étienne came to himself, to kneel at once.

"Sire, I blush for my looks. But your zealous soldiers would not let me from their clutches. I am just come from killing Paul de Lorraine."

"What! the spy Lucas?"

"Himself. And when I left the spot by way of the window in some haste, I was not expecting this honor, Sire."

"Nor do I think you deserve it, ventre-saint-gris!" the king cried. "Though you come hatless and coat-less today, you have been a long time on the road, M. de Mar."

"Aye, Sire."

"You might as well have stayed away as come at this hour. Marry, all's over! Go hang yourself, my breathless follower! We have fought all our great battles, and you were not there!"

Scarlet under the lash, M. Étienne, kneeling, bent his eyes on the ground. He was silent, but as the king spoke not, he felt it incumbent to stammer something:

"That is my life's misfortune, Sire."

"Misfortune, sirrah? Misfortune you call it? Let me hear you say fault."

"I dare not, Sire," M. Étienne murmured. "It was of course your Majesty's fault. We cannot serve heretics, we St. Quentins."

"Ventre-saint-gris! You think well of yourself, young Mar."

"I must, Sire, when your Majesty invites me to dinner."

The king burst into laughter, and his temper, which I believe was all a play, vanished to the winds.

"Pardieu! you're a glib fellow, Mar. But I didn't invite you to dinner for your own sake, little as you can imagine it. So you would have joined my flag four years ago, had I not been a stinking heretic?"

"Aye, Sire, I needs must have. Therefore am I everlastingly beholden to your Majesty for remaining so long a Huguenot."

"How now, cockerel?"

M. Étienne faltered a moment. He was not burdened by shyness, but before the king's sharp glance he underwent a cold terror lest he had been too free with his tongue. However, there was naught to do but go on.

"Sire, had I fought under your banner like a man, at Dieppe and Arques and Ivry, M. de Mayenne had never dreamed of marrying his ward to me. I had never known her."

"The loveliest demoiselle I ever saw!" the king cried. "I shall marry her to one of my staunchest supporters."

The smile was washed from M. Étienne's lips. He turned as white as linen. In one moment his youth seemed to go from him. The king, unnoting, picked a parchment off the table.

"To one of my bravest captains. Here's his commission, my lad."

M. Étienne stared up from the writing into the king's laughing face.

"I, Sire? I?"

"You, Mar, you. You are my staunch supporter, perhaps?"

"Your horse-boy, an you ask it, Sire!"

He pressed his lips to the king's hand, great, helpless tears dripping down upon it.

"If I ever desert you, I am a dog, Sire! But the fighting is not all done. I will capture you a flag yet."

"Perhaps. I much fear me there's life in Mayenne still."

M. Étienne, not venturing to rise, yet lifted beseeching eyes to the king's.

"What! you want to get away from me, ventre-saint-gris!"

My lord, who wanted precisely that, had no choice but to protest that nothing was farther from his thoughts.

"Stuff!" the king exclaimed. "You're in a sweat to be gone, you unmannerly churl! You, a raw, untried boy, are invited to dine with the king, and your one itch is to escape the tedium!"

"Sire –"

"Peace! You are guilty, sirrah. Take your punishment!"

He darted across the room, and throwing open an inner door, called gently, "Mademoiselle!"

"Yes, Sire," she answered, coming to the threshold.

The peasant lass was gone forever. The great lady, regal in satins, stood before us. She bent on the king a little, eager, questioning glance; then she caught sight of her lover. Faith, had the sun gone out, the room would have been brilliant with the light of her face.

M. Étienne sprang up and toward her. And she, pushing by the king as if he had been the doorpost, went to him. They stood before each other, neither touching nor speaking, but only looking one at the other like two blind folk by a heavenly miracle restored to sight.

"How now, children? Am I not a model monarch? Do you swear by me forever? Do you vouch me the very pattern of a king?"

Answer he got none. They heard nothing, knew nothing, but each other. The slighted king chuckled and, beckoning me, withdrew to his cabinet.

So here an end. For if Henry of France leave them, you and I may not stay.

www.ingramcontent.com/pod-product-compliance
Lightning Source LLC
Chambersburg PA
CBHW020926310726
48980CB00005B/406

* 9 7 8 1 5 9 8 1 8 5 5 8 4 *